Shades
of
Right

Robyn Braemer

Halstad House

Other Books by Robyn Braemer

The Heart Key

The Horse Keeper

Dark Thunder

Huron: Descendants

Shades of Right

Robyn Braemer

This story is based on a true event. On November 18, 1862 38 men from the 9th Minnesota Regiment held up a train in Missouri to help a slave save his family who were being shipped to Kentucky to be sold. 41 men were court martialed and sat in prison for two months until the Secretary of War ordered their release. Upon hearing of this event I wondered what slave would be brave enough to risk going up to a complete stranger and asking for help to save his family from the auction block. What sort of men were those 38 who risked everything to help a stranger? This is the tale as I imagine these men to be.

Everything but the fact that a slave asked for help of men from 9th Minnesota Regiment and that 38 of those men held up a train to help him is completely fictional.

Chapter One

Isaac

I was five years old when Master Meadows bought me.

Master Meadows said he had not meant to buy a slave that day. He had gone to the auction with his old friend, Samuel Taylor, who was in need of a household slave for his daughter's wedding gift. Master Meadows said he spotted me up on the block and felt his heart stir in a grand way.

There I was, five years old, all alone, with the biggest brown eyes and a determined expression. That was what Master Meadows said often over the years when people asked him whyever did he buy a little boy. I stood with my shoulders straight and faced the crowd of buyers with the expression of a condemned man facing his execution with bravery and honor.

I don't remember much of anything before going home with Master Meadows. I guess that means my life started up on that auction block.

My memories of my mother were vague even before the day Master Meadows bought me. I was separated from her long before finding myself standing on that auction block surrounded by a sea of white faces. I didn't know if it was weeks or months when last I saw my mother. It seemed like forever by the time I found myself climbing up on the platform with the auctioneer waiting for me.

It was hot that day. Sweat dripped down the faces of the men gathered to buy workers for their plantations, factories, and households. There were women holding parasols over their heads, fluttering paper fans in front of their faces to stir up a breeze. They needed to create a breeze because there was not a drop of stale, baked air circulating on its own.

My mother became but a compilation of senses. Sometimes when the lavender was in bloom I would get a bit of memory of a smiling woman cutting bunches of lavender and putting the stems laden with their purple flower into a flat woven basket. For years the smell of lavender made me think of sunshine and laughter. Even that faded.

I didn't even really know for sure if the fuzzy image of the smiling woman was an image of my mother or some other woman. I liked to think it was my mother. I had so little memory of her that I wanted to hold onto the few that images that remained.

There were other memories as well, though not so pleasing as the memories stirred by the scent of lavender. Sometimes, when it would rain hard at night, even if I was bone tired and needed to sleep before morning came so early, the sound of a woman crying would haunt my thoughts. They were not gentle sobs but great wracking sobs full of grief and pain. The memory would keep me from falling asleep until late many a rainy night.

Standing up there on the wooden stage in front of all those hot, sweaty faces was a horrible thing to experience. Master Meadows always liked to say that I looked so brave, that I was facing what came with a stoic determination. I don't remember feeling any of that.

All I remembered was missing the feeling of my mama holding me in her strong arms and knowing that I would never see her again. Mr. Hobbs had told me I would never see Mama again as he took my hand and led me out onto that stage.

"I miss my mama," I had said to Mr. Hobbs while we were standing down at the foot of the stairs leading up onto the auction block.

"You ain't never gonna see yo mama again, boy," Mr. Hobbs had said. "No bawling now. You keep that brave face on and do what yo new owner tells ya without quibble and it'll go all right wid ya."

"But I miss my mama," I said in a low whisper.

Mr. Hobbs was staring at my feet. "Didn't ya get shoes, boy?" he said, frowning.

They had given me a pair of shoes that morning to wear up on the auction block. They were worn and scuffed but had no holes in the soles. They also pinched my feet and hurt my toes so I had taken them off and left them in the holding area behind the auction block. I remembered wearing shoes before but mostly being barefoot most of the time.

I was thinking about never seeing my mama again as I climbed those wide wood planks up and up until we were standing above the crowd. The wood had been worn smooth and polished by many feet climbing to the raised platform. There wasn't much interest in me. People wanted to buy a slave old enough to work a full day, not a child.

All those eyes in those faces filling the area below the platform were scary. I clutched Mr. Hobbs' leg. He pried my fingers loose and gave me a small push on my back. I took two stumbling steps forward and stopped. The sun was hot on my freshly shaved head.

A lot of people in the crowd below the auction block looked away, chatting with each other and studying the sales bill for what was coming up next. I needed to keep a brave face on so that was what I focused on, looking brave instead of crying for my mama.

There was some talking going on between the auctioneer and some people standing about in front of the platform but I wasn't really paying mind to what was being said. Those people standing about, asking the auctioneer questions wanted to know something about me.

The auctioneer was the man standing by the podium with a pile of papers containing information on each slave being presented for purchase that day. The day before he had walked through the holding area, asking questions, writing stuff down. I don't know what they had written down about me.

A man raised a white handkerchief in his hand, fluttering the bit of cloth to get the auctioneer's attention. "Did you say Summerset Plantation?" he asked the auctioneer.

The man was almost right in front of me. He wore a white straw hat over pale hair and his jet black beard was trimmed so that the sides of his jaw were bare. He had blue eyes and wore wire-rimmed spectacles that made his eyes look even larger. I never did see another man with skin so white as that man's skin.

A woman next to the man in the white hat stopped flapping her paper fan and glared at him, eyes narrowing. Her hair was curled into lots of spirals that framed her face under her wide brimmed hat. She was not young but she was pretty. Her dress was white and fluffy with a purple band around her middle. I stared at her, hoping she would take me home with her.

The auctioneer read from his papers but his voice sounded like it was muffled in cotton through the roaring in my ears. The woman said something about "not letting him buy a boy" and several heads turned in interest.

A man standing next to the gentleman in question said something to the woman in a low voice. She blushed so hard that her cheeks and throat turned red and she started moving her paper fan so fast that it turned into a blur. Right after that she stepped back and around some other people in the crowd so that there were people between her and the man who's words had made her face turn red.

I kept my eyes on the fluffy woman, willing her to take me away with her but she never did look back up at me. She watched the two men who had upset her for a time then turned to talk to a woman beside her. The other woman was holding a piece of paper and they bent their necks over the paper, studying whatever it was written there.

A man wearing denim trousers, a red kerchief tied around his neck, and no hat and that man in the white hat were the only people who raised their hands when the auctioneer started talking in a funny voice while I was on the block. The man with no hat did not have a beard but had also not shaved for several days. He had combed his thinning hair over his balding head and the strands of hair were soaked in sweat and where the hair did not cover his scalp his head was red.

When the man with no hat looked at me it took all my effort not to cry. I stiffened my shoulders and stared straight ahead. He was a bad man. I did not know why but I knew that it was important that he did not buy me that day. If I didn't look at him it was like he wasn't even there.

The sun had shifted in the sky enough that it peeked out behind a tree back behind all those white people looking to buy slaves, making me have to squint to see the people spread out below the auction block. A glow of white light struck directly behind the man in the white hat so that I could only see his outline.

The man with no hat and scruffy face had visited the slave quarters before the auction. He was looking for replacements for the boys who kept dropping like flies. I don't know what he did to those boys but the auctioneer looked uncomfortable around the man.

"This one's too young," the auctioneer said when the man with no hat stopped to look at me. "Only five. Barely five."

"Young," the man said, nodding as he stared at me. "But cheap."

"Sold!" the auctioneer had called out, slamming his gavel on the podium. "To Mr. William Meadows for $3.00."

The man in the white hat smiled and nodded his head in pleasure at having just purchased me. His friend slapped him on the back and congratulated him. The man with no hat scowled but faced the auction block, ready for the next one up to bid for his replacements.

Mr. Hobbs took my hand and led me back down the auction block stairs. Instead of taking me back into the holding quarters Mr. Hobbs led me into the crowd to the man with the white hat. The man with the white hat and magnified blue eyes smiled down at me as he took my hand from Mr. Hobbs. His hand felt squishy soft after Mr. Hobbs' rough, calloused hand.

"This be Master Meadows," Mr. Hobbs said to me, bending down almost at eye level with me. "He's yo new master now. Understand?"

I nodded. I didn't understand but I knew enough to know that Mr. Hobbs was expecting agreement from me. Mr. Hobbs straightened and gave Master Meadows a piece of paper. "Good day," he said, nodding his head at Master Meadows.

"What a beautiful child," his companion said upon seeing me close up. "What are your plans for him?"

Master Meadows laughed. "I must confess," he said with a grin. "I had not thought that far out. I only knew that I must have him."

I stood next to my new master in the blazing sun, my hand in his. At first his hand had felt cold but it did not take long to get all sweaty and hot from our shared heat. At least standing facing the auction block meant the sun was behind me instead of in my eyes. My back and top of my head were getting mighty hot though.

Up close I could see that the man had more gray hair than blonde hair and his partial beard was fake black. I knew that it was fake black because the heat was making black sweat drip from his face. His skin sagged around his mouth and on his neck. The back of his hand holding mine was so white with paper thin skin that I could see the blue veins running under the skin. There were brown spots on his hand also.

Master Meadows looked down at me. "I think I should get you out of this hot sun, boy," he said. He had a kind voice, soft and light. "What say you?"

I didn't' say anything. I didn't know what he wanted me to say and I had nothing I wanted to say so I chose to remain silent. That didn't seem to bother my new master at all. He turned to his companion and made farewells before leading me out of the crowd.

It felt good to be out of the crowded press of people. There was a slight hint of a breeze on the edge of the crowd and the smell of sweating bodies faded away. There was fierce bidding going on behind us, with the auctioneer rattling off what sounded like gibberish in a steady stream as he watched the crowd below the stage.

I glanced over my shoulder as we walked away from the auction. There was a black man wearing cotton, cropped pants but no shirt standing on the block. The man stood with his shoulders slumped, head down, gaze locked on his bare feet. His shirt was folded and set neatly on his shoes next to him.

One of the auctioneer's helpers stepped up to the man and pulled his pants down, leaving him standing in nothing but a piece of cloth covering his privates. The man stepped out of the pants at his feet and put both his hands over that little bit of cloth to cover himself the best he could.

I wanted to ask Master Meadows why the man had to remove his clothes in front of all those people. I didn't know my new master well enough to know if he would get angry with me for asking questions so I kept my mouth shut.

Master Meadows took me home and passed me into the care of Lisbett, the housekeeper. Lisbett was always old. Her hair was gray and she had wrinkles fanning out from her eyes. I remember being afraid of her at first. Lisbett was not happy that Master Meadows came home with a little black boy without any warning.

"He'll need clothes," Lisbett had said, staring down at me with a stern expression, making wrinkles appear across her forehead and deepening the wrinkles on her cheeks.

"Old Hank can go to the store in the morning," Master

Meadows had said. "Put him in an old shirt for tonight."

"He'll need a bath," Lisbett had said, sniffing.

"Then give him a bath," Master Meadows had said.

"I don't know nothing about raising no child," Lisbett had said, turning her scowl from me to Master Meadows. "What you thinking, buying an child? You think I'm gonna raise this boy?"

"He's just a little person," Master Meadows had said. "Feed him and I'll take care of the rest."

"What you thinking?" Lisbett had asked again, staring at Master Meadows. "Buying a little black boy? He ain't no good for nothing."

"Rockforque was in the crowd," Master Meadows said.

"Rockforque?" Lisbett said, her ebony face scrunching up so tight that her eyes seemed to pop. She looked like she just bit into a sour berry. "That man still buying boys?"

"What do you mean you don't know nothing about raising no child?" Master Meadows said with a grin, changing the subject. "You practically raised me when Mother took to the bottle."

"Hmph," Lisbett muttered. "Never did neither. Don't you go talking like that."

"Sure enough, you did," Master Meadows said.

I was a bit in shock watching them argue. First, I had been put on an auction block and sold, which was a little hard to understand for a five year old boy. I had never seen a black woman going after a white man, sassing him like anything. The white man did not seem to mind. He smiled quite fondly at the woman scolding him so gruffly.

"Sure enough he's a beautiful face, isn't he?" Lisbett said, staring down at me. "It be those eyes. Feels as though he can see right into my soul. Such an old soul in a boy's body."

"Yes, the eyes," Master Meadows said. "Those eyes grabbed me and I knew I had to have him."

"Hmph," Lisbett muttered, staring at Master Meadows. "Rockforque, huh?"

"Does he remind you of anyone, Lisbett?" Master Meadows asked. Lisbett didn't even look at me. "You saw it, too!" he said.

"Never did see anything," Lisbett muttered.

While they stood discussing me over my head my stomach growled. The sound made Lisbett's curly haired head snap around like someone had sounded a canon in her kitchen. Her face melted. I could never forget that sight. All her wrinkles just melted away and the anger with Master Meadows went with the wrinkles.

"Didn't they not feed you, child?" Lisbett had asked, looking down at me with her big, brown eyes.

Slaves working at the auction had come through at dawn with a pot and a ladle and filled a rusty tin cup with the liquid. Though the woman handing me the cup of soup had said it was bean soup it was mostly just watered broth with a few beans and two pieces of mushy carrot. Once I drank what was in the cup the slave woman took it and moved on to the next person.

I hadn't gotten anything since dawn and it was late afternoon. I was afraid to speak so I just shook my head. Lisbett put her hand over her heart and took a deep breath. Lisbett glanced over at Master Meadows and shook her head before she hurried to the larder and pulled out paper wrapped bundles of food. Lisbett pulled down several pans from their hooks above the stove and set them on the burners.

Chapter Two

That woman was the best cook east or west of the Mississippi. She bustled about the kitchen and in no time the room was filled with the smells of cooking food, which made my stomach growl even harder. I had not moved from my spot in that whole time, not certain what I should do, not realizing that the food she was making was meant for me.

"Sit at the table, boy," Lisbett said, with a plate of steaming food in her hand.

I obeyed, eyeing the food she set in front of me on the table as I slid onto the chair next to the table. Master Meadows settled into a chair opposite me, eyeing the food on the plate. I didn't even know what the food was, never having seen it before.

The smell of it made my stomach growl though so it must be good. My stomach growled so hard that it hurt. I didn't know what the food was but my stomach sure did.

Master Meadows looked at me eyeing the food. "Do you know what it is, boy?" he asked.

I shook my head. Master Meadows pointed at each thing as he named them. There's corn bread with butter. Bacon. And eggs," he said.

There was steaming coming off the corn bread that had been cut in half with big globs of butter melting into the centers of both halves. Strips of bacon leaned against the corn bread. Two eggs with golden yellow yolks stared up at me.

I looked over at Master Meadows. The food must be meant for him instead of me. With regret I slid the plate across the table towards the man. Lisbett pushed the plate right back to me. "You want something, too?" Lisbett asked Master Meadows. "Roasted ham for dinner tonight. With mashed potatoes and corn on the cob. So don't go filling up now."

"Just a little then," Master Meadows said, sniffing the odors drifting up from the plate in front of me. "Some of that corn bread. With butter and syrup on it." He looked at me. "You want some syrup on your corn bread, boy?"

I shrugged. I didn't know what syrup was. Master Meadows was sure eyeing that plate in front of me. Though the smell of the food made my stomach ache and growl even louder I could not eat. I was certain all that food wasn't really meant for me. It must be a trick and if I tried to eat it the penalty would be a beating.

Lisbett returned to the table with a plate for Master Meadows as I started sliding the plate in front of me away again. The woman set the second plate in front of Master Meadows and pushed the first plate back at me.

"This be for you, boy," Lisbett said. "You pick up that fork and eat up now." I nodded. I didn't know what a fork was. Lisbett picked up a piece of metal with pointy ends. "Eat, child," Lisbett had said, putting the fork in my hand.

I obeyed. I picked up the bacon with my fingers of my hand without the fork and took a bite. My mouth filled with joy and I ate the rest of the bacon strip as fast as I could before someone could take it away. Lisbett watched me eat for several minutes until I was feeling that I was doing something wrong. I set the fork down.

"Don't you stop eating until that plate is clean, mind you, boy," she said. She handed me the fork again and I held it in one hand while I used my free hand to pick up the corn bread. "Do you speak, boy?" I nodded. "Then say something!"

"Let the boy eat, Lisbett," Master Meadows had said.

"Does he have a name?" Lisbett had asked Master Meadows. She turned to me before Master Meadows had a chance to answer.

"What's yo name, boy?"

"Isaac," I whispered after swallowing the bite I had just taken.

Lisbett nodded. "That's a good name," she said. "Isaac. A good, strong name. Quit dawdling. Eat."

I was getting full but the angry woman had told me to eat everything on the plate. I reached for an egg. The egg with its golden yolk was slippery and the gold globe broke when I picked up the egg. Gold liquid ran all over the plate. I cringed, afraid of being smacked for breaking the egg but they just watched me.

The eggs were the best part. I used my fingers to get every drop of the yellow liquid then leaned over the plate licked all the spilled yolk. The whole time I ate I held that fork in my left hand.

I had never eaten so much food at one time in my life before. I was feeling mighty full but I had not dares disobey the large woman towering over me, watching every bite I took. It had gotten tougher and tougher but I ate every crumb of one half of the corn bread.

Master Meadows was watching me. "Are you full, boy?" he asked.

I looked over at Master Meadows then back up at Lisbett. I nodded as I took a bite of a second piece of bacon. I was starting to feel like there was no more room for any more bites no matter how hard I tried to follow Lisbett's orders.

"Miss Lisbett might have overestimated the size of your stomach," Master Meadows said, glancing at Lisbett meaningfully. "If you're full you can finish the rest later."

That was a relief. I took a deep breath and leaned back on the chair. I was not used to so much food. Most often I got some gruel in the morning and some bread at end of day so my stomach was used to going without.

Master Meadows had not taken more than a bite of his corn bread. They were both staring at me with long faces. Master Meadows sighed and used his fork to lift a bite of corn bread to his mouth. Lisbett cleared her throat.

"I'll just save this for you, Isaac," she said. "If you get hungry before dinner you can finish it." She took the fork out of my hand when she took the plate from the table.

"Have you ever used a fork, Isaac?" Master Meadows asked. I shook my head no. "You will learn," he said.

"Next a bath," Lisbett said, returning to the table from putting away the plate with my leftover food.

That was the start of my life in the household of Master William Meadows. I even had my own bedroom with a real bed, right next to Master Meadows' bedroom up on the second floor.

Old Hank went and bought homespun clothes appropriate for a slave boy. Master Meadows sent Old Hank back for clothes he felt were suitable. I was dressed like a fine young gentleman in linen trousers, white lawn shirts, and a linen jacket. I did not have to wear the jacket in the house but I did have to wear it if we ever went out in public. I even had shoes that were properly sized for my feet. They didn't pinch or hurt at all.

My days started with Lisbett's big breakfasts. Lisbett was determined to put some meat on my bones. According to her I was nothing but a feather. After breakfast I headed for Master Meadows's office for educating or some days we stayed in the kitchen at the table.

Master Meadows taught me to read and write. Master Meadows said I was an apt pupil, a joy to teach. Numbers came easy to me. Once I learned how to read I read whatever I could get my hands on.

My favorites were stories of faraway lands full of magic and possibility. Over the years I read the classics. I read modern books. I read The Bible. I read newspapers. I read magazines. I devoured every book Master Meadows owned.

As I grew older I had to do chores, such as emptying the ashes from the kitchen stove once a week. I had to clean out the fireplace grates but Master Meadows hired a service to clean the chimneys. I helped Lisbett in the garden. Every morning I did chores for a few hours then sat with Master Meadows at the kitchen table while he explained lessons and went over my assignments from the day before. After lunch was my time for studying and reading.

By the time I was in my teen years I was helping Old Hank with the horses and cleaning the stables. Master Meadows never asked me to work in the stables but Old Hank sure appreciated the help. It was getting harder and harder for him to move around. Old Hank's hands looked more like claws than human hands as the arthritis took over.

The whole time I was growing up and approaching becoming an adult Master Meadows was teaching me advanced mathematics, geometry, and history. Master Meadows started giving me his accounting books to double check when I was only fifteen. He owned several businesses in town and did a lot of speculative investing which rewarded him with a healthy bank account.

Master Meadows taught me investment also. In fact, Master Meadows taught me everything he knew about business and finances. The only catch was that I was not allowed to tell anyone. Ever. If word got out that Master Meadows was educating me he could face fines and even jail time. Despite his warning to keep it a secret he didn't seem worried about it.

Master Meadows treated me like a son he never had. Master Meadows was a confirmed bachelor. He had never married and never expected to marry. Master Meadows often said that I was his family. I never called him dad, father, or papa though. He was a good man but a black boy calling a white, confirmed bachelor father was not done, even by Master Meadows.

One day the sheriff came to see Master Meadows. I was in the kitchen helping Lisbett shell peas. I had been with Master Meadows for over two years then. Master Meadows did not invite the sheriff in so they stood in the foyer. Their whole discussion could be heard back in the kitchen. We were just down the hall from the front door.

"I've been hearing complaints that you're educating the boy," the sheriff said.

"What nonsense," Master Meadows had said.

"Nonetheless, I have to investigate," the sheriff said.

"Who is the busy body sticking their nose in my business?" Master Meadows said.

"He was seen reading the milk man's cart," the sheriff said.

I remembered that. I had not paid attention to what was around me when I saw the milk cart. Below the word Milk was painted the word Confectionaries. I had never seen that word before. I remembered trying to say it under my breath, to feel the word on my tongue.

"Looking at words doesn't mean he was reading them," Master Meadows said.

"His mouth was moving," the sheriff said.

"The boy is sharp," Master Meadows said. "It doesn't take an educated man to see a milk man come every day and figure out that the sign says milk."

"I suppose," the sheriff said slowly, considering. "But you know, William, you can't go educating a slave. Why not so long ago that school for blacks was found out in Dayton. They arrested the couple and burned down the building."

"What nonsense," Master Meadows said. "I am not running a school for blacks. If the boy picks up things from me, why it can't be helped. He's a smart boy."

"Yes, sir," the sheriff said. "Maybe it would help if he wasn't so smart."

"I will keep that in mind, sheriff," Master Meadows said. "I apologize for not inviting you in but you caught me on my way out. Walk with me, will you?"

Their voices had faded as they left the house. Lisbett had been sitting at the kitchen table, head turned slightly to catch the whole conversation. When Master Meadows and the sheriff left the house she looked across the table at me.

"Don't you go get Master Meadows in any trouble, boy,"

Lisbett said.

"What did I do?" I asked, confused.

"Don't go reading outside this house," Lisbett said. "Not even signs."

"Yes, ma'am," I said.

"Don't you go ma'aming me," Lisbett snapped. She reached across the table for the bowl holding the peas I had shelled and dumped them into her bowl. She stood and carried the peas to the stove. "Grab a basket and collect the green beans that are ready before lunch. And don't go reading nothing out there."

"There's nothing out there to read," I said, stepping away from the table and grabbing a wicker basket from its hook near the kitchen door.

"Then maybe yo can manage to get by without doing it," Lisbett said.

"Can you read, Lisbett?" I asked, turning at the door.

"Lord, no," Lisbett said, looking up at me in surprise. "Don't even say such things."

"Don't you want to know how to read?" I asked.

"I've gotten along this long fine without no reading," Lisbett said.

"If I couldn't read it'd be like someone taking my eyes," I said, unable to comprehend life without being able to read. The world evolved with written words.

So I learned not to let anyone know that I could read and write and do arithmetic. I did not want Master Meadows to get into trouble for educating me. It was easier than I thought it would be. I just did not move my mouth when sounding out new words on signs and no one noticed.

I learned to memorize a new word and look it up in Master Meadows' big dictionary later. That book was so big with so many words that it had its own pedestal in the salon. I was determined to learn every word in that giant book but there were just too many. I put a fair dent in it though.

Most of Master Meadows' real family was not very close. He had one nephew that came to visit Master Meadows at the house only twice in the time I was growing up there. Though the nephew did not visit the house but those few times, Master Meadows regularly went to the nephew's house for visits. There were holidays, special events, and the first Sunday of the month Sunday dinner like clockwork where Master Meadows went off to spend the day or evening at his nephew's house. I never once visited the nephew's house, of course.

In addition to the nephew, Master Meadows had a sister who lived over in Atlanta with her family and two brothers who lived near St. Louis with their families. I never met them. Master Meadows never talked about them either. His nephew who he did see was the son of a brother who had died in a boating accident.

Master Meadows did have other visitors who were not family. His friend who had been at the auction with him the day he purchased me, Samuel Taylor, often spent time at the house. They had a great friendship and spent a lot of time together.

Sometimes Master Meadows would have big parties and all sorts of people would come to the house. I stayed in the kitchen with Lisbett during those grand parties. Master Meadows hired people to come in and make food and serve the food. When I was older I liked to sneak down the hall and watch all the laughing people in their fancy clothes.

Servants dressed in clothes as fine as the guests walked around the rooms holding up trays filled with glasses of champagne or plates of bite-sized food. There were little squares of toast with caviar, egg salad, or roast beef. There were melon slices wrapped in bacon. There was all sorts of food that made my mouth water.

Not only did the pieces of food look mighty appealing, they smelled like heaven. The hired cook called them hors d'oeuvres. The servants would stop in front of guests and offer the filled glasses, collect empty glasses, and offer the hors d'oeuvres. Back in the kitchen the cook made up little plates for Old Hank, Lisbett, and me with samples of those hors d'oeuvres.

Lisbett would get all ruffled that there was another cook in her kitchen. She didn't care that the cook came all the way from France and refused to be called cook. He was a chef. He wasn't like other white people in Jefferson City. He talked to us like we were really there.

As huffy as Lisbett got over Master Meadows bringing a man to cook in her kitchen, she got huffy about having to cook for all those people when he had smaller parties and didn't hire staff for the event. When the French man calling himself a chef would make up plates of his bite-sized food Lisbett would eye the plate and wait until he wasn't looking to eat up every crumb on that plate, even licking her fingers and wiping them across the emptied plate.

I thought they were saying horderves the first time the French people came to the house to cater a party but I couldn't find the word in the dictionary the next day. Master Meadows said the term was French so it wouldn't be in an English dictionary. I wanted to learn French then but Master Meadows said that he would have to hire a tutor to teach me French and that would draw unwanted attention.

Chapter Three

Both Master Meadows and Mr. Taylor would travel. Sometimes they went together and sometimes Mr. Taylor went without Master Meadows. Mr. Taylor traveled more often than Master Meadows. Whenever Mr. Taylor traveled on some business trip without Master Meadows he would come visit as soon as he returned.

Mr. Taylor would bring me small gifts or new books whenever he returned from his travels, delighting in my enthusiasm at such wondrous portals into the world outside Jefferson City. The books were definitely my favorite gifts.

If Master Meadows was a father to me then certainly Mr. Taylor had taken on the role of uncle. I did have a family of sorts. Master Meadows was my father, Mr. Taylor my uncle, Lisbett my grandmother, and Old Hank my grandfather.

Mr. Taylor had arrived from abroad with gifts of books in hand one day near my fifteenth birthday. I am not sure if my birthday was listed on the papers about me that Master Meadows kept locked away in his safe or if Master Meadows just made up a day. However it came to be, Mr. Taylor would always give me a gift of books and Lisbett would bake a cake.

"You spoil him," Master Meadows said to Mr. Taylor with a smile.

"He deserves books," Mr. Taylor said, settling onto the settee in front of the window. "He absorbs them like a sponge. That brain of his was designed for great things, William. Not rotting away with no use."

"He's hardly rotting away," Master Meadows said with a short laugh. Though he smiled I could see that what Mr. Taylor said disturbed Master Meadows' peace of mind. "Isaac, run and fetch the tea tray Lisbett is preparing."

"Yes, sir," I said, giving the two books a lingering caress before setting them down.

The feel of the pressed leather covering the book under my fingers was a fine thing. The one rule Master Meadows had about me reading was that I never carried a book out of the office or salon. Even my books, gifted to me, had their place on Master Meadows' book shelves.

I was returning with the tray of tea and treats when I heard them still talking about me. Now, I am not one to eavesdrop, yet I stopped in my tracks at what they were saying. They were talking about my future. I had never considered a future before that day.

"If ever someone deserved a college education, it's Isaac," Mr. Taylor was saying.

"He would never be admitted," Master Meadows said. "Don't go giving him hope of something that he can never have."

"He could study in Europe," Mr. Taylor said.

I was so stunned at the idea that I missed a bit of what they said. Study at university? Travel all the way to Europe, where there were no slaves. The idea made my heart race in excitement and fear all mixed together.

"Hetty has family in England," Mr. Taylor said. "Perhaps I could convince her to sponsor him."

"Hetty?" Master Meadows said with a short laugh. "She would refuse just to spite me. You know your wife bears me no affection."

"Her lack of affection for you does not include the boy," Mr. Taylor said. "He would do well in England. Maybe even stay if it suited him."

"Neither does it mean she would have affection for the boy," Master Meadows said with a snort. "You delude yourself to think she would assist him in any way."

"She might," Mr. Taylor said, voice fading in doubt at his own words.

"Relatives in England?" Master Meadows said. "Some distant cousins. Right? Even if she agreed to it, that's a lot to ask of relative strangers."

"They are relatives," Mr. Taylor said.

"I know you mean well," Master Meadows said, voice softening. "I appreciate the thought, Sam. I really do. I love that you care for him so."

"I just thought he could use the best education," Mr. Taylor said.

"I give him the best education I can," Master Meadows said.

I was feeling guilty at remaining out of sight in the hall listening to their discussion even though it was the most exciting discussion I had ever heard. I tiptoed backwards a few steps then walked loudly down the hall towards the salon door. They were quiet as I entered the room. I tried to keep my face expressionless but it was difficult to fool Master Meadows.

"Mr. Taylor was just suggesting that you would gain with a college education," Master Meadows said, watching me set the tea tray on the short table in front of the sofa. My head jerked up in surprise. "What do you think of that, Isaac?"

My mouth moved but no words came out. I took a deep breath. "I don't know, sir."

Master Meadows nodded. "We'll have to think about it," he said.

The idea seemed to make him sad. My heart raced as I considered the idea. I had never been farther than St. Louis to the east one time and Kansas City to the west two times. England was a long ways away. I would be gone for years, if I even came back.

"Someone should learn how she does it," Mr. Taylor said, taking a bite of Lisbett's custard cake. "Just heavenly."

"You plan to publish recipe books now?" Master Meadows

asked Mr. Taylor in a teasing voice.

"Perhaps," Mr. Taylor said. "Perhaps."

Looking at Master Meadows I realized that was his fear, to lose me forever. The years passing were making Master Meadows look more and more frail. He would be all alone if I went off to Europe. Well, except for his nephew and Mr. Taylor.

An idea struck me and I grew hopeful. "Perhaps we could both go," I said to Master Meadows.

"I am too old to start over in Europe," Master Meadows said. He poured a cup of tea and handed it to Mr. Taylor. "What family I have is here. When you get older family means everything, Isaac."

It was years before I would come to realize that Master Meadows meant that nephew who welcomed Master Meadows into his house and his two brothers and sister who he so seldom saw meant everything to him. Family loyalty ran deep in Master Meadows. Family did mean everything to him, even if they didn't feel the same.

I nodded, understanding. Mr. Taylor was not as understanding. "It would be good for the boy, William," he said, wiping the custard from the corner of his mouth with a heavy, damask napkin.

"He's young yet," Master Meadows said, tapping the corner of his own mouth to indicate that Mr. Taylor had missed some custard on his face. "We have time to consider the possibility in the future. Enough about that." Master Meadows smiled at Mr. Taylor. "Are you staying over tonight?"

Mr. Taylor nodded. "Hetty is visiting her mother," he said. "I hate staying in that house alone."

"Then let's drink away the night while you tell me of your adventures of your latest trip," Master Meadows said. "Isaac, open two bottles of the burgundy, will you?"

After I opened the two bottles of wine and set them on the side table to breath I walked over to the laminated wood globe standing on one of the book shelves. I spun the globe, stopping it with my fingertips. Europe was sure a long way away from Missouri.

"Don't you have homework before bed?" Master Meadows asked me.

That was his way of saying he wanted some private time with Mr. Taylor. Master Meadows enjoyed listening to Mr. Taylor's stories of his trips. As much as I would have liked to hear the stories, the first night was always just the two of them. Mr. Taylor would repeat the stories again. He always did.

I bid goodnight to them both and walked out of the room, head filled with thoughts of what it would mean to go to university, to attend an actual school. It probably wasn't possible though and really I wasn't even sure if I was brave enough to go off on my own like that. Still, it filled my head for a long time.

We never discussed it again. Soon after that though, Master Meadows gave me the full-time task of maintaining his business books. On Tuesdays I went to the printing house and collected their ledgers, returning them at end of day. On Wednesdays I went to the tannery for their books. They thought I was just the runner. No one knew that I was the one auditing their accounts. On Fridays I went to the lumberyard at the end of the day for their ledgers and returned the books on Monday mornings.

Chapter Four

Days had the habit of whisking on past in the blink of an eye. I was busy doing tasks that kept my mind occupied. I was mostly happy, almost content. Though I had realized early that the world saw me differently than I felt who I was in Master Meadows' house, I learned to keep my head down and my mouth shut. Most of the time.

We never talked again about my going off to college somewhere but we did talk about Master Meadows freeing me. I was seventeen and restless when I first brought up my desire for my freedom.

The idea of going North consumed me. Up North, in a state where slavery was abolished, I could be free to do what I wanted. No matter how good Master Meadows was to me, the older I became the more the shackles of slavery chaffed my soul.

Twice that year the sheriff came to talk to Master Meadows about me getting into trouble. I had not stepped back and allowed two ladies complete access to the sidewalk. I had moved to the side to allow them to share the sidewalk but that was not good enough. I had been expected to step completely off the sidewalk.

When the sheriff came to the house I knew instantly why he was there. I led him into Master Meadow's office and retreated. "Isaac, wait," Master Meadows called out. I turned back to the office. "Jim, would you like some tea?" Master Meadows asked the sheriff.

"I won't be here that long," the sheriff said.

"Isaac, take a seat," Master Meadows said, gesturing to a chair just inside the door along the back wall.

"It's about your boy that I'm here," the sheriff said.

Master Meadows nodded. "I figured," he said.

"He needs to learn his place, William," the sheriff said, shaking his head. "I got complaints that he didn't move over for two ladies on the sidewalk."

"Is that true, Isaac?" Master Meadows asked, looking at me.

"There was room," I said softly.

Bordering the right side of the sidewalk was a stretch of open dirt. It had rained earlier in the day and the dirt had turned to mud. I had edged over so that my shoes were almost hanging off the edge of the sidewalk. They were brand new shoes and I had not wanted to ruin them with stepping in the mud.

"But he didn't step off the sidewalk," the sheriff said to Master Meadows.

"It was muddy," I said to Master Meadows. "I moved over as far as I could."

Master Meadows nodded. He turned to the sheriff. "I appreciate you delivering the bad news yourself, Jim." He made a tsking sound with his tongue. "My, my, what is the world coming to when two white ladies have to share a sidewalk with a blackie."

The sheriff frowned, looking at Master Meadows suspiciously. "You mocking me, Mr. Meadows?"

"I would never mock you, Jim," Master Meadows said. "I voted for you myself. I think you do an upstanding job keeping the fine citizens of Jefferson City safe."

Something in the tone of his voice kept the sheriff on edge and he remained stiff and on guard. "There was a complaint, William," he said.

"Those ladies had every right to go to you," Master Meadows said. "Their delicate constitutions were most certainly unbalanced by the proximity of Isaac here that close to their persons when all they was doing was walking down a sidewalk."

The sheriff relaxed, appeased by Master Meadows' honeyed words. "I have to follow through on complaints, William," he said.

"Besides, flagrant disregard for the welfare of our whites by the darkies is often the first step to insurrection. We can't have that."

"Thank you, Jim," Master Meadows said, standing and stepping around his desk. "I will see that he does not infringe upon the fine ladies of Jefferson City again." Master Meadows led the way out of the office and the sheriff fell into step beside him.

I waited. They talked at the door for a few minutes. I could hear their voices but I did not pay much attention to what they were saying. I heard a few bits of weather and upcoming elections then Master Meadows' shuffling footsteps coming back down the hall.

"It was muddy next to the sidewalk," I said, going on the offensive as soon as Master Meadows returned to the office. "I moved to the very edge. There was plenty of room."

Master Meadows nodded. He sighed and sank into the chair next to me against the wall. "As gentlemen we sometimes must sacrifice our shoes to chivalry," he said.

"There was plenty of room," I said again.

"Next time, keep your eye out for what's ahead," Master Meadows said. "Then you can avoid being in such a dilemma."

"Keep your eyes ahead. Keep your head down," I muttered. "Which is it to be?"

"Both," Master Meadows said. He stood and cupped the side of my face with his hand. "You can do it, Isaac. Just remember that wiping off mud from your shoes is much easier than dealing with a whipping."

I hung my head. "Yes, sir," I said.

Master Meadows walked back to his desk. He stood next to the desk for a moment, rubbing the polished wood with his fingertip. "No matter my influence in this town, there are some things that won't be strong enough to stop. Not moving over for a white lady could cause you more grief than not. I can't protect you every moment."

I nodded. "Yes, sir," I said. I looked up at him. "It isn't fair!" I said, voice rising.

"No," Master Meadows said, sliding into his leather chair behind the desk. "It isn't fair. But it's how it is."

The second visit from the sheriff was only a month later. That time he settled into a chair in the office and tossed his hat on a neighboring chair. Lisbett brought a tea tray and I poured for both of them. Master Meadows held the steaming tea cup up to his face, breathing deeply. There were dessert plates and a crumble cake with blueberries as well but the sheriff settled for just tea.

"Ah, a nice orange pekoe," Master Meadows said. "Some people like coffee but I prefer my tea. There's honey, Jim. Try a piece of that cake."

The sheriff shook his head and launched into why he was there. I had looked a white man in the eye when he had spoken to me. He had yelled at me about being uppity and gone straight to the sheriff. The man had said he was fearing for his life from Meadows' wild buck.

Master Meadows had snorted into his teacup at the term wild buck. "What nonsense," he said.

"He feared for his life, William," the sheriff said.

"I am sure he did," Master Meadows said, looking over his tea cup at the sheriff.

"They start out as little things," the sheriff said, nodding at me when I held up the teapot. I poured more hot tea into his half empty cup. "I know your boy is not a bad 'un but you get someone like Ol' Josiah there getting his pants all twisted up and pretty soon it's a lynching for the smallest offense."

"Isaac is not a wild buck," Master Meadows had said, setting his cup down on the side table.

"Look at him, William," the sheriff said, gesturing at me. "He towers above all of us. Once he really fills out someone is bound to lynch him out of fear whether it has a basis or not."

"So he has to learn to walk with his head down?" Master

Meadows said, twining his fingers together over his knee. "Is that the solution?"

"It'll save a lot of heartache in the end," the sheriff said. "It helps that you are who you are but that will only hold them back so far."

"Who I am," Master Meadows said slowly. "You mean that I own half the town?"

The sheriff shifted in his seat in discomfort. "You know that's what I mean," he said. "That and where you come from. Next they'll be looking at you more closely."

"I know there are rumors," Master Meadows said. "No one has the gumption to say it to my face but I see it in their eyes."

"There will always be talk about anyone in your position," the sheriff said. "If you took a wife that would help matters."

"I do not need to subject some poor woman to my peculiarities to silence rumors," Master Meadows said. "Besides, I'm way too old to take on a wife. Let them talk. They have no reason to."

"Of course not," the sheriff said quickly. "You know that and I know that. People talk though."

I had no idea what they were talking about. No one shared rumors with Master Meadows' slave boy. No one ever talked about Master Meadows around me. I didn't even know people ever said anything about Master Meadows that they couldn't say to his face.

After the sheriff left, Master Meadows sat on his chair for a long time, deep in thought. I collected the tea dishes and carried the tray back to the kitchen. When I returned to the salon Master Meadows was still sitting motionless on the chair.

"I'm sorry," I said.

Master Meadows looked up at me in surprise. "For what?" he said.

"For causing trouble," I said.

"You did nothing wrong but be born with dark skin," Master Meadows said. He sighed. "But maybe you could try harder to be docile in public." He stood and paced. "It boils my blood that those words came out of my mouth. But the sheriff is right. If someone gets it into their head that you overstepped yourself they might not go to the sheriff next time."

"If you freed me I could go North," I said.

"Free you?" Master Meadows said, coming to a sudden stop in his pacing. He didn't wait for me to answer. He shook his head. "What would you do? I can't risk it."

"Risk it?" I asked, puzzled.

"It's a piece of paper," Master Meadows said. "I've heard stories of slaves being given their freedom and being enslaved by people who just tear up their papers. That would be so much worse. At least with me you're safe. I can make your life the best it can be for a man in your position."

I had been giving it a lot of thought lately. The North was a magical land where all men were free and I had the strongest desire to head North. I wanted to live in a land where a man could walk with his head high. Up North I could work for a living, provide for myself, make my own way in life. I was almost eighteen and considered myself as a man grown and the desire to be free was growing stronger every day.

"It's worth the risk," I said, growing emotional. "I would not give them my papers without a fight."

Master Meadows nodded. "That is another fear," he said. "Resisting would get you killed. You are young and strong. Too tempting for some unscrupulous slave runner. They go out looking for runaways and take anyone they find, free or not. I've had friends send slaves out on errands and be abducted. Most get them back as stolen property but not all."

"If I was free they could not take me," I insisted, confident in my youthful certainty.

"For now just keep your head down and stay ten feet away from any white lady," Master Meadows said. "Even if you have to wade through mud up to your knees."

"I thought you loved me," I said, voice rising in volume, not ready to give up yet. "Like a son. Why would you deny me my freedom?"

Master Meadows' face fell. "I am protecting you, Isaac," he said. "Have I not been good to you? Have I not loved you as my son? Why do you want to leave me so badly?"

I had hurt him. That was not my intent. "I'm sorry, sir," I said in a lower voice, a normal voice. "You just don't know how hard it is when I step outside this door. To be treated like dirt on the bottom of their shoes."

I was angry. I was not angry with Master Meadows. I was angry with the situation that made the conversation come up. But if he really loved me he would give me my freedom. It made no sense to me that he would continue to hold onto me as property. It made no sense at all.

"Oh, Isaac," Master Meadows said. He looked like he was ready to cry. "Going north won't stop that. You're young and idealistic. There are bad people everywhere you can go."

"But I would be free," I said. My throat felt dry and I coughed to clear it. It was not that I was fighting back tears. "I would be free," I added in a lower voice.

"What would you do with your freedom?" Master Meadows asked.

"Anything I want," I said without hesitation.

Master Meadows sighed. "It's too dangerous, Isaac," he said. "Not yet. Perhaps one day. But not yet."

"They call me uppity," I admitted. "I can see the fear in their eyes. The sheriff is right. Just by being me they are afraid of me."

"Who's afraid of you?" Master Meadows asked.

I shrugged. "A lot of people," I said. "Sometimes I walk with my shoulders back and meet their eyes like I'm equal. Just to see their reactions. And sometimes I act like a timid rabbit to see the difference."

"Stop doing that," Master Meadows snapped.

"Doing what?" I asked.

"All of that," Master Meadows said, waving his arms in the air. "Just be yourself."

"Who am I?" I asked. "Your son or your slave?"

"You think you're the only one who has to show a different face to the world?" Master Meadows snapped. He took a deep breath and continued in a controlled voice. "You are my slave, Isaac. For now you are my slave. I have given you the best life I could. But the reality is that you are a black man in a world where black men are slaves."

The words hurt. The words stung like nettles under the skin. For a long time after they were said they continued to burn and irritate.

Weeks passed but I did not let it rest. I hounded him. "I could go North," I said. "Where I could be a free black man. Up North even black men are free."

Master Meadows sighed. "Who is really free?" he muttered.

He was free. I did not say that though. I knew that the argument was going nowhere so I stopped talking. I sulked for months. I kept my head down when outside the house and I gave any white lady a wide berth. And I sulked.

"It would be a shame for your talent to go to waste," Master Meadows said when I brought up my request for freedom yet again.

"What?" I asked.

"You think you can go on up to some state where there isn't slavery and everything will be smooth as silk for you?" Master Meadows said. "You think some white man will hire you to keep his accounts? That someone will listen to your advice for investments?"

"Yes," I said with conviction.

"You'll only find some menial job," Master Meadows said. "That's all that will be available to you."

I think he believed that. I didn't. "I'll do what I need to," I said.

"Your talent can't be wasted," Master Meadows said. "Here I can keep you safe. Stepping off sidewalks and keeping your head down, that's little matters. Here you're safe."

"You have no faith in me," I said.

"Oh, Isaac," Master Meadows said sadly. "It's the rest of the world I have little faith in."

Chapter Five

A few months after our last argument Master Meadows decided to go to St. Louis. He wanted me to go with him, to drive the buggy. Master Meadows had never been fond of driving the buggy and lately he really didn't like driving much, not even short trips across town.

Old Hank used to drive him if he had to go any distance but Old Hank was even older and in tougher shape than Master Meadows by then. He said it was getting harder and harder to see and he didn't trust himself to not run off the road and the horse was foolish enough to go where directed. I didn't think much of it.

It took a good part of the day to reach St. Louis. Master Meadows got a room at a hotel that was the grandest building I'd ever seen. When we walked in through the glass doors my jaw dropped. There was red velvet draped all over the place, with gold tassels. There was even paintings on some of the walls.

A man standing behind a long, curving desk looked up when we entered the building. There was a whole wall of wood cubbyholes behind him, with little metal numbers nailed below each cubbyhole. Master Meadows limped from the door to the desk. Seeing Master Meadows limping made me forgot about ogling the hotel lobby. The trip must have been harder on him than I realized.

"No blacks in the lobby," the man behind the desk said.

"I require his assistance," Master Meadows said. "Your finest room, please. And a pallet for the boy."

The man eyed the gold coins Master Meadows set on the desk, looked up at me, and then back to the gold. "Very well," he said. He slid a ledger in front of Master Meadows. While Master Meadows signed the register the clerk reached into a cubbyhole behind him and took a key. "Room 114. Do you need assistance with your bags?"

"The boy will get them," Master Meadows said.

In the morning Master Meadows took me with him to a grand bank in St. Louis. I stared around me in awe as we entered the building. The ceiling was so high I could barely see it way up there. The ceiling was made of embossed tin. From where I stood it looked like it was a gold ceiling. Marble statues stood on stone pedestals. The marble floor was so shiny I could see myself in it. It was slippery under my shoes also.

A man dressed in a uniform, wearing a holstered gun around his waist stepped in front of us. "Sir, no darkies in the lobby," he said.

"I require his assistance in my task," Master Meadows said. He handed the guard a business card. "Tell Mr. Poole that I wish to see him in a private office."

The security guard took the card, looked at it, looked at Master Meadows, and nodded. "Wait here please, Mr. Meadows," he said.

Master Meadows walked to the sofa against the wall where the security guard had gestured. I followed but stood behind Master Meadows. A young couple entered the bank while we were waiting. The woman gasped and covered her mouth with her hand when she saw me. The man with her stepped around her so that he was between her and us.

"Next they'll allow goats in the lobby," the man said, glaring at Master Meadows.

"You'd think they've never seen a black man," Master Meadows said, staring after the couple. "Idiots."

The security guard returned with a short, balding man. Master Meadows stood and they shook hands. "Mr. Meadows, what a pleasure to see you again," the man said.

"Mr. Poole," Master Meadows said.

Mr. Poole held out his arm. "This way, please," he said.

I kept my head down as I followed them, aware of everyone in the bank staring at me. It was a relief when we entered the small office and Mr. Poole shut the door against the stares. There was a desk with a stool behind it and two leather upholstered chairs in the room. The chairs were positioned facing the desk. One wall was lined with metal file cabinets and one wall was lined with built in wood file cabinets.

"What can I do for you today, Mr. Meadows?" Mr. Poole asked as he settled onto the stool behind the desk.

Master Meadows sat on one of the chairs across from the desk, the leather creaking as it took his weight. I remained standing. Master Meadows looked back at me. "Sit here, Isaac," he said. He turned back to Mr. Poole. "I would like to open an account and a security box."

"Very good," Mr. Poole said. He opened a desk drawer and pulled out several pads of pre-printed forms.

"The name on both accounts will be Isaac Williamson," Master Meadows said.

"A joint account?" Mr. Poole asked.

"No," Master Meadows said. "Solely Isaac Williamson."

"Please spell that," Mr. Poole said, busily writing on the top paper of one of the pads of paper.

I looked at Master Meadows in surprise. Master Meadows did not even look at me. He spelled out the name Isaac Williamson and answered all of Mr. Poole's questions. Mr. Poole spent several minutes filling out other forms with the same information. When he finished he pushed the prepared papers across the desk at me.

"I want the box paid for twenty-five years," Master Meadows said.

Mr. Poole looked up in surprise. "So long?" he asked. "Normally it's paid annually."

"Yes, yes," Master Meadows said. "I want to pay for twenty-five years."

Mr. Poole nodded. He scribbled the multiplication on his pad. I looked at the annual fee for the box and automatically did the multiplication in my head. It was a habit for me.

"Please sign here," he said, pointing to a line. I looked at Master Meadows and he nodded. I wrote Isaac. "The full name, please," he said, tapping the paper next to my name. "Isaac Williamson. How you will always sign it."

It was an unfamiliar name to me but I signed every paper he gave me with Isaac Williamson. When I finished all the papers he gave one of them to me as well as a small key. "Keep these somewhere very safe," he said. "Without the account numbers you won't be able to access the account and box."

The piece of paper was thick velum with squiggly lines decorating the four corners. The name Isaac Williamson was written in a fine hand as fancy as the decorated paper. Below the elaborately written name was my signature. Below my signature were two sets of eight numbers.

Mr. Poole handed me a second piece of paper. It was thin and only a few inches in height and width. It was a receipt for a deposit of one hundred dollars to the account of Isaac Williamson and the same eight numbers as was written on the other paper.

"I'll be right back with the security box," Mr. Poole said.

Mr. Poole left the room, shutting the door behind him. I stared at the papers in my hand. I was in a bit of shock. The need to travel all the way to St. Louis and the false name suggested Master Meadows wanted this to remain a secret.

"Does this mean you are giving me my freedom?" I asked Master Meadows.

"As much as I dare," Master Meadows said. "If something ever happens to me, you have this. It's yours to do with as you wish, Isaac. That signature is your identification. Always sign it the same so there's no questions."

"Does that mean my name is Williamson now?" I asked.

"No," Master Meadows said. "It's a way to keep it private."

"Private?" I asked. "I don't understand."

"One day you will," Master Meadows said.

"But why?" I asked, confused.

"So that there's no paper trail back to me," Master Meadows said. He sighed. "I love my nephew but if he was aware of this money he would find a way to take it. This is the only way I could think of to keep it out of his hands."

"William son," I said, looking at the name on paper. "Son of William."

Master Meadows smiled. "Technically you are a Meadows but I thought it a nice twist to use Williamson," he said. "Surnames are a recent invention, you know. Only a few hundred years. It was common for someone to take or be assigned a surname simply as an identifier. Larson, son of Lars. Baker, for being a baker. Or even a town or location. I suspect our family back in England lived by a meadow or owned several meadows. I considered using Summerset for this for you. Williamson gives me more satisfaction."

Summerset? The name sounded familiar but I couldn't place it, the memory just out of reach at the back of my mind. It tickled senses, of heat and the smell of sweat mixed with lavender. It wasn't important. As Master Meadows grew older he repeated the same stories, forgetting who he told what. I had heard the history of surnames so many times that I barely listened, merely waiting for a chance to speak what was on my mind.

"What good does it do me when I can't even enter this bank?" I asked, holding up the paper with the account numbers written on it.

"You do it by mail," Master Meadows said. "Or hire a courier to deliver written requests. You should know that. I don't personally visit every bank outside of Jefferson City."

I nodded. I was just a bit shaken by the whole thing and hadn't thought of that. I was disappointed that he was still holding onto me.

I was torn on how to feel about his opening an account for me. That piece of paper in my hand did not bring me any closer to my freedom but I knew that having money was important if I did gain my freedom.

"Thank you, sir," I said.

I didn't see what Master Meadows put inside that box. When Mr. Poole returned he set the metal box on the desk and left the room again. Master Meadows pulled a canvas bag from his inside jacket pocket and put it in the box. I could see sharp edges pushing against the canvas, like a book maybe. He used the key to lock the box and handed the key back to me.

Mr. Poole returned to the private office a few minutes later. Master Meadows stood and took Mr. Poole's hand. "I am eternally grateful to you for your assistance, John," Mister Meadows said.

"Anything for you, William," Mr. Poole said, putting both his hands over Master Meadows' hand and shaking vigorously.

"You are a dear friend for doing this," Master Meadows said.

Mr. Poole picked up the lock box and carried it out of the room as he walked with us. When we left Mr. Poole gave the box to a man behind the teller window to put in the vault. Though I was curious as to what Master Meadows had put in that box I didn't ask.

The box required my key to open it but it was as out of reach as could be, all the way over in St. Louis in a bank where I wasn't allowed to enter on my own.

I didn't want to know what he put in there. That's what I told myself as we left the bank. I looked back as we walked through the large foyer. I did want to know what was in that box. One day I would make it a point to find out.

We headed back for Jefferson City without lingering after we left the bank. I guided the horse through the traffic with difficulty. I wasn't used to driving a buggy with so many other vehicles in our way and people walked right in the way. Twice I almost knocked someone over because I wasn't expecting them to dart in front of us.

It was a relief when we cleared the congestion and left the city behind. Near the city the road stretched out smooth and straight ahead of us. It had been a dry summer and the road was packed nice and hard. Even the ruts had been mostly knocked down by wagon wheels of summer traffic.

The road was not as packed the farther we went from the city. Dust coated the horse's back and the ruts in the road rocked the buggy.

The trip to St. Louis bothered Master Meadows for some reason. He started taking pulls from a flask he carried in his inside jacket pocket. He stared out at the countryside we passed, lost in his own thoughts. They did not appear to be happy thoughts. He scowled at his thoughts.

We were halfway back to Jefferson City when I asked him about the box. "What did you put in the box?"

"If it was something I wanted to show you now I wouldn't have bothered getting the box," Master Meadows said, taking a drink out of his flask.

"Couldn't you at least tell me?" I asked.

"Just be sure to collect it before the twenty-five years are up," Master Meadows said. "Did I ever tell you that I was named after my father?"

"No, sir," I said, "His name was William also?"

"William Senior," Master Meadows said. "He owns a plantation up north a bit. I haven't seen him since I left home when I was twenty years old. Except once. Just once."

It was a surprise to learn that Master Meadows' father was still alive. He never mentioned him. I always thought that the man was dead years ago. Master Meadows had told me a little bit about the brothers and sister but never talked about either of his parents.

"My mother could have stood up for me but she didn't," Master Meadows said. His words were becoming slurred.

"They are both alive?" I asked.

"No," he said, shaking his head back and forth several times in slow motion. "I wasn't allowed at the funeral. Old Pops though, he keeps going. Much to my brothers' regret. Old Jackson's got his eyes on that plantation. Old Pops is too stubborn to die. He'll stay alive just to spite Jackson. And he likes Jackson."

"Jackson? That's your oldest brother?" I asked. I was thinking but didn't add, *"The brother who lives by St. Louis. Right where we just were without your going to see him?"*

"He's got his own plantation," Master Meadows said. "Right next door. Bought it a good thirty years ago. Named it Autumn Rise Plantation." Master Meadows giggled. "Jackson never did have any imagination."

The buggy wheel hit a bump just as Master Meadows put the flask up to his lips, causing whisky to splash all over his face. Master Meadows wiped away the spilled liquor with his hand and took a generous swallow. "It'll be the biggest plantation in the state when he combines the two," he said.

At least that's what he meant to say. What he actually said was, "Id be biggesh pandation in shtate when he combs de tchew."

Master Meadows took a long pull from his flask, emptying it. He tossed the steel flask on the floor of the buggy. A wagon filled with slaves lined up on each side approached us on the road ahead. A driver and an armed man sat on the bench in the front. Two armed men rode on horseback behind the wagon.

My stomach started feeling queasy when I saw that wagon and I tried to keep my head down and gaze averted even while trying to pay attention to the road. It was hard to look at those poor souls sitting in the back of that wagon. The buggy had a canopy to shade us from the sun. They had nothing giving them a break from that sun beating down on them.

Chapter Six

The faces of the men and women sitting in the back of the wagon had the look of resignation. Empty eyes stared down at their feet without ever looking up. Whatever their fate, to be sold, a work party heading to St. Louis, or returning home to St. Louis from being loaned out, they had given up on life.

They wore little more than rags, the simplest of clothes only meant to cover. One man wore what looked to be a burlap sack with a hole cut at the top for his head to fit through and slits in the sides for his arms. Several men wore rectangles of oiled canvas with holes cut for their heads to fit through and twine wrapped around their waist to hold the canvas in place.

The wagon rattled as it approached us, the sound of metal bouncing on wood. The wheels and horse's shod hooves kicked up dust, which settled over the men and women sitting in the open back. They were coated with dust.

"I hear chains rattling," Master Meadows said. He frowned as he tried to focus his eyes.

The wagon was the widest vehicle we had met on the road. I guided the horse over to the side of the road but it was still a tight squeeze and both me and the other driver slowed, keeping an eye on the wheels as we passed. The man seated next to the driver stood up and leaned over as he watched our wheels getting closer and closer. It was close but we managed to pass without the wheels scraping.

"Where ya'all headed?" Master Meadows yelled.

"St. Louis," the driver yelled back.

The moment our wheels were clear he cracked a whip over the

horse's heads and the wagon moved ahead quickly. The sound of rattling chains thundered in my ears.

One of the riders escorting the wagon of slaves stopped and looked into the buggy. "Mr. Meadows?" he asked.

I stopped the horse. A soft cloud of dust drifted back over the front of the buggy. It was a dry year all across the state. Better a dusty road than a muddy road. I kept my head down and eyes straight ahead. I was used to being invisible.

Master Meadows tried to look sober. "Do I know you?" he asked, straightening his back and talking slowly.

"Horace, sir," the man said. "Theodor Horace."

Master Meadows giggled. "Now that's a name," he said. He reached inside his inside jacket pocket, frowning when he didn't find his flask. He pulled his hand out from inside his jacket and patted the front with his palm. "To home, Isaac! I have run out of magic liquid."

I flicked the reins and the mare started up again. The man on horseback in the middle of the road looked after us for a moment then snapped the reins against the horse's side. The horse leaped into a steady canter after the retreating wagon. Master Meadows' head sagged down until his chin touched his chest.

The next morning Master Meadows did not come down to breakfast until late, almost nine o'clock. He sat at the kitchen table holding his head in his hands, his elbows on the table, occasionally emitting a low groan. He stank of stale booze.

"I drank the whole flask," he muttered. "Wine does not carry such a punch."

"Stick yer head in a bucket of water," Lisbett said.

"Shhh," Master Meadows whispered. He raised his head and peered at me with one bloodshot eye, the other squeezed shut. "Did we meet someone I know on the road?"

"A Theodor Horace," I said, nodding.

Master Meadows groaned. "Ugh. Now I have to find a way to

apologize without coming across as a drunken ass," he said. "If his father wasn't a respected friend of a friend I would not bother. The son is a slave runner. I have no time for such men."

"Slave runner?" I asked.

"He collects runaways," Master Meadows said. His voice was muffled. His forehead was almost touching the tabletop. "Goes around buying up slaves to take to auction."

"So those slaves in the wagon were runaways?" I asked.

"Perhaps. Or just as likely he was going about buying them cheap so he could sell them for profit," Master Meadows said. He raised his head and looked at Lisbett. "Coffee. I need coffee."

Lisbett pursed her lips together but poured a steaming cup of coffee and set the cup in front of Master Meadows. He wrapped his hands around the cup and breathed deeply of the aroma drifting up, his face wreathed in the coffee steam.

"Where's that flask, Isaac?" he asked.

"Floor of the buggy," I said. I had forgotten to go get it after dragging him out of the buggy and up to his bed.

"Throw that beast away," he said.

"The horse?" I asked in surprise.

"The flask," Master Meadows said.

"Yes, sir," I said.

"No, don't," he said. He still had his eyes closed, his face over the cup of hot coffee. "It was a gift. I think it's even engraved."

"No one told you to drink it all at once," Lisbett said.

"I was chasing away old memories," Master Meadows said. "It worked, too."

"What memories of yours need that devil brew?" Lisbett asked in a crossed tone.

"My father," Master Meadows said, opening his eyes and looking up at Lisbett.

Lisbett's face softened. "Those be old memories, Master Meadows," she said. "Let the past stay in the past."

"Sometimes the past knocks on the door whether you were expecting it or not," Master Meadows said. He raised his coffee cup in a toast. "To my father, William Meadows. May be rot in hell."

"Don't go saying such things!" Lisbett said, eyes going wide. "Yer to honor your father and mother."

Master Meadows snorted. "He's beaten men to death because they irritate him. He rapes young girls because he feels he has the right as they are his property. He starves his people to save a dollar yet will toss twenty dollars on the table for a bet over a horse," Master Meadows said to Lisbett. "Where in that does he deserve my honor? Where in that does he feel the right to judge me?"

"Was he like this the whole trip?" Lisbett asked me. I shook my head no.

"I'm right here, Lisbett," Master Meadows snapped. He took a deep breath. "I'm sorry. They are my demons, not yours. You're a good woman, Lisbett."

"Let's get some food in yer belly," Lisbett said. "Yer still drunk." She turned to me. "Get on upstairs and unpack, Isaac."

"Yes, ma'am," I said, jumping to my feet and hurrying out of the room. The mad ramblings of Master Meadows were making me uncomfortable anyway. He wasn't making any sense.

Since I was eight years old Master Meadows had been giving me a dollar every month for an allowance. The first few months I had spent the whole dollar right away when I went to the store with Master Meadows but as I got older I realized that it was better to save part of it.

There was a loose board behind a shelf in my bedroom closet and every month I put half my dollar into a burlap sack and stuffed it into that hole behind the loose board. When we returned from St. Louis I folded up that piece of paper with my account information and stuffed it into the burlap sack along with the key for the box the bank kept.

I was twenty years old when the elder Master Meadows passed

to the great beyond. One day he did not wake up. We were at the breakfast table and Master Meadows had not come down. Lisbett asked me to go up to his room to see what was taking him so long.

Chapter Seven

My name is Philip Henry Hansohn but everyone calls me Hank. I was born in Duren, Germany but I have no clear memory of Germany. My parents immigrated to America when I was a young child. I was only five when we made the long journey across the ocean. We lived in New York that first year then moved on to Chicago for a year.

I have vague memories of life in those cities. So many people crammed into little, dark rooms stacked next to each other and even on top of each other. The streets were muddy and dangerous, especially for children. Gangs of older boys roamed about even during the day when they should be in school.

The stench of garbage and sewage in the streets was especially strong in the heat of the summer months. Piles of horse manure littered the dirt streets. Winter wasn't much better but the smells weren't so bad.

Dad worked as a butcher in New York and we lived in a one room apartment. We didn't go to school there. Mom set up a schoolroom in our tiny apartment and taught us like we were in school. Everything she taught us she used English no matter how much we groaned. Though we knew English it was so much easier to do our studies in German.

The move to Chicago was not much better. Dad worked for a furniture maker there and once again we were crammed into a small apartment that had a living room and a bedroom that had a leaking roof. In the winter the wind whistled into the rooms through the windowsills and cracks in the walls. In Chicago we went to school during the day. Our classroom wasn't much warmer than our apartment.

Mom made lace and knitted hats, socks, and sweaters for the store down the block. If she wasn't cooking or cleaning she was knitting or tatting. Once she put us to bed she worked by candlelight. The click of wood needles was our nightly lullaby.

Every Thursday morning before the store opened Mom took what she had made that week to the store and collected the monies she had earned from sales the week before. All that money went into a tin box under the bed.

Once the store owner came to the apartment asking Mom for more of her items before Thursday. "People are coming in asking for your hats and socks," he said. "On Thursday they are waiting

"I am working nonstop to make what I do make," Mom explained. "You need to raise the price. That will slow them down."

The store owner nodded. "Just more hats and socks," he said.

The higher price did not slow down the demand but the store owner did not come to the apartment again. Mom used some of the money to pay our neighbor, Mrs. Dulanio, to cook dinner so that she could spend more time making items for the store. Dad, the most frugal man I have ever known, was against Mom paying someone to do her cooking for her.

"I pay her half what I make selling one hat," she said. "In the time I save by not cooking I can make two, sometimes three hats."

"But she makes strange food," Dad complained, though his argument was half-hearted. That extra money was needed.

Mrs. Dulanio was a marvelous woman. Dad might not have liked the food she made but all of us boys sure did. She would sing while she was cooking. She talked funny and when she sang it was with words that none of us understood. Mrs. Dulanio was a widow and had no children. She had moved to America with her husband so she was all alone in the city.

Every night when we ate Mrs. Dulanio's dinners she would sit down to dinner with us. She would tell us stories of when she was a child in Italy. Even Dad warmed up to Mrs. Dulanio and her cooking. They tried convincing her to move west with us when it was time to go but she wouldn't leave Chicago.

"I like to cook for you," she said, shaking her ahead when they once again brought up the topic of her going with us. "I like to cook big meals and it's only me so I cook for you. But I'm a city girl. No farming life for me."

After a year of struggling in Chicago, my parents moved west into the frontier. Minnesota Territory was giving away land to anyone who would live on that land and cultivate it. They had been so frugal that they had saved enough money to buy two wagons, two horses, two mules, dry food supplies for the first year, and a milk cow.

Once we arrived in Minnesota Territory Dad bought two cows, two pigs, two sheep, and a dozen chickens. The first thing we did was build a one room house. It was late spring and Dad was impatient to get crops in the ground. We all helped build that shed we called home for the summer.

Once the crops were in Dad set about building a real house. Wilhelm and Piotr were old enough to do the work of grown men and the rest of us helped fetch and carry and it was our job to take care of the animals so that Dad and the oldest brothers could concentrate on getting the house built.

By the end of summer he had built a two story house with a kitchen, living room, and bedroom on the main floor and two bedrooms upstairs. There wasn't time before winter to build a barn so the one-room house became the winter quarters for the livestock. There were other settlers who brought their livestock right into their house for the winter but Mom was having none of that idea.

I loved our new farm. There was always something needing doing but I still had time to explore, go fishing, and do my studies. My best memories are of growing up in Minnesota Territory.

I'm the youngest of five boys, Wilhelm, Piotr, August, Hans, and then me. My oldest brother, Wilhelm remembered Germany pretty well. At least he talked like he did. Wilhelm was sixteen when our family left Germany so he had better memories of it than I did. One day I hoped to travel there, to see where we came from. I can't imagine it being any more beautiful than Minnesota.

My parents farmed just west of New Ulm Township. We were close enough to walk into town for school. When the weather turned cold in the heart of winter sometimes Dad would take us into town in the wagon. As hardy as we were, we were no match for walking miles in Minnesota winters. Sometimes Wilhelm brought us into town, until he left to go to school back east. If it wasn't too cold we still walked into town.

Some farm kids rode horses into town and put them in a lean-to shack behind the school but Dad didn't let us take the horses and leave them sitting outside the school all day. When the butcher found out that Dad had worked as a butcher in New York he asked Dad if he'd work for him in the winter. So for three days a week every winter Dad worked in town and for two whole weeks before Christmas he worked every day for the butcher.

Once the barn was built Mom used the original house that had been used as a barn for her work room. We spent a week cleaning it until she was satisfied. Dad built attached long boards on one wall for her to use as a work table. Hans and I had to help her clean the shorn wool from the two sheep and help comb the wool to make roving. Dad had built her a spinning wheel and she spun the wool into yarn.

Some of the wool she left its natural color but some of it she dyed. She was like a crazed scientist in her converted house to barn to wool room, trying all sorts of things to stain the wool colors that she wanted. That's what Dad said, that she was a crazed scientist. It just made her laugh when he said that.

I personally thought it was a waste of good blueberries when we found a patch of wild blueberries and she used half of all the berries we picked to color her wool. Mom was sure happy with the blue-purple yarn. So were the ladies who bought her yarn in the store in New Ulm.

Some of the settlers didn't have much money to buy the yarn at the store so they would trade with what they had. Mom always took the trade even when Dad complained that we had more need of cash than more chickens or some old lace. The first year Mom did not even have any yarn leftover to use herself. She sold every hank she had.

Mom tried ground up crickets, ground up stones, and all sorts of spices to make dyes for her wool. She even set us to catching butterflies and used those. Some worked. Some did not work. There were little patches of wool tacked all along the walls with notes on what she had used to dye them.

"They make dyes you can buy," Dad said, wrinkling his nose at the smell inside the building when he stepped inside after an especially adventurous experiment.

"Where's the fun in that?" Mom said with a laugh.

Dad looked down the line of square samples she had made for testing the colors. "Such a waste though," he said. "There's enough wool there for two sweaters for the boys. Just a waste."

"It's an investment," Mom corrected.

"But if you just bought dyes from someone who knows what they're doing you can save all that wool for making something worth making," Dad said.

"These are worth making, Jakob," Mom had said, giving him a look.

When Mom gave Dad that look he stopped arguing. He was the only one who got that look from her. I don't know what it meant. I only know that once Mom got that look on her face and that look was directed at Dad any further discussion was over.

In the end she did let Dad order dye powders from back east but she still experimented with whatever she could think of to make new colors. She told Dad that one day people would order dyes from her. He just smiled and shook his head.

Mom made enough money selling her yarns that she bought two new sheep. They were funny looking sheep, bigger than the normal, plain sheep we had started with. They had such thick wool growing under their chins and down their chests that it looked like they had beards. Plus, they had big balls of wool growing on top of their heads.

Dad nicknamed them Old Men even though only one was male and the other a ewe. They did look like old balding men with shaggy beards and a clump of hair right on the top of their head. Merino sheep, Mom called them. Yarn made from their wool was soft and not itchy at all.

The first time Dad sheared the four sheep I was surprised to see that the new, big sheep were actually smaller than the regular sheep under all that wool.

A few years after we moved to New Ulm we had a new sister. She arrived in March and died in May. Mom took her death hard. We all grieved but Mom took it really hard. That was when she started drinking.

I must have been nine but closer to ten years old when I met Walking Moon. Maniyanhanwi his brothers called him. Piotr and I had taken the farm horses, Donder and Blitzen, out to the Cottonwood River about a mile or so south of the farm and ridden along the river until we found a good spot.

Donder means thunder in German and Blitzen is lightning. I'm not rightly sure how they got such distinguished names. The two horses were but shaggy, brown beasts with little spirit.

Just a guess, but I think Blitzen was named for the white blaze on her forehead and Donder for the farts. I don't know for sure since the horses were older than I was. I was stuck riding Blitzen because Piotr, being older and bigger than me, chose Donder.

It wasn't because Donder had any more spirit than Blitzen that Donder was always the preferred horse when it came to riding. It was that Blitzen had a ridged back that wasn't the most comfortable to sit on when riding without a saddle.

We had started out the day intending to catch some fish for dinner, the reason Dad had allowed us to go off on a perfectly fine summer afternoon. Mom had been in a bad way for days so it was good to get away from the house for a while.

Dad had a favorite spot along the river where the bank was low and there were river rocks that formed a sturdy bank that was comfortable to stand on and walk on. Sometimes the clay and mud would suck our boots right off our feet in other areas. That was the spot where we headed for.

The river gurgled as it passed by our fishing spot, the current occasionally broken with a splash. That splash could have been a fish breaking the surface or a frog jumping. I was in a hurry to drop a line to find out if the fish were active.

The river made lots of sounds. We had actually baited the hooks and dropped the lines when Piotr spotted wolf tracks. The soft clay of the river bank just off the rocks held a perfect impression of the large paws.

"Might be dog," I said, crouching down next to a track and studying it intently. It looked like a dog print to me but I didn't know much.

"Too big," Piotr said. "Besides, what's a dog doing out this far?"

"Coyote?" I asked, tilting my head. It looked like a coyote print to me.

"Too big," Piotr said. He handed me his fishing pole and headed off in the direction the tracks were going.

It didn't take me long at all to pull the lines out of the water and follow Piotr. He looked back at me. "You can't leave the horses alone," he said.

I ran back to the horses and led them behind me as I followed Piotr and the wolf tracks. The two animals meekly followed me as we wound around fallen trees and soggy river bank that looked like it could suck up a small boy whole. Piotr ducked and climbed the fallen trees and jumped over the occasional puddle.

"It's just one," I called up to Piotr. "Don't wolves travel in packs?"

"Hush," Piotr said, looking back at me over his shoulder. "If it's near you'll scare it off."

Maybe it wasn't such a bad idea if some wolf knew that we were there and ran off to hide. I was starting to remember all the nursery rhymes that Mom had told us growing up. That one wolf, the one trying to trick Little Red Riding Hood, was big enough to swallow a man whole.

"Maybe we should go back," I said, slowing a bit so I could look around for any hint of a furry body in the trees lining the river. "Those fish aren't going to catch themselves."

Piotr was only five years older than me but a lot bigger already. He was almost an adult and wasn't afraid of anything. Not that I was afraid of any possible wolf which was most likely cut back and stalking us even as we stalked it. I started looking back as much as I was looking into the trees around us.

Donder and Blitzen meekly trudged behind me. What they lacked in spirit they made up for in being mild-mannered and obedient. They weren't worried about any wolf hiding or sneaking up behind us.

Just ahead was a break in the high river bank, where the earth sloped up gently away from the river. The grass was beaten down and the mud by the river fairly trampled from hooves and paws. Piotr stopped and looked up the game trail.

"He's gone up the trail," Piotr said.

"Oh, well, those fish aren't going to catch themselves," I said.

I heaved a sigh of relief tinged with disappointment. It would have been exciting to see an actual wolf but following tracks along a muddy river bank was a lot easier than across prairie grass. There was no way of following the tracks up there. As much as I liked the idea of seeing a wolf, meeting up with one in the flesh was a bit unnerving.

Piotr took Donder's reins. He wiped most of the mud off his boots by scraping them on the rough grass on the side of the game trail. "Let's go up," Piotr said. He turned Donder so that the horse was downslope from him, grabbed a handful of mane, and swung onto Donder's bare back.

I had been looking forward to fish for dinner. I looked back at the river and sighed before turning Blitzen so that she was slightly downslope from me. I had to jump onto Blitzen on my stomach then swing my leg over her rump as I sat up.

The mud stuck to my boots felt like it weighed a good ten pounds. I looked down at my feet, considering climbing back down and trying to knock some mud off like Piotr had thought to do. Donder was already climbing the game trail. I turned Blitzen and she followed Donder without any coaxing from me.

There was an Indian boy riding a brown and white painted horse across a meadow as we climbed up out of the river bank. He was riding at a full gallop. My full attention was on the horse. That was a horse with spirit.

Chapter Eight

The horse flowed across the grasses. Though the horse's legs ate up the ground beneath it vigorously the boy on its back looked like he was gliding across the meadow. I watched them running at full speed. It was a sight of beauty.

Back then seeing Indians was common. The boy looked more frightened of us than we were of him when he spotted us coming up over the riverbank. He pulled back on his horse's reins. The paint's back legs bent and his front legs stuck out in front of him as he stopped abruptly. Bits of grass cut by the horse's hooves and dust billowed up in a cloud around the horse's hooves.

Even before the horse had completed the stop the boy was turning the horse, bending the horse's neck back to the side. The boy leaned over the horse's neck and the animal straightened and lunged forward in the opposite direction.

The boy was looking back at us over his shoulder. When he realized that it was just Piotr and me he slowed his horse and turned him in a wide arc so that they were facing us again. The horse loped toward us then slowed to a trot. The Indian boy stopped the horse about thirty meters short of reaching us.

He yelled gibberish at us, waving his arm. Piotr slowed his pony and held his arm out to the side to signal for me to stop. I pounded my pony's sides with my heels and rode around Piotr, straight up to the Indian boy. The boy continued to yell at me the whole time in his native tongue.

He looked older than me but younger than Piotr. He wore buckskins and had his hair braided into a single braid down his back.

The braid nearly reached the small of his back it was so long.

"Do you speak English?" I asked, pulling back on the reins until my mare grudgingly stopped.

The boy shook his head. That made no sense. If he didn't speak English how had he known that I asked him if he spoke English. The boy's horse was shaking his head, sniffing the air, and pawing the ground.

Piotr rode up next to me and stopped. "What are you doing going by me?" Piotr asked me. "That mare is in heat and that's no gelding."

"I wanted to meet him," I said, gesturing at the boy on the brown and white horse in front of us. "He doesn't speak English though." I turned back to the Indian. "Sprechen Sie Deutsch?" I asked.

"Hiya," the Indian boy said, shaking his head.

"How does he know what I'm saying if he doesn't speak English or German?" I asked Piotr.

"He's probably saying no to anything you say," Piotr said.

"Did you see elephants in the river?" I asked the boy.

"Hiya," the Indian boy said, shaking his head. He struggled to maintain control of his horse.

"Elephants in the river?" Piotr asked me, smacking my arm.

I rubbed the sore spot. "Ouch," I muttered. "I just wanted to see. You said that."

"That's a nice horse though," Piotr said, studying the brown and white painted horse.

The horse was heavily muscled, with a fine, curved face. It towered above our two nondescript brown farm horses. Instead of a bit and bridle, twisted bands of leather formed a halter with a thicker band across the horse's nose. Leather wrapped feathers dangled from the halter up by the horse's ear. The reins were attached to the halter.

The Indian boy noticed our interest in his horse and scowled at us. There was a red hand print on the horse's hindquarters. I looked at that hand print more closely. Someone had spread paint on their hand and smacked it against the horse's hindquarters. Paint had dripped down from the shape of the hand.

"Why do you put a hand on the horse?" I asked, forgetting that he couldn't understand me. "Can you really control him without a bit?"

"He's not going to have control long," Piotr said, eyeing the stallion.

Two riders appeared in the meadow, coming out of the trees behind the Indian boy. Startled at the sound of hoof beats he looked over his shoulder. Piotr and I both watched with interest as the two riders approached us at a full gallop.

When the boy on the brown and white paint saw who rode towards them his head dropped and his shoulders slumped. Up closer the boy on the brown and white paint looked much closer to my age than Piotr's age. The two Indians approaching were older than Piotr, almost young men. My mom would still call them boys.

The new riders circled us at a full gallop, looking us over. I watched in amazement at how well they rode. It was like they were part of their horses. They only circled once before they slowed their horses to a stop right next to the younger Indian boy. Dust and dried grasses swirled into the air around us.

When they stopped their attention was on the younger Indian boy. They didn't even pay attention to Piotr and me. The oldest of the pair scolded him sharply in their language. I had a longing to know what they were saying to each other. It looked like it would have been interesting.

"What are you two doing here?" one of the pair asked, finally looking between me and Piotr.

"More like what are you three doing here?" Piotr said.

"We are searching for our brother," the taller, long-faced teenager said. He rode a dun gelding.

Blitzen raised her head and whinnied. Her whole body vibrated from the force of that whinny. I could feel it between my thighs. The brown and white paint pointed its head up to the sky and curled its upper lip back as it savored the mare's scent.

The second of the pair, short and stocky, astride a buckskin mare smacked the boy on the paint across the shoulder, almost knocking him off the horse. The boy on the paint curled his shoulders in and his chin was almost down to his chest. The stallion snaked his head and bugled. The boy's fingers were turning white from pulling on the reins to keep the stallion under control.

No one had to tell me for me to know that all three were brothers. They acted like older brothers. I felt bad for the boy on the paint. They clearly felt they were in the right though and by the way he kept his head down he must have done something to deserve their scolding him. Still, I didn't like it.

"Leave him alone," I said, nudging Blitzen closer.

"Oooh oooh, the puppy growls," the oldest of the three said. He laughed and turned his attention from the boy on the paint to me. "You're just a puppy. What are you gonna do to stop me?"

"Leave my brother alone," Piotr said, riding up past me and grabbing Blitzen's reins before I could ride any closer.

As if that was going to stop me. I slid off Blitzen's bony back and promptly fell on my face. The mud under my boots had dried and I had forgotten about it. Inches of caked mud threw off my balance. Everyone laughed, even Piotr.

I faced them, hands in fists raised up, which just made them laugh even harder. At least Piotr stopped laughing but he was still grinning. It was like the grin was stuck on his face. He kept trying to keep a straight face but that grin kept popping out.

The boy on the paint looked up at me. I couldn't be sure if he even knew what was going on but he gave me a smile. Not the laughing grin of the others but a real smile.

"You shouldn't be here," the long-faced teenager said. "You are on agency land."

"No," Piotr said. "The boundary is at least five miles west yet."

"What are you doing here, so close to agency land?" the teenager asked.

"We were following a wolf," I said, dropping my fists.

My excitement transferred to the Indian boys. The boy astride the buckskin mare looked up at me in interest. He said something in his language and the boy on the paint looked up, eyes widening. I had the attention of everyone.

Chapter Nine

"You saw the wolf?" the Indian teenager asked.

"Tracks," Piotr said. "But they were fresh."

"I am Catches Pebble," the boy on the dun gelding said.

"Talks With Fist," the stocky boy said. He pointed at the younger boy. "Walking Moon."

"I am Piotr Hansohn and this is my brother, Hank," Piotr said.

"Growling Puppy," Talks With Fist said, pointing at me.

"Tell Walking Moon that he has a wonderful horse," I said to Catches Pebbles.

"If it was his horse I would," Catches Pebbles said.

"It is our father's prized stallion," Talks With Fist said, hitting Walking Moon's arm with the back of his hand. "We have been chasing him to bring him back."

"Where are those wolf tracks?" Catches Pebbles asked.

We started out looking for the wolf. First Catches Pebbles and Piotr rode back to the river so that Catches Pebbles could see the tracks. When they came back Catches Pebbles took the stallion's reins and Walking Moon pushed himself onto his knees on the stallion's back and slid onto the back of the buckskin mare behind his brother. Talks with Fist and Walking Moon went down to the river to see as well.

While we waited for them, Catches Pebbles and Piotr struck up an instant friendship, laughing and talking like old friends. Most of the talk seemed to be about troublesome younger brothers.

There was no sign of the wolf up away from the muddy river bank so we headed back to the tree line, hoping to see if the wolf had circled back to the river. Their rush to retrieve Walking Moon and their father's horse got waylaid by the search for the possible wolf.

Eventually we ended up sitting in a massive oak tree that had a large branch growing out right over the river. Piotr was asking what the Lakota word was for things and I listened carefully as Catches Pebbles translated everything Piotr could think to ask what it was in Lakota. Walking Moon walked out on the tree limb as nimbly as a goat.

"Don't even think about it," Piotr said to me when I eyed the limb, debating on if I had the courage to follow Walking Moon.

"I wasn't," I said even though I was. It was a relief that Piotr wouldn't let me try because I wasn't so sure I could have.

Walking Moon grinned and pivoted around. The branch wobbled under his weight. Catches Pebbles stopped in mid-sentence, staring at Walking Moon. He looked down to the area below Walking Moon, tilting his head as he studied the river below the branch. "I hope you feel like a swim," Catches Pebbles said to Walking Moon in Lakota. He translated what he said. Piotr laughed.

Walking Moon said something to his brother in Lakota, a grin splitting his face. He bounced on his toes, making the branch swing up and down. Catches Pebbles crawled a few feet out onto the branch, his added weight bending the branch down closer to the water. Walking Moon laughed and ran along the branch, jumping over Catches Pebbles.

Dad wasn't happy when we returned home without any fish. At least we remembered to go back to the fishing hole and collect the poles before heading home. We'd have really been in trouble if we'd returned home without fish or the fishing poles.

Whenever we could sneak away that summer the five of us could be found together. We never did catch up with that wolf but by the end of the summer I learned the Lakota language and became great friends with Walking Moon. In Lakota his name was Maniyanhanwi but I couldn't manage to say the name at first so I called him Mani. Likewise, Walking Moon learned English.

They never called me Hank. Their name for me was Growling Puppy. I didn't really like that name but they called me that anyway. I wasn't a puppy. I tried to talk them into changing it to Growling Wolf or Soaring Eagle. They just laughed and told me that I was always a Growling Puppy. Even Piotr called me Growling Puppy when we were with Catches Pebbles and Walking Moon.

"Why don't you know English like your brothers?" I asked him once at the end of the summer.

Though Walking Moon had learned English I had learned Lakota better than he had learned English. So we normally talked in Lakota. Walking Moon could understand most of what we said in English but he had a difficult time saying the words so he didn't like to use English words very often.

"They learned English at boarding school," Mani said. "Until they ran away."

"Boarding school?" I asked. "Back east?"

"Indian school," Walking Moon said. "I hid. Bad place." He shook his head.

"I like school," I said.

"Indian school is different," Walking Moon said. "At Indian school they change you into white people. But we're not white people. We're Indians. How do we stop being Indians?"

That was a mystery to me also. "At my school we just learn history and math," I said. "And geometry. And geography. English too, I guess."

"That's because you're already white," Walking Moon said.

That made sense. An idea flared to life inside me. "You should come to my school instead then," I said.

Walking Moon shook his head. "I'm not white," he said.

"We can ask," I said. "My dad always says it never hurts to ask."

"Maybe I don't want to go to your school," Walking Moon said, growing agitated.

"But you can learn to read," I said.

"Can I read in Lakota?" Walking Moon asked.

"It's English," I said. "But you're smart. You'll get it."

"Why do I need to read in English?" Walking Moon said. "They should teach it in Lakota."

"I had to learn English," I said, shrugging. I didn't understand why it was making him so huffy.

"You're white," Walking Moon said.

"I'm from Germany," I said in German. "A lot of us came from Germany, Norway, even Sweden." I repeated what I'd said in German in English so that he could understand me.

Walking Moon calmed and grew thoughtful. "I will think about it, Growling Puppy," he said in English.

Well, no matter what Walking Moon said, I planned to ask Dad if Walking Moon could go to my school. I forgot about it for a few days but remembered when we were out walking the cornfields to check the progress of the plants.

"Dad, can Walking Moon go to school in New Ulm?" I asked.

"If he wants to, I suppose," Dad said, squatting on his heels and studying the leaves of a corn stalk. "Does he want to?"

"I don't know," I admitted. "But if he wanted to he could, right?"

"He couldn't do it living out at the agency," Dad said, straightening and walking farther down the row.

"Why not?" I asked.

"Well, that's too far to travel every day," Dad said. "And I don't know if he has the money to pay for school."

"It costs money?" I asked in surprise.

Dad squatted next to another plant. "Everything costs money, Hank," he said. He straightened. "Everything looks good. Should be a good harvest."

"Well, he should go to school," I said with conviction.

Dad looked over at me. "Why do you care so strongly, Hank?" Dad asked.

"He's my friend, Dad," I said. "You always say education is important."

"And it is," Dad said, nodding. "Aren't there schools for the Indians? He wouldn't have to pay to attend those schools."

"He doesn't want to go there," I said, shaking my head.

Dad put his hand on my shoulder. "It is his life to live, Hank," Dad said. "Being a friend doesn't mean you force your friend to share your values."

"I was just seeing if he could go to my school," I said.

"If he wants an education he can go to the Indian school," Dad said.

"He said they try to turn Indians into Whites at the boarding schools," I said. "He's not white, Dad. He's an Indian."

"Then he has no need of schooling," Dad said. "The schooling is to help them adjust to civilized life. If that's not what he wants then it's a waste of his time."

I didn't say anything. There was nothing more to say. Dad just didn't understand. Walking Moon couldn't go to an Indian school because that meant going away. They would cut his long braid and beat him if he spoke Lakota. Catches Pebbles had told him all the bad things that happened in those schools, the reason Catches Pebbles had run away from the school.

I only went out to the agency with Walking Moon once. It was in September the first year I met him. Piotr had gone there several times with Catches Pebbles but I hadn't gone with those times. I was curious to see a real live Indian village and asked Walking Moon if I could see his home.

It wasn't what I expected. There were teepees but there were also wood lodges and across the dirt cart road was a cluster of log buildings where the traders lived and traded with the Indians. Tar paper had been used the winter before to insulate the buildings against the cold wind. Several corners of the tar paper had come loose from the building and it fluttered in the wind with a rasping sound as it flapped and rubbed against the building.

The grass had been trampled to dirt around the buildings and teepees. There were no trees. Dogs and children ran around laughing, barking, and screaming. Many of the smaller children were naked.

Women crouched around campfires, performing various tasks. There was a woman grinding grain with a slab of stone and pestle. Two women had their hands and arms up to their elbows in a large wicker basket, moving their whole bodies back and forth. Mixing something I figured.

We rode through the labyrinth of teepees and buildings to Walking Moon's home. Everyone stopped what they were doing to stare at us as we rode through. I heard a few women teasing Walking Moon that he had better ask his father before bringing a pet home. Walking Moon stopped in front of a large teepee with paintings on the outside and we dismounted.

A woman carrying wood kindling into the village dropped several branches and another woman hit her over the shoulders with one of the dropped branches. I stared in shock as the woman was beat until she dropped to her knees, dropping all the kindling she had been carrying.

My first impulse was to go to the woman being beat and help but Walking Moon put his hand on my arm when I took a step in that direction. "Do not interfere," he said. "That is my aunt's slave. It would dishonor her to interfere."

"Slave?" I asked, looking at the Indian woman cowering below Walking Moon's aunt. "But she's an Indian."

"She's Chippewa," Walking Moon said. "My uncle captured her when she was a child."

"Slave?" I muttered again. The woman with the stick had dropped it and walked away. The slave was on her knees picking up all the dropped kindling, walking on her knees to reach all the scattered wood.

"Come," Walking Moon said, heading for the teepee entrance nearest us. "I will show you my new bow."

I followed Walking Moon to the teepee, pausing to look back at the Indian slave. An Indian man approached her, talking to her as she stood and brushed away dried grass from her clothes with her free hand. With his back to me I couldn't hear what he was saying. Walking Moon ducked his head back out of the teepee, wondering what was taking me so long.

"That is my uncle, Water Over Rock," Walking Moon said, looking over at the two talking. "He is thinking of marrying Spotted Fawn, which is why my aunt, his wife, is so angry with her."

"He can marry a slave?" I asked in surprise.

What I knew about slaves was only what I had read about. I'd never seen a slave, not even in Chicago or New York. I thought slaves were negroes.

"Well, she won't be a slave anymore if he marries her," Walking Moon said in a tone that suggested I was an idiot for not knowing that.

"She won't?" I asked, following him into the teepee.

"My aunt wants to send her back to the Chippewa so that my uncle doesn't marry her," Walking Moon said.

"Would she be a slave there?" I asked, thoroughly confused.

Walking Moon laughed. "Of course not. It was my uncle who captured her," he said. He held his side as he laughed. "You are so funny sometimes, Growling Puppy." When he calmed from his laughter he picked up his bow to show me. "See? Feel how smooth the wood is."

The bow was nice. I ran my thumb along the wood, noting how smooth it was. There was not a single bump or jagged area on the entire bow. I was still thinking about that woman who was a slave even though she was an Indian. It suddenly hit me that Walking

Moon said that his uncle's wife did not want his uncle to marry the slave.

"Indians can have more than one wife?" I asked in surprise, forgetting about the bow.

"If they can afford them," Walking Moon said. "Are we going to talk about some stupid slave or my beautiful new bow?"

Walking Moon's mom entered the teepee. She stared at me with a solemn face before turning to Walking Moon. "Did you offer our guest a meal?" she asked.

"He's not a guest," Walking Moon said to his mom, brow furrowing. "He's Growling Puppy." He looked at me. "I'm sorry. I will fetch food."

"You speak Lakota?" his mom said as Walking Moon opened leather pouches and put together a meal of jerky and dried berries. I nodded. "Maniyanhanwi has spoken highly of you, Hank of New Ulm."

"He has?" I asked in surprise.

She smiled at me and removed a pack from her back. She swung the pack around and set it upright on the floor of the teepee. A baby inside the frame stared back at me.

Walking Moon gave me the jerky and dried berries, saving a piece of jerky for himself. I took a bite of the dried meat, not certain if it was beef, deer, buffalo, or even raccoon. One never knew. It was tough to bite into and I had to hold it with my teeth and pull to get a piece bitten off. It was salty and dry but had a good taste once I started chewing it enough to soften it up.

I looked over at the baby inside the wood frame. I didn't know if it was a boy or girl. Babies all looked the same to me.

"What is that?" I asked Walking Moon.

"A baby," Walking Moon said.

"No," I said. "I mean, what's the baby in?"

"A cradleboard," Walking Moon said. "Don't you use them for your babies?"

"No," I said. "We put our babies in cradles. You know, baby beds."

"How do you carry a baby around in a bed?" Walking Moon asked.

"You don't," I said. I pointed at the cradleboard. "That's a good idea."

"You go now," Walking Moon's mom said. "It's better that you are not here."

Chapter Ten

Isaac

When Master Meadows passed to the great beyond it was completely unexpected. One day he did not wake up. There had been no hint the night before that he was even feeling ill. We were almost finished with breakfast and Master Meadows still had not come down. Lisbett sent me to fetch him.

"His food's gone cold," Lisbett said, frowning at the plate of food waiting on the table. "It's not like him to dally in bed so late. Go fetch him. Tell him his plate's in the warming tray but it's not gonna taste much good much longer sitting there."

I ran up the stairs two at a time. It wasn't that I was in a hurry or concerned. It was because I was young and full of vigor. The need to stretch my muscles was always on my mind.

First I knocked and called his name. A full minute passed with no response so I knocked again. Another minute passed. I tried the door handle. On nights Master Meadows did not want to be disturbed he would lock the door. There had been no visitors the night before so I did not expect the door to be locked and it was not.

I opened the door a few inches and pressed my cheek up against the panel carved on the door. The painted wood was smooth and cold against my cheek. "Master Meadows," I said. Nothing. I opened the door wider. I could see him lying on the bed. "Master Meadows," I called out. "Lisbett has your breakfast warming for you. Master Meadows?"

It was a feeling. Despite the knocking and calling out his name repeatedly, Master Meadows had not even stirred once on the bed. I felt a strange sinking sensation in the pit of my stomach and took another step into the room. I knew somehow. I didn't call his name again because I knew that he would not answer.

I took a step further into the room. My legs trembled. I took another step and another. When I reached the side of the bed I could see Master Meadows. It looked like he was just sleeping but he was not breathing and his eyes were half open. With a trembling hand I reached forward, touching his cheek with my fingertips. I jerked my hand away instantly. Master Meadows was cold.

Instead of going down to tell Lisbett right away I sat on the floor next to the bed and cried. The grief was overwhelming. Not only had I lost a man who was a father to me but the world had lost a wonderful man. He had not even been ill. There had been no hint the night before that he would succumb to something in his sleep.

I don't know how long I sat on the floor and cried but long enough that Lisbett came looking for me. Climbing the stairs made her out of breath so she stood at the doorway huffing and trying to catch her breath. It did not take long before she realized what had happened and she started crying and clutching the door knob to keep from falling to the floor in anguish.

I jumped to my feet and took Lisbett's arm, leading her to a wing-backed chair next to the bed. Lisbett sank into the chair. Tears ran down her cheeks, filling the cracks in the wrinkles. "Is he? Is he? Is he gone?" she asked between sobs.

I nodded. "He's cold," I said.

Lisbett clutched my hand. "Lord have mercy on his soul," she said. "Might be he was a sinner but he was a good man for all that and really we are all sinners."

"He was a wonderful man," I said, wiping the tears from my face. I sniffled. "What do we do?"

"I suppose we'll need to send word to his nephew, Mr.

Andrew," Lisbett said, gaze turning to the man on the bed. "But no hurry. We can do our grieving first. There might be no more chance once they know."

"I'll go tell Old Hank," I said.

I was going down the stairs when I thought of the papers Master Meadows kept in the safe. It could be my only chance to know what was written on the papers from the auction block. It seemed cold hearted to be concerned with that with Master Meadows lying in his death bed.

I hesitated, debating. It was the only chance I would get. I knew that. Master Meadows would understand. Master Meadows kept the combination written down on a piece of paper in his desk.

Instead of going straight out to the stable I turned in the opposite direction from the staircase. My heart thudded in my chest as I opened the drawer and stared at the numbers written on the paper. I wasn't stealing, yet I felt like a thief as I walked to the safe and turned the dial.

I hurried, glancing up at the door several times. The safe lock clicked and I swung the heavy door open. I did not look at the other papers, pushing them aside as I searched for the thick slab of folded parchment that the auctioneer had given Master Meadows the day he bought me.

I had seen him stuff them in there a few days after the auction and I knew they'd still be there. I didn't know what I'd find, not really expecting anything in particular. The papers were near the bottom of the pile of various documents in the top shelf. I carefully opened the tri-folded collection of papers and read the first page.

It really was my actual birthday that Master Meadows celebrated all those years. I had come from a plantation that kept disciplined records. My mother's birth date was listed as well. She was only fifteen when she gave birth to me. My father's name was listed as unknown.

There was nothing noted about why the plantation owner had

sent me to the auction block when I was only five years old, why he would take me from my mother. I read the whole document, memorizing every detail, afraid that I would forget something important.

My mother's name was Eveline and I was born on Summerset Plantation. The plantation owner was William Meadows. The name startled me until I remembered that Master Meadows' father shared his name. He must have known. Yes, certainly he knew that I came from his father's plantation.

I reached the last page. I glanced at the doorway, uncertain how long I had been crouched in front of the safe reading. I looked at the last page. Master Meadows had insured me. The last paper was newer than the rest of the papers in my hand. It was only a year old. I had been insured for three thousand dollars. I was a valuable slave.

I stared at the insurance receipt. Master Meadows had taken out an insurance policy on his slave. I had been his property after all.

I refolded the papers and put them back where they had been in the pile of documents, shifting everything to exactly how it had been before I opened the safe. I shut the door and spun the dial.

I went out to the stable and told Old Hank the news about Master Meadows then I went to the sheriff and told him that Master Meadows had died but I did not know how to reach his nephew to tell him the news. The sheriff was sad to learn that Master Meadows had died in his sleep.

"You just go home, boy," the sheriff said in a somber voice. "I'll go fetch the younger Mr. Meadows and he'll take care of everything."

Master Andrew Meadows inherited me from his uncle. The elder Master Meadows, Master William Meadows, was a lot different than the nephew Master Meadows.

Living with the elder Master Meadows had meant almost not being a slave. Almost.

Almost not being a slave is not the same as not being a slave even when my owner was as great as the elder Master Meadows. When I stepped out the door of Master Meadows' house I was always aware that I was a slave. Going into the younger Master Meadows' house made me aware of being a slave every minute of the day.

God works in mysterious ways. At first I was angry that elder Master Meadows had died without freeing me first. I would have gone north, where black men are free. I had given it a lot of thought. I was so confident that Master Meadows would eventually free me that I gave a lot of thought to what I would do as a free man.

I would head north. Chicago or Boston, it didn't matter to me. The name of the city meant nothing. Living north meant being free. Any city in The North would have been fine by me. I could get a job, have my own place, and live as a free man.

But Master Meadows had not freed me upon his deathbed. There had been no hidden emancipation papers to be revealed upon his death. Instead he had left me to his nephew as the property I was. I was a bit in shock the first few days following the death of my almost father.

Within an hour of returning from telling the sheriff that Master Meadows had passed in the night five men had arrived at the house. I knew one of the men by name, Mr. Shay, Master Meadows' lawyer.

One of the men was a doctor who went straight up to the bedroom where Master Meadows slumbered in his eternal rest. Mr. Shay went straight to the office. After a few minutes he came out looking for me.

"Do you know the combination of the safe, boy?" Mr. Shay asked me. I shook my head no. "Damn," he muttered to himself, turning to stare into the office in deep thought. "I'll have to send for a locksmith." Mr. Shay looked over at me again. "Don't you touch nothing. Until we get things settled you stay in the house but out of the office. Do you understand me?"

I nodded but said nothing. The reality that Master Meadows was really gone was sinking in and I could not hold back the tears welling in my eyes. It had been so sudden and unexpected. Yet I was glad that he had gone so peacefully in his sleep.

"We'll start with you," Mr. Shay said, nodding at the other men. They stepped up to me and without any warning stripped off my jacket and then my shirt. My first impulse was to struggle against their manhandling but I stood numbly instead.

Being stripped and examined like a piece of livestock to assess my value was the first bitter taste of losing elder Master Meadows' protection. It was humiliating. One man even stuck his filthy finger in my mouth and felt my teeth.

"Big boy like him would fetch over a thousand five hundred for sure," the man probing my mouth said to the man behind him.

"He's insured for three thousand," the man said.

The man's eyes widened. "He ain't no smithy," he said. "What else is worth so much?"

"Nonetheless, that's his value," the other man said.

There I was, standing buck naked in the salon with four men looking at me, poking and prodding me and talking amongst themselves like I wasn't even in the room. I felt fear that day. Genuine fear. My stomach tightened in knots and I kept forgetting to breath. I thought they were getting ready to put me up on the block.

The first time I opened my mouth to speak I was cuffed alongside the head like a disobedient dog and told to not speak unless directly asked a question. I had just wanted to know what was going to happen to me. It took great effort not to speak again. My head was spinning with questions.

"Don't you give no trouble, boy," one of the men said. He held a ledger and was making notes.

"Old William spoiled his blackies," the man checking my teeth said. He stared into my eyes, leaning his head closer to me. It took all my self-control to not pull back away from him. His breath smelled of tobacco and rot. "You're going to behave for Mr.

Meadows now, ain't ya?"

I was confused. "Mr. Meadows?" I asked without thinking. Did the man not realize that Master Meadows had died?

The man raised his hand to cuff me again but the man with the ledger stopped him with a curt command. "Don't, James," the man with the ledger said, standing. "Isaac, isn't it?" he said to me, coming to stand in front of me. "Your late master's nephew has inherited you. He will come by tomorrow to collect you. Do you know Andrew Meadows?"

Learning that I was not going up on the block but being moved to the nephew's residence was some relief. I nodded. I had met the younger Master Meadows a few times and the elder Master Meadows often spoke highly of his nephew.

I don't know how to explain the disappointment at realizing that the elder Master Meadows had not seen fit to give me my freedom upon his death. I had been so sure that he would set me free. Not only had I lost a man I loved but I felt betrayed.

I told myself over and over again that Master Meadows had not freed me because he thought he was protecting me but a real father would have let me take my chances in the world. Disappointment left a bad taste in my mouth.

It was too late by then when I suddenly realized that I could have forged emancipation papers and put them in the safe. It just never dawned on me that there would be a need. It was too late once the sheriff informed the family. I couldn't even imagine the great punishment should I have attempted such a thing and been found out in my crime.

Mr. Shay spent the day going through Master Meadows' office and eventually found the piece of paper with the safe's combination written on it. I recognized the stack of papers in his hand when he left that evening.

It was a good thing I had not thought to forge emancipation papers when I had the chance. Any legal documents were given to

Mr. Shay and he would have known that anything I wrote up would be a forgery. If that man with him knew what Master Meadows had insured me for then they likely knew if there had been other papers or not.

My grief and shock had clouded my thinking. Master Meadows would not have created emancipation papers and willed me to his nephew both. Someone was watching out for me that day by not allowing me to think of making forgeries before the lawyer and his men arrived at the house.

Lisbett stayed in the bedroom until they carried Master Meadows down into the salon and put him in his coffin. For two days a steady stream of visitors moved from the front door, through the salon, and back out again. Ladies and gentleman came to pay their parting respects to Master Meadows.

Samuel Taylor stood at the coffin and cried for over an hour. His wife and two daughters came with him but left again without him after only a few minutes. I was curious about meeting Hetty Taylor since Mr. Taylor had suggested that she would help me go to university.

Hetty Taylor was a stern looking woman who did not give me a second glance. I could just as well have been a chair in the room for all the attention she gave me. I think Mr. Taylor was being overly optimistic to think she would have been interested in helping me.

Mr. Taylor was Master Meadows' greatest friend and his grief touched my heart. I don't believe that he would have wept so hard had it been a member of his own family in that coffin instead of his closest friend. They certainly enjoyed each other's company over the years, hardly apart more than a day except when one was traveling.

Eventually Mr. Taylor wandered into the kitchen where Old Hank, Lisbett, and I sat at the kitchen table. Old Hank's eyes were swollen and red but he sat in complete silence. Lisbett's eyes were red and she occasionally wailed and snuffled in her grief. Mr. Taylor sat down at the kitchen table next to me and burst into tears all over again.

"I loved him so," Mr. Taylor said before dropping his head into his arms on the table.

"He was a great man," Lisbett said. "I loved him as if he was my son." She pulled out a hankie and wiped her face. She took a deep breath, pressing her lips together. "We should celebrate his life. Grieving his death is done."

Mr. Taylor's shoulders shook in great wracking sobs and he remained bent over the table with his face buried in his crossed arms. The urge to put my hand on the man's back and comfort him with my touch came and went. Though he was almost like an uncle to me, physically comforting Mr. Taylor was not in me. Mr. Taylor was still a white man and I was a slave.

"Mr. Meadows grew up on a plantation north of here," Lisbett said. "I was working in the house, in the kitchens. He was the third born. I always knew he was special even as a little boy."

Mr. Taylor raised his head and looked at Lisbett. "How old are you?" he asked in surprise.

"I've lost track a few times." Lisbett said. "I was twenty years old when Master Meadows was born."

"You're over eighty years old?" Mr. Taylor said, eyes widening.

"If you say so," Lisbett said. "Master Meadows brought me and Old Hank with him when his mother died. He was good to us and I will miss him."

"Amen," Old Hank said.

Lisbett looked over at Old Hank. She put her hand over the back of his hand. "We been married all these years thanks to Master Meadows," she said. "Usually a marriage gets automatically dissolved when a wife or husband gets sold. But Master Meadows, he kept us together. All these years."

"I met William in school," Mr. Taylor said, trying to smile through his tears. "We were both so young and full of energy. We lost touch for a few years but found each other again. His was the greatest friendship." Mr. Taylor burst into fresh sobs.

I listened to them talk. I felt numb inside. The betrayal I felt was stronger than the grief. Master Meadows had named me in his will as property to go to his nephew. I was to be transferred into another's household without any say in the matter.

The younger Master Meadows did not come collect me as the lawyer said he would but after a few days Mr. Shay came to the house and escorted me himself to my new home.

It was with a heavy heart that I entered the younger Master Meadows' household. The very atmosphere of the place was like night and day from the elder Master Meadows' house. Master Meadows had never married and his quiet bachelor holdings in the middle of town consisted of me, Master Meadows, old Hank, and Lisbett.

The younger Master Meadows, Andrew Meadows, was married with a young family and a handful of slaves plus a paid servant who did all the cooking and managed the house slaves. The house was out on the very edge of town, a sprawling three story mansion on twenty acres of land. There was a pasture behind the stables, orchards, and almost an acre sized vegetable garden.

There was Andrew Junior, who looked to be about twelve years of age. The boy was at that awkward stage in life where he was growing so fast his joints ached. He was a mannerly child, not kind, nor mean spirited, though he did enjoy teasing his younger siblings. Young Andrew Junior already knew a slave's place in the world but did not treat us badly as long as we understood our place as well.

Ulysses was a few years younger than Andrew Junior. That boy with the name that twisted my tongue was driven by a curiosity that drove anyone around him batty. He would latch himself onto a person and ask questions from sunup to sundown. Ulysses wanted to know everything. Ulysses did not ever quite understand a slave's place in the world and more often than not forgot that we were slaves.

The youngest Meadows when I arrived in the household was Miss Constance. She was a vivacious seven year old. Miss Constance looked just like a living doll all dressed up in her finery with curls that spiraled around her face. The first time I saw her I stopped in my tracks and just stared in surprise. I had never seen such a pretty sight.

The middle-aged black woman with the child glared at me and whisked her away. The woman was Ham, the upstairs maid and nanny to the little girl. Ham's full name was Hamilton but everyone but Master Meadows called her Ham.

Miss Angeline was born a year after I arrived at the house. After Angeline there was one more boy Meadows come into the family. He was a sickly baby. I never even ever saw him. He never left the nursery and he died within a year of being born.

When he was struggling to live there were a lot of whispers about him being deformed. I overheard Ham and Betsy whispering in the kitchen about Mistress Meadows being upset that she had given birth to such a baby. When he died in his sleep one day Tildy told me that Ham thought Mistress Meadows had put a pillow over the baby's face.

Even huddled on our bed whispering, such speculation was dangerous. I listened but did not say anything. "Ham said he was fine that day. No coughing or wheezing," Tildy whispered. "Then in the morning she woke up and found him blue in his cradle." Tildy paused as she thought about it. "Mistress Meadows never did like that baby. It upset her to think she had given birth to a monstrosity." Tildy never mentioned it again.

Ham left the household soon after the baby died. Betsy was upset and spent the day walking around with tears rolling down her cheeks. Bannister was upset, thinking Ham had run away. I knew that Ham had been sold because I saw the receipt. No one ever mentioned the baby again. I don't even know what or if they named him.

Bannister was the butler. He opened the door and kept an eye on anyone visiting the house. There were a lot of visitors to the house so Bannister was kept very busy. He seemed to have a knack of knowing when someone was approaching the door. Bannister never forgot a face and always remembered what a visitor liked to eat or drink.

I met Betsy first. She was the cook's assistant and downstairs maid. Betsy was in the kitchen peeling back the corn husks from a big pile of corn cobs when I arrived from the elder Master Meadows' house. When she spotted me her eyes got all round and she stared at me with her mouth forming a big oh.

There was a white woman in the kitchen wearing an apron. She was tall and bony thin with dark brown hair pulled back from her face. "Who are you?" the white woman asked in a sharp voice.

"Isaac," I said.

"What are you doing in my kitchen, Isaac?" she asked, eyes narrowing.

"Mr. Shay told me to go around to the kitchen while he talked to Master Meadows," I said.

The woman nodded. "Go sit outside and wait," she said.

I learned later that the white woman in the kitchen was Dorothy Jennings, a hired servant. She wasn't there very long. Within a year of my arrival she gave notice and headed west.

Lisbett and old Hank did not come with me to the new place. The elder Master Meadows had signed papers giving them their freedom and a pension so that they could remain in his house until they died. He had even thought to stipulate the house and all it contained. Upon their natural deaths the house would go to Mr. Taylor. Not that I begrudged either of them their new found freedom but I have to admit that was painful news to hear.

Chapter Eleven

The younger Master Meadows did not know what to do with me so he put me in the stables until my fate could be determined. I slept on a thread-bare blanket tossed on the hay in the loft. I did not have any possessions. All of my things remained in the house, except for a change of clothes. I used the spare clothes as a pillow.

Lisbett promised to keep an eye on my books until I could collect them. We both knew that would never happen. At least they had a good home. All my things remained in my second story bedroom next to Master Meadows' bedroom. I could have packed up the items scattered about the room and dragged them along with me but I didn't know if they would be taken from me so I left them safe in the bedroom.

The stables were under the care of a middle-aged black man by the name of Lucas. Lucas was on the short side and I towered above him. Most of Lucas' teeth were missing and the few he still had were outlined in black.

Lucas was not quite friendly but not antagonistic either. He never told me to do anything and when I performed tasks without being bidden he did not care either. I think Lucas had pretty much given up on life and just existed. When I looked in his eyes he looked dead inside.

The second day of waiting Mr. Ulysses found me in the stable. He was a friendly little fellow, pestering me with questions but his heart was in the right place so it was difficult to get too frustrated with him even though he made my head hurt with the bombardment of nonstop chatter. Lucas had conspicuously vanished the moment

Ulysses stepped into the stable.

"Who are you?" Ulysses asked upon spotting me up in the loft.

"Isaac, sir," I said, intending to descend the ladder. He was just a boy but I still didn't want to lounge about up in the loft while the master's son was in the stable.

Ulysses was fast though and I didn't expect him to go directly to the ladder and climb up to join me in the loft. My escape was blocked. "What are you doing here, Isaac?" Ulysses asked.

"Waiting," I said. "Sir," I added as an afterthought.

Ulysses remained standing on the ladder's upper rungs, his hands on the top of the ladder. He leaned forward, sticking his head through the top of the ladder so that he could see me clearly. "Can I wait with you?" the boy asked.

"Whatever sir wants," I said.

"Have you been waiting long?" Ulysses asked.

"A second day is all, sir," I said.

"How long will you have to wait?" Ulysses asked, swinging back on the ladder, allowing his body to bend back as far as his outstretched arms allowed.

"As long as necessary," I said.

"Aha, you forgot sir that time," Ulysses said in delight, leaning through the opening between two ladder rungs again. "Why do you have to say sir all the time? Only blacks say sir to me. Everyone else just calls me Ulysses."

"Yes, sir," I said.

"You're mighty tall, Isaac," Ulysses said. He had shifted his weight to his stomach over a rung and let his legs dangle.

His constant contortions with the ladder were making me a bit nauseous. It was not my place to warn him that he was hanging from a rickety ladder high enough from the stable floor to do some serious damage should he misstep and fall.

"Yes, sir," I said, breathing a little easier when he put his feet back on the ladder rung and slid his slim form out from between the space between two rungs with his hands firmly on the sides of the ladder.

"How come you're so tall, Isaac?" Ulysses asked. He wrapped his right elbow around the ladder and swung around so that he was facing the stable below. Only one foot was on a ladder rung. He swung his other foot out as far as he could reach.

"Don't rightly know," I said, looking over the edge of the loft. It was a long way down for a little boy like Ulysses to fall.

"Maybe your daddy was tall," Ulysses said. His foot on the ladder slipped and he hung for a moment from his right arm before he got his foot back on the ladder rung again. I think I groaned. I don't know. "Was your daddy tall, Isaac?"

"Don't know," I said. I wanted to close my eyes so I didn't see him fall but I was afraid if I closed my eyes he would actually fall.

The older Meadows boy entered the stable, gaze up on Ulysses on the ladder. The boy looked at me then back to Ulysses.

"Hi, Andy," Ulysses said in delight at seeing his brother. "This is Isaac."

"I know who he is," Andrew Junior said. "You were warned to stay away from the new blackie, Ulysses. Father warned you."

"Ah, he's all right," Ulysses said.

"If you don't get out of here in one minute I'll tell Mother," Andrew Junior said.

There was no hesitation from Ulysses. "Bye, Isaac," Ulysses said, descending the ladder. "It was nice meeting you," he called up before his head vanished over the side of the loft.

I fell back into the hay in relief. I had been so sure that boy would fall and break his neck. In addition to his lack of respect for the height of the ladder he was performing his antics upon, his nonstop questions tired my brain.

A few minutes later Lucas appeared below. "Boy sucks my brains," Lucas said, peering out the door to make sure Ulysses was really gone.

The days passed with me sitting in the stables with not enough work to do to engage my mind, not knowing my fate. I began to fear that I was headed for the auction block after all. Unless I made a run north. I spent many an afternoon sitting up in the loft, staring out the single window at the blue sky, thinking and planning.

If I went up on the block I could be sold to a plantation and put to work in the cotton fields. Plantation owners had need of young, strong men like me. There were other jobs just as difficult as plantation work. I had seen men come into town to help load wagons and freight cars, some had visible white, raised scars on their arms and backs.

The first time I had noticed the scars on a man loading a wagon I had stopped in surprise. Looking up at the sullen face of the man who bore such scars I had seen that same dead expression as Lucas had. Except a light did flare to the surface for a moment as he looked back at me. A light of anger, of resentment. The man looked at me in my proper linen suit and hate filled his glare.

At first I was startled and took a step back in fear. I must have been about fourteen or fifteen at the time. I did not understand why that sullen man who had just hoisted a hundred pound seed bag on his shoulder with ease would hate me so when he did not even know me. Gradually I realized that it was not me specifically who he hated.

The scarred man was likely only a few years older than me. It was not easy to tell. He had already lived a hard life and there I was, young and fresh. I represented everything that he did not have. I represented everything that had been taken from him. We were both slaves but he lived on a plantation where he was worked like a dog and beaten when he resisted how he was treated or even for a misstep while I lived in a cozy house with a man who treated me like a son.

I could not survive living on a plantation. I had to run North. Up North I could be free. If I was caught I would be whipped. I could even be crippled just enough to prevent me from running but allow me to continue working.

The idea of running consumed me. The problem with growing up in a cozy house in town was that I had no idea how to survive in the wilderness. I could calculate how long it would take me to travel the distance separating me from freedom but I could not figure out how to survive in the time it would take me to get there. I would be spotted and captured if I stuck to the roads. I would be lost and helpless off the roads.

I had seen a runaway slave once. His captors went through town as they dragged him back to where he had run from. His bare feet were caked in mud created from blood and dirt from the road. He walked behind men on horseback, his arms behind his back, tied with his hands on his elbows.

One shoulder was bent and the position did not look natural. His clothes were dirty and torn. Cockle burrs were stuck to his hair and clothes. One of his eyes was swollen shut and his face was bruised. Children pelted him with rotten fruit and stale bread as he walked past them.

"What did he do?" I asked Master Meadows, horrified at the sight. I was under ten years old at the time.

"He ran," a man standing next to us said. He spit on the ground. "If he survives the trip back he won't run again."

Master Meadows had stared at the man, his face a mask. When that mask slid onto Master Meadows' face it usually meant that he was hiding feelings of dismay or anger. The people around us were the type of people that would not understand why a white man would be angered at the sight of a runaway slave being punished appropriately.

"They'll cut his tendon," Master Meadows said in a slow voice. "Make him a cripple."

"If he survives," the man next to us said, nodding.

The memory of that runaway slave kept me from dashing

blindly out of the younger Master Meadows' stables. It was a sight that stayed with a person for the rest of their life having seen it. I needed a safe plan of escape so I did not encounter that same fate. Yes, I was afraid.

About a week after Master Meadows died Samuel Taylor came to see me. He stepped into the stable, carefully watching where he placed his feet. I was up in the hay loft, daydreaming about flying north when I spotted Mr. Taylor. At first I thought I was imagining the man in the stable but he was really there.

Joy filled me at seeing that familiar face. Hope filled me at what it could mean that Mr. Taylor had come to see me. I jumped up from my bed of hay and raced to the ladder resting against the side of the loft. I clambered down the ladder, ignoring the threat of slivers as I slid the rest of the way down. My feet hit the floor with a loud thud.

"Isaac," Mr. Taylor said, when I reached him. He smiled up at me but he looked sad.

"Mr. Taylor," I said, nodding my head. "It is good to see you."

"You too, boy," Mr. Taylor said, eyes turning weepy. He took a deep breath. "I came to talk to Andrew. I just came from him. I hoped to buy you from him."

Exaltation and relief both filled me at the same time. I felt like a hundred pounds of weight had been lifted from my shoulders. I had not even considered the possibility of Mr. Taylor coming to rescue me. Slowly it dawned on me that what he had said. He had hoped to buy me.

"The price is too high, my boy," he said. My heart dropped to the ground. "I'm sorry, Isaac. He named a ridiculous price. Ridiculous."

"I could repay you," I said. "If you bought me and freed me I would go north. I would work. I would repay you."

Mr. Taylor cringed with every word I said. I could not control the tone of desperation in my voice. I was desperate.

"Yes, yes," Mr. Taylor said. "But the thing is that I cannot come up with such funds to begin with." Mr. Taylor patted my shoulder in an attempt to sooth me. "I tried."

"There must be a way," I said. "I would repay you."

"With what?" Mr. Taylor said, an edge to his voice. "Even if you went north and worked in some factory it would take you your whole life to pay back such a sum. You can't afford yourself, boy."

"I would make the money," I said, confident. "You know I would."

"I know no such thing," Mr. Taylor said, taking a step back. "I'm telling you that I tried. But your fate lies in the hands of Andrew now. William always spoke highly of his nephew."

"He should have freed me before he died," I said, voice growing heated. The frustration ate at me.

Mr. Taylor slapped me. The blow stung but was merely a sting. "Don't you speak ill of him," Mr. Taylor said in a shrill voice. "He treated you better than you deserved."

I rubbed my cheek, staring down at Mr. Taylor in surprise. "I would never speak ill of him," I said slowly. "I just wish... I just wish he had thought more highly of me than to pass me over to his nephew like I was nothing to him."

Mr. Taylor turned his head. He was breathing hard. His eyes shone with unshed tears. "I miss him so," he said, more to himself than me. "It was his wish that you go to his nephew. I should have respected that."

Mr. Taylor left without another word to me. I stared after the man, hope having risen fell that much harder. I was not aware that Lucas had been standing in one of the stalls the whole time until he stepped out. Lucas stared out the wide door, watching Mr. Taylor hurrying away. Mr. Taylor never looked back.

"Don't do it," Lucas said, turning to me.

"Do what?" I asked. I continued to rub my cheek as I stared out the doorway.

"Run," Lucas said. "Don't do it."

I turned to Lucas in surprise. "I have no intention of running away," I said. It was an outright lie.

Lucas studied my face. "Yeah, you are," he said. He turned his back on me and walked away. "Don't do it," he said as he headed back to the stall he had been cleaning.

I followed Lucas. "Did you ever consider it?" I asked.

Lucas picked up the shovel he had leaned against the stall wall. "I'm still here, aren't I?" Lucas said.

"I saw a runaway slave captured once," I said, shivering at the memory.

"Then you know," Lucas said. He looked up at me thoughtfully. "That stops you, don't it? 'Membering that runaway?"

I nodded. There was no use in denying it.

"That's why they parade 'em," Lucas said. "To scare you." Lucas turned back to shoveling the manure and used straw from the stall floor. "Don't do it," he said yet again.

"I'm still here, aren't I?" I snapped.

"I see you up there," Lucas said. "Staring out north. Thinking. Planning. Hoping. Waiting."

"Waiting, yes," I said. "I'm waiting for Master Meadows to decide my fate."

Lucas ignored me. I grabbed a shovel and went into the neighboring stall. Some physical labor actually appealed to me. I needed to distract my mind from my own thoughts. Seeing Mr. Taylor had made things even worse for some reason. I slid the shovel under the straw bedding. The metal blade scraped the wood floor as I pushed.

Mr. Taylor could have tried harder. I could hear Lucas' shovel scraping behind me as he scooped up piles of manure and horse urine soaked straw. If I had to spend my days doing nothing but tending to horses I would become dead inside, the same as Lucas. I needed more.

Then I met Tildy. If elder Master Meadows had freed me I

wouldn't have met Tildy. I was sulking in the stable, considering the risk of running away when the most beautiful girl in the world walked past me on her way to the garden. I went from the darkest regions of despair to the highest heights of wonderment in one moment.

It was the girl's legs I noticed first. I had been staring at the hard baked ground of the driveway leading up to the stable when a pair of bare, black legs came into view above bare feet. She had hiked up her skirt for working in the garden.

I looked up in surprise and our eyes met. Deep, mysterious brown eyes looked back at me with interest. The enchantress smiled and ducked her head as she hurried past me. She carried a woven basket in the crook of her left elbow. A pair of garden sheers peeked over the top of the basket and gloves were draped against the side so I figured out pretty quick where the angel was headed.

I had played with girls in the neighborhood. Though I had enjoyed their company none had ever left such a lasting impact as this girl. I knew that something important had happened the moment our eyes met.

It only took me a minute to decide to follow her. I don't know if it was the long, lean legs or that mischievous smile that hooked me but I fell in love with that girl the moment I met her. As I hurried past the stable to the garden all thoughts of running north left my head.

Chapter Twelve

The nephew was strict but fair in most cases. As long as I kept my head down, my mouth shut, and did as instructed it was not too bad and I would do anything to be with my Tildy. I like to think that over the years Master Meadows had grown to appreciate my contribution to his business holdings. That might be a daydream.

One day after weeks spent waiting in the stables I was summoned into the office. Like his uncle, the younger Master Meadows had many enterprises and often worked from his office in his home. There was a letter near Master Meadows' hand, sitting open on the desk as if he had just been studying it. I recognized the handwriting on the paper as the elder Master Meadows' handwriting.

"My uncle informs me that you are educated and that you've been keeping his books for years now," Master Andrew Meadows said. There was unmistakable anger in his voice. "Slaves are not supposed to be educated. My uncle broke the law."

I was not about to argue with the younger Master Meadows. I was also not going to agree with him. I knew that Master Meadows educating me was frowned upon but I didn't know what my being educated could mean to me. Master Meadows could have been fined. I didn't know what they would do to me since I had no money to pay any fines. So I said nothing.

Master Meadows picked up the letter and read a few lines then looked up at me for a moment before going back to his reading. I waited. Master Meadows tossed the letter on the desk and sat back in his chair, steepling his fingers as he studied me.

"He never said anything all these years," Master Meadows said.

"I thought he bought you for other purposes."

Master Meadows stared at me, as if waiting for me to say something. I did not know what he was inferring. It seemed better to keep my mouth shut.

"Did he ever, uh, well, in that house," Master Meadows said, stumbling over his words. He cleared his throat. "Were there trysts?"

"I don't understand, sir," I said.

"Trysts," Master Meadows said. "You know, trysts."

"I don't understand," I said. "Master Meadows did not have women stay over, if that is what you mean, sir."

Master Meadows gave a short bark of laughter that had no humor to it. "I know very well that my uncle did not entertain women in his house," Master Meadows said.

I was thoroughly confused by the discussion. If Master Meadows knew that the elder Master Meadows had never entertained women in his house I did not understand why he asked me about Master Meadows having trysts with women in the house. Once again I relied on saying nothing more.

The younger Master Meadows continued to stare at me from behind his massive oak desk until I felt the urge to squirm under his blazing scrutiny. I felt quite strongly that Master Meadows was displeased with me. I kept my gaze respectfully down, careful not to meet his gaze directly.

"You can tell me, boy," the younger Master Meadows said. "I know about my uncle."

"Yessir," I said, bobbing my head. "But I don't understand, sir. As I said, Master Meadows did not entertain women in the house."

"So proper," Master Meadows said. "Rumor has it that he bought you for a play toy."

Once again I was at a loss for words. The younger Master Meadows was making no sense. I was not familiar with the term play toy. I decided that it was better to wait out the questioning with silence.

"Come, boy," Master Meadows said. "I understand that you like women. It isn't your fault if my uncle used you for his own pleasure. Though I did not expect him to use boys. Did he sneak into your room at night? Or maybe he preferred his own bed for your liaisons?"

My mouth dropped open. "He never!" I gasped. "You think he… he never," I said. He was like a father to me but I wasn't going to say that to the younger Master Meadows.

"You're telling me you did not engage in sexual relations with my uncle?" Master Meadows asked me.

The idea stunned me to my core. "No sir," I said.

"From the look of your face I am guessing that you did not even know that my uncle preferred the company of men over women," Master Meadows said, raising a single eyebrow. "Either you are not the genius he claims you are or he was even more discreet than I realized."

Memories surfaced. Samuel Taylor and Master Meadows spending almost every day together. The warm smiles between the two. But Mr. Taylor was married. With two children. All the times Master Meadows said he would not marry to stop the rumors. Mr. and Mrs. Taylor did not have a good marriage. Because Mr. Taylor loved Master Meadows, not Mrs. Taylor.

"Well, naïve then," the younger Master Meadows said, watching my face as the realization dawned on me.

"Master Meadows never… he was just a bachelor, sir," I said.

If anyone ever thought that Master Meadows preferred the company of men over women in his bed someone would have hurt him. Maybe even killed him. Being a homosexual was even more dangerous than being a runaway black man. At least a black man had monetary value.

"You think you're the only one who has to show a different face to the world?" Master Meadows had said that day we had been arguing about my desire for freedom.

I had not known. Memories of all those times we had argued crashed down on me. I felt overwhelmed. Master Meadows had had his own burdens to bear and yet he had never complained to me or blamed me. Master Meadows had been a good man. The best man I had ever known.

Learning his secret only compounded my great admiration and respect for my surrogate father. He lived a great life, full of warmth and love, despite knowing that if the wrong people discovered his secret he would be in great danger. He carried that secret without ever complaining.

My shoulders sagged. The death of Master Meadows, being trapped in a stable for weeks with nothing to do but think, not knowing my fate, and then hearing the nephew say that the elder Master Meadows had lived a secret life, so secret that even I had not known, it all took its toll. I was willing to accept my fate and at that moment didn't even care. I just needed to know what was ahead so that I could deal with it.

"Yes, a bachelor," Master Meadows said. "We shall let his secret go to the grave with him."

I nodded. "Yessir," I said.

"I had to be sure that you weren't like my uncle," Master Meadows said. "I can't have a pervert in my household. A pervert slave has no place here."

I nodded, staring at my feet. "Yessir," I said.

"Naïve then," Master Meadows said. "Once the truth is exposed you understand."

"Yessir," I said automatically. I wasn't really even listening to him anymore.

I just wanted the interview over with. I took a deep breath and waited for whatever verdict Master Meadows was about to deliver. Thinking about Master Meadows was difficult. I missed him so much.

Master Meadows opened the top right drawer in the desk and

pulled out an envelope. He slid his thick fingers inside the envelope and pulled out a folded letter. He read the letter then tossed the paper on the desk in front of him. It was also written in the elder Master Meadows' handwriting.

I looked at the letters, trying to read them upside down but the second letter covered most of the first letter and the second letter had fallen closed again along the folds. I could see the date of the first letter, marking it over five years old.

"Well then," Master Meadows said. "I am a business man, boy. The only use I have for slaves is hard work. Since I already have slaves to take care of all the tasks needing doing I am not sure what is left over for you."

Chapter Thirteen

The next year, in early summer Blitzen dropped a painted foal. It was a colt. I loved that colt. He followed me around like a puppy. Dad named him Ritter. Everyone else in the family called him Hank's Shadow, which turned into Shadow. It was difficult to believe he came from Blitzen because he was a magnificent animal, full of spirit and clever as could be.

I thought he could be mine but Father said he was going to give him to Wilhelm. Wilhelm was supposed to be back from college by the time the colt was old enough to be weaned and start his training.

When the time approached for Wilhelm to come home I grew sad. Though I missed Wilhelm and was looking forward to seeing my oldest brother again, it meant that he would get Shadow. Wilhelm had been granted a homestead, just north of us, even nearer New Ulm. He was going to farm and set up a veterinary practice.

Wilhelm was please to get the yearling as a graduation gift. The night he returned home and Dad presented Shadow to him was the hardest day of my life. Wilhelm ran his hands over the colt and declared him in fine shape. He would make a good saddle horse for visiting the farms when he had calls to make.

I spent the night out in the barn with Shadow while everyone else was in the house welcoming Wilhelm home. Wilhelm found me there, sitting in the stall with Shadow's head in my lap. I had been crying.

Wilhelm stood at the stall gate for several minutes, watching me. "I hadn't realized how much the colt means to you, Hank," Wilhelm said.

"He's mine," I said, sniffing. I wrapped my arms around Shadow's neck. "At least he should be mine."

"I don't want to take your colt from you," Wilhelm said. "I'll talk to Dad."

Dad came out to the barn a few minutes after Wilhelm went back inside. "What's this nonsense?" Dad asked me.

"I don't know why you'd give Shadow to Wilhelm," I said. "He's mine. Shadow is mine."

"You're too young to have your own horse, boy," Dad said. It seemed to puzzle him that I even thought I could. "Just because you let that Indian pony at poor Blitzen you think the colt is yours?"

"Yes!" I wailed. "I love him!"

"It's just a horse, boy," Dad said, shaking his head. "Horses eat grain. Take time. You're too young to take care of him. When you're old enough you can have your own horse."

"But I want Shadow," I said. "Not just any horse."

"That's enough now, Hank," Dad said in a firm voice. "Time to come back inside and make your brother welcomed home."

"I don't want to leave Shadow," I said, voice rising enough to startle the young horse.

Shadow pulled out of my embrace and scrambled to his feet. Instead of moving away he rubbed his mouth over my head, wrapping his lips over my hair and tugging playfully. He blew air out through his nostrils right into my face.

"It's just a horse, boy," Dad said, a little softer than the first time. He watched Shadow trying to make me feel better. "It *is* just a horse. Wilhelm won't be that far away. It's not like he's going to a place you'll never see him."

Shadow wasn't just any horse. He was my horse, even if Dad thought he could just give him away to my brother. It helped to be reminded that Wilhelm was going to live only a few miles away. I would still get to see Shadow at least. That helped. It did not completely ease my soul but it helped.

It was time to go back to the house. Mom had made a cake and they were probably playing games. Besides, the barn floor was getting cold under my butt and legs.

I got to my feet, gave Shadow one last hug, and followed Dad back into the house. Wilhelm was telling stories at the kitchen table and Mom was smiling as she bustled about the kitchen, getting the cake ready to serve. It was the happiest I had seen Mom in a long time.

When my baby sister had been born a few years ago she had only lived a few months before a fever took her. Mom had been so distraught that she had taken to drinking during the day. It had gotten worse and worse until it seemed that she was always drunk. That night with Wilhelm home Mom was actually sober.

There was a fire crackling in the fireplace. The house felt so nice and warm after the cold barn. Wilhelm had changed. He still looked like the brother I knew but all those years away at college had turned him into a man.

Mom carried the iced cake to the kitchen table and set it down in front of Wilhelm. "My boy," she said ruffling Wilhelm's hair. "You're all grown up now. But it's so good to see you."

"It's good to be home," Wilhelm said, smiling up at Mom.

"Promise me you won't go away again," Mom said.

"I have no plans to go away again," Wilhelm said. "Except for one short trip."

"What's that?" Mom asked, freezing in place.

"I met someone, Mom," Wilhelm said. "We got married before I left, a few weeks ago. I have to go back and collect her."

"You married someone?" Mom asked. "Without telling us?"

"I'm telling you now," Wilhelm said.

"Well, tell us about her," Dad said, straddling a chair next to

Wilhelm.

"Yes, tell us about her," Mom said, pushing the cake away from Wilhelm, to the center of the table.

Wilhelm smiled, his whole face lighting up as he thought about his new wife. "You will like her," he said, head turned up to Mom. "She's sweet and amiable. She's so pretty and her laugh fills my heart with love."

"Her laugh," Mom said, walking back to the liquor cabinet. She pulled out a bottle of elderberry wine. "Let's toast your new bride."

Wilhelm looked around the table at the faces of his brothers. Our reactions varied but it was clear that no one was happy that Mom had pulled out the wine. Once she started drinking she got a bit ornery lately. It hadn't started out that way but it was almost always that way anymore.

I looked around the table, seeing what Wilhelm saw. Dad had gotten a mulish look on his face. When Mom started drinking he shut down. Hans and August exchanged glances then looked everywhere but at Mom. August ducked his head and stared into his lap. I met Wilhelm's questioning gaze and shook my head.

"Let's save the toast for when she arrives," Wilhelm said.

"Why wait?" Mom asked, setting the bottle on the table and moving further into the kitchen for glasses. "We can toast her again when she arrives. You didn't say her name."

"Caroline," Wilhelm said. "Her name is Caroline."

Mom returned to the table with two glasses but only poured wine into one glass. "To Caroline," Mom said, raising her glass in the air before drinking the wine in one swallow.

"Elise, no," Dad said, taking the bottle before Mom could refill her glass.

"I want another," Mom said, grabbing for the wine bottle.

"Not tonight," Dad said.

"I said I want another," Mom said through gritted teeth.

"Wilhelm is home," Dad said. "Not tonight, Elise. Not tonight."

"Wilhelm," Mom said softly. She stared at the wine bottle in Dad's hand and licked her lips before turning to Wilhelm. "We are going to have cake. To celebrate Wilhelm's return home."

She waited until everyone went to bed. In the morning she was sleeping on the kitchen floor with several empty wine bottles on the kitchen table and one bottle cradled in her arm. Hans and I were the first ones up and found her. Dad was not far behind us.

"Go on out and do your chores," Dad said as he picked up the empty green bottles.

Wilhelm was home a month, working on his homestead, getting everything ready for his new bride. We helped him build the house. Walking Moon and Catches Pebbles came and stayed with Wilhelm, helping also. I loved the smell of fresh cut lumber and the sound of hammering. Walking Moon was not so handy with the hammer and had sore thumbs for the whole month.

Catches Pebbles was very handy with carpentry and Wilhelm insisted that Catches Pebbles did the work of two men. Piotr was off at university then, learning how to be a dentist, but the rest of pitched in and every afternoon after doing our farm chores we headed over to Wilhelm's homestead and worked until the sun was gone. Dad helped also but not every day like the rest of us.

The house was almost done when three Indian men rode into the yard looking for Catches Pebbles. They came to fetch Catches Pebbles home. There was some trouble with the Indian agent and his father wanted Catches Pebbles there to help.

"I am helping Wilhelm," Catches Pebbles said to the Indian men. "What is so important that it cannot wait?"

"It's almost done," Wilhelm said. "If your father needs you then you must go."

Wilhelm went into the house and returned with a small bag of money to pay Catches Pebbles. He handed the bag to Catches Pebbles and Catches Pebbles slipped the bag into a pouch he wore around his waist without even looking inside.

Walking Moon only stayed another day after his brother left then he went home also, leading the cow Dad had given him and Catches Pebbles for helping Wilhelm.

Wilhelm brought his bride home. She was so pretty. She had long blonde hair and bright blue eyes and an easy smile. Every time Wilhelm looked at her his face melted. It just got all soft and mushy. At first it bothered me to see my big brother acting like a love struck puppy around this stranger.

Mom was on her best behavior the day she met Caroline, Wilhelm's new wife. She smiled pleasantly but I saw her scowling when she thought no one was looking. I wasn't sure why Mom was so against Caroline but I held back on making up my own mind about Wilhelm's bride until I saw which way the wind was blowing.

The very next day after Wilhelm returned with his new bride Dad told me to take Shadow on over to him. It took me a long time to walk that two miles with Shadow on a lead beside me. Shadow danced beside me, kicking up his heels and shaking his head in play. He must have sensed that I was sad and he came up behind me and butted his head against my back until I laughed.

Wilhelm was laying fence posts back where the barn was going to go. I kicked clumps of grass in the dirt as I walked past the house. It wasn't fair. Shadow was my horse, not Wilhelm's horse. Caroline came out of the house and walked beside me.

"So this is Shadow?" she asked, looking at the colt.

"Yep," I said, watching my feet.

"What a pretty colt," Caroline said. That traitor Shadow went right up to her and nuzzled her. Caroline giggled when Shadow blew air against her neck. "Oh, what a lovely creature."

"You talk funny," I said.

"Maybe," Caroline said with a smile. She reached over and tousled my hair with her fingers. "Not as funny as you talk though."

"He's my shadow," I said, ducking my head out of her reach. "That's his name. Hank's Shadow."

"Yes, I heard that," Caroline said. "Wilhelm and I were talking about this very colt just last night. With all the work he's got to do he just isn't going to have any free time to train this pony properly."

I listened, not certain where she was going with that. We had almost reached Wilhelm. He had taken his shirt off and dirt stuck to the sweat covering him. He wrapped his arms around a post, lifted it, and dropped it into the hole he had just dug. Caroline forgot about me and Shadow for a moment, eyes locked on her husband.

She got that same mushy face when looking at Wilhelm that he got when he looked at her. I spotted another clump of grass and kicked it hard enough to tear it up by the roots. It went flying. Shadow danced beside me, snorting at the clod of grass.

Caroline cleared her throat and turned back to me. "So I was wondering if you would train Shadow," she said, glancing out of the corner of her eye at her husband, my brother, who was wiping the sweat from his forehead.

A wave of exhilaration filled me. "Really?" I asked, looking over at Wilhelm. Why was she peeking over at him like that? "And Wilhelm agrees?"

"Oh, yes," Caroline said. She stared boldly at Wilhelm now. "Oh, he distracts me," she muttered. She turned so that her back was to Wilhelm. "Where were we? Yes, we would like you to take care of all of Shadow's training. As a saddle horse, of course. Can you do that, Hank?"

I grinned up at her. I swear there was a halo around that woman. The sun seemed to shine all around her, lighting up her hair and covering her white paisley gown with the brightest glow. I had a sister now and I loved her with all my heart.

"Yes!" I said, jumping up in the air.

Wilhelm had walked up to us. I hadn't seen him behind the glow around Caroline, my new sister. "I take it Caroline asked you to help with Shadow?" he said with a grin. He leaned over and kissed the top of Caroline's head.

"Yes," I said. My face hurt from smiling so hard. "Thank you!"
I wrapped my arms around Wilhelm and hugged him, not even
caring about the sweat.

I did a dance around Shadow and then hugged him also. I turned
to Caroline then hesitated. I didn't really know her that well.
Caroline smiled and opened her arms. I threw my arms around her
and hugged her, too. She smelled nice.

"But won't you need him for plowing and stuff?" I asked.

Wilhelm shook his head. "We're getting two Belgiums.
Wedding gift from Caroline's parents," he said.

"Your parents farm, too?" I asked Caroline.

She laughed. It was like the twinkling of stars across a brook. At
least what I imagined stars would sound like. "Mercy no," she said.
She turned to Wilhelm. "I think you need a break, husband."

Wilhelm looked down at her and his face got all mushy. "Hank,
time for you to head home," he said without even looking at me. He
only had eyes for Caroline.

"But I just got here," I said. "I need to introduce Shadow to his
new home. Let him adjust."

"It's all right," Caroline said, licking her lips.

"Just don't come near the house then," Wilhelm said, taking
Caroline's hand. "I mean it. Don't come in or even near the house
until I come back out."

"Sure," I said. They'd already forgotten about me and were
almost running to the house. I watched them for a minute then led
Shadow to the corral where Wilhelm's two carriage horses were.

The horses were interested in Shadow and stuck their heads over
the railings. There was a lot of blowing through the nostrils and one
of the horses squealed at Shadow but that was it. They went back to
eating hay out of the hay rack. I led Shadow around the yard,
explaining to him that there wasn't a barn yet but there would be
soon enough.

We walked along the line of post holes Wilhelm had dug, trying to figure out where he was building the fence. If he was going to be a vet he would need plenty of room near the soon to be built barn for farm animals people brought to him though he would mostly go out and visit farms to check the livestock.

There were strange sounds coming from the house. Shadow was interested in the sounds and stared at the house, his ears pricked forward. I cocked my head, trying to make out what the sounds were. It sounded like Caroline was begging for help.

I took a step towards the house then stopped. No. Wilhelm had said to stay away from the house. I couldn't hear her anymore so I led Shadow in the opposite direction, away from the house.

Dad had planted alfalfa before Wilhelm came home and Shadow and I checked on how it was doing. It was ready for a first cutting already. I was ready to go home and Shadow was safely in the corral with the other horses before Wilhelm finally came out of the house.

I had been sitting on the bottom rail of the corral fence waiting and jumped to my feet the moment the door opened and Wilhelm stepped out. "Alfalfa's ready for a cutting," I said, running over to him. "And I hope you aren't beating your wife."

"What?" Wilhelm said in surprise.

"Alfalfa's ready for a cutting," I said.

"I would never harm Caroline," he said. "Where did you get that idea?"

"She was making a racket," I said, shaking my head. "She all right?"

"I told you not to get near the house," Wilhelm said, swinging his arm to cuff me.

"I didn't," I said, dancing out of the way of his arm. "I heard you all the way out there." I pointed to where I had been when I heard her.

Wilhelm turned and studied the house. His face turned a bright crimson. "Windows are open," he muttered. He turned back to me. "Don't worry. She saw a spider."

I closed one eye to concentrate better and tilted my head. "Spider?"

"Yep," Wilhelm said. "A spider."

"She must be mighty feared of spiders," I said, shaking my head. "She was sure wailing."

"Mighty feared?" Wilhelm asked, looking down at me. "You picking up bad habits from the locals, Hank?"

"I like how it sounds," I admitted. "Tom Guhrt likes to say that."

"Well, don't you go using that," Wilhelm said. He looked off in the distance thoughtfully. "Guhrt. Is that Maria Guhrt's brother?"

"Yep," I said. "He sits next to me in school." It was getting late. The sun was heading towards the horizon. I had to head for home. "Wilhelm," I said. "Thanks for letting me train Shadow."

Wilhelm nodded. "Thank Caroline," he said. "It was her idea."

"Okay," I said, heading for the house.

"Not now," Wilhelm said quickly. "She's resting. That spider wore her out."

"Okay," I said, heading down the driveway. Girls and spiders. They just didn't like crawly things at all. Imagine being so scared of a spider that it wore a person out and forced them to take a nap. Only girls.

Chapter Fourteen

A few weeks after Caroline arrived Catches Pebbles and Walking Moon came to visit again. I was at Wilhelm's farm, working with Shadow, so they came there to find me. Both of them were impressed with the two giant draft horses that shared the corral with Shadow and the two carriage horses.

"That is the largest horse I've ever seen," Walking Moon said, staring with awe at the two Belgiums. "And there's two!"

"They're draft horses," I said.

"What's that mean?" Walking Moon asked, gaze glued to the horses.

"They can pull a lot, I guess," I said, shrugging.

Catches Pebbles studied the horses without saying anything. He turned and walked away from the corral. Walking Moon stayed with me by the corral while Catches Pebbles headed for the house.

The door banged open and Caroline stepped out on the front porch with a rifle cradled in her arm. She raised the rifle, pointing it right at Catches Pebbles. Walking Moon and I looked at each other then we both headed for the house at a full out run. Catches Pebbles stopped and stared at the woman on the porch in surprise.

"Don't you come any closer," Caroline said. "Wilhelm! Wilhelm!" she yelled at the top of her lungs. I'll bet they heard her in New Ulm.

Walking Moon and I reached the house before Wilhelm. He was out walking the wheat field and I don't know if he could even hear her. Caroline swung the gun at Walking Moon then kept moving it between Walking Moon and Catches Pebbles.

"It's all right," I yelled, stepping between the gun and Walking Moon. "This is Walking Moon and this here is Catches Pebbles."

For a moment there I wasn't sure if Caroline wouldn't shoot me too. Eventually Caroline lowered the rifle so that it pointed to the dirt in front of Catches Pebbles but kept her finger on the trigger. "They're Indians," Caroline yelled at me. "Get behind me, Hank!"

"Yep," I said, stepping forward slowly. I wasn't sure if she wouldn't shoot Walking Moon right through me.

"Wild Indians," Caroline yelled, leaning forward.

"Well, not really wild Indians," I said. I looked back at Walking Moon. "You wild, Mani?"

"Not now," Walking Moon said, shaking his head.

Wilhelm had heard her screams after all. He came running into the yard, looking all around for what had set Caroline to screaming. Seeing nothing he slowed, panting to catch his breath. "What is it?" he asked between gulps of air.

"She saw wild Indians," Catches Pebbles said.

"Huh?" Wilhelm asked Catches Pebbles, confused. Then it hit him. He trotted up to the house and took the rifle out of Caroline's arms and set it against the wall. "It's all right, Caroline. This is Catches Pebbles and this is Walking Moon. They are our friends."

"Friends?" she asked. Her whole body trembled in fear. "You are friends with Indians?"

"Sure," Wilhelm said, wrapping his arm around her shoulders.

Catches Pebbles walked up to the house. He bowed. "Pleased to meet you, Mrs. Hansohn," he said. It was like she had not just been pointing a gun at him a moment ago.

"Um, likewise," Caroline said though she did not sound at all pleased to meet Catches Pebbles.

I nudged Walking Moon in the side with my elbow. He scowled at me. "What?" he muttered.

I nodded my head in Caroline's direction. Walking Moon was not as quick to forgive the woman for pointing a gun at him. Sullenly he stepped forward and did a half-hearted bow. "Hello," he said. Catches Pebbles scowled at him. Walking Moon did another half-hearted bow. "Pleased to meet you, wife of Wilhelm."

"Everything's all right at the agency?" Wilhelm asked Catches Pebbles.

Catches Pebbles shrugged. "The traders rob us and the government is slow in paying," he said. "But my being there won't help anything."

"We came to help with the barn," Walking Moon said, gaze on Caroline.

"Good," Wilhelm said, nodding. "Good." He patted Caroline's arm. "You all right now?" he asked her. Caroline nodded but her eyes were still as large as saucers and she had not taken her eyes off Walking Moon. "Okay, let's go take a look," Wilhelm said to Catches Pebbles, releasing Caroline's arm and taking a step forward.

Caroline grabbed Wilhelm's arm. "You can't leave me," she said.

"We're just going to look at the barn foundation," Wilhelm said. "You're all right." Caroline's fingertips were white from gripping Wilhelm's arm so tight. "Hank, stay here with Caroline, please."

"Okay," I said.

I wanted to go hear the plans for the barn but I could tell that Caroline was scared. I'd come to like her and I didn't want her to be scared. So I stayed while Wilhelm and Catches Pebbles headed for the plot of land designated for the barn. I settled down on the steps and Walking Moon plopped down next to me.

"How much you think those horses weigh?" Walking Moon asked.

"About as much as four or five horses combined, I guess," I said.

"That's what I'm thinking," Walking Moon said, nodding. "A lot. You'd split yourself in half trying to ride one."

I had tried to ride one and it had split me in half. I nodded, glancing behind me at Caroline to see if she was paying attention to us. Wilhelm had said not to try to ride them so I didn't want to tell Walking Moon that I had tried just that if she was listening. She was still standing wide-eyed in the same spot. Not only had she not moved, I wasn't sure if she was breathing.

"Maniyanhanwi!" Catches Pebbles yelled. Wilhelm gestured for Walking Moon to join them.

Walking Moon got to his feet and trailed after them. Caroline made a strange sound deep in her throat and I looked back at her again. She was sort of sagging. She waved her hand about until she finally found the rail and grabbed it like it was the only thing holding her up.

"Indians," she muttered. "Indians in my yard."

"There are lots of Indians around here," I said, getting to my feet and climbing the stairs to stand next to her. I pointed west. "The agency is only about twenty miles or so that way."

Caroline stared out where I pointed. From the front porch she couldn't see anything but rolling hills, trees, and planted fields, of course. "Agency?" she asked.

"Indian land," I said.

"That close?" she asked in a breathless voice. She looked like she was going to fall down. The color sort of drained out of her face.

"Mani is my closest friend," I said. "Well, him and Guhrt are both. I don't see Mani much in the winter so then Guhrt is. But in the summer Mani is."

"Who's Mani?" Caroline asked.

I pointed at Walking Moon's back. "Walking Moon," I said. "In Lakota his name is Maniyanhanwi. When I first met him I couldn't say it so I started calling him Mani and it stuck."

"Why didn't you just call him Walking Moon?" Caroline asked. Some of the color was returning to her face as we talked.

"Because his name is Maniyanhanwi," I sad. I didn't add the "duh" that I was thinking.

Caroline almost smiled. She was looking more herself again. "A boy's logic," she said.

"You never saw an Indian before?" I asked.

She shook her head. "I've heard lots of stories though," she said. "Like, they scalp people. They run around naked. If they look at you for more than three heartbeats that means they are claiming you as their property.

I stared at her with my mouth hanging open. She looked at me and laughed softly. I snapped my mouth shut. "Even the women?" I asked.

"What?" she asked.

"What tribe runs around naked?" I asked. "That would be a sight to see."

"Tribe?" she asked.

"Well, there's Apache, Lakota, Cheyenne, Chippewa, Wahpeton, and Black Feet. Crow," I said, slowing down as I tried to remember the names of all the tribes in Minnesota and Dakota Territories I'd heard of. "Apaches are out west. Maybe they do."

"Are you thirsty, Hank?" Caroline asked. "I could use a lemonade. Wilhelm brought lemons from town yesterday."

"Okay," I said, following her into the house.

"You keep talking about the Indians while I make the lemonade," she said.

"What do you mean?" I asked, sliding onto a chair at the table. The house still smelled of fresh lumber.

"Are they so different?" Caroline asked. "From tribe to tribe?"

"I suppose," I said. "Mani would be able to tell you better."

"I'm not sure I'm up to asking, uh, Mani," she said.

"Why not?" I asked.

"Well, because he's an Indian," she said. She set a cutting board and a bag of lemons in front of me. "Here, roll the lemons around on the board."

"Okay," I said. "Why am I doing that?"

"It releases the juices," she said.

I rolled each lemon back and forth across the cutting board. Caroline took them from me when I was done and cut them in half. She had a wood pestle she used to squeeze the juice out of the fruit into a pitcher of sugar water. She even used a paring knife to peel long strands of lemon skin and put that in the pitcher as well.

"Were you afraid of me when you met me?" I asked, watching her make the lemonade.

Caroline turned in surprise. "Of course not," she said.

"Then why are you afraid of Mani?" I asked.

Caroline didn't say anything for a long time. She stared out the kitchen window as she stirred and stirred the lemonade. "Sometimes things you aren't familiar with can be scary," she said at last.

That didn't really make sense to me but I thought about it. "Like having to get up in front of the class and talk?" I asked.

"Yes, I suppose," she said. "Are you afraid to do that?"

I shook my head. "Nope," I said. "But Guhrt is. He can talk and talk but if he has to stand in front of everyone at once he clams up and can't say a word."

Caroline poured four glasses of lemonade and put them on a tray. "Can you carry this much out to the others?" she asked.

"Sure," I said.

"Go ahead," she said. "I'll be fine now."

I picked up the tray and Caroline opened the door for me. It was a bit heavier than I expected but other than being a little slow going down the steps because I couldn't see them very well I managed all right.

"Hank," Caroline said just as I stepped off the last step. "Thank you."

"Sure," I said.

I had no idea what she was thanking me for and my concentration was on holding the tray level. The glasses were suddenly wanting to slide around on the spilled liquid on the bottom of the tray.

I reached the barn area without losing a glass. Wilhelm took the tray from me and passed out the glasses of lemonade. I sipped mine, eyes widening in amazement. It was the best lemonade I'd ever had. Walking Moon and Catches Pebbles drained their glasses after the initial sip they took.

"Do you mind staying at my parents while we work on the barn?" Wilhelm asked.

Catches Pebbles nodded. "That will work," he said.

I climbed up behind Walking Moon on his pony when it was time to leave. I had to walk to Wilhelm's so it was nice to get a ride back home.

"That woman does not like us?" Walking Moon asked me.

"Back east they tell tales," I said. "She thought Indians walk around naked."

Catches Pebbles and Walking Moon both laughed for a long time at that. "Maybe the Mandan do," Catches Pebbles said, laughing again at his own joke.

Chapter Fifteen

Isaac

I stood in front of the desk with my head slightly bowed. It had not taken me long to realize that the younger Master Meadows liked deference from his slaves. Whenever I was around him I kept my head down and bowed my shoulders in instead of maintaining the straight shouldered posture that the elder Master Meadows had worked so hard to instill in me.

I could smell the books in the room. The leather and the paper were like perfume chasing away the lingering odors of horse shit and straw that had filled my nostrils the past weeks. That nasty feeling of my stomach tightening in knots had started again as I listened to the younger Master Meadows.

"Well then," Master Meadows said. "I am a business man, boy. The only use I have for slaves is hard work. Since I already have slaves to take care of all the tasks needing doing I am not sure what is left over for you."

It sounded like Master Meadows was going to put me on the block after all. As much as I worried about being sold to some cotton farmer and being put out into the fields, a brutal life for a slave, my new worry was more that I would be taken from Tildy when I had just found her.

"My uncle said that you would be of great use to me," Master Meadows said.

I glanced down at the letters lying open on the desk. Master

Meadows picked up the top letter, uncovering the first letter. The sight of that familiar handwriting stirred a great sadness. I could read upside down but not without being obvious about it. I tried to look away but kept turning my gaze back to that letter.

On that piece of paper was written the explanation for why Master Meadows had not freed me. I would be of great use to his nephew.

"Take a look at these," Master Meadows said, sliding two ledgers across the desk at me.

"Yessir," I said.

"Yessir," Master Meadows said, glaring at me. "Don't get fresh with me, boy. Address me properly."

"I don't understand, sir," I said, not understanding.

"Just look at the books," Master Meadows said, jerking his head.

I wasn't sure what he wanted. The outside of the ledgers were identical, long, heavy, leather bound, dark blue books with metal trimmed corners. I opened the first ledger, caressing the leather with my thumb as I slid my first finger under the cover to lift it.

The ledger contained the financial records from a shipping company. I looked at the first page, noting the costs and revenues as well as volume and frequency of the cargo being moved. I flipped the page and studied the next page and then the next page. Everything looked standard and well recorded.

He had given me two ledgers so I opened the second ledger next to the first ledger, studying the first few pages. The second ledger was for a hardware store. There were several mathematical errors in the second ledger. Several times numbers were added when they should have been subtracted. I noticed that cotton and lumber was going out but nails and lumber were coming in to the hardware store.

I became so engrossed in the story the ledgers told that I forgot that I was standing in front of Master Meadows, bent over his desk. I was not sure why Master Meadows chose to bring in lumber when he was also shipping it out at a lower price. There was more. I continued to flip pages, comparing the two ledgers. Whoever was tracking for the hardware store was making more and more mistakes.

"Well?" Master Meadows said, reminding me that he was there.

I straightened. If the elder Master Meadows was sitting in front of me behind that desk I knew what I would say but the nephew made me nervous. I wasn't sure what the right thing to say was. I had learned in the past few weeks that being honest and forthcoming was not the right route to take in this new life. I stood there in silence, struggling with my internal thoughts.

"When it comes to anything in this office you may speak your mind, boy," Master Meadows said, leaning forward in his seat. "My uncle said that you have a gift for books. I could see it in your face. You found the errors the moment you saw them."

"Yessir," I said cautiously.

I had forgotten that Master Meadows did not like that response but I did not know the correct manner he was looking for so I kept quiet. Master Meadows let the slip pass. He looked excited, happy even.

"It took my accountant a full day of careful scrutiny to find the errors," Master Meadows said. "You spotted them the second you saw them." He leaned back in his chair again. "Go on. Tell me what you see."

I spun the ledgers on the polished desk top so that they faced Master Meadows and flipped the pages back to the first error. "This here, it's been added when it should have been subtracted, sir," I said, putting my finger on the page to show him. "And here, the numbers were carried wrong. And here. And here."

Master Meadows looked closely at each place I pointed to, nodding occasionally. "And that money is not accounted for," he said.

"I don't see it anywhere," I said. "Two thousand three hundred and forty-seven dollars and thirteen cents is unaccounted for."

Master Meadows' head jerked up in surprise. "That's right," he said. "You just looked at it and you came up with the same figure as the accountant."

"Yessir," I said automatically. "And the revenue of the lumber being shipped out is lower than the lumber you are bringing in. You are losing one thousand two hundred dollars doing that. Maybe you have a reason for bringing in lumber when you are already shipping it out but, well, maybe you have your reasons."

"I will have a desk brought in for you," Master Meadows said, slamming the ledgers shut. "Every morning at seven o'clock you will come to this office."

"Yessir," I said, nodding in acceptance of the order.

I had a place in Master Meadows' household. Relief made me almost giddy. I was not going to lose Tildy. The months passed with me spending my days in Master Andrew Meadows' office and my evenings courting Tildy. Her smile brightened my day. The sound of her voice soothed my restless soul. Thoughts of heading north were long faded out of my head.

The next step was marrying Tildy. I didn't know how to go about that. In many of the books I read a man approached the girl's father for permission to marry his daughter. Since Tildy had no father to ask I approached Master Meadows out of courtesy, telling him that Tildy and I planned to marry.

"No," Master Meadows said. He sat at his desk in the office and I sat at my desk. "I forbid it."

I stared in surprise, twisted on my chair in order to face him. "But why?"

"How dare you question me," Master Meadows said, eyes narrowing.

"No, sir," I said, dropping my gaze. "I was just hoping I could understand, sir."

"You aren't human," Master Meadows said, looking back to his papers spread out across his desk. "Livestock can't legally marry."

We were property. Nothing else. Tildy and I weren't allowed to marry. Master Meadows decided that Tildy and I could not marry so that was that.

I was crushed. I moped for days. I even avoided Tildy for a while, not wanting to have to tell her that Master Meadows would not let us marry. Instead of spending my evenings in her company I hung out in the stables with Lucas. His company was what I was in the mood for. The man barely said more than three or four words in a row.

Though slave marriages were not technically legal it was common for owners to allow a ceremony. I don't really know why Master Meadows was so against Tildy and I getting married. I had merely asked Master Meadows out of courtesy, never expecting him to deny us getting married. Even Lucas was surprised that Master Meadows wouldn't allow Tildy and me to marry.

"I was married," Lucas said. "Once."

"You were married?" I asked in surprise.

Lucas nodded. "She lived on a neighboring plantation," he said. He shrugged. "Then I got sold. To Master Meadows."

"So you don't see her anymore?" I asked.

"Too far away," Lucas said. Life moved into his eyes for a moment as he thought about his wife. He shook his head, losing that spark of life. "Too far away."

"What is her name?" I asked.

"My wife's owner even made us a cake," Lucas said, staring out through the open stable door. Lucas grew thoughtful as he remembered. "We had a little cabin to ourselves when I visited. They put the broom down at the door sill and we stepped over it into the house and was married then on. Old Nellie said the words." Lucas cleared his throat. "Miss my wife and children."

I stared at Lucas in amazement. That was the most Lucas had ever talked. "Maybe Master Meadows will let you go visit them," I said.

Lucas shook his head. "Been way over ten years now," he said. "The plantation fell on hard times when the master died. The master's children split it all up when the master died. My family was in the first round sold off."

"Maybe they ended up in town?" I said hopefully.

"Nah," Lucas said. He pressed his lips together and shook his head. "They long gone. Long gone." Lucas cleared his throat again. "But yo and Tildy don't need no permission to marry. Mistake was asking. If yo had just gone and done it the deed would be done."

"I don't know," I said, picturing Mistress Meadows finding out after the fact that Tildy and I had married. "That woman gets her innards all twisted if she isn't in control of everything. I can see her selling Tildy or me or even both to spite us if we went behind her back."

Lucas knew who she was without my having to say Mistress Meadows' name. Lucas considered. "True story," he said in agreement. "But yo don't need no ceremony. It's just between yo."

"What is your wife's name?" I asked Lucas again, thinking maybe he didn't hear me the first time I asked.

Lucas shook his head. "Don't matter," he said. "She's gone."

So we said the words. Thirteen years ago Tildy and I whispered the words in the darkness of her bedroom. There was no preacher. There weren't guests. There was no cake with lemon filling and sugary frosting. There was only the two of us lying on her bed with its worn blanket, promising to God that we were man and wife no matter that the masters wouldn't allow us to be married.

"Shouldn't we find a broom for jumping?" Tildy asked.

"Nah," I said. "I don't want to jump over no broom."

"But we aren't really married if we don't jump over a broom," Tildy said, frowning at me.

I shook my head. "Broom don't mean anything," I said. Tildy opened her mouth to protest and I cut her off. "The English use jumping over a broom to say it's a sham marriage. We aren't gonna have a sham marriage."

Tildy looked at me in surprise. "But everyone does that," she said. "Jumps over a broom."

I shook my head. "No, ma'am. Only slaves," I said. "Because it isn't real."

Tildy giggled when I called her ma'am. I liked the sound of her giggle so I called her ma'am all the time back then. "How you know so much?" Tildy whispered.

"I read," I said. "There's so much in books, Tildy. On those pages are the past, the present, and the future. The whole world is in those books. The law is there. And history."

"That stuff about the broom is in books?" Tildy asked in her soft voice.

"And newspapers," I said. "Every morning I read the newspaper. Master Meadows, uh, the elder Master Meadows, had newspapers come in from England and all over the United States. The new Master Meadows only has the St. Louis newspaper but it's still something."

"So much on paper," Tildy said in awe.

"I'll teach you to read, Tildy," I said.

Tildy's eyes widened and she pulled back. "Don't ever!"

"It's all right," I promised, pulling her back into my arms. "No one will ever know."

There was no hiding it when Tildy grew heavy with child. When Tildy first got pregnant with Sam, Master Meadows was not happy that Tildy and I had created a baby together.

Two lashes I got for sleeping with Tildy and putting a child in her. Four more lashes for getting married even though Master Meadows had forbidden it. Only time I got the lash. Just thinking about the lashing makes my knees tremble. Master Meadows had been so angry that he had ordered the lashing at the height of his strong emotions.

It was Mistress Meadows who had convinced her husband that it was only natural for the livestock to form bonds. Providing more slaves was an economic advantage for the family. As long as Tildy did not shirk her duties then she was allowed to have as many children as she wished.

Mistress Meadows also said that saying the words did not qualify as a marriage. Too bad she had not pointed that out before I got the lashing. Mistress Meadows wanted a real fake marriage for the sanctity of the children we were creating.

There was no cake but Mistress Meadows organized a small ceremony where we jumped over the broom into our own little cabin behind the house. Mistress Meadows hired a preacher who did slave weddings.

Though I did not want to jump over a stupid broom the slave preacher said it was not legal unless we did. So I jumped over a broom with Tildy at my side. Even if it was a fake marriage at least it was one step up from just saying the words.

A few years later, shortly after Benji was born, I overheard Mistress Meadows complaining to one of her friends that her slaves were breeding like rabbits and eating like starving dogs. I took note of that brief moment of overheard conversation. I wouldn't put it past Mistress Meadows to send the children off to the auction block. That was always a concern for me.

The idea of gaining our freedom and heading north began to stick in my head again. Up North no one could take away my family at their whim. Running with children was not an option. I had to figure out a legal way of gaining our freedom.

A plan began to form. Chance favors the prepared mind. I read that somewhere. The elder Master Meadows used to say chance favors the prepared man but I think he changed the quote. I couldn't remember who said it. Maybe one of the Greek heroes.

I wrote a letter and slipped it into the pile of mail I dropped at the post office. I collected the mail every day on my trips to the various businesses that Master Meadows owned. I was more worried about the post master intercepting my correspondence than Master Meadows ever finding it.

If I was going to buy my family's freedom I had to have money. I borrowed one hundred dollars from Master Meadows' household account. He seldom looked at that account and Mistress Meadows never looked at the account except to see how much money she had available to spend. Within two months I was able to return the one hundred dollars to the account and no one was the wiser.

Borrowing that money was the most daring thing I had ever done in my life. Though I only chanced it because I knew that Master Meadows would never see it, I did not sleep well until the money was returned to the account.

The next step was to find out if Master Meadows would be willing to sell us to me. Or at least take our sale value and grant us our freedom. It took me a long time to work up the nerve to ask him. Months passed. Every day I considered how to bring up the subject. Something always stopped me from taking that step.

Chapter Sixteen

One day, when Master Meadows was in an especially jovial mood, I took a deep breath and blurted out my question. "Sir, would it be possible for me to buy the freedom for me and my family?" I kept my head down but could see his face in my periphery vision.

Master Meadows jerked a bit in surprise, his eyes widening as he digested the question I had asked. There was no taking back the words once they were out. I cringed, my shoulders tightening up onto my neck as I waited for his response.

"Buy your freedom?" Master Meadows said at last, settling back in his chair and studying me across the room at my desk. "Just how do you propose to do that? You have no money."

"Yessir," I muttered. I took a deep breath. Normally I knew better than to argue with Master Meadows but I was feeling motivated that day. "But maybe you could bank some of the investment funds for me. All of it to go to buying my family and me. The investments I find for you. Like a finder's fee."

Master Meadows stared at me for a long time. It was hard to breathe as I waited. Eventually he turned his head and stared out the window. His right thumb tapped the desk top, a nervous tick he had when he was deep in thought. At least he was thinking about the idea.

"You think you're entitled to that money, Isaac?" Master Meadows asked, gaze still locked out the window.

I had to be careful. "Not entitled. No, sir," I said in a calm voice though my insides were churning. If it wasn't for me he wouldn't have made those investments that made his bank balance grow and grow faster than all his other business incomes.

"I will think about it," Master Meadows said, turning his head and meeting my gaze.

I dropped my eyes. "Thank you, Master Meadows," I said politely.

I went back to my work, comparing a pile of receipts and invoices against the entries in the ledger from the printing house. I held little hope that further thinking on Master Meadows' part would inspire the man to set up a credit account for me with the goal of using it to buy our freedom. Master Meadows had not outright said no at least.

"I thought you were happy here, Isaac," Master Meadows said a few minutes later.

I looked up in surprise. "Yessir," I said.

"So why this sudden urge to leave my household?" Master Meadows asked.

I was at a loss for words. "I worry about losing my children," I blurted out without thought.

Master Meadows nodded thoughtfully. "I have no intention of selling your children, Isaac," he said. "Even if I don't feel you are entitled to my money, you do enable me an income that I can afford to raise your children."

"Yessir," I said. I nodded my head. "Thank you, sir."

There would be no account set up but I did achieve relief in learning that Master Meadows had no intention of selling my children. Though Mistress Meadows ruled the household Master Meadows was quite firm in ruling the finances of the household. Let Mistress Meadows complain of the costs. She would not be selling my children without Master Meadows' permission.

A few months after I approached Master Meadows about buying our freedom there was an article in the newspaper about the Dred Scott case. Dred and Harriet Scott had sued for their freedom because their owner had taken them north into Minnesota Territory, where slavery was banned.

The Supreme Court verdict had come back that, as slaves, the Scotts were considered property that could be taken anywhere by their owners, regardless of whether or not a particular place banned slavery.

The court went even further, declaring that slaves were not citizens and had no right to bring cases to court in the first place. According to Chief Justice Roger B. Taney, African Americans had no rights which the white man was bound to respect and that the negro might justly and lawfully be reduced to slavery for his benefit.

Master Meadows had tossed the newspaper down on my desk as soon as he walked into the office from his breakfast, folded so that the article was centered. "See that? Don't go getting ideas," Master Meadows said, walking over to his desk.

The story had been ongoing for years. The Scotts had won and lost their freedom as the courts listened to appeals and more appeals. I had followed the story with mild interest. Though it was interesting to see slaves going through the courts to gain their freedom, their circumstances were too different from mine to feel a connection.

The only new news stated in the story was that the Chief Justice Taney had declared that African Americans had no rights. That was really nothing new. That accepted attitude of thinking was what every slavery state held to be true.

"No, sir," I said, glancing at the newspaper briefly before setting the paper aside so that I could focus on my work.

"Is that what you would do with any monies I set aside for you?" Master Meadows asked, sliding into his chair. "Pay a lawyer to sue me?"

"No, sir," I said, startled at the idea.

"Well, I'm not going to give you the chance," Master Meadows said. "I have no intention to set up any freedom fund for you."

"Yessir," I said. The news was not a surprise and since he had already promised not to sell my family I did not give it further thought. Thinking about such things kept a man up nights and the only thing that came of it was losing sleep.

We had been blessed with five beautiful children. The two girls were the spitting image of their mama. My heart swelled with love every time I laid my eyes upon those sweet little girls created with loving Tildy. The three boys made my soul swell with pride. They were fine, strapping young boys.

Even Master Meadows had said to me on more than one occasion how fine those boys were. I was glad, mighty glad, that Master Meadows was happy with the children. Our cabin was feeling mighty small and cramped but I did not mind. As long as we were together that was what mattered.

Now I don't want to give the impression that Mistress Meadows has a softer heart than her husband. In many ways Mistress Meadows puts the fear in my heart much more than Master Meadows ever did.

When I sometimes happened to look directly into that woman's eyes I couldn't look away fast enough. They were hard eyes, as cold as glass. I wasn't supposed to look her in the eyes anyway but sometimes it happened purely by accident.

Mistress Meadows had pale blue eyes with nothing behind them. Sometimes she would stare at me. It made me nervous when she did that. I didn't know what she was thinking. Mistress Meadows would just stare at me and even if I didn't look at her I could feel her staring at me. I don't know what she went through her head when she stared so hard at me but it could not be anything good.

I made the mistake of mentioning once to Tildy how Mistress Meadows stared so long and hard at me. Tildy said Mistress Meadows wants to know what I do in bed that makes Tildy so happy.

"You so good looking even the white women want you," Tildy said with a grin.

Tildy thought she was teasing me but the idea made my chest tighten in fear. My first thought was to deny such a thing. It didn't take long for my thoughts to jump to how beautiful Tildy was.

"Has Master Meadows ever tried touching you?" I asked, torn between anger and fear.

I wanted her to deny it. Tildy did not quite deny it but almost. She shrugged. "Not really, no," she said.

"What do you mean, not really?" I asked. The blood roared in my ears at the thought of Master Meadows putting his hands on my Tildy.

"He used to put his arm around my shoulders. Sometimes," Tildy said, growing thoughtful as she remembered. "When I was little. I remember." She shrugged the memory away. "There was another girl here once. Before Miss Jenkins. He made her use her hands and mouth a few times. When Mistress Meadows was carrying Miss Constance. Until Mistress Meadows found out."

That other girl was really Tildy. I knew it for sure. Tildy thought she would protect me by claiming some other girl used her hands and mouth to satisfy Master Meadows but the way she wouldn't look at me when she said it told me that it was Tildy who Tildy was talking about.

"If he ever touches you that way I will kill him," I said in a low voice.

Tildy put her fingers on my lips. "Hush," she whispered. "Walls can have ears. Don't ever, ever, ever say that again, my love."

"I mean it," I said, jerking my head out of the way of her fingers.

"Don't even say it, fool," she hissed, angry with me now. Tildy started to cry. "They would not just kill you," she whispered against my cheek in a raspy voice. "They would kill you slow."

My cheek was wet with her tears. "I'm sorry," I said, bringing her fingers back up to my mouth and kissing her fingertips.

It took a long time for Tildy's tears to dry up. Just when I thought she was done fresh tears would pour from her eyes. "I can't bear to picture it," she said. "Promise me. Promise me you won't ever think or say such a thing again."

My own anger at the thought of Master Meadows pestering my Tildy cooled. It did not die completely. One thing a lifetime as a slave had taught me was when to keep my mouth shut and my feelings off my face. I couldn't promise to never think it but I could promise to never say the words aloud again.

"I would never do anything to put you or the children at risk," I said. "I won't ever say anything to risk you any harm. I promise."

Tildy stared at me thoughtfully for a long time, considering my promise. Eventually she nodded in satisfaction. Tildy snuggled up against me with her cheek on my chest. I rested my chin on the top of her head.

"I don't think Master Meadows makes Mistress Meadows happy in their bed," Tildy said. "Let her look and wonder. It feels good to know that I am the lucky one with the right man in my bed."

I didn't say anything. I didn't want to talk about it anymore. If Master Meadows wanted to rape Tildy he could and there was nothing either of us could do about it. The law wouldn't even consider it rape. I really don't know if I could stand by and do nothing. Tildy was right. If I even threatened Master Meadows with words I would be lucky if they just killed me.

No matter what Tildy said, I did not like Mistress Meadows looking at me. My biggest fear was that she would decide one day to see what I could do in her bed. That scares me more than ten lashings. A black man touching a white woman gets a rope and a tree. If a white woman touched a black man that black man still gets a rope and tree.

It don't matter none at all if that black man didn't want that white woman touching him. Tildy might think that Mistress Meadows wanted to test me out in her bed but I thank God every single night that Tildy must be wrong. All Mistress Meadows ever did was stare at me with her cold, blue eyes, nothing more than stare.

Though I spent my days working for Master Meadows keeping track of his business accounts I still had other tasks in the house. One such task was to stand in the dining room every dinner when they entertained. I didn't have to do anything, really, just stand by the wall and look like I was there for some reason.

Appearances mattered a lot to Mistress Meadows. For some reason I never understood, having Lucas and I standing in the dining room while the Meadows and their guests ate their dinner made some important social statement.

I watched Tildy as she served the family. She held the bowl of steaming green beans in the crook of her left arm and held the serving spoon in her right hand. Around the table Tildy went, scooping up beans and dropping them on a guest's plate, performing her duty without any recognition from anyone at the table.

Tildy wasn't showing yet but we were going to have a sixth child before the year was out. I was looking forward to the new baby but a bit worried that Mistress Meadows would be angry. After the incident with her last baby our children seemed to irritate her more than before.

Tildy's main job in the house was to do all the sewing as well as keep the garden and orchard. She made all the dresses and altered clothes. Mistress Meadows would show Tildy a picture from a magazine and Tildy would figure out by just looking at the picture how to make the dress Mistress Meadows wanted. It took a lot of time to sew a dress.

Like me, she was put to work serving whenever Mistress Meadows entertained. It was almost like Mistress Meadows dressed up all her slaves and paraded us in front of her guests. Betsy entered the dining room with a platter of roast beef and Tildy headed for the kitchen once everyone got their green beans.

Neither Betsy nor Tildy even existed for the people sitting at the table. It was like anyone with dark skin was invisible. To me Tildy was the most beautiful person on the face of the earth. I never tired of looking at her, even if she was serving green beans.

God does indeed work in mysterious ways. If the elder Master Meadows had freed me in his last will and testament I would have never met Tildy. Thinking of the elder Master Meadows made me sad and I stared out the window to hide the feelings. If Mistress Meadows noticed anything out of the ordinary she would ask me about it later.

Lucas stood on the other side of the buffet table, looking straight ahead with his hands clasped behind his back. We wore matching tuxedo suits. Once dinner was over and the guests had gone the first thing we would do would be to remove the tuxedo suits so that Mistress Meadows would put them away until the next time visitors came for dinner.

Normally Lucas did the driving and tended the horses but like me when there were dinner guests he was recruited into being a human book end during the meal. That's how I was sure we looked, like human books ends, each standing at the end of the buffet table with our backs to the wall, just standing there staring straight ahead.

Lucas barely even moved a muscle the entire meal. I don't know how he did it. I found standing still for hours boring beyond my ability to deal with almost. I say almost because imagining the punishment for any behavior Mistress Meadows did not approve of kept me from bouncing up and down on my heels or gaze wandering all over the room.

I would pick a spot out the window across the room and daydream, sometimes glancing over at Tildy. I never grew tired of looking at that woman, my wife. Seeing Tildy helped give me the strength to deal with almost anything.

Chapter Seventeen

Hank

When Wilhelm's barn was completed he invited everyone over for a big party. Mom went over in the morning and helped Caroline cook all sorts of good food. She didn't drink all day. I liked it when she didn't drink.

Caroline had not pulled a gun on Catches Pebbles or Walking Moon again. She kept her distance from the two brothers and as long as there was some distance between her and them she was fine. She was more relaxed the night of the celebration. I think she was relieved that they were heading home in the morning.

Catches Pebbles had a big appetite and ate more than Wilhelm and Dad combined. It was good food and I ate until I was stuffed. Wilhelm and Dad had roasted a whole pig in a pit. They had started the pig roasting the day before. Mom and Caroline had made salads and vegetables fresh from the garden as well as deviled eggs and corn muffins.

I could tell what Mom had made and what Caroline had made. I always thought that my mom was a terrific cook but Caroline made food that made my mouth explode with flavor. Some of it I didn't even know what it was but I ate it anyway. There was even chocolate cake with chocolate icing. It was only the second time in my life I had chocolate cake.

Mom did pour herself a glass of wine while we were eating. I watched her, hoping that she did not drink more than the one glass.

For some reason, since Caroline had arrived, Mom had gotten a little better about her drinking. Dad said that she didn't feel so alone, having a woman in the family now.

Wilhelm waited until everyone was finished eating and stood up to make an announcement. "We would like to share that there will be a new Hansohn come this winter," he said with a grin.

Everyone but Mom looked at August. Mom stared at Caroline. August looked around the faces of everyone seated round the plank table in the barn. "What? I think he means they're having a baby."

Everyone laughed. I really had thought it meant that August was getting married. He had been courting Annabel Holbert for over two years. August was only twenty years old and Dad was always telling him that he had to wait four more years. Now that Wilhelm had gotten married so young August would probably start pestering Dad again.

It finally dawned on me. Wilhelm was going to have a baby. I was going to be an uncle. Mom started to cry.

Dad patted Mom's arm. "It's all right, Elise," he said.

"I'm going to be a grandmother," she said. She pushed her glass of wine away and wrapped her arms around Caroline.

Mom and Caroline both cried and hugged each other. I looked at Hans and he looked at me. We both shrugged. I really didn't understand why the two women were crying and carrying on so. I thought Mom and Caroline were happy about a baby but there they were, holding each other and bawling.

A few weeks after the barn was done I was working with Shadow when I spotted Walking Moon riding toward Wilhelm's yard. He waved as he galloped into the yard, stopping at the corral. He carried a blanket wrapped bundle in front of him, across his lap.

I eyed the bundle in curiosity. "Hi, Mani," I said. "What are you doing here?"

"I brought a gift for Wilhelm's new baby," he said.

"Oh, the baby's not here yet," I said.

"I know that," Walking Moon said. "It's for when it comes."

Wilhelm was working on the pasture fence again. He was almost done, just the gate left. The fence had been put on hold until the barn was done. The horses were in the pasture now and he had strung rope across the gate opening for the time being. He walked over to the corral when he saw Walking Moon.

"A gift for your baby," Walking Moon said. He was still sitting on his pony. He handed the bundle to Wilhelm but Wilhelm didn't take it.

"I'll get Caroline," he said.

"Your woman, she doesn't like me," Walking Moon said. Wilhelm did not speak Lakota so Walking Moon was forced to use his English.

"She just hasn't gotten to know you yet," Wilhelm said. Without another word he headed for the house.

"She doesn't like me," Walking Moon said to me in Lakota.

I shrugged. There was no use denying it. "You may as well get down. You'll be here a while," I said. "We should go up to the house anyway."

I took the bundle from Walking Moon and he dismounted. Whatever was wrapped in that blanket, it was heavy. Once Walking Moon had tied his pony to the corral fence I handed back his gift so that he could present it.

Caroline came out of the house with Wilhelm as Walking Moon and I walked that way. She held onto Wilhelm's arm and pasted a smile on her face as we approached. Walking Moon looked uncomfortable and hesitated. I nudged him in the side and he started walking again.

"For your baby," Walking Moon said in greeting to Caroline, holding out the bundle.

Caroline hesitated then reached forward and accepted the bundle. She pulled back the blanket and revealed a cradleboard. Tucked inside the cradleboard was a small buckskin dress. Caroline stared at the cradleboard and dress then pulled out the dress and handed the cradleboard to Wilhelm.

The small dress was embroidered with beads and porcupine quills. Wilhelm held up the cradleboard. Soft, downy feathers dangled from a strap around the top of the cradleboard. The inside was lined with a leather pouch where the baby could be placed and the strings cinched up to hold the baby in place. A roll bar at the top of the cradleboard protected the baby's head if for some reason the cradleboard fell.

"What is it?" Caroline asked, looking at the cradleboard Wilhelm held.

"For can carry baby or set baby down when you work," Walking Moon said, staring at his feet. He didn't like speaking in English but he did for Caroline.

"Did you make it yourself?" Caroline asked, running her fingers over the smooth, polished wood that curved out over the top of the cradleboard.

Walking Moon nodded. "But my sister make dress," he said. "I give her leather and she make it."

Tears rolled down Caroline's cheeks. She hugged the little dress to her face. Suddenly she dashed forward and threw her arms around Walking Moon and gave him a huge hug. Walking Moon's eyes widened so much I thought they'd pop out of his face.

"Thank you!" Caroline said, stepping back. She looked at Walking Moon and gave him another giant hug. Walking Moon stood with his arms straight at his sides.

Ever since that day Caroline has always treated Indians like anyone else and she treated Walking Moon like a brother. Walking Moon was embarrassed by all her attention and grumbled under his breath a lot that women were as fickle as the river in spring but he was not immune to Caroline's charms. Any time he came to see me he always had to go say hello to Caroline. Maybe it was because she always gave him sugar cookies when he visited her.

Mom was so busy making baby clothes and blankets that she went days and then weeks without a drop of alcohol. She was happy and looking forward to the new baby. She even started making yarn again, singing as she sat at her spinning wheel.

When Wilhelm and Caroline's baby arrived it was a cold winter day. It had snowed the day before so the air was crisp even if it was bitterly cold. Dad harnessed up Donder and Blitzen and we rode the few miles in the wagon to Wilhelm's place. I unhitched the two horses while everyone else went into the house.

I led Donder and Blitzen into the barn and put them into stalls then stopped to give Shadow a carrot I had snuck from the root cellar. The barn was almost warm from the heat generated by the animals but cold enough that I didn't linger long.

Everyone was in Wilhelm and Caroline's bedroom. Mom was holding the baby while Dad, August, and Hans stood in a semi-circle looking down at the newborn. Wilhelm stood behind Mom's chair, beaming so bright he looked ready to burst. Caroline was in bed, almost buried under piles of blankets. She looked tired. She even had brown circles under her eyes.

It was a baby girl. Mom told me to quit dawdling and come look at my new niece. I stepped up next to August and peeked around him. Not sure what the fuss was all about. She was kind of red and her head was pointy and she had no hair.

Suddenly her little fists started shaking and she opened her mouth and wailed. I mean wailed. I had to cover my ears with my hands to block out that high pitched scream of torture.

Caroline and Mom both smiled as that red-faced little thing wailed her displeasure to the world. I backed out of the room to escape. Mom stood and handed the baby to Caroline. Mom stayed in the room but Dad and my two brothers bolted out so fast they almost trampled me.

Eventually Wilhelm came out and joined us in the kitchen. He looked tired also. Tired but happy.

"Have you settled on a name?" Dad asked.

"Lydia," Wilhelm said. "Lydia Elise Katherine Hansohn."

Though she wasn't much to look at when she was born, I have to say that she grew into kind of a cute baby. She was all soft and happy. She made funny gurgling noises and waved her arms a lot. By spring Caroline was putting that cradleboard to good use.

For no apparent reason at all, Mom started getting drunk again but only at night and not every night. I had really thought that she was done with her drinking, having Caroline nearby to keep her from being lonely. I didn't understand it at all. Sometimes I thought she wanted to stop drinking but it was like she couldn't.

She was teaching Caroline to spin to make yarn and to knit the yarn she made. As hard as she tried, Caroline could not do it as well as Mom though. Caroline was better at sewing than knitting or spinning. Wilhelm sent off for a sewing machine.

When it arrived we all gathered around and watched Caroline sew. She moved her foot up and down on a foot pedal and that machine whirled and clicked as the needle went in and out of the fabric faster than the eye could see. Mom's eyes lit up as she watched the machine stitch a whole side of a pair of trousers faster than a person could sew a few inches.

Winter lost its grip and the snow melted. School was still in session but with the ground thawing out we were busy getting ready for spring planting. Caroline was nervous about her first garden but Mom promised to help her with the planting and learning about gardening.

August and I went over to help Caroline start her garden. First we had to plow up the ground where Mom had chosen to place Caroline's garden. Lydia slept in the cradleboard under a tree within sight of the where we were working. I was looking forward to trying out the Belgiums but Wilhelm said that I was too young so August got to hitch up one of the big beasts ahead of the plow.

I walked behind August, kicking the clods of dirt that were too big. The smell of freshly turned soil filled my nostrils. Mom had stuck sticks into the four corners to mark where she wanted the garden to go. The sun glinted on something turned up by the plow and I reached down and brushed the dirt away. It was an arrow head.

More things were coming up to the surface as the plow blade scored the ground. I picked up a piece of old matted basket, more arrow heads, some charred wood, and bones that had weathered to a deep yellow. I started a pile next to Lydia under the tree. Caroline had been watching August to make sure that he stayed true with the furrows but she walked over to see what I was piling up under the tree.

Caroline picked up an arrow head, running her fingers across the ridges in the center. "Why so many?" she asked, looking down at the pile.

"There was probably a village here," I said. "Or a campsite."

"They lived here?" she asked, looking up at me in surprise."

"Sure," I said. "This was all Indian land before we came."

"I thought the agency was miles away," Caroline said.

"That's just the land the government makes them stay on," I said. "They used to move around a lot before."

I went back to following August behind the big brown Belgium. The horse pulled the plow without any effort and he was moving fast. Caroline remained standing for a long time over the pile of relics I was finding buried in the ground.

At the end of the row August turned the Belgium. The reins drooped low as the horse turned but the plow was still pointing forward. August struggled to turn the plow but the front was lodged against something. I found a whole handful of arrow heads and picked them out of the dirt while I waited for August to get the plow turned.

I trotted back over to the tree with my find. Caroline had walked back to the other end of the garden plot to be able to look down the furrows, to watch that they remained straight. It was almost done,

only a few more rows to plow. Lydia was squirming in her
cradleboard but her eyes were still closed. Anticipating her famous
wake-up wail, I turned to tell Caroline that the baby was waking.

It all happened so fast. While struggling with the stuck plow
August had allowed too much slack on the reins and they drooped to
the ground. The Belgium had stepped on one of the reins just as
August freed the plow from what had been keeping it from moving.

The plow slammed into the horse's back ankles. Startled and in
pain, the horse tried to move away from the plow but the rein was
trapped under its front hoof. The horse charged forward in fear,
trying to escape. The plow turned on its side and slid under the
horse's back hoofs.

Blood splattered the side of the plow blade and the rein snapped.
The horse bolted across the freshly plowed garden, the plow
bouncing behind it. For every third step the horse took the plow
blade bounced up high enough to hit its back ankles. I stared in
shock as the horse came right at me. Me and the baby.

Caroline screamed when she realized what was happening. She
picked up her skirts and ran towards me and the baby. Going through
the garden was the direct route but the freshly plowed dirt was soft
and her feet sank into the dirt with each step she took. August was
running also but he was sinking into the soft soil as well.

I threw myself over the baby, wrapping my arms around the
cradleboard and ducking my head. The horse swerved around me but
its hoof still caught my back. I cringed but resisted the urge to arch
my back from the pain. It could have been worse. Though he had
clipped me with his shod hoof it was just a glancing blow and I
didn't get squashed under his full weight.

The plow blade slammed into my side and leg. Below me the
baby was screaming. "Sorry," I whispered to her. My apology did
not calm her. I think my ears hurt more than my leg.

I felt kind of funny, like the world was spinning. Maybe the
hoof had clipped me harder than I thought. It was kind of quiet

except for the wailing baby. She was hiccupping now. I raised my head to look around.

August had reached the Belgium and had his hands on the reins. The plow blade was wedged into the side of the tree a few feet from me. Red smears and splatters made a line down the side of the plow blade.

I looked over at the Belgium. Blood covered its back legs. I hoped no tendons had been severed. It was hard for a horse to recover from such a wound. Beyond the Belgium and August I could see Wilhelm running towards us.

"Don't move," Caroline said between gasps for air. "Don't move! Don't move!"

"It's all right," I said, loosening my arms from the cradleboard. "August has him. She's all right. See?"

"Don't move," Caroline said again, dropping to her knees next to me. "Oh, Lord! Don't move."

She had her hands on my leg. I looked back and down. I could see my own bone in my leg and my leg was twisted all funny. It should not have been twisted like that. I did not faint. Men don't faint. I am sure it was the loss of blood making me lose consciousness. The body needs blood in it. It's just a coincidence that the sight of my bone in my leg was the last thing I remembered until I woke up in a bed.

Chapter Eighteen

There was a man sitting next to the bed. He smelled of tobacco and lye soap. When he saw that I was awake he reached over and pulled each of my eyelids up so he could look into my eyes. He nodded and sat back.

"So you're a hero," he said. "Being a hero often comes at a cost."

"Who are you?" I asked.

"Doc Larson," he said. He stood and opened a black bag next to him. He looked back at me. "You're lucky your brother is a veterinarian. Saved that leg, he did."

"It hurts," I said. I could feel it throbbing under the blanket. I lifted the blanket and looked. My whole leg was wrapped in gauze and plaster.

"You'll be in bed for a few weeks," Doc Larson said. He put a stethoscope up to his ear and the other end over my heart. "Good strong heart. That's why you don't know me. You Hansohns are a hearty lot."

Mom was standing at the bedroom door. I looked around the room, realizing that I was not in my own bed. I was still at Wilhelm's house. Mom was crying but she didn't look drunk. Since Lydia had arrived she was drinking less and less, only a few nights a week.

Mom stepped further into the room, hesitated for a moment, then ran to the bed and wrapped her arms around my head, squishing me against her chest. I struggled to move my head so that I could breathe. She smelled of stale alcohol even though she seemed sober.

"Mein Junge," Mom said, crying even harder. "Oh, mein Junge."

At least she was calling me her son and not her baby. "I'm all right," I said. I don't know if she heard me because my head was still buried against her chest and my words were muffled. "How is the baby?"

"Sie gerettet," Mom said. "Mein Junge. Sie gerettet."

"I'm glad she's all right," I said.

Caroline entered the room next, carrying Lydia. Caroline was crying also. She stood on the other side of the bed. "Thank you, Hank. Thank you. Thank you."

"You're smothering me," I said to Mom, trying to squirm out and under from her arms.

Wilhelm was next. He came into the room and stood next to Caroline. "How are you, Hank?"

"Save me," I said to Wilhelm.

Wilhelm grinned but made no move to save me from the smothering embrace of my mother and the tearful thanks from Caroline. It wasn't long before Dad and Hans were in the bedroom as well. August lingered at the doorway. Mom finally released me but sat in the chair the doctor had vacated and held my hand.

"How's the Belgium?" I asked.

"He'll be all right," Wilhelm said. "Some cuts but no tendons were cut."

"That's good," I said in relief. I had been worried that he would have had to be destroyed.

August still stood in the doorway. He looked uncomfortable and wouldn't look right at me. "Are you all right, August?" I asked him.

"I'm sorry," August said in a soft voice.

"For what?" I asked.

"For what happened," August said in a firmer voice.

"It wasn't your fault," I said. It wasn't his fault.

"I shouldn't have let him take out the Belgium," Wilhelm said.

"I should have stayed by Lydia," Caroline said.

"I should have been here," Dad said.

I looked around the room at all the faces taking the blame. "Can't turn the clock back, can we?" Doc Larson said. He picked up his black bag and left the room. August had to move into the room to allow the doctor space to get out. The doctor looked back over his shoulder. "I'll be back in a few days to check on you," he said.

"So what did the plow get stuck on?" I asked August. "A stump?"

He shook his head no. "An old buffalo hide," he said, perking up a bit. "We're going to dig it up."

"Probably an old, abandoned teepee," Dad said.

"It must be old to get covered up like that," I said. I was getting tired and my leg throbbed. I felt like crying but I couldn't cry in front of everyone. "We should tell Walking Moon and Catches Pebbles."

"We'll see," Dad said. "You need some rest. Everyone out."

"If you need anything, and I mean anything, just call my name," Caroline said. She leaned over and kissed the top of my head. Lydia squealed and grabbed at Caroline, afraid she was going to fall. "Anything." Caroline straightened and shifted the baby on her hip. "Maybe we can get a bell for you to ring."

"Out," Dad said, gesturing.

"Uh, Dad," I said before he followed everyone out.

"Yes, son," he said.

"How am I supposed to get to the outhouse?" I asked.

"I'll help you for now," Dad said, shutting the door. He reached under the bed and pulled out a bedpan.

It was the worse summer of my life. I was stuck in bed all spring when I longed to be out. Winter had just loosened its hold and I had been looking forward to spring and summer to do all the summer things and I was stuck in bed. By the time the doctor said I could get out of bed I was as weak as a baby.

Worse, Caroline was serious about wanting to take care of me. It was embarrassing. I didn't mind her serving me meals in bed but I didn't like her giving me sponge baths. I held a towel over my privates and stared at the ceiling as she scrubbed me down with a soapy wash cloth and then scrubbed me down with plain water to rinse away the soap. I drew the line at having her help me with the bedpan but she still emptied it.

Mom came to Wilhelm's every single day and sat with me, sometimes for an hour, sometimes the whole day. Between her and Caroline I was cleaner than I'd ever been in my life. They washed and fed me until I shone and my belly grew into a bump.

Eventually the doctor said I could get out of bed for short stretches. I could only get out of bed for an hour a day for the first week. Then I had to hobble around with a cane because my leg was still wrapped in hardened plaster. The doctor visited me every so often to change the plaster cast and check on my progress.

Walking Moon came to see me once. He was uncomfortable coming into the bedroom. His eyes darted everywhere. He had a growth spurt over the winter and looked like he'd shot up a foot. He brought me tea that the medicine man made and a spirit totem inside a leather bag that he put under my pillow.

"What is it?" I asked, looking at the pillow. I was dying of curiosity.

"If you look inside you break the medicine," he said.

Caroline made a cup of the tea he brought and I tried to drink it but it was so awful that I couldn't take more than two swallows. "You must drink it all," Walking Moon said. "It keeps the infection away."

I tried to drink again but it made the tip of my tongue sting. In fact, my whole tongue was tingling after a few minutes.

"What is it?" I asked.

Walking Moon shrugged. "I'm not a medicine man," he said. "I had to drink it when that deer stuck his antler in my side. You can drink it."

"Did it work?" I asked.

Walking Moon twisted and lifted up his shirt. There was a puckered scar under his ribs. I leaned forward and looked more closely at the scar. It was an interesting scar. It almost looked like a ghost face.

I pinched my nose with my fingers and downed the rest of the tea without stopping. That was the most horrid stuff I had ever tasted. But if Walking Moon could do it I could do it.

Tom Guhrt came to see me also even though he lived five miles on the other side of New Ulm. His sister Maria and his mom came with him. They brought an apple pie. It was so tart that it made my eyes water.

"Mom ran out of sugar and the apples were just coming in," Guhrt said. I set the plate down beside me, unable to eat another bite. "You gonna eat that?" he asked, pointing at the piece of pie.

"Go ahead," I said. "I ate just before you came and I'm still stuffed."

"I heard you got hurt saving a baby," Guhrt said. He picked up the slice of pie and ate it in three bites.

Guhrt was always taller than me and he seemed to have shot up even higher since the end of school only a few months ago. The girls liked Tom. I don't know why. They giggled and whispered to each other behind their hands. They never did that for me.

Guhrt also brought schoolwork for me. The accident had happened two weeks before school was scheduled to end for the year. "Master Harris said that your marks are high enough to pass into seventh grade but if you do the homework before school starts this autumn you won't lose points," Guhrt said.

"Thanks," I said. The idea of doing schoolwork was actually inviting. I had already spent a lot of time bored in bed.

"I'm surprised Maria wanted to come," Guhrt said. "She was mad in love with Wilhelm before he went off east."

"Really?" I asked.

"When she heard he'd gone and gotten himself hitched while back there she went to her room and cried for a week," Guhrt said.

"How did she even know him?" I asked.

Wilhelm was done with elementary school before we came to New Ulm. Since my life was school and the farm I couldn't imagine anything outside of that.

"At one of the town socials, I reckon," Guhrt said.

"You think she'll fight with Caroline?" I asked, not sure whether to be nervous or excited at the idea of the two fighting.

Guhrt shrugged. "Probably not. Maria's not a fighter," he said. "Did you see how huge those Belgiums are? And one stepped on you?"

"Just grazed me with a hoof," I said. "The bruise is almost gone. It was the plow blade that got me."

"Can I see?" Guhrt asked, looking at the lump under the blanket where my wrapped leg was.

"Nothing to see," I said even as I pulled the blanket aside.

Guhrt reached over and wrapped the cast with his knuckles. "Does it hurt?" he asked.

"No," I said even though it did when he knocked it like that. I pulled the blanket back over my cast so that he wasn't tempted to do it again.

I had to stay at Wilhelm's house even once I could get out of bed. Caroline wanted to take care of me. Besides, I think Mom was drinking too much to take care of me. After the first month she didn't come see me every day anymore. The summer was half over before Doc Larson removed the cast and I still had to take it easy on the leg.

It was glorious having that hard plaster cast off though. It had been so hot and within days of the doctor changing it for a new one it started itching. The doc said it was from my sweat. No wonder it itched because my leg was always sweating.

There was a long scar down my leg but by the end of the summer I was fully healed and back to normal. Just in time for harvest and school to start.

Before leaving Wilhelm's house to return home I opened the small leather bag that Walking Moon had put under my pillow. Inside was the mummified corpse of a mouse with a broken leg, an eagle feather folded to fit into the bag, and some dirt with dried grass. It was a good thing Caroline hadn't opened it.

Chapter Nineteen

A few weeks after I returned home from Wilhelm's house Caroline came to visit the farm. She took Lydia into the house to see Mom. Wilhelm was not with her. Sometimes they came over on a Sunday or sometimes we went there on a Sunday. Caroline had never come by herself. It wasn't even Sunday.

She wasn't in the house more than a few minutes when she came back out without Lydia. She went to the wagon and lifted out a woven basket. Hans and I were up on top of the hay rack, settling the hay into place as Dad lifted it up with his hay fork. We had cut it a few days before and it was hot enough that it had already properly dried.

"I have something for Hank," Caroline said, approaching the wagon that Dad was standing in.

Dad stopped and looked down at her. He nodded. "Hank, come on down," Dad said.

I clambered down the hay rack, not even thinking about my injured leg as I slid down the last few feet. "What is it?" I asked.

Caroline lifted a towel that covered the basket. A fluffy brown puppy head popped up over the side of the basket. I stared in disbelief, looking over at Dad. He nodded. I ran to Caroline, eyes only for the puppy.

"You can pick him up," Caroline said.

The puppy squirmed and whimpered as I lifted him out of the basket. I held him up and twisted him to look to be sure. Yep, a boy. I hugged him against my chest and he wiggled and licked my face and neck.

"It's really all right?" I asked Dad. "He's for me and I can keep him?"

Dad nodded. "You're responsible for him," he said. "But I think you're old enough now to take responsibility."

Hans slid down the hay stack and came up beside me to see the puppy. The puppy licked his fingers. I kissed the top of the puppy's head. He was so soft and smelled like puppy. He was a dark brown with a patch of white on his chest and two white back paws. I lifted one of those paws.

"Look at the size of those paws," Hans said.

"He'll be big," Dad said.

"Does he have a name?" I asked Caroline.

"You get to pick one," Caroline said.

"Lydia all right?" Dad asked, looking over at the house.

"She's sober," Caroline said.

I looked up in surprise that Caroline had said it out loud. We all knew that Mom drank too much liquor but no one talked about it or said aloud anything to do with her drinking. Dad just nodded and pick up his hay fork.

"That hay's not going to stack itself," Dad said.

"What do I do with him?" I asked. "One of the horses could step on him if I put him down."

"I'll put him in the barn," Caroline said.

"When we finish with the hay you can build a pen for him," Dad said. "Until he's big enough to watch out for himself."

It took me a few days to decide on a name for the puppy. I thought of all sorts of elaborate, clever names but none seemed to suit him. In the end I settled on Patches. Everyone fell in love with Patches.

When school started up I was a hero. Somehow the teacher and kids had all heard about my valiant rescue of my brother's baby. All the kids wanted to see my scar so during recess I would raise my pants leg so they could get a good look.

Guhrt returned to school with a scar also. He was still wearing the plaster on his forehead, covering his left eyebrow when school started. When the plaster came off there was a white X across the bottom part of his left eyebrow. No hair grew there and the skin was raised and white.

My scar and heroics was forgotten and since Guhrt refused to talk about what had happened to give him the scar there was a lot of speculation, all of it making Guhrt the greatest hero of all time. Guhrt protested that he was no such thing but since he wouldn't share what had actually happened the stories only grew in stature.

When Piotr returned from university he opened up a dental office in New Ulm. The town wasn't big but everyone came from all over so he had a busy practice right away. August headed off to university the year before Piotr returned. All five of us had not been together since the first year we arrived in Minnesota Territory.

August had gone north to Chicago to study architecture but changed to philosophy and then to veterinary medicine all in the first year. In April that year Dad went up to Chicago to visit with August. He was gone for almost two weeks. When he came home he didn't say anything about what had happened during his visit but he told Mom that August had settled on a field of study.

Patches grew like a weed. He was smart and easily learned all the tricks I taught him. Mom really took to him. Patches seemed to really like her also. As he grew older his ears started to stand up straight. First one ear went up. He looked pretty funny for a while with one ear up and the other ear floppy down. About a week later the second ear stood up.

At Sunday dinner in October that year Wilhelm and Caroline announced that they were going to have a second baby. Lydia was walking around if she had something to hold onto. It was her favorite thing to have one of us walk behind her while she held our hands. She could keep going longer than us but if we stopped she would plop down on her butt and squeal until someone grabbed her hands again.

Patches loved Lydia. He would lick her face and she would laugh and laugh. Whenever Lydia visited he wouldn't leave her side if she was outside. He would sit by the front door and not move the whole time she was inside.

At Christmas Wilhelm gave me Shadow as my Christmas gift. "He was always your horse anyway," Wilhelm said.

I looked at Dad. He nodded. I could keep Shadow. It was the best Christmas ever. Patches and Shadow were best friends. Patches slept every night in the barn in Shadow's stall.

With everyone going off to university and starting their own lives it meant more work for the rest of us. I had less free time than I had when I was younger. I only had one more year of school left in New Ulm after the current school year. The county school only went through eighth grade. This was Hans' last year of school before he went off to university.

A whole year passed without Walking Moon coming to see me. Dad declared a free day one sunny fall day and planned a trip to the river to do some fishing. We had all spent weeks of long hard days harvesting the crops so it was good to relax.

Wilhelm had helped with our harvest and we had gone over and helped with his harvest. Caroline put Lydia in a pen at the end of the field so that she could work. Patches stayed right by Lydia, guarding her. Mom worked right beside us. When it came to harvesting everyone had to work to get it done in time.

Even though a day of sitting beside the river fishing sounded ideal, I decided to ride Shadow out to the agency and see if I could find Walking Moon. It would be good for Shadow to stretch his legs also. I didn't know why Walking Moon had stayed away for so long and I missed my friend.

I had been out at the agency once the first summer I met Walking Moon but had not been out there since. I rode with Dad and Hans to the river, Patches running alongside us. He was growing into a big dog but Dad said he wasn't done growing yet even at a year old.

We were almost in the same exact spot where Piotr and I had first spotted the wolf tracks and then met Walking Moon, Catches Pebbles, and Talks With Fist. I smiled as I remembered that day. We never did see a wolf in all the time we lived there.

"I think I'll ride on out to the agency," I said as we neared the fishing spot Dad liked so much.

Dad was not happy about my wanting to ride over to the agency. "Nor a good time, son," he said. "I've been hearing rumors."

"I'll be all right," I said. "I just want to see Walking Moon. He didn't come by at all this past summer."

"There have been some young Lakota men riding around causing trouble," Dad said. "I'd feel better if you didn't go out there right now."

"I'll be fine," I said. "That's up north. Not here."

"Hans, go with him," Dad said.

"But I wanted to do some fishing," Hans said. Dad gave him a stare. Hans sighed. "All right."

We hadn't gone far when we encountered five Indians riding east away from the agency. One of the Indians grabbed an arrow from behind his back, raised his bow, and shot Patches. The dog yelped and fell, rolling over and over in the grass. I dropped from Shadow and ran to Patches.

The arrow had pierced him in the side. I didn't know what to do. The arrow had not gone all the way through but had lodged inside him. If I pulled the arrow shaft out it would just hurt him more. He whined and licked my hand then lay panting. He sighed once and stopped breathing.

"No," I whispered. I gathered him in my arms and carried him to Shadow.

Hans had dismounted and was holding the reins of both our horses. He looked at the limp dog in my arms and tears flowed down his face. I handed him Patches and turned my attention to the five riders who thundered up to us. The Indian who had shot Patches dismounted and approached me.

He started to say something but I didn't give him a chance to speak. I yelled the loudest war whoop I could manage and charged him. I lowered my head and butted him right in the stomach. Caught off guard, he bent in half and I could hear the air whoosh out of him. He had killed Patches. For no reason.

Hands grabbed me and feet and fists pummeled me. I swung back wildly, my fists making contact most of the time. I thought all five of them were beating me but it was actually only two. Hans grabbed me around the waist and pulled me back. I accidently elbowed him in the jaw before I realized that it was him grabbing me.

The Indian I had charged was still sitting on the ground trying to catch his breath. I had knocked the wind right out of him. Two were still sitting on their horses and two were standing in front of the Indian on the ground. The two standing were panting from the exertion of beating on me but they stayed back.

The sound of pounding hooves heralded the arrival of more riders from the northwest. They crested the small rise of land we were standing on. At least forty Lakota rode in the approaching group.

I recognized the horse of the man leading the party. It was Walking Moon's father's horse, Shadow's sire. I didn't recognize anyone else in the party though. I took a second look and spotted Talks With Fist. It had been years since I had seen Talks With Fist.

"Um, I think we should leave," Hans said, looking around. Even more riders were approaching from the southwest.

"No," I said. I stood with my hands clenched into fists at my side. "He killed Patches for no reason."

"You're on agency land," one of the men standing beside the Indian sitting on the ground said.

"I was looking for Walking Moon," I said.

The larger party had reached us in time to hear what we said. Walks With Fist edged his horse up next to his father and spoke to him in a voice I could not hear well enough to know what he was saying. The man listened, nodded, and guided his horse closer to me and Hans.

"You are Hank Hansohn?" the man asked in English. I nodded. "Why are you on agency land?"

"I was looking for Walking Moon," I said. I pointed at the Indian who had shot Patches. "He killed my dog! For no reason."

Walking Moon's father did not seem bothered by the news. "Tall Grass was perhaps rash in shooting the animal," he said.

"He has no business on agency land," the Indian I had head-butted said, getting to his feet. "He's lucky I put an arrow through his dog and not him."

"Go home, Hank Hansohn," Walking Moon's father said. "Walks With Fist, go with him as far as the river."

I jumped up on Shadow's back and Hans handed Patches up to me. I laid the dog's body across my thighs. Hans mounted Donder and Talks With Fist led the way back east.

"I am sorry about your dog," Walks With Fist said, guiding his horse next to me. I nodded, not trusting myself to speak. "You fought with Tall Grass?" he asked.

"He had no right to kill Patches," I said.

"You are brave or foolhardy," Talks With Fist said. "Tall Grass would have hurt you if he got the chance. He is angry with all the white settlers stealing our land while we starve."

I stroked Patches' ear and ran my hand down his back. It wasn't fair. He was such a good boy and he didn't deserve to die for no reason. Tears ran down my cheeks. I quickly wiped them away before Walks With Fist could see that I was crying.

"Walking Moon is not here," Walks With Fist said. "He went west, up to Big Stone Lake. You came for nothing."

Patches died for nothing. I was responsible for him and I let him down. I wished with my whole heart that I had made him stay home. It was my fault that he was dead.

I buried him behind the barn. Everyone came out to say farewell. Dad had to hold Mom's arm to keep her from falling. She had been drinking since she heard that Patches had died. Hans had ridden over to tell Wilhelm and Caroline and they had come as well.

I had dug a hole and piled up several large rocks next to the hole. Patches lay next to the hole. I had left the arrow in him but Dad had broken the shaft off.

"You were a good dog, Patches," I said, sniffling.

"Good-bye, Patches," Hans said. "I hope there are squirrels in heaven for you to chase."

"I loved him," Mom said. She swayed next to Dad. "I lose everyone I love. I miss Germany. No one died in Germany."

"Paws. Paws," Lydia said, leaning forward in her mother's arms, trying to get to Patches. That was as close as she could get to saying Patches.

"You had a short life but a good life," Caroline said. "Good-bye, Patches."

Lydia squirmed, trying to get down. Wilhelm reached over and took her from Caroline. Lydia forgot about Patches, intrigued with Wilhelm's moustache. She grinned as she slapped her chubby hand on Wilhelm's face.

"There's a lot of unrest on the agency," Wilhelm said to Dad as I used my hands to pull loose dirt out of the hole. "If they'll shoot an arrow through a pet who's to say they won't start shooting people?"

"Always a bad apple in the lot," Dad said somberly, gaze on the hole I was filling.

"They resent us," Wilhelm said. "They've lost so much. They have nothing to do but sit around waiting for government payments that are late and stolen by the traders."

"His name was Tall Grass," I said, pausing in my shoveling. "It wasn't they. It was him."

"Hank tackled him," Hans said, still in a bit of awe that I had done that.

"You inherited your mother's lack of fear," Dad said.

I looked up at Dad in surprise before looking at Mom. She was so drunk she could barely stand. If Dad didn't have his arm around her she would have fallen. Her legs wobbled and Dad pulled her upright.

I picked up Patches and gently laid him in the hole, straightening his legs and brushing dirt from his fur. I kneeled next to the grave, saying my final farewell in silence. Mom cried as I shoveled dirt over Patches.

"Stay away from the agency," Dad said. He turned, leading Mom back to the house.

I filled the grave then stacked the rocks on top. Hans helped me with the rocks. Though I had dug deep the rocks were to stop little creatures from digging to reach the body. Wilhelm and Caroline stayed until the last rock was in place.

"You listen to Dad," Wilhelm said. "You stay away from the agency. This Tall Grass might hold a grudge against you for attacking him."

"I'm not afraid," I said.

"No, I didn't think you were," Wilhelm said. "That's why I'm telling you to listen to Dad."

Wilhelm and Caroline walked back to their wagon and headed straight home without going into the house. Mom was in a mood so no one really wanted to be around her. Hans and I stayed outside.

I sat next to the freshly dug grave, mourning the loss of Patches while Hans wandered off into the barn. If only I could take it back. I wouldn't have brought Patches with me. I would have sent him home. He had been having so much fun running along with us. I wished with all my heart that I could take it back.

Chapter Twenty

For over thirteen years I had been going to that office every morning and spending the day bent over Master Meadows' ledgers, business reports, and newspaper to assess likely investments. Master Meadows flourished from my hard work. At my suggestion he even subscribed to more newspapers eventually. I could not convince him to order the newspaper from London, however.

Having more newspapers helped me decide on whether an investment was good or not. The more information I had the better I could see the whole picture. A drought in Warsaw County meant it was good to buy wheat early because it meant the prices would go up. Fashions were a good study in sound investing.

It took a few years before Master Meadows trusted my advice enough to actually follow my suggestions. When he did he made money. His capital increased in value year after year.

Not once did he ever thank me or even say that I was doing a good job. He expected it of me now. I didn't need recognition. It was enough for me that I was able to spend my days working at a task I enjoyed and my nights with Tildy and our children.

Then the war came. The war had steadily been encroaching on our lives. At first it was subtle. Everyone expected the war to end after only a few months. No one expected the war to really impact us. It affected us. It affected us a lot. Not only financially but our very lives. Armies marched and fought all across Missouri.

Mr. Andrew Meadows Junior was a man grown by the time the war started and he went off to fight with the Confederacy. Mistress Meadows was proud of her son yet terrified of what would befall him in a war. Some days her moods had the whole household walking on tiptoes. Master Meadows had the good fortune of being able to escape the house and spend his work day at one of his business sites when Mistress Meadows was in one of her moods.

Ulysses vanished a year into the war. Rumor was that he joined the Union side of the war. Rumors started that he had been killed in his first battle but no official word of his death ever came.

No letters from him arrived either. Not a single one, ever. Andrew Junior sent letters home at least once a week. To this day I don't know what happened to Ulysses. For all I know he could have sunk into a bog on his way north, if he was even heading north.

I felt bad about Ulysses vanishing and hoped that he was alive somewhere and just too lazy to write his family. He was a good boy with a good heart and a lot of enthusiasm for life. But as the years passed and no word came I expected the worse fate had befallen him.

I opened the newspaper one day to see in bold letters that President Lincoln had declared a Proclamation of Emancipation of all slaves. I stared at the headline in stunned silence. With one stroke of the pen the president could do what I had been hoping for my entire life, what the elder Master Meadows had not done for me.

My heart filled with swirling emotions. Freedom. We would go north, was my first thought. Though I had lost the urge to head north when I met Tildy, the very word north filled me with a hope of a grand future. Just because the president said we were free did not mean it would be safe to remain in Missouri.

I read further. The decree would go into effect on January 1st of the next year, months away yet. He had freed the slaves in the ten rebelling states. My heart filled with lead and sank to the floor. Missouri belonged to the Union.

The state was divided in how it felt about the secession but in the end had stuck with the Union. Missouri was not on the list of states where President Lincoln had freed the slaves. Because Missouri was still a part of the Union the state's slave owners were safe from losing all their slaves.

I closed the newspaper and set it on the desk beside me. Master Meadows had already read the newspaper that morning. He normally read it while he ate breakfast then brought it into the office for me to read. Master Meadows had not said a word about reading about the Proclamation of Emancipation.

I did not know what to think of the news. If the Confederacy won the war then slavery would continue, of course. If the Union won, would the president free the slaves in the rest of the states? That must be his plan.

I was no longer the naïve boy who had argued with Master Meadows about going north to live happily ever after. If we were going to be free I would need a plan. We would need money. Cash.

That canvas bag holding my saved allowance from the elder Master Meadows was still hidden away at the house. It should still be safely waiting in its hiding place. I had left the key to the lock box in the bag. I needed to fetch that key. One day soon.

None of the other newspapers mentioned the big news. Before the war the newspapers from New York, Chicago, and Atlanta were a week behind. Since the war started they would arrive even later, sporadic at best. The last newspaper from Atlanta had arrived three weeks after printing and we hadn't received a new one in weeks.

"You think you going to be freed, boy?" Master Meadows asked from his seat behind his big oak desk. He had been watching me read the article after all.

"No sir," I said. I opened a ledger and flipped through the pages.

"South's gonna win," Master Meadows said.

"Yessir," I said.

"Don't go thinking you're going anywhere," Master Meadows

said. "You're nothing but property."

"Yessir," I said, gaze fixed on the ledger in front of me.

"Just because their president boldly declares all slaves be free men don't mean nothing," Master Meadows said.

Their president. Master Meadows was one of the men who had voted to secede. In his mind Missouri had no part of the Union. I didn't need him reminding me that though Missouri was part of the Union I was still a slave. No matter which way the war went, I needed to plan a way to escape Missouri. Eventually. Somehow.

The past year had impacted Master Meadows' holdings. The war had torn the country apart. Master Meadows was determined to make up the losses from his businesses with investments. I wouldn't recommend any investments. There was too much turmoil. I didn't feel confident about investing in anything.

The railways were hit hard with the war. Fields were destroyed with armies battling on them or camping on them. What crops weren't destroyed were often left fallow in the field because there was no one to harvest. Farmers with cattle to sell were dumping all their livestock on the market at once. Whole shipments of goods were destroyed when trains were caught in the cross-fire of generals and their armies. Wagon trains were even more vulnerable than rail trains.

"My stores are sitting empty," Master Meadows complained. "My income has dwindled to almost nothing."

"Yessir," I said. It wasn't almost nothing but it had definitely slowed. "But investing would take away from your capital. I don't see anything worth the risk right now."

"Guns and steel," Master Meadows muttered. "That's worth investing now."

"Steel's all up north, sir," I said.

"Well, Missouri's part of the Union," Master Meadows said. "I don't see why I can't get part of the wealth the steel makers are raking in with this war."

"War will be over soon, sir," I said. "I think it's best to hold onto your capital and wait to see what results from the war."

"Well I think you're a chicken waiting on the sidelines in fear," Master Meadows said.

"Yessir," I said. "Them's mighty big cats squabbling in the yard. Better to stay out of the way if you're a chicken."

"You calling me a chicken, boy?" Master Meadows said in a low, angry voice.

"No, sir," I said without hesitation. "I'm the chicken watching those cats."

"Well I'm not a chicken," Master Meadows said. "You're afraid to choose investments but I'm not."

"Yessir," I said, turning back to my books.

Master Meadows had gone ahead and made some bad investments anyway. I saw the losses, of course. At least he had not thrown away all his holdings.

It was a hard lesson to learn, however. Even though I had been against the investments Master Meadows still blamed me for the loss of his money. The family was not in any financial danger but the funnel of income coming in had noticeably tightened.

Funny thing I noticed about these men of fortune. They never seemed to be satisfied with enough. Take Master Meadows, for instance. He had this nice house and all us slaves to take care of it for him. There was food aplenty even when others impacted by the war were starving.

Mistress Meadows had new clothes made for her and the family all the time. If there was a special party or occasion coming up Tildy would often work late into the night hurrying to finish new gowns for Mistress Meadows and the girls. Even with the war going on that did not change.

The boys could always wore the same clothes for a while before they left but Mistress Meadows and her daughters had to change their clothes multiple times in a day and they always needed new clothes before the old clothes were even worn in. Yet there never seemed to be enough money coming in to make them happy.

They still had enough money to take care of their every need but they worried when they did not have enough money to waste on silly things. I kept all these thoughts to myself, of course. What Master Meadows did with his money was his business. My job was to keep track of his money and help him make more money.

When the War of the States started Missouri was at war with itself. Money got even tighter. Yet that household never changed its habits. That was important because as money got tighter the Meadows family began to look at ways to save money. Slaves eat and require clothing, which costs money.

Now my children wore hand-me-down clothes from the Meadows children but Mistress Meadows still included the cost of clothes for the slaves in her household budget. Tildy would take the hand-me-down dresses of the two Meadows girls and remake them into dresses suitable for our girls by removing any ribbons or lacing, replacing pearl buttons with wood buttons.

So there was no cost for covering our children's backs, yet every month Mistress Meadows would hand over a list of her household budget and costs for slave clothing was on that list. I would enter those figures in the books even knowing that they were a lie. If Mistress Meadows wanted to lie to her husband that was not my concern.

Though the children were put to work doing household chores at a young age they were still considered an overhead cost with no benefit by Mistress Meadows. They helped weed the garden and collect the vegetables. They cleaned and helped in the kitchen. Mistress Meadows never understood the amount of work those children actually did for her.

My oldest boy, Sam, was turning thirteen a few weeks after I first got hint that something was up. I had been worrying about him for a while. He shared the stable chores with Lucas. I am proud to say that he was a hard working young man. My first born, with a strong resemblance to myself, I could not love him more. That stable was the cleanest, most organized stable in town.

When the fighting delayed supplies and hay and grain became scarce, as happened from time to time, Sam went out into the fields and cut grass for the horses. He loved those horses as much as I loved my books.

Every night we gathered in the small, one-room cabin that Master Meadows had allowed to be built for Tildy and me and I taught my children to read and write. I had taught Tildy to read and write the first years we were together and though she was sharp and learned quickly she did not want to teach the children.

Tildy never lost her fear that she would get into trouble for knowing how to read and write so she found little joy in it. "You're going to get us in trouble," she said, watching Sam sound out the words I had written on a slate.

"Don't think it's illegal for a black man to teach a black child," I said. "White people can't teach blacks but blacks can teach blacks. That's the law."

I didn't really know that for sure but it sounded reasonable to me and put Tildy more at ease. I can't say she ever fully relaxed but at least she didn't argue any more about me teaching our children. I had more free time as well.

Tildy's day was often much longer than mine. Sometimes Mistress Meadows would set me to doing tasks about the place but for the most part once my day was done in the office I was done working for the day.

I taught our children mathematics. I borrowed books from Master Meadows' office and every night I would read stories about Jason, Aladdin, and the Greek gods, so that they could hear the classics and expand their minds beyond our small world in Missouri.

I don't think Master Meadows ever noticed me sneaking books out of the office every night because he never said anything. I was always careful to return them in the morning.

The cabin was only large enough for a full-sized bed against one wall and sleeping pallets stuffed with straw lined up against the remaining walls for the children. At least the cabin had a wood floor instead of bare earth and a closet in the corner for our spare clothes. The bed was the only real furniture in the room so that was where we gathered every night.

Sometimes, when a battle was close enough to be heard in the distance, we would huddle on the bed instead of studying, hoping and praying that the battle stayed in the distance. The steady boom boom of canon fire made sleeping hard. Except for Shonny.

Shonny could fall asleep on the ground in a thunderstorm. That girl moved and moved and moved without ever slowing down but when she did get tired she would drop off to sleep wherever she stood or sat.

One day, after their schooling, the children settled down on their pallets and fell asleep. Sam lay on his stomach, a candle next to his pallet to light the book he was reading. In the past few months Sam had been on a growth spurt and was growing so fast that I swear I could see his legs getting longer as I watched him while he read. Tildy watched me watching Sam.

"Our baby has sure grown into a fine young man," she said, smiling as she followed my gaze to our son.

"What will happen to him?" I asked, turning to Tildy. I spoke in a whisper so that Sam would not hear. "He's almost a man grown. What will happen to him?"

Tildy frowned. "Not a man yet," she whispered. "He's still my baby boy."

"I can hear you," Sam said without lifting his gaze from his book.

"Close your ears," I said.

Sam turned a page in his book. "What? I can't hear you," Sam said.

A fine boy, my Sam. Sharp as a tack. Good natured. The thought of Master Meadows putting him up on a block and selling him to some plantation owner to pick cotton or dig trenches and getting the lash for speaking his mind or even moving too slow did not sit well with me.

I am not a violent man, yet a rage built inside me as I thought of my boy being poked and prodded, his teeth examined by some stranger sticking his dirty finger in my boy's mouth. Though I had been but five years old when I went up on the auction block I still remembered it clearly. I did not want my boy going through that.

"He's a hard worker," Tildy said. I could see the worry in her eyes. "That Lucas has nothing on my boy. If they want to get rid of someone it should be Lucas."

"What did you hear?" I asked Tildy. That too present knot formed in the pit of my stomach.

"Master Meadows was asking Lucas about me," Sam said, looking up and over his shoulder.

I didn't say anything. I could imagine Mistress Meadows doing the calculations in her head. How much she could save with one less mouth to feed. How much they could earn with the sale of a fine, young boy like my Sam.

"They can't sell him," Tildy whispered. "No selling of slaves in Missouri. I heard her say it. She was angry enough to forget I was there. She said it wasn't right that they weren't allowed to sell their own property."

Chapter Twenty-One

I highly doubted that Mistress Meadows forgot that Tildy was there. Mistress Meadows simply did not care if Tildy heard her. "They can sell slaves in Kentucky. They ship them off to Kentucky to be sold," I said. "Did she say anyone in particular?"

Tildy shook her head. "No," Tildy said. "She was just fussing in general."

I did not sleep well that night. It could have been Mistress Meadows angry that she could not have a new dress. Mistress Meadows was more and more on edge lately. Andy Meadows, her oldest boy, had gone off to join the Confederacy side of the war. Sometimes Andy's letters home came once a week or more and then sometimes weeks would go by without hearing from him.

Master Meadows had not said a word about selling any slaves. If they were planning on selling Sam surely Master Meadows would have said something.

There was enough money coming in to take care of their needs. Supplies were the problem, not the money to buy the supplies. Blockades and blown up railroads slowed down shipments of goods. If Master Meadows planned on selling anyone I would hear about it. Selling Sam would not make the supplies available.

Still, I worried. On the first day of the year 1863 President Lincoln had declared that all slaves were free with his Proclamation of Emancipation. All slaves in other states. In Missouri slaves were still slaves even if Missouri was still in the Union. Still, it had people like Master Meadows worried. What if the president declared all slaves freed?

I had been so focused on what it meant to me to be freed that I had not considered the other side of the coin. I tried putting myself in Master Meadows' shoes. He would lose a lot of money if we were suddenly freed. But if he sent us off to Kentucky and put us on the block he would make a lot of money. Master Meadows was fretting a lot about money these days.

I tossed and turned until Tildy punched me in the arm. "Sorry," I muttered.

I slid my arms around my wife and pulled her close. It had started to rain and I could hear the steady drum of the raindrops on the roof. Our cabin was warm and dry. Lucas and I had built it all those years ago for when Tildy and I got married. Lucas was mighty handy with construction tools and I was fair at following his instructions. Sam blew out his candle and the pungent aroma of candle smoke filled the room for a few minutes.

I dreamt that night of a woman sobbing. It had been years since a rainy night had disturbed my sleep with memories of that woman sobbing. I knew that it had to be my mother's sobbing that I heard. For the first time I realized that she was crying because I was being taken from her.

In the morning I woke to Shonny jumping on me. Instinctively I curled into a ball to protect my full bladder from being hit by a bony elbow or wayward knee. I opened one eye and looked up at the little hellion. She was staring down at me, head tilted, her face only inches from my face. Shonny grinned when I opened my eye.

"Get up! Get up!" Shonny said, bouncing up and down on her knees next to me.

"What's so special about today?" I asked.

"The sun is shining," Shonny said, slowing down enough to point at the window. "See!"

I scooped her up and held her laughing, squirming body above me. I tilted her to the left and to the right while she squealed in delight. She weighed hardly anything and I could feel her ribs under my hands. Shonny was tall for a three-year old but she burned off anything she ate before it had time to stick to her ribs.

"Shonny, get dressed," Tildy said. She was sitting cross-legged on the floor with Arice sitting in front of her.

After Sam we tried to be careful to avoid getting pregnant and Benji was three years younger than his older brother. Then we slipped and Arice came only a year after Benji. We managed to make it three years before Willie came along and again three years to Shonny.

Those are my children, Sam, aged almost thirteen, Benji, aged ten, Arice, aged nine, Willie, aged six, and finally Shonny, aged three. Though all five came from me and Tildy they were as different as it was possible for any children to be.

Sam was the serious, responsible one. I swear that boy was born a full grown man already. He was obedient, mannerly, and sharp as a tack. Anything said to him was absorbed and digested. The boy forgot nothing and was always thinking six steps ahead.

Benji was smart but easily distracted. He spent his days looking for adventure. Or bugs. He was fascinated with bugs. It had taken a firm scolding and then a curt spanking to stop him from bringing his bugs into the cabin. Finally we settled on a corner of the stable for his bug collections.

Arice was sullen and moody one day and happy and carefree the next day. Tildy called her the drama princess. Everything was about the drama. Arice felt everything deeply and did not understand why no one else felt the same. Tildy assured me that she would outgrow the drama but to me it seemed that the passing of time only made matters worse. When Arice grew quiet we all walked on eggshells. It meant that she was thinking.

Willy was the clown in the family. He liked to make everyone laugh. He was as happy go lucky as Arice was sullen. Willy tended to take everything in stride as it came.

Then there was Shonny. My little bundle of sunshine wrapped

up in hummingbird wings, was my Shonny.

I dropped Shonny on the bed and she laughed as she bounced. I had to relieve my bladder. I stepped around Tildy and Arice and left the cabin for the outhouse. When I returned Shonny was dressed and sitting in front of Tildy for her turn at having her hair done.

As active as Shonny was, Arice was as quiet as a mouse that morning. She was sitting quietly, patiently, watching Tildy try to work on Shonny's hair. Shonny kept forgetting that she was supposed to be sitting still and would lean over sideways or jump to her feet spontaneously. Tildy was used to Shonny's antsy pants and easily directed the girl back into position each time.

The boys were picking up the sleeping pallets and stacking them neatly in a pile. Sam left the cabin, heading directly for the stables, to feed the horses before eating his own breakfast. Tildy hurried out after Sam but headed for the house. It was up to the middle children to watch Shonny and bring her to the house after they cleaned the cabin.

Master Meadows would rise early and need breakfast but Mistress Meadows liked to sleep in a bit later than her husband. Betsy would make breakfast for Master Meadows and me first. Master Meadows ate in the morning room while I ate in the kitchen.

After making our breakfasts Betsy would feed the children and the rest of the slaves in the household. Finally, Mistress Meadows would have breakfast, either in the morning room or served up in her bedroom. Since Ham left Betsy did all the cooking in addition to the cleaning.

It was a normal spring day. I ate my breakfast in the kitchen while Bannister served Master Meadows in the morning room. I had to be in the office before Master Meadows but Tildy would warn me when he had finished his biscuits and bacon.

That morning Tildy was making breakfast because Betsy had gotten sick. It was some bug that upset her stomach. Betsy was still expected to do her cleaning tasks sick but not to cook while sick.

Being sick wasn't an excuse to getting out of work but even Mistress Meadows drew the line at the woman cooking everyone's food while burning with fever and stopping in the middle of frying eggs to vomit in a bucket next to the sink.

The children sat at the kitchen table with me while Tildy dished up porridge with a slice of fried bacon stuck in the porridge in each bowl. Tildy put her finger to her lips and dropped two strawberries on each bowl as well. The children quickly ate their berries first before being spotted by someone who would tattle to Mistress Meadows. I savored my single slice of bacon then hurried to the office.

Master Meadows entered the office a few minutes after I'd settled in front of my desk. "I'm expecting a visitor this morning," Master Meadows said as he settled into his leather upholstered chair behind his large mahogany desk. "When you bring the ledgers back set them on your desk then make yourself scarce until he's gone."

I nodded but did not respond. Master Meadows did not require acknowledgement from me. He had given instructions and expected them followed. Acknowledging his order would only irritate Master Meadows. When I nodded Master Meadows was not even looking at me. The nod was an automatic reaction.

Though I was curious as to whom his visitor was I did not ask. It was not my concern. If Master Meadows wanted me to know he would have told me when he gave his instructions. It was not who the visitor was that compelled Master Meadows to have me out of the office. He did not want anyone to know that I worked in the office.

I left the house at the normal time to walk down to collect the ledgers at the printing house. The younger Master Meadows had inherited the elder Master Meadows' businesses. There were many trees in full bloom, filling the air with a heady perfume. Fresh blue coats swarmed around the train station. I slowed my steps as I walked past them, listening to their chatter without being obvious.

The Union soldiers had come from St. Louis to watch over the
railroads. This group talked funny. All Northerners talked funny but
this new group was especially odd sounding. They talked fast with
an accent so heavy that it was not easy to understand them as I
walked past. One man stood apart from the rest, probably overseeing
others. It was not easy for me to tell what they were doing.

My steps slowed even more as I approached the man standing
alone on the train platform. He was staring at me. It was not an angry
stare, nor even a curious stare. He was a slender man of average
height. His blonde hair swept in waves down the side of his head and
his beard was as blonde as his hair. I glanced around at the men
moving about the train station. They all looked the same, mostly
blonde hair and blue eyes. Some were tall and some average height.

I turned my gaze back to the man in front of me. He was still
staring at me. I dropped my gaze and ducked my head, careful to
avoid eye contact. He did not say anything as I walked past him on
the way to the printing house.

When I returned the same route after collecting the books they
were all still there. The man who had been watching me stepped into
my path. I stopped walking, waiting for him to speak.

"Excuse me, sir," the blonde man said in his funny accent. I
glanced behind me, thinking someone must have come up behind me
without hearing them. "You there, with the books," he said. I looked
up at him in surprise. He had called me sir.

"Me, sir?" I asked in confusion.

He smiled. "Yes, you," he said. "Can you tell me where Becker
Street is?"

"Yes, sir," I said. I twisted and pointed slightly behind me to the
left. "Four blocks east and you'll be on it, sir."

"Thank you," the man said. He turned and walked away.

I stared at his back in stunned silence. He had thanked me. The
man in the blue coat had treated me like a peer, like an equal. I had
not felt that in so many years. He had not told me to tell him where

Becker Street was. He had called me sir and then thanked me.

A man from the south would have said, "You, boy. Point out Becker Street."

There would have been no asking and no thanking. They weren't the first Union soldiers to show up in Jefferson City. They were different though.

On a whim I turned off the direct path back home and walked the two blocks east to the elder Master Meadows' old house. The elder Master Meadows' house was looking a bit in need of a paint job but otherwise was being well-maintained. I had not walked by the house in a long time.

When I first started collecting the books for the younger Master Meadows I had walked past the house a few times but it brought back memories that pulled at my heart so I stayed away. I wondered if my little stash of money was still in its hiding spot in my old bedroom. A lot of years had passed. I didn't even know if Lisbett and Old Hank were still alive.

I had visited the old housekeeper and servant a few times the first year after moving to the younger Master Meadows' house but then life had gotten so busy and the days so short that I had not been able to visit and then time had slipped away. I considered going up to the house, to see who was on the other side, but I did not have time that day either.

I hurried back to the house. Master Meadows was sitting behind his desk in his office. His visitor was a man with a professional air about him. Despite the sweat dripping down his temples and neck he wore a full wool suit with cravat and shirt points. Neither man paid any attention to me as I slipped into the room, set the ledgers on my desk, and slipped out again like a ghost.

I stood in the hall outside the office for a moment, debating on whether to go back to the train station to learn more about the new soldiers or to spend the free time with the children. Tildy would likely appreciate a few hours of my occupying Shonny. The rest of the children had household chores to do.

"You selling him?" Master Meadows' visitor asked.

"No," Master Meadows said. "He is most definitely not for sale."

I did not want to be caught eavesdropping as much as I wanted to hear their conversation. I took a step forward then stopped.

"The train is the most effective method," the visitor said. "But Sherman has been focusing his attention on the train lines."

"It's got to be the train," Master Meadows said.

I wanted to know what they were talking about. I took another small step forward. I heard footsteps coming down the hall. Fearing Mistress Meadows catching me lurking at the office doorway I hurried down the hall, turning the corner to come face to face with Tildy.

"What are you doing?" I asked in a low voice.

Tildy was carrying a tree of tea and pastries. She raised the tray slightly "Can't you see?" she said, giving me a stink eye expression. "It's heavy. Move out of the way."

"Where's Bannister?" I asked.

"Bannister came down with Betsy's bug," Tildy said.

"I'll take it," I said. "I have to stay away from my desk while he's got company anyway."

"Shoo," Tildy said, trying to sidle around me in the hall.

"Do you know who's in there with him?" I asked.

"It's heavy, Isaac," Tildy said. "Move."

I turned so that she could move past me. Tildy stopped and looked over her shoulder at me then continued on her way to deliver the tea tray to the office. I did not go back to the train station. I went to the kitchen. Shonny was sitting at the table sorting buttons.

"What are you doing, Shonny?" I asked, sliding onto a chair opposite her.

"Finding all the blue ones," Shonny said. There were a lot of blue buttons in both piles she had in front of her on the well-worn tabletop. As well as white, pink, green, and brown.

"Can you show me a blue one, little girl?" I asked. I glanced up at the clock on the opposite wall. It shouldn't be taking Tildy so long to deliver a tray.

Shonny held up a pale brown button with a pearl finish on the edge. "This is not blue," she said, placing the button in the pile in front of her. She reached into the pile beyond the pile in front of her and picked a green button. "Is this blue?" she asked.

"That's green," I said, glancing at the clock.

Shonny set the green button in the pile in front of her and reached for another button in the pile beyond the pile in front of her. She picked up a sky blue button. "That's not blue, right?" she said, frowning at the button.

"Yes, that's blue," I said.

Shonny tilted her head as she studied the button. She picked up a cobalt blue button from the pile in front of her. "This is blue," she said, holding the darker blue button up for me to see. "Not this." She studied the two buttons, frowning.

"They are both blue," I said.

"But that's blue," Shonny said.

I stared at the clock. It should not be taking fifteen minutes for Tildy to deliver the tray. Shonny continued to pick up new buttons from the big pile and hold them up for me to see. I soon realized that she was putting every button she looked at into the pile closest to her whether they were blue or not. I watched her sorting the buttons, smiling at the way her face scrunched up in concentration.

Mistress Meadows wandered into the kitchen, stopping in her tracks when she saw me sitting at the table with Shonny. "What are you doing in here in the middle of the day?" Mistress Meadows asked.

"Master Meadows has a visitor," I said. "I'm to stay away from the office."

"Oh," Mistress Meadows said, chewing on her lower lip. "I

forgot that was today." I was ready to get to my feet, expecting her to send me out to perform whatever task she could think of. My muscles tightened in preparation to stand when she surprised me. "Very well," she said. She smiled. Mistress Meadows smiled at me. Her gaze moved to Shonny. "What is she doing?"

"Sorting buttons," I said.

Mistress Meadows giggled. I almost looked right at her, I was so shocked. Mistress Meadows walked to the stove and poured herself a cup of coffee from the pot on the stove. She sipped her coffee, watching us over the coffee cup rim.

"I don't know what I'd do if the war interfered with me getting my coffee," Mistress Meadows said.

I said nothing. In the almost fourteen years I had been in the house Mistress Meadows had never, not once, ever made small talk with me. I glanced at the clock. Almost thirty minutes had passed since Tildy had entered the office with the tray of tea and pastries. Tildy walked into the kitchen, gaze going immediately to Mistress Meadows.

"Sorry for keeping you waiting, Mistress Meadows," Tildy said, hurrying to the stove. "I'll bring your breakfast right to you. Your room or the morning room, ma'am?"

"It hasn't been that long," Mistress Meadows said in an amiable voice. She smiled. "Were you delivering tea to my husband?"

"Yes, ma'am," Tildy said, pulling a plate from the warming drawer and filling it with scrambled eggs, biscuits, and gravy. She pulled a small bowl of strawberries and peaches from the ice box.

"Where's Bannister?" Mistress Meadows asked.

"Stomach bug, ma'am," Tildy said. "Same one as Betsy."

"I'll take breakfast in the morning room," Mistress Meadows said with a smile. She floated out of the kitchen in the direction of the morning room.

"She been drinking?" Tildy muttered, sparing the time for a brief, confused look in the direction Mistress Meadows had gone.

"What happened?" I asked, jumping to my feet. "In the office?"

"What?" Tildy said without pausing in preparing the breakfast tray for Mistress Meadows. She put the warm plate on the tray with the bowl of fruit up in the corner and a carafe of coffee. Tildy picked up the tray then set it back down. She grabbed a napkin and silverware and placed it on the tray then carried it out of the kitchen.

"Is this blue?" Shonny asked, holding up a button.

"Yes," I said, glancing at the cobalt blue button between her dainty little fingers.

Shonny carefully placed the cobalt blue button in the growing pile in front of her and reached over to the original pile. She picked up a pink button, wrinkling her nose as she studied the button. "This isn't blue, is it?" Shonny asked, holding the button up for my inspection.

"No," I said, feeling impatient and distracted. "It's pink. Where is your sister? Why are you sorting buttons? Why do you need blue buttons?" I asked, sounding a little harsher than I intended. I wanted to hear from Tildy why she had been in Master Meadows' office for thirty minutes with the visitor.

"Mama axed me to," Shonny said, dropping the pink button into the pile in front of her. "I don't know 'bout the rest."

Tildy returned to the kitchen with the empty tray and walked right past me to the sink. I followed her. "Well?" I asked.

Tildy looked up at me. "What?" she asked.

"What happened?" I asked. "In the office?"

"Oh, that," Tildy said, pumping the water pump arm several times then turning the nozzle to fill the pan sitting in the sink. "He was an insurance man. Mr. Norton. Or Morton."

"Insurance?" I asked, puzzled. Master Meadows had not mentioned needing more insurance.

"Set this on the stove for me, dear," Tildy said, gesturing at the pan filled with water.

"Is this blue?" Shonny asked from the table.

Tildy glanced over at Shonny. "Yes, it's blue," she said.

"Are you sure?" Shonny asked.

I picked up the pan filled with water and set it on the stove so that the water could warm for washing the breakfast dishes. "But why were you in there so long?" I asked Tildy.

"Mr. Norton wanted to know about the children," Tildy said. "Master Meadows wasn't sure how old they were and then they asked what they could do."

Chapter Twenty-Two

"The insurance is for the children?" I asked. Sweat dripped down my neck.

"I guess so," Tildy said, gathering the dirty dishes and preparing the sink.

"This is blue," Shonny said, holding up another button.

"Why is she doing that?" I asked. "She's just putting them all in the same pile anyway."

Tildy stopped what she was doing and stared up at me. "It's busy work. It's not always easy to get things done with her underfoot," she said. Tildy tilted her head. "What's wrong with you today?"

I debated on telling her my fear or waiting until I was sure if it meant anything. I could be wrong. It might not mean anything that Master Meadows had been discussing with the visitor about using the train and getting insurance on the children. I didn't think I was wrong though. With the war going on it would make sense to put insurance on slaves being shipped on the train to Kentucky for selling them.

The bell in the breakfast room dinged. Tildy sighed. "Pour the water in the sink before it boils," she said as she headed for the breakfast room.

Arice and Willie wandered into the kitchen. Arice carried a basket filled with berries and Willie had red smeared all over his mouth and chin. Arice skipped across the kitchen dropping berries as she went while Willie stopped at the table and eyed the two piles of buttons with interest.

"We was picking berries," Arice said, showing me the basket.

"That's a fine selection," I said, looking into the basket.

Arice smiled. "Mama said she'd make cobbler and we can even have some," Arice said. "So we picked all we could find."

"Indeed you did," I said, noting the green berries mixed in with the red and blue.

Arice set the basket on the butcher block and joined her brother and sister at the table. It did not take long for Arice to take control of the button sorting and squabbling soon filled the kitchen as Shonny protested. I grabbed a towel and wrapped it around the pot handle and poured the water into the sink just as Tildy returned to the kitchen.

"Master Meadows is with Mistress Meadows in the breakfast room," Tildy said. "He said to tell you your books still be needing done today."

I escaped the growing commotion in the kitchen for the quiet solitude of the office. The office was empty. I sat at my desk and opened the ledgers. The numbers danced wildly and would not cooperate. My mind was in turmoil.

I don't know how long I was alone before Master Meadows joined me in the office. He settled into his chair behind his desk without a word and picked up a newspaper. Every fiber in my being wanted to ask him if he was meaning to sell my children but I kept my mouth shut. I tried to concentrate on my work but concentration escaped me.

I glanced up at Master Meadows. He was staring at me. I ducked my head back down to the ledgers sitting open in front of me.

"Well?" Master Meadows said.

I looked up and over at Master Meadows. "What, sir?"

"Go ahead and ask," Master Meadows said.

"Are you taking out insurance on the children?" I asked.

Master Meadows nodded. "The premiums are acceptable," he

said. "Go ahead and write out a check to Mr. Norton for me to sign. The figures are here on my desk."

Master Meadows pushed a piece of paper across his desk in my direction. I stood and walked to his desk. My hand trembled as I reached for the paper. The invoice included Tildy as well as the children. I looked up from the paper to Master Meadows.

"You're shipping them to Kentucky?" I asked. "To sell them?"

Master Meadows nodded. "With the war going on it's a risky venture sending them by train but it's a risk I'm willing to take," he said.

"But why?" I blurted out. Emotions were running high.

"They're valuable livestock," Master Meadows said. His eyes narrowed slightly at my questioning his actions but for some reason he was making an effort to let it slide. "The war is not going well. If Lincoln has his way I won't ever be able to sell them if I wait."

I nodded. "I don't see my name on here," I said.

"Oh, I'm not selling you, boy," Master Meadows said, shaking his head. "No. You're too valuable." He sat back in his chair and waved his hand. "Get to work now. You'll have to keep your head down to get through everything today."

I stood with the piece of paper defining the insurance worth of my family, unable to move my feet, unable to think coherently. "When?" I asked.

"Don't you never mind that," Master Meadows said. "It'll be awhile yet. Now get to work."

I nodded but my feet still would not move. A squeezing band of pressure tightened across my chest. Master Meadows was going to send my family away. They were my life. Without them my life was not worth living. Breathing was difficult. I exhaled slowly, pushing all the air I could out of my lungs then taking a deep, deep breath.

Master Meadows was looking uncomfortable. "Maybe this is a bit for you to take," he said, watching me purposely exhale a second time. "Why don't you take the books back and you can skip the printing house books this week?" Master Meadows was fingering the third drawer handle on his desk. "A walk will do you good."

There was a gun kept in the third drawer. I nodded. "Yes, sir," I said, setting the piece of paper back down on his desk. "A walk will do me good."

I grabbed the ledgers and headed out of the office. I paused at the doorway and looked back. "Thank you, Master Meadows," I said. "For a chance to clear my head. It's an awful lot to take in."

Master Meadows relaxed. He nodded but did not say anything. Master Meadows was no longer sitting at an odd angle to reach the third drawer. He picked up his newspaper again and gave it a shake before holding it up and consequently hiding his face from my view.

I felt the tears burn my eyes even before I reached the sidewalk outside the house. I had been worried about Sam. It had never dawned on me that he would ship off everyone to be sold. Even Tildy. Even Shonny. I couldn't imagine anyone paying more than a dollar for Shonny. Shonny was worth billions of dollars but no slave buyer would understand her worth.

Imagining my children up on the auction block tore my heart into pieces. They were too young. Sam might fetch a good price. He was young but not too young and would make a good worker in a stable. I really thought the Meadows would let Lucas retire and replace the man with Sam. My boy worked so hard.

Benji might also fetch a fair price. He was young but sharp and had some talent. Arice with her moods would have a hard time. Someone was likely to beat her into behaving. Arice needed a gentle hand. Willie and Shonny were too young to be separated from Tildy. Just too young.

I couldn't even think about losing Tildy. She was the love of my life, the mother of my children, my heart. I walked blindly, tears filling my eyes. Even considering my family being sold like livestock, shipped off to Kentucky, never to see them again was overwhelming. Rage battled with an urge to drop to the ground in despair.

Someone was approaching me on the sidewalk. I wiped my face with the back of my hand and stepped off the sidewalk. I was near the train station by then and I walked across a field of grass bordering the train platform. There were still a few blue-coated soldiers lingering at the station but most had gone.

I had gained control of my crying by the time I reached the printing house. I took the ledgers to the manager's office, telling him that Master Meadows did not have time to go through the books that day. The manager eyed me with concern but did not question me. I must have looked a mess with my red, swollen eyes.

I wandered for a while. I don't know how long or even where I went. I stopped when I saw the same blue-coated soldier who had asked me for directions earlier in the day. He was with four of his comrades walking in front of me. I trailed behind them just because they were going in the same direction I wanted to go.

"Sherman's got a thing for railroads," one of the men said. He was a tall, lanky fellow with bony arms and legs and a perfectly straight nose. His blonde hair curled up under his cap.

The statement made the other men laugh. "All we gotta do is keep these tracks in one piece while he's out blowing up the rest," a short, husky man with dark hair and a thick moustache said. There was more laughter.

They distracted me with their laughter and strange accents. I listened to them banter amongst themselves without really listening that closely. I was staring down at the sidewalk in front of my feet and almost stepped right into them when they suddenly stopped. Startled, I looked up and stepped back, intending to go around them.

"He looks just like Edward Patrice back in Mankato," the stocky man with dark hair said, staring back at me. "The smithy."

"He does!" the tall, lanky man said, eyes widening. He turned to the man who had had asked me for directions. "Even their hair is the same, all curly. Except Edward's is blonde. Do you think that means

Edward is a negro?"

"And Edward Patrice has arms the size of Lechemann's legs," the skinny man with big ears said. "And Edward Patrice has missing teeth. His two front ones. Someone said a mule kicked him. Right in the face. Knocked out the top two. That's because they stuck out over his lower lip. Kinda hard to miss 'em when they stick out like that. Looked like a rabbit. When he had those teeth. Which he doesn't anymore."

"I think it means that we're all men of God and the color of our skin doesn't make us who we are," the man who asked for directions said. Several of the other men nodded thoughtfully. He looked directly at me. "Are we blocking the sidewalk, sir?"

"Excuse me, sir," I said, ducking my head and averting my gaze. "I was just thinking hard. Don't pay no never mind to me. I'll be out of your way."

It really made me uncomfortable that he kept referring to me as sir. If someone not wearing a blue-coat heard him I could be in serious trouble. The last thing I needed right then was to get into trouble for being uppity.

I hurried around them and continued on my way. They trailed behind me, almost keeping pace. They continued their easy banter as they strode along the sidewalk to their destination. Their destination turned out to be the train station. Once we reached the platform they stopped while I continued walking.

I couldn't let Master Meadows sell my family. I didn't know how I would stop him but I only knew that I was not going to let him send my family away from me. I had helped him earn far more money over the years than he could ever get from selling my wife and children.

Master Meadows owed me. He owed me my family for all I had done for him. He had promised me he wouldn't sell them.

Determined, I headed back to the house with my head high and my shoulders straight. If Master Meadows sold my family I would no longer help him run his businesses, advise his investments. I was going to tell him that. Master Meadows could whip me. Master Meadows could threaten me. Master Meadows could not force me to do my work with his best interests in mind.

When I returned to the house the office was empty. Master Meadows had gone to visit one of his businesses and would not be home until late. Tildy eyed me with some misgivings when I wandered into the kitchen. Twice in one day I was loitering in the kitchen instead of working in the office.

Tildy was looking a bit harried. She was standing at the butcher block with a large roast in front of her. There were still dirty dishes in the sink, the soapy water having gone cold and the suds flat. Working in the kitchen was not her normal job so she was feeling out of her element.

Betsy sat on a chair in the corner with a blanket wrapped around her shoulders, giving instructions between bouts of coughing. Soon after I entered the kitchen Betsy groaned and bolted out of the room, holding her hand over her mouth.

It was not the right time to discuss what was going on so neither of us said anything but I could see Tildy looking at me in puzzlement. I was so upset that I could barely even think. My world was crashing down around my head and my brain was filled with a fog.

I collected the children and took them out to the garden. I showed Willie and Arice the proper berries ready for picking and we filled another basket, minus any green berries. Shonny found a toad and was following it around the garden. Benji and Sam pulled weeds and checked the progress of the vegetables. It had not rained for a while and the soil was dry so I told Sam to water the beans.

Sam cocked his head, studying the garden. "Are you sure?" he said. "Doesn't seem that dry."

"Just do it," I said.

He was probably right. I wasn't a gardener. I just needed to keep them busy. I needed to think and I couldn't do that while surrounded by them. I was close to breaking down and I could not let them see that.

I sent the younger children back to the kitchen with the berries and left Benji diligently pulling weeds while Sam filled a watering can from the rain barrel. I found Lucas in the stable. It was getting harder for him to grip the tack with his gnarled fingers but he managed to do it, just slow about it. Lucas was sitting on a stool with a bridle on his lap, wiping oil onto the leather to keep it conditioned.

"He's going to sell my family," I said in greeting.

Lucas looked up at me. I couldn't tell at all what he was thinking. He just sat there on his three-legged stool, his legs stretched out in front of him, the leather bridle draped across his lap, a rag soaked in oil clutched between his thumb and first finger.

"He's going to sell them all," I said.

Lucas nodded, once. He looked back down at the leather straps that made up a horse's bridle. "I'll miss Sam," Lucas said. His eyes turned red but he shed no tears. Lucas cleared his throat. "I'll miss that boy."

"I can't let him do that," I said.

Lucas looked up at me. "What can you do?"

"Stop him," I said.

"Don't go doing anything stupid," Lucas said. He looked back at the bridle and wiped the rag in his hand over the leather strap. He looked up at me again. "I been hearing rumors that Lincoln's going to free the slaves. All the slaves. There's black men fighting with Lincoln."

"He only freed the slaves in the rebel states," I said.

"But if The North wins this war all the slaves will be free," Lucas said. "Then you can find your family. When we're all freed."

"I can't risk that," I said. "What if The North doesn't win? What if they win and the rest of us aren't freed?"

"Don't you go and do nothing stupid," Lucas muttered, shaking his head.

"I need your help, Lucas," I said.

Lucas squinted up at me, face going hard. "I ain't doin' nothin' stupid either."

"I need you to convince Master Meadows how valuable Sam is to this household," I said, going down on one knee so that we were level. "I need you to tell him how much Sam does around the stable."

Lucas turned his head, nodding at his own thoughts. Slowly he turned his head back to me, looking me square in the eyes. "You see this floor? Clean enough to eat off," Lucas said. "You see those horses? Look how they shine. Their coats are polished and their manes are combed."

"That's my Sam," I said.

"That's your Sam," Lucas said, nodding. He ran his tongue over his teeth with his mouth closed. I could see his tongue stuck up under his upper lip. I waited. "Don't you think that Master Meadows don't notice," Lucas said at last.

"But you could tell him anyway," I said.

"That boy takes those horses out every day," Lucas said. "Let's 'em run and graze on green grass." Lucas twitched, raising his chin. "Don't you think Master Meadows don't notice." Lucas glared at me. "You think I be afraid to tell him how much that boy does. I tell him."

"But-" I started to say.

Lucas cut me off. "No," he said, leaning forward. "That's why Master Meadows going to sell the boy. Master Meadows don't care 'bout those horses any more than he cares about you and me. He cares 'bout getting money for that hard working boy. He gets lots of money for that boy and the horses are left with me."

The truth in his words hit me hard. I felt helpless. There was going to be nothing I could do to save my family from the auction block.

"That Lincoln, he'll free the rest of us," Lucas said, going back to rubbing his bridle with the oiled rag. "Then you can go find them. Once we're all free you be free to go find them."

"What if he doesn't?" I said, each word catching in my throat. "What if the Rebels win? What if The North wins and we still be owned?"

"Then we go on the best we can," Lucas said.

"How could I even find them?" I said, more to myself. "He's shipping them all the way to Kentucky. Someone from Georgia could buy them. They could be split up all over."

"Pick a meeting place," Lucas said.

"A meeting place?" I asked, confused.

"Tell everyone to head for one spot," Lucas said.

"How would Arice get to some town on her own?" I said. "If Willie got sold to someone in South Carolina how would he get back to Kentucky on his own?"

Lucas did not respond. He turned his attention to his task and effectively tuned me out. I didn't care. I wasn't looking for answers from Lucas. I couldn't rely on Lincoln freeing all of us. I had to do something before they headed for Kentucky. I just didn't know what I could do to stop it in time.

Chapter Twenty-Three

Master Meadows returned that evening with three slaves from his daughter Constance's household. There was Mindy, a girl in her early twenties who had been working as a maid. There was a man about my age, Thomas. There was a middle-aged woman named Dorathea. Tildy brought in pallets for them to sleep in the kitchen.

"What's going on?" I asked Thomas. But I knew. In my gut I knew instantly that the hour was coming mighty quick. If Master Meadows meant to sell his slaves, fearing he'd lose money if we were freed, he would want his daughter to do the same.

"Getting shipped to Kentucky," Thomas said. "Auction block."

They sat at the kitchen table while Tildy cleaned up the kitchen for the night. Shonny crawled into Mindy's lap and hugged the crying girl. Dorathea sat next to Mindy, staring off into nothingness. She seemed to be in shock. Thomas seemed resigned.

Mistress Meadows wandered into the kitchen. She frowned when she saw the pallets. "What's this?" she asked, gesturing at the pallets.

"For the visitors," Tildy said.

"Nonsense," Mistress Meadows said. "It's a kitchen not a bedroom. They will share your cabin for the night."

"Yes, ma'am," Tildy said, glancing at me with a worried frown.

"Now I'm not sure how much anyone knows," Mistress Meadows said, crossing her arms in front of her chest and looking at each of us in turn. "But we have decided to send you all to Kentucky tomorrow. To new owners. Mr. Meadows and I are sure that these new owners will appreciate you as much as we have."

Tildy stared at Mistress Meadows in horror, her mouth dropping open. I took two steps toward my wife even as she ran into my arms, burying her face against my shoulder. I wrapped my arms around Tildy, fighting the urge to join her in crying. She trembled in my arms and I tightened my embrace.

"Now, just in case any of you get the stupid idea of running, don't," Mistress Meadows said. "Mr. Meadows has hired two guards who will be watching the house all night and escorting you to the two o'clock train tomorrow. They will shoot you if they feel you are trying to run."

"I like to run," Shonny said in a bright voice.

"Hush, child," Mindy said in a low voice.

Shonny squirmed out of Mindy's arms and off the young woman's lap. She ran around the kitchen, arms held out to her side. Mistress Meadows grabbed Shonny's arm the second time the girl circled her. She jerked Shonny hard. "Stop it. It's a different kind of run," Mistress Meadows said. She dragged Shonny to Tildy and me. Tildy turned and picked up Shonny.

Shonny squirmed in Tildy's arms, trying to get down. "I want to run," Shonny said.

"I won't miss that," Mistress Meadows said, glaring at Shonny.

I reached around Tildy and took Shonny in my arms. Shonny calmed slightly though she swung her legs repeatedly. One leg was kicking the back of my legs and one was digging into my front thigh.

"So soon," Tildy said in a ragged voice. "There's no time to prepare."

"Prepare?" Mistress Meadows said, frowning. "Prepare what? You have nothing to prepare."

"I have two dresses for you in process. The fat in the ice box needs rendering," Tildy said. "I have bread rising for in the morning. The green beans are ready for picking."

"We have a woman coming in the morning to take over those tasks," Mistress Meadows said. Mistress Meadows looked around the kitchen at the glum faces. "So we will have no trouble, right?" Her gaze landed on me as she asked that question.

I remained standing where I was, holding a squirming Shonny, Tildy standing in front of me but leaning back so that she was touching me. I wrapped my free arm around Tildy's chest and pulled her against me. I could feel her heart racing under my forearm.

"Well?" Mistress Meadows snapped.

I looked up, meeting her gaze. The woman was staring right at me. I dropped my gaze immediately. "No, ma'am," I said.

There was a spattering of "no, ma'am"s around the room. Mistress Meadows nodded, gave each of us a hard look, and left the kitchen. No one moved or spoke for a long time after she left. Eventually I let Shonny slide down to the floor. Once her feet touched the floor she ran around the kitchen again. When Shonny realized that no one cared about her running in the kitchen any longer she lost interest and started pulling wood out of the wood bin.

Arice had entered the kitchen at some point. She was standing behind me, leaning against the doorframe between the kitchen and the breakfast room. "I don't want to go," Arice said.

I turned. Arice ran up to me and wrapped her arms around my legs. "Hush, child," I said, putting my hand on her head. "It will be all right."

"No it won't," Arice said. Her voice was muffled against my shirt. "I don't want to go. I don't want to go. I don't want to go."

Sam was there also. He picked up all the wood and put it back into the wood bin then took Shonny's hand. "Willie is looking for you. He found a nest of bunnies," Sam said to Shonny.

Shonny's face lit up. "Bunnies!"

"They're babies so you have to be careful," Sam warned as he led Shonny outside.

"Go with your brother," I said to Arice, pushing her back.

"I don't want to go!" Arice said, diving back to me and wrapping her arms around me.

"He found bunnies," I said.

"I don't care about no stupid bunnies," Arice screamed.

"Go with Sam," Tildy said in a firm voice.

Arice took a step back, glaring at her mother, but she obeyed. She wiped her face with her sleeve as she followed Sam and Shonny out of the kitchen.

"What are we going to do?" Tildy asked me once the children were gone.

I shook my head. "I don't know," I said. It was too sudden. I needed time.

"There's nothing to do," Thomas said.

"Your friend, Mr. Taylor," Tildy said, hope filling her face. "Maybe he can help."

"Mr. Taylor?" I hadn't thought of him in years. "I don't know what he can do. He can't buy us. That's why Master Meadows is shipping us to Kentucky."

"Maybe he can go to Kentucky and buy us?" Tildy said. She took a deep breath. "Maybe someone will buy all of us together."

"They aren't selling me, Tildy," I said in a low voice.

Emotions flashed across Tildy's face as she absorbed what I said. There was confusion, surprise, and horror. "No," she whispered. "Oh, dear God, no." Just as quickly hope filled her face. "You'll be safe here. They'd split us up anyway, wouldn't they? Oh, Isaac!"

"I'll figure something out," I whispered against her cheek as I held her against me. Tildy's knees crumpled but I held her up.

"My babies," Tildy cried. "My babies."

I couldn't hold back the tears. They ran down my cheeks. I felt my wife's pain as strongly as I felt my own pain.

"There's nothing you can do, Isaac," Tildy said, groaning.

"Lucas suggested we pick a meeting place," I said. I had to soothe her somehow. "Maybe the president will free all of us. Soon. Soon."

"It'll be too late for us," Tildy said.

"We can find them," I said, rubbing her shoulder with the palm of my hand. "There will be records. We can find them."

"Bannister and Betsy," Tildy muttered, pulling away from me. "They're both sick. They can't travel sick."

In the morning Betsy was feeling better, able enough to ride on a train, but Bannister was still in bed with a fever and sweats with a bucket next to his bed. Bannister was clearly too ill to travel. Shonny became ill overnight, as did both Mindy and Dorathea. Mistress Meadows had no choice but to delay their departure. Later that morning Tildy was struck with the fever, aches, and nausea.

I had a late start to head to the tannery for the ledgers because Shonny had kept us up most of the night. Everything was in chaos with so many sick people in the house and Mistress Meadows upset that their plans to ship everyone off to Kentucky that afternoon had to be changed. No one made breakfast so I told Sam to take the older children to forage in the garden for something to eat that morning.

"She'll be mad," Sam said, gazing in the direction where Mistress Meadows could be heard yelling at Betsy to stop being sick.

I stuck a bucket in his arms. "Pretend you're picking stuff," I said.

I had to go. I was trying to think of a way to save them and I could not think with all the chaos. I had to save them. I could not let my family be shipped off to Kentucky to be sold.

I left the house and made my way in the direction of the tannery at the other side of town. My feet knew the path well and I did not have to think about where I was going. I paused at Kennelly Street then turned east towards the elder Master Meadows' old house. I went directly to the kitchen door and knocked.

An elderly black woman peered out through the window in the top half of the door, scowling at me in puzzlement. She swung the door open and faced me with her hand on her hip as she scowled at me. "Who you be 'n whadda want?" she asked in a booming voice.

My biggest fear, that someone else lived in the house now. I did not have time to mourn Lisbett right then. I struggled to not let my impatience show. "I am Isaac," I said, nodding my head once in greeting. "I used to live here. With Master Meadows. I'm looking for Lisbett. Is she still living here or does Master Taylor own the house now?"

"You talk mighty fancy for a black boy," the woman said. The woman's scowl cleared from her face. "Lisbett talks 'bout you all the time."

My heart lifted. "She's still alive then?" I asked.

The woman gave a curt nod. "She's slowed a bit the past year," she said. "Master Taylor has me looking after her."

"Old Hank?" I asked hopefully.

"Gone a year at least now," the woman said.

I hung my head for a moment in mourning the loss of the man. I only had a moment to give him. "Can I see her?" I asked, taking a step forward.

The woman hesitated then nodded and stepped out of the way so that I could enter the house. "Upstairs," the woman said.

I did not wait for any further discussion. I raced up the stairs two at a time. Master Meadows' bedroom was still empty. It looked identical to how it had been the day Master Meadows had passed away in his sleep.

Lisbett was sleeping in my old bedroom. I tiptoed into the bedroom, stunned at the sight of the formerly robust woman now barely a handful of bones held together with shrunken, leathery skin. Most of her hair was gone and what was left stood up in tufts over her head.

I knelt next to the bed and took the woman's hand in mine. Her hand felt so fragile under my large hand that I was afraid I would break her. Lisbett's eyes fluttered open upon my taking her hand. She stared at me for several minutes before recognition finally dawned on her.

"Isaac?" she whispered. "Is that you, Isaac?"

Tears rolled down my cheeks. "It's me. It's Isaac," I said. "I'm so sorry I stayed away so long."

"Hush, child," Lisbett said with a small smile. "You here now." Lisbett raised her free hand and put it over my hand on her hand. She patted the back of my hand my hand. "Such a fine young man."

"I'm sorry to hear about Old Hank," I said, squeezing her hand as gently as if it was a newborn chick.

"Such a fine young man, Isaac," Lisbett said. "What is wrong?"

I smiled. "Nothing gets past you," I said. Tears were rolling into my mouth so I used my elbow to wipe my face without disturbing our hand clasp. "It's my problem to deal with, Lisbett."

"Men," Lisbett said with a small snort. "Always too proud to ask for a hand."

"No one can help me," I said.

"You here for your hidden allowance?" Lisbett asked, trying to sit up.

"Don't get up," I said.

"I will too get up," Lisbett said, pulling her hands from mine. I slid my arm behind her back and helped her to sit, stuffing pillows behind her to support her. "Stop your fussing," Lisbett said, pushing me away.

Lisbett swung her legs from the bed and slowly but steadily got to her feet. She walked across the room to the closet, pulling out the piece of wood covering the cubby hole I used to hide my valuables as a child. Lisbett turned with the small bag in her hand and held it out for me.

"How did you know it was there?" I asked as I took the bag.

"I always knew," Lisbett said, walking to a chair next to the bed. "You going to tell me what's happening?"

"They're shipping my family to Kentucky," I said, throat feeling congested. I cleared my throat. "To the auction block."

"You gonna run, Isaac?" Lisbett said, nodding at the bag in my hand. "With children?"

"I have to do something," I said.

Lisbett nodded. "You need help," she said. "You go to those men in blue scurrying around those train tracks and ask them for help."

"They can't help me, Lisbett," I said.

"You ask them," Lisbett said. "I got a feeling about them. You just ask them for help."

"How do you know about the Union soldiers?" I asked in surprise.

"I know," Lisbett said. She stretched out her arm towards the bed. "Hand me that throw, Isaac." I picked up the blanket and wrapped it around her frail shoulders. Lisbett patted my hand and clutched the edges of the blanket together with her gnarled hand. "Promise me, Isaac. You go ask them for help. Those men in blue with the blonde hair who talk all funny."

"They can't help, Lisbett," I said again. "They aren't here to help runaway slaves."

"Promise me, Isaac," Lisbett said.

"If I ask them to help us run away they'll just turn me in," I said. I shook my head. "I can't risk that."

"Just tell them your family is being shipped away and you need help," Lisbett said. "They'll do the rest."

"It is nice of Mr. Taylor to send over a woman to help you out," I said. "Have you seen him recently?"

"Don't go changing the subject," Lisbett said. Her eyelids drooped then she sat up abruptly opening her eyes as wide as they'd go. "Promise me, Isaac. Promise you will ask for help. Sometimes we just need to rely on help from others."

"I promise I will ask for help," I said reluctantly.

Lisbett took a deep breath in relief. "That's a good boy, Isaac," she whispered. Her eyelids fluttered for a moment then closed. "Always a good boy, Isaac," she whispered, voice trailing off as she fell asleep.

I scooped her into my arms and laid her back on the bed. Lisbett felt like she weighed less than Shonney even, just a bit of bones held together with a covering of skin. I adjusted the blanket around her, tucking the ends under her slight form.

"I have to go, Lisbett," I whispered, stroking her forehead. She felt so cold that I checked to see if her heart was still beating. I pressed my ear against her bony chest, listening until I heard the faint heartbeat that meant that she lived.

Chapter Twenty-Four

I stuffed the bag into my inside jacket pocket as I left my old bedroom, turning at the door to look back. No matter what transpired in the days ahead I knew that I would never step foot in this house again. Memories stirred like the fine bits of dust motes drifting in the ray of light shining through the window.

My first night in this room had been twenty-four years ago yet I remembered. I remembered sliding into the cool envelope created by the crisp cotton sheets on the mattress. Lisbett had put one of Old Hank's undershirts on me for a night shirt, leaving my legs bare from the knees down. She had scrubbed me from head to toe first.

"No dirty child is laying on my clean sheets," she had muttered as she poured buckets of warm water over my head to rinse away the soap suds.

Even squinting my eyes shut had not completely blocked the soap from irritating my eyes. The soap burned. When I tried to rub the soap from my eyes Lisbett had knocked my hands away and poured more clean water over my head. The water in the laundry tub I stood in was a dingy brown from the dirt Lisbett had scrubbed off me.

Lying in the strange bed in the strange room in the strange house surrounded by strangers had been too much for my young self. I had cried for my mother. I had still missed her so much. I missed her warmth and her arms holding me tight.

I don't think Master Meadows had heard me crying. I had learned young to cry in silence. I think he had just stepped into my room to check on me before retiring for the night himself. My heart had pounded in my heart when I realized that he was standing beside the bed. I expected a beating for sure.

Instead of being angry with me, Master Meadows had sat on the edge of the bed and wiped away my tears with his thumb. "It will be all right, Isaac," Master Meadows said. "It's all so much, isn't it?"

I nodded, sucking the snot up my nose so that it did not run out. "I miss my mama," I had whispered.

"Of course you do," Master Meadows said softly. "We will have to make do for now without her. I shall tell you a story. How would you like that?"

I did not know what a story was but I nodded politely. Master Meadows had smiled and began to talk. He talked about some king and queen in a faraway land who desperately wanted a child but had no such luck as each year passed without a child coming to their house.

Master Meadows had such a soothing voice that my eyelids grew heavy as he talked. I wanted to ask Master Meadows what a king and queen were but instead I pretended that I understood what he was talking about. I hadn't understood why a little, old man could give them a child but he did. Only if they promised to give him the precious child when it turned five.

It was getting tougher and tougher to concentrate as Master Meadows talked. I was trying so hard to stay awake to hear the story but sleep was stronger than my will. I fell asleep while Master Meadows was rattling off all sorts of names.

I smiled remembering. Every night, for years and years, Master Meadows came into my room and told me a story. I almost always fell asleep to the sound of his voice in my ears. He had been a kind man, in his own way.

I said a silent farewell to Lisbett as she slept on the bed in my old bedroom then hurried down the hall and down the staircase. The woman who had let me in was in the kitchen, stirring a big, boiling pot on the stove. She looked up when she heard my footsteps.

"How is she?" the woman asked.

"Sleeping," I said, heading straight for the door. I stopped and turned. "How does she know about the bluecoats at the train station?"

"We walk every afternoon," the woman said. "She likes to sit at the train station to see all the people coming and going."

"She walks all the way to the train station?" I asked in surprise.

The woman nodded. "Sure enough," she said. She smiled. "Takes us a bit of time but we get there. Then we rest for a while. Then we walk home."

"And the bluecoats," I said. "Do they talk to her?"

The woman shrugged. "There's one man who tips his hat and says good morning to her," she said. She shook her head. "But other than that, no. Lisbett likes to listen to them talk. They talk funny."

"They do," I said in agreement. "I have to go. Thank you."

"Good luck, dear," the woman said in farewell.

I had to hurry to get to the tannery. It had taken longer at the house than I had planned. I stretched my muscles in as long of strides I could take without breaking into a run. The bluecoats were milling about the train station again. Going past the train station to the tannery was actually out of the way. I did not see the man who had asked me for directions. A few men glanced at me but no one gave me much attention.

I collected the ledgers and hurried back to the house, slowing as I walked past the train station once again. There was the man who seemed to be in charge. I slowed even more, dragging my feet. I had promised Lisbett to ask for help but I could not take the risk. He had his back to me, talking to a handful of men. They were listening to him, occasionally nodding in unison.

If there was anyone there who I could risk asking for help, that was the man. He was busy, giving orders to his men. I could not interrupt him. I had no business going up to him while he was surrounded by all those soldiers. I kept walking.

Mistress Meadows was in the office yelling at Master Meadows when I returned. I stood in the hall waiting, not wanting to intrude. It took Master Meadows a few minutes to notice me standing out in the hall.

"How long have you been waiting out there?" Master Meadows yelled out to me. "Get to work."

"Yessir," I said, ducking my head and heading for my desk.

"He's already causing trouble," Mistress Meadows said. "I don't understand why you won't sell him along with the others."

"His value is beyond an auction block's understanding," Master Meadows said.

"That doesn't even make sense," Mistress Meadows said. "All he does is sit in here. Lounging about, reading the newspaper. Oh, I see him reading."

"You must have understood that he could read," Master Meadows said, voice rising in anger. "What did you think he was doing in here all day every day?"

"I don't interfere with your business dealings," Mistress Meadows yelled back. "If he's so valuable he should go on the block."

"No," Master Meadows said.

The single, abrupt word silenced Mistress Meadows instantly. She stared at her husband for a few moments. I sat at my desk with my shoulders hunched forward, trying to at least pretend to be working but finding that impossible with them fighting and Mistress Meadows being in the room. In all the years I'd been living in the younger Master Meadows' household she had never once entered the office during the working day.

"But Andrew," Mistress Meadows said in a calm, soft voice.

"The topic is closed," Master Meadows said. "You would be better suited in your time trying to nurse those slaves back to health so we can get them on their way."

Mistress Meadows puckered her lips in a gesture of distaste.

"You know I don't do well in the sickroom," Mistress Meadows said, a whine creeping into her voice. "Betsy is almost recovered. She can do it."

"Suit yourself," Master Meadows said.

"They will go tomorrow," Mistress Meadows said in a firm voice. "No matter what. They can recover on the train."

"Or the day after," Master Meadows said.

"Fine," Mistress Meadows snapped. She left the room without another word.

"I can't believe that woman isn't aware of your talents," Master Meadows said, staring at the doorway his wife had just passed through. "After all these years." I didn't say anything. Unless Master Meadows told his wife what I did in the office there was really no reason for her to have any idea. Master Meadows turned to me. "What took you so long?"

"I had a late start this morning," I said.

"John Wells came by a bit ago. Said he saw you walking past the train station," Master Meadows said. "That's out of your way. What were you doing there?"

John Wells was the runner for the printing house. "Just looking," I said. "Is there a problem at the printing house?"

Master Meadows nodded. "That's what he said, that you walked straight on through," Master Meadows said. "You're not going to cause any trouble, Isaac. Are you?"

"What can I do, sir?" I said, looking up and meeting his gaze for the briefest of moments. "Is there a problem at the printing house, sir?"

Master Meadows studied me for a moment then nodded in satisfaction. "Very true, Isaac," Master Meadows said. "I'm glad you understand that. No, no problem. I had asked for a mid-term report. I want you to take a look at why the revenue is dropping."

"Yessir," I said.

We both knew why the revenue was dropping. There was a war

going on. At least I thought we both knew that.

For a moment I thought of how the elder Master Meadows had distracted a scared five-year old boy with night time stories to lull me to sleep when I was missing my mother. The younger Master Meadows was going to distract me with more work. More work was not going to chase away my loss.

"I was actually hoping that I could spend the time with my family," I said. Once the words were out of my mouth I held my breath in anticipation.

Master Meadows considered. Finally he nodded. "Very well. The report can hold for another day or two," he said. "Finish up the ledger audit today and the rest of the day is yours."

"Thank you, sir," I said.

"After you return the ledger to the tannery," Master Meadows added.

"Yessir," I said.

Master Meadows left the office a few hours later. As soon as he was gone I closed the ledger and went looking for Tildy. She was in our cabin lying in bed with Shonny. Sam was trying to get Shonny to drink water from a ladle. Shonny kept turning her head away. The front of her dress was soaking wet.

"Hello, baby girl," I said, sliding onto the bed next to Shonny. Shonny crawled into my lap and put her head against my chest. The heat poured from her little body.

"She won't drink," Sam said.

I took the ladle from Sam's hand. "Can you drink, little girl?" I asked Shonny. She nodded but when I held the ladle up to her mouth she pressed her lips together and turned her head. "Just a little," I coaxed.

"Let me try," Tildy said, struggling to a seated position.

I touched Tildy's forehead. "You're burning up," I said.

"I know," Tildy said, reaching out and pulling Shonny out of my arms. Tildy took the ladle from me and held it to Shonny's mouth.

Shonny obediently sipped the water.

"There's no way you'll be in any shape to travel tomorrow," I said.

"She still plans on sending us out tomorrow?" Tildy asked, looking up from Shonny to me. "Oh, lord," Tildy muttered, pushing Shonny away and leaning over the bed. Sam was quick to put a bucket under his mother's face, just in time.

"I have to run back to the tannery," I said to Sam. "But when I come back the rest of the day is free. Can you hold up until I get back?"

Sam nodded. "I'm fine."

"You're a good boy, Sam," I said, putting my hand on his shoulder.

I leaned over and kissed the top of Sam's head then hurried back to the office to retrieve the ledger. I went the direct route to the tannery, surprising the manager. He was not expecting me that early in the day.

"Just put it in the office," he said.

"Yessir," I said. I went up the stairs to the office. As I leaned over the desk to set the ledger down I noticed the open drawer. It was only open a few inches but it was enough to see that it was filled with cash.

My first thought was to wonder why the manager was holding so much cash in the office. As I stared at all that money it crossed my mind that it would be enough money to get us north. I straightened but remained standing in front of the desk.

I've never been a thief. But I'd never faced such a critical point in my life before either. The manager would know instantly that I had taken it. Yet again, the office door was unlocked, the desk drawer left open for anyone to see. Anyone could steal the money.

I leaned forward and slid the drawer shut. I was still not a thief. I turned, jumping guiltily when I saw the manager standing in the doorway.

"What are you doing, boy?" he asked, shutting the door as he stepped further into the room.

"Shutting the drawer, sir," I said. My heart raced. I had not done anything wrong. Yet my heart raced.

The manager stepped around the desk, opening the drawer. He looked inside the drawer then looked up at me. "Why you lingering?" he asked, sliding the drawer shut again. "Get out of here."

"Yessir," I said, hurrying out of the room.

I went out of the way and walked past the train station on the way home. He was there. Standing apart from the others. I took a deep breath and slowed my steps. The soles of my feet scraped the ground as I dragged my feet slower and slower. The man in the blue coat watched me approach, cocking his head slightly as he studied me.

I couldn't do it. I picked up my feet as I neared him and stretched my legs in long ground-eating strides. The man nodded his head at me in greeting as I passed then turned his attention to the bluecoats nearest him.

I could not risk it. If the bluecoat turned me in I would not be able to help my family. I did not know him to be able to trust him. I had only one option. I was pinning my hopes on Master Meadows' greed for money. The delay due to their sickness had given me the extra time I needed.

Years ago I had asked him about buying my family and he had turned me down. He had turned me down because my coming up with enough money was but a theory. I hoped that the money being real would spur Master Meadows to agree.

Master Meadows had not returned to the office by the time I returned from the tannery. I tried to embrace the time left with my family, unsure if it would be the last night with them or the eve of the first day of a great adventure. I had come up with a plan but plans have a way of going awry.

Tildy was actually recovering already. Her fever had broken but she still could not hold anything down. Fortunately no one else was getting sick. Unfortunately Shonny was still burning hot with her fever.

"She's too sick to travel," Tildy said, stroking Shonny's forehead.

"Maybe she won't have to go anywhere," I said.

"What are you up to?" Tildy asked, looking up at me.

"Nothing," I said. I did not want to get her hopes up.

"You just want us out of here all that faster?" Tildy asked.

"Yes, that's it," I said.

Tildy stared at me. "Don't you go doing nothing stupid," she said. "We can still plan on a meeting place when the president frees the rest of us. Better to do that than have them hang you for running."

"What if he doesn't free everyone?" I asked. "What if the South wins? What if the North wins but everything goes back to how it was?"

"It won't ever go back to how it was," Tildy said. "We'll find each other. Don't go doing nothing stupid."

"Sometimes life isn't worth living if it's been lived without what matters in life," I said.

Tildy's eyes narrowed. Whatever she was about to say was interrupted with Shonny throwing up all over herself. The smell of vomit made Tildy gag. Sam brought water and rags and helped me clean up Shonny while Tildy leaned over the side of the bed dry heaving over a bucket.

When things calmed down Tildy lay on her side with Shonny snuggled up against her and fell asleep. I gathered the rest of the children and herded them to the kitchen. They still needed to eat dinner. Arice was in a cooperative mood, fortunately. Betsy was on the mend and was moving a little slow but was managing to function.

"Only a simple meal tonight," Betsy said, turning from the stove and watching us file into the kitchen. "Oatmeal. But there's berries with the oatmeal. And some ham. What's she going to do about some ham?"

"How is Bannister doing?" I asked.

Betsy shook her head. "I don't know," she said. "Haven't seen him today."

"I'll check on him," I said. I turned to my eldest daughter. "Arice, help Betsy."

Arice got a mulish expression on her face, her chin jutting down but she nodded. The last thing I needed was to get into a squabble with Arice so it was a relief that she was going to cooperate.

"I can check on him," Sam said.

I shook my head. "No," I said. "You keep an eye on Arice and Willie."

I walked down the hall from the kitchen to the back of the house. Betsy and Bannister had small, cramped rooms at the rear of the kitchen area. Neither room had a door. I peered inside the last room where there was just enough space for a single mattress strung over a frame. The smell of sickness was almost over powering.

"Bannister?" I asked from the doorway.

There was no response, no movement from the bed. I could see his form, covered by a blanket. A bad feeling crept into me. The lack of response reminded me of when I had found the elder Master Meadows dead in his bed. I stepped into the room.

Chapter Twenty-Five

Hank

The War Between the States began just a year after Minnesota gained statehood. First thing, Wilhelm joined the First Minnesota Regiment and went off to fight to keep the Union together. August joined with him. The First Minnesota Regiment was making a name for itself, doing Minnesota proud.

I had recently returned from back east after earning my degree at university and had set up a law practice in New Ulm. I had met Miss Katherine Baker while attending university in Boston. We married the year before I returned to New Ulm. We had a nice little house near my office.

When Wilhelm told Caroline that he was joining up with the First Minnesota Regiment she did not take it well. They were always fighting about it before he left. He closed his veterinarian practice and moved Caroline, Lydia, and the two boys into New Ulm, not wanting her to be out on the farm alone.

The war was supposed to only last a few months. August joined up with Wilhelm. August was not married yet but he was engaged to Miss Annabel Holbert. The Holberts farmed about fifteen miles northwest of New Ulm, very close to the agency boundary. Annabel was more forgiving than Caroline. August had promised they would marry as soon as he returned.

Piotr was newly married to Maria Guhrt with a new baby on the way when the call to arms came. Piotr, Hans, and I stayed behind that first round. We followed the progress of the war, reading the reports in the newspaper. Every time a letter came from either Wilhelm or August we all gathered in the kitchen on Sunday and listened while Mom or Dad read the letter or letters that came that week.

Katherine was a good sport about leaving her family for the wilds of Minnesota. I think she fit in pretty well, despite finding the frontier town a bit rustic after having spent her life in the more sophisticated Boston. Little Lucas was born before we left Boston and Emily came less than a year after I opened my law office so she was kept busy.

My law office was doing all right. Most of my work was setting up land claims and property deeds. A lot of people were moving into Minnesota and settling the land so I had a steady influx of work. There were a few incidents with the Lakota on the agency land to the west of New Ulm but for the most part they got along well with the new settlers.

The incident with Tall Grass and Patches had been my only bad experience with them. The Indian Agent Galbraith was treating them unfairly and there was a lot of grumbling. They had every right to grumble. The government had promised them payments and no payments were coming.

Their payments per the treaty were so far behind and the traders weren't doing anything on credit anymore. I heard that it was the war down South delaying the payments. Excuses didn't soothe the Indians with starving children. I hadn't seen Walking Moon in years but Catches Pebbles still visited my parents and occasionally came into town to see me.

A year passed and Wilhelm and August were still fighting the war down south. Hans was considering joining up with the Union army but Mom kept talking him out of it. Mom had not liked that Wilhelm and August had signed up to fight and she convinced Hans that he was needed at home. He was the only one of us boys still living on the original farmstead.

In 1862 President Lincoln called on us for more men to fight down south. The war was not going as quickly as expected. I gave it serious consideration and decided that it was my duty to join the army and fight to keep the union intact.

I had not joined the 1st Minnesota Regiment because my wife, Katherine, was about to deliver our second child. The war was not going as easily as expected so when the president made the request for more men to aid in defending the Union in July of 1862 I felt it was my duty to heed the call to arms.

Katherine was not happy with my decision and we discussed it for several days. In the end I remained firm in my decision.

"Maybe I won't be here when you get back," Katherine said.

"Then you aren't the woman I thought I married," I said. It made me angry that she thought to blackmail me out of doing my duty.

"I'm sorry," Katherine said, immediately contrite. "I just feel so helpless. I don't want you to go."

I held her, rubbing her back with my hand. "I won't be long. A few months," I said. "With the added men we should wrap up this war in no time."

We both knew that was being overly optimistic. Wilhelm and August had left years ago, believing then that the war would be a few months. Instead of ending quickly, the fighting grew more and more intense. We wanted to believe that the Union was stronger, with right on our side, that the Confederacy was just a ragtag band of seceders.

The Confederacy had proven to be a formidable foe. Their spirit and determination helped them win several key battles. Often it seemed that they would win but the Union was just as determined to hold the States together, so the war continued long past the few months expected.

It was difficult to leave the children. I knew how fast children could grow. Lydia had sprouted up like a weed while I was off at school, looking like a young lady already. I didn't want to miss all their growing up but it was my duty to go.

I closed my law office and left Katherine, secure in the belief that she would be fine. Caroline and Piotr and his wife were living in New Ulm so she wasn't completely alone.

"You come back to me," she said.

"I intend to," I said, giving her one last hug.

I kissed the children good-bye. It was even harder leaving them than I had expected. I had already said my farewells to the rest of my family the Sunday before. Tom Guhrt was waiting out on the front steps of my house. We had both signed up.

Guhrt and I headed to Fort Snelling to enlist in the Union army and do our duty to battle the Rebels. We were both assigned to the Ninth Volunteer Regiment of Minnesota, Company K.

The Ninth was still at Fort Snelling, wrapping up training, when the news came. The Sioux were murdering settlers. The first incident started with the murder of five people on Robinson Jones' property over in Acton Township in Meeker County. Meeker County was west of Fort Snelling.

It all started with Brown Wing, Breaking Up, Killing Ghost, and Runs Against Something When Crawling. One day they were heading home from visiting some relatives for a hunting trip. The hunting trip had not been successful and they were hungry.

They spotted a farm house and lingered near the house, eyeing the eggs in a chicken nest. After much consideration and some dares, Brown Wing worked up the courage to steal the eggs and decided along the way to start killing people. The blood lust had begun and they killed more settlers as they encountered scattered farmsteads on their way home. Innocent civilians were murdered without warning.

It seemed at first that it was an isolated incident, some rogue Indians taking out their frustration on some unfortunate souls who happened to be in the wrong place at the wrong time. The Jones settlement had a post office and trading store on their property so it was frequented by Indians of the area.

It was unsettling but not too alarming since Acton was so far north of New Ulm. I began to fret though. New Ulm was less than thirty miles from the Lower Agency border. My parents and brother were too close to the Lower Agency to ease my mind. If there was trouble I fully expected Dad would take Mom and Hans into New Ulm where they would be safe. Yet I fretted.

"I need to go check on my family," I muttered upon hearing the news.

Tom Guhrt was standing next to me. He had come up with me from New Ulm to Fort Snelling. Guhrt also was unsettled by hearing the news of the murders over in Acton Township.

"Just some renegades," Guhrt muttered under his breath but he was staring off into the distance with a worried look on his face.

I shook my head. "I don't know, Guhrt," I said in a low voice. "There was a lot of grumbling about late payments. I have a feeling. I have a feeling this is the pot simmering over before the lid starts rattling."

Guhrt turned and looked at me. "Strange choice of metaphor," he said. "You *are* rattled."

I shrugged. "What if it's just the start of something?" I asked. "I need to make sure my family is okay."

"You go anywhere and it's desertion," Guhrt said. "You belong to the army now. You can't just go off on your own."

"My feet are restless," I said. "My heart is heavy."

Guhrt nodded. "They will be all right," he said. "Catches Pebbles will warn them if anything is going to happen."

Guhrt hadn't mentioned Walking Moon. I hadn't seen Walking Moon in years because he had become bitter about the large number of whites taking over Indian land. Catches Pebbles still visited. Dad and Wilhelm both sent food back with him before Wilhelm left to go to war. Food had become a problem on the agency.

Catches Pebbles often showed up at harvest time, helping Dad and Wilhelm both. They appreciated his help and gave him bushels of grain, vegetables from the garden, and the occasional cow in payment for his hard work. When Wilhelm went off to war Catches Pebbles continued to help Dad.

Reports of more murders reached the fort. They managed to talk Little Crow into making war with the settlers. Many other chiefs refused to participate in Little Crow's war. It gave me hope that the uprising would die down before it reached the area around New Ulm.

Little Crow had listened to the four men who had done the killing up in Acton when they called for war against the settlers. Little Crow had listened and decided that it was time to rise up against all the white settlers moving onto the land that had been theirs. Though many chiefs refused to join Little Crow's war, some did. The number of Lakota scouring the countryside for settlers to murder climbed.

Only they weren't warring on the whites. They were massacring innocent families who lived on farms, innocent men, women, and children who had been granted their land by the government. Families, like mine, who put their sweat into succeeding on the rustic frontier land. Families who struggled to survive on land that provided their livelihood. Families who had been good neighbors to the Lakota.

It was no war. It was out and out murder. Bands of Lakota descended on farms and burned, killed, and took women and children as hostages. Not all women or children were even taken. Some women were raped and killed next to their husbands and children.

Word came that settlers trying to escape had been ambushed on the road to Fort Ridgley. Two families had reached the Larson homestead, outrunning Indians who had burned their farms behind them. All three families had gone from the Larson homestead towards Fort Ridgley.

They had met a small band of Indians led by a Lakota man who they knew. He had talked them into going back to their farm and once they reached the farm they had been met by more Indians. Both bands came together and began the slaughter. Some of the children managed to escape, hiding in the cattails lining the road.

The Indian they knew, Prawn, was telling Mrs. Larson that he would spare her son if she would go with him but she was refusing. Her husband lay next to the wagons, shot in the stomach. Prawn dragged her three year old son out from the wagon and smashed his head in with the butt of his rifle.

The oldest boy, nine-year old James Larson, crawled through the underbrush away from the road, dragging his five year old sister and one year old brother with him. He managed to reach Fort Ridgley on foot two days later. Pete Lackly had been shot in the leg and back and a bullet had grazed the side of his skull so the Indians had left him for dead. He came to later that night and managed to reach Hutchinson a week later.

Wandering through bogs and swamps to get to Hutchinson had not helped his wounds. He was in rough shape when he arrived but he managed to tell what had happened. Panic gripped the area and settlers were evacuating as fast as they could, some heading for Fort Ridgley, some skirting the fort and heading farther east.

Each passing day brought more disturbing news of settlers being murdered without warning. The only thing that kept me from running to New Ulm was the news that soldiers were marching down to Fort Ridgley. Better yet, Sibley had been given four companies of men and was headed for New Ulm.

"I could ask to go on a hunting trip and slip down there," Guhrt said one day as more news of murders reached our ears.

Guhrt had gained a reputation as a top hunter and scavenger. That man would eat anything that didn't poison him. Sometimes I thought he might even be immune to poison. He often went out with a small party of men to supplement our food stores.

Guhrt was a favorite with most of the officers. As a soldier he excelled. Guhrt was a spot on marksmen, well disciplined, and did as told without hesitation. In hand to hand combat no one could beat him. In comparison, I was just average.

I shook my head. "It would take you too long to reach New Ulm," I said. "I don't want you to get into trouble. It's my responsibility."

"My family is there, too," Guhrt said.

"Then we'll both go," I said.

"You'd just slow me down," Guhrt said. "You know it's true."

Guhrt asked anyway. With all the commotion going on he was denied permission to leave the fort even for a hunting expedition. We weren't the only ones who feared for our families. A lot of men training at Fort Snelling had family down in the area under attack.

Major Harrison approached Guhrt later the same day he had asked to leave the fort to do some hunting. He nodded at me and asked Guhrt for a word in private. They stepped away and talked for several minutes. Guhrt nodded often as he listened to the major. When the man left Guhrt told me what they had discussed.

"He's going to push for that hunting trip," Guhrt said. "He wanted to know how long it would take me if I ventured a little farther south than normal."

"How long would it take you?" I asked, feeling relief.

"By myself, on the major's horse, I could reach New Ulm in eight hours," Guhrt said. "He's got family down there also. Over by St. Peter."

Guhrt vanished that night. He didn't even tell me that he was going. Major Harrison covered for him, telling Major Candon that he had sent him on an errand. Guhrt and I reported to Major Candon. He wasn't too happy to lose Guhrt for a few days but it was too late to supersede the orders.

It wasn't a well-kept secret that Guhrt was headed south to

check on settlers in the front line of the uprising. Before he had asked permission the first he had gone up to everyone he knew had family down that way and asked who he should look for if he happened to end up that way during his hunting.

Then a letter came from Katherine. Catches Pebbles had convinced Dad to go into New Ulm. A few days later a letter came from Dad telling me that he had moved Mom and Hans into town. Mom and Dad were staying with Caroline and Hans was staying with Katherine. I could finally breathe again. A letter came from Hans the next day.

Catches Pebbles had arrived only hours before a band of Indians had descended on the farm. Catches Pebbles had stood outside the house, guarding my parents and brother all day and all night. At the first chance the next morning he had escorted them to New Ulm. Later in the day they could see smoke coming from the direction of the farmstead.

Worse than anything was getting the news days after it happened. The letter was over a week old. I penned a quick letter, telling Hans to get everyone out of New Ulm. I asked him to bring the Guhrt family with them and go up to St. Paul where they would be safe.

I posted the letter, hoping it would reach them in time. Training continued while we waited for our orders. There was speculation about where we would be heading. The popular thought amongst the enlisted men was North Carolina.

It didn't seem right to me to ship us down south when we were needed right at home. Orders finally came in. We were heading to Alabama by the end of the week. Guhrt still wasn't back. He had been gone for four days. I wasn't the only one worried about my friend. After the third day Major Harrison was often standing up in the guard tower staring off to the southwest.

Before we could head out for Alabama new orders came in. We were to sit tight a while longer. General Pope had convinced the president that the Lakota uprising was a serious threat and not an isolated incident.

Guhrt returned to Fort Snelling mid-morning five days after he left. He looked like he'd lost twenty pounds in those five days. Dark circles were etched under his eyes. As the farm horse he rode trotted into the fort he sat with his shoulders slumped forward. He pulled back on the reins and the sweating horse came to an immediate stop, head dropping, sides heaving.

Guhrt was swarmed by soldiers, those who had family down around the Redwood River area bombarding him with questions. He apologized to Major Harrison because the major's horse had been shot out from under him. Guhrt slid off the gelding and handed the reins to the major.

Chapter Twenty-Six

Even Major Candon didn't pretend that Guhrt's errand had been anything but a run to get word on what was happening. Major Candon waded through the gathered crowd.

"Well, what's the news, Guhrt?" Major Candon asked.

Guhrt eyed Major Candon for a moment then launched into his tale. I don't know if anyone but me noticed that Guhrt was leaning back against the gelding's shoulder in order to stay on his feet. Several times he opened his eyes wide to keep them from drooping shut.

Guhrt had ridden all night, pushing the borrowed horse pretty hard to reach St. Peter by morning. The closer he got to St. Peter the worse the destruction. Most homesteads were burned. Some appeared to have been abandoned before they were burned since there were no bodies. It had been difficult for him to leave the bodies he had seen but the living were more important at the time.

The roads had been filled with settlers escaping the carnage. Guhrt had asked them all for names so that he could pass on the names of those he'd been asked to check on. Many a soldier heaved a sigh of relief as Guhrt called out the names he had heard. He had also asked everyone he passed for the names he'd been asked to check on.

Unfortunately he had also heard names of families who had been murdered. From St. Peter he had gone on to New Ulm. The town had been evacuated by most of the residents but filled again with refugees looking for safety. The Indians had attacked New Ulm but had been held back.

"Your house is gone," Guhrt said, looking at me. "Burned. But your family already left along with my family. They headed for Mankato long before the attack on New Ulm."

"They're safe?" I asked.

"They're safe," Guhrt said.

"Thank God," I said. The relief was so great that my knees almost buckled at hearing the news.

The major's family was safely on their way to St. Paul. Major Harrison gladly took the aging gelding in trade for his lost horse even though it was just a farm pony and his horse had been a purebred. There were several soldiers that had not received good news of their loved ones. I noticed Major Candon noting which soldiers had learned that their families had not been so fortunate to escape the carnage.

Major Candon told Guhrt to go get something to eat and hit the infirmary building so that he could be ready to take up his duties the next morning. Guhrt said that with some food he would be ready to go that day yet but Major Candon refused to release him to duty until the doctor had seen him.

Grudgingly Guhrt headed to the mess hall. Major Candon went up to each man who had gotten the bad news and said a few words of consolation. There was a small ceremony that evening for those who had lost loved ones and for those who wanted to console their friends.

As soon as I was off duty I headed for the infirmary. Infirmary was a fancy word for an outbuilding with two rooms, one with cots lined up against two walls and a room where the doctor could operate if needed. The doctor wouldn't let me in to see Guhrt. He was sleeping. I could see him on one of the cots behind the doctor. Guhrt was the only one in the room.

He slept all afternoon, all evening, and through the next. The next morning he reported to duty looking more himself again. There was a haunted edge to his eyes though. He didn't want to talk about what had happened.

It was only later that I heard stories of what Guhrt had done on his wild ride. As settlers drifted into Fort Ridgley and even up to St. Paul they talked about the tall, thin man wearing a Ninth Regiment patch who had shown up everywhere like an angel. He was even marked with a cross on his forehead.

The mystery soldier had single handedly shot eight Indians attacking a line of wagons trying to escape St. Peter, scattering the rest of the band. He had ridden through a party of Indians attacking a farmstead east of New Ulm, joining forces to fight off the attack. That was when Major Harrison's horse had been shot out from under him.

That family had given him one of their precious horses, hitching up the oxen to the wagon even though it meant slowing down their escape. In the morning he had led the way as they escaped their home, staying with them until he felt he could leave them on their own.

Guhrt was in New Ulm when the attack came. He was critical in helping the remaining townspeople and the refugees hold their ground. He could have gotten out before the attack but when he realized that the Indians were going to attack the town itself he had chosen to stay. Because so many in New Ulm knew Guhrt it had not taken long to put a name to the mystery angel all the saved settlers were talking about.

Some people thought it couldn't have been the same man being in so many places in such a short time. I believed it. They didn't know Guhrt like I did. Stories continued to circulate but Guhrt wouldn't confirm or deny anything. Whatever had happened, Guhrt only wanted to put it behind him.

Word came that New Ulm had been attacked a second time, just two days after the first attack. It was a larger attack and 68 people were killed and over a hundred injured. Every house outside the brigade in the center of town where the townspeople and refugees had made their stand was burned. But they had pushed back the Lakota and held the town.

The new orders came at last. Washington had finally recognized the threat terrorizing Minnesota and we were being dispatched to deal with the Lakota uprising. Some companies headed to Fort Ridgley, some down to Mankato. Our company went to Mankato.

The first chance I got once we reported in, I went looking for my family. They were all staying in a house. Katherine ran into my arms and I held her close. Mom was holding Lucas. He had grown so much. I pulled Mom into my embrace with Katherine and kissed the top of Lucas' head.

I kept my arm around Katherine as everyone stepped up for a hug, Caroline, Hans, Dad, and even Lydia. Wilhelm's boys held back until Caroline pushed them forward.

"I can't stay long," I said. "I just had to see you. Be sure you are all safe." I looked around. "Where's Piotr? I thought everyone got out."

"He's got a place across town," Dad said. "The rooms above a shop."

"And the Guhrts?" I asked.

"Near Piotr," Dad said. "They're talking about heading for St. Paul but not until things calm down."

I looked over at Caroline. "Any word from Wilhelm or August?" I asked.

"They're still all right," Caroline said. "They were in Missouri but heading east again."

"They're in separate companies now," Dad said. "They split up the First."

"Catches Pebbles saved us," Mom said. "I'm so worried they'll hurt him for helping us."

She was sober. I pulled her in for another hug, still not releasing my hold on Katherine. "I'm sure he'll be all right," I said. "Any word of Walking Moon?"

Dad and Hans exchanged looks. "I heard Walking Moon was in the group that murdered the Larsons," Dad said. "His father, Chief Sun Eagle was one of the chiefs refusing to join Little Crow but Walking Moon joined Little Crow anyway."

"He promised he'd take care of the animals but I don't know how he can hold them off on his own," Mom said.

"I'm sure they took the animals before Catches Pebbles could return," Dad said.

"Shadow?" I asked, hardly able to say the name.

"Catches Pebbles rode him out," Dad said. "We hitched up Hickory and Mabel and put the Old Men in the back of the wagon, along with a few keepsakes. I'm sure the rest is gone."

"We should have stayed," Mom said in a fury.

"Stayed?" I asked in shock. "You were lucky to get out alive, Mom. If not for Catches Pebbles they would have killed you. Or worse."

"With Catches Pebbles we could have held them off," Mom said.

It was disappointing to hear that Walking Moon had joined the uprising. Maybe that was wrong. Maybe someone had mistaken another Lakota warrior for Walking Moon. Yet, deep down, I feared it must be true.

"Your mother was determined to save the farm," Dad said, shaking his head. There was a sparkle of pride in his eyes as he looked at her though. "Bravely foolish woman."

"There were too many," Mom admitted.

"The only reason Catches Pebbles was able to hold them off was that they weren't willing to hurt him to get to us," Dad said.

"You were lucky to get out alive," I said. "They almost took New Ulm. Do you think they would have let one lone Lakota stand in their way to get to you?"

"I wasn't afraid," Mom said, chin jutting out.

I shivered, the hair on the back of my neck tingling. "You

should have been," I said.

At the same time Dad said, "I know you weren't, Elise. But you also used your head and that's as important."

"I was afraid for you," Mom admitted, putting her hand on Dad's chest.

I held Lucas for a few minutes then Emily. "I have to go," I said handing Emily to Katherine. "I hope to see more of you later when I get the chance." I kissed Katherine then left. I headed back to the barracks with mixed feelings, relief that they were so close and safe and regret that having found them I had such a short time to visit.

I found Guhrt staring with remorse at a wood crate holding a ham, a canvas bag of oats, and two pies. He looked up at me as I approached. "I wish they wouldn't do that," he said.

Since arriving at Mankato word had gotten out that the Mystery Ninth Angel, as he was dubbed, was stationed there. Small gifts of food had been showing up every so often ever since.

"They're saying thank you," I said.

Guhrt might not have liked the constant stream of food but the rest of the company appreciated the home cooked food and meat. Army issued food was enough to keep a man functioning but not much more could be said about it.

We were stationed in Mankato for a year. The uprising was quelled in just a few months but just as things quieted down there would be another series of attacks on settlers. Our presence in Mankato kept them away from Mankato but there were still areas in the Redwood River Area being targeted by bands of renegade Lakota.

By December of 1862 over a thousand Lakota were housed in prisons around Minnesota. There were trials and 303 Lakota were convicted of murder and sentenced to hang.

The president had requested all the paperwork from the trials and had gone through the sentences, choosing only the ones who had murdered and raped women and children for execution, pardoning the rest. President Lincoln pardoned 265 of the prisoners and ordered the execution of the remaining 38 go on as scheduled.

The war officially ended with the sentencing and hanging of the 38 Lakota convicted of murder. Someone forgot to convince the Lakota that their war was over and they continued to harass settlers and there were sporadic murders even after the war officially ended.

It was the largest mass hanging ever in the history of the United States and it took place in Mankato. I was in the detail set to keep out the general population and reporters. I kept my back to the gallows built just for the occasion. When the trap doors snapped open behind me I cringed, unable to help it.

There were 38 men behind me dead or dying. The lucky ones had their necks snap from the fall. The unlucky ones choked to death from the rope around their necks if the fall didn't kill them. Even knowing that the ones hung that day were the murderers of women and children, death was a serious affair.

After we put a stop to the war our orders were to chase all the Indians out of Minnesota. Little Crow had escaped. Rumor had him up at the winter camping ground along the shores of Devils Lake over in Dakota Territory.

General Sibley headed for Devils Lake with eight thousand troops. He advanced so slowly that Little Crow snuck away from Devils Lake long before Sibley reached the campsite. While Sibley's focus was up north the killings started again down by the Redwood River. Thirty settlers were killed despite the large military force tasked with keeping the settlers safe and ridding the area of Indians.

It was a hard task, chasing down the Lakota and pushing them off of the land promised to them by our government. It didn't seem right, punishing every Indian for the actions of a few Lakota. The settlers weren't comfortable any longer having Indians living so close. The government wanted the land settled and the settlers to feel safe so they came down on the Lakota with a heavy hand.

Things had settled down again when word came in that a war

party had been seen south of Hutchinson. It was a band of about nine Lakota warriors and they were recognized as having attacked another homestead a few weeks earlier. Major Candon was given the orders to go out and find them.

We were riding northwest from Mankato to Hutchinson when we saw smoke in the distance to the west. We raced out to the homestead but we were too late. The house and barn were smoldering but had had time to burn to shells. A man lay in the middle of the yard, shot in the stomach six times. He had pulled his shirt open in pain as he lay dying.

Behind the man, halfway between the house and barn was a woman. Her dress had been cut open below her waist and she had been raped. It wasn't clear if the shot to her head had killed her before or after she had been raped. Her hair was silver gray.

Two girls were just beyond the elderly woman. Both had been raped even though they were just children. A woman with brown hair lay face down next to one of the girls, her hand outstretched to her dead daughter.

"One's still alive," Private Jenkin said, dropping to his knees beside the young girl.

He tried pulling her skirt over her legs but it had been shredded with a knife and would not reach to cover her. He took his jacket off and covered her from the waist down before bending over her to examine her head wound.

"Fire burned hot but it's only been a few hours," Guhrt said, looking around the yard. He pointed south. "They went that way."

Major Candon gave orders for several men to stay behind and deal with the bodies and get the girl some medical help. The rest of us headed south to chase down the party of Lakota that had attacked the farm.

We came across them camped next to the river. We might have missed them but for a thin trail of smoke escaping the trees lining the river. We dismounted and secured the horses then formed a semi-circle and crept slowly and silently on foot towards the source of the smoke.

Guhrt led the way, as silent as a ghost. He crawled up a knoll and carefully peered over to the river bank below. He backed down the knoll and held his arm up, rolling his hand into a ball. They were there. He gestured to where the Indians were below then swept his arm out and back, signaling where we should move.

We had gained experience over the months hunting Indians. We moved silently through the prairie grass, barely causing the grass to even ripple from our passing. Even if they couldn't see us because of the rise of the river bank, we had learned to never be over optimistic.

We carried nothing metal in our pockets and wrapped anything metal on our uniforms. No one talked. We moved in silently, trapping them against the river.

As we crested the river bank I could hear a girl screaming and crying. Two men were laughing as they pushed her between them. She stumbled but before she could fall one would pull her upright and push her to the other man. Two boys were tied to a tree near where the two men toyed with the girl.

The boys were yelling threats at the men even as they cried helplessly. They wouldn't have heard us approach unless we had ridden in bugles blaring. The man set to be a lookout was sitting up on the crest of the riverbank but was turned so that he could watch the entertainment below him.

Guhrt gave the signal and we all stood and moved in. Lechemann put his gun against the lookout's shoulder and gave him a nudge. The men playing with the girl looked up at us and the girl took advantage of their distraction to stumble over to her brothers and hide behind the tree they were tied to.

They gave up without a struggle. We outnumbered them and there was nowhere for them to go. When I saw Walking Moon in the band I dismounted and walked up to him. Two of my fellow soldiers yelled out in surprise. The Indians were still armed.

"Maniyanhanwi," I said in Lakota. "Mithakhola. What are you doing with these murderers?"

Walking Moon switched to English. "My friend? We are no longer friends," he said.

"Tell me you did not murder these people," I said in Lakota. "Khola."

"They have stolen our land," Walking Moon said, reverting to Lakota without thinking about it. "Like white slugs they come. More and more. We have nothing and they have everything."

"The children?" I asked in Lakota. "Women raped. I just came from a farm where the women and little girls were all raped. Little girls, Maniyanhanwi? Little girls!"

Walking Moon looked away. "Sometimes the fighting lust is strong," he said. "They were going to die anyway."

"It is not a war to kill innocents," I said. "It is a slaughter."

"As whites have done to us," Walking Moon said, looking up and meeting my eyes.

My companions had moved in and secured the prisoners while Walking Moon and I argued. Private Tom Sampson stepped up and took Walking Moon's rifle and knife. Walking Moon stood perfectly still as they disarmed him and put manacles around his ankles.

"You are right, Walking Moon," I said in English. "You are no friend of mine."

"I should have been a chief!" Walking Moon yelled at me in Lakota as I turned away. "I should have been a chief of my people. But a chief of what? We have nothing left. You have taken it all from us. We fight because we are men."

"Men do not war on women and children," I said, turning on my heel and marching back to Walking Moon. "Soldiers make war on soldiers."

"Soldiers! Hah!" Walking Moon yelled. He spit on the ground at my feet. "We destroyed your soldiers at Redwood Ferry and again at Birch Coulee. Your soldiers *are* women!"

Several of the manacled Indians behind Walking Moon chuckled in agreement. Though the soldiers taking the band into custody did not understand our conversation they didn't like that what Walking Moon said made the prisoner laugh. Several soldiers used their rifles as clubs to strike the Indian in front of him, mostly across the back but a few heads got walloped as well.

"Enough!" Major Candon yelled. "We are all disgusted by what these men have done but they are our prisoners and as our prisoners we treat them fairly." Every man dropped his rifle at the first word from Major Candon, some looking guilty as he continued to talk. Not all looked guilty for having caused a few bruises to the prisoners.

Major Candon barked an order and soldiers roughly started the prisoners moving away from the campsite. Guhrt stepped up behind Walking Moon and pushed him between the shoulders to get him walking. Walking Moon shuffled forward, glaring at me as he walked past me.

"It's good to know that you speak their language," Major Candon said to me, watching the prisoners shuffle past. "We should find a wagon to put them in or it will be a long walk back to Mankato."

"He used to be my friend," I said, more to myself than to the major.

I felt personally betrayed that Walking Moon had joined the uprising. Having seen what they did to the settlers was by far worse than hearing about it and hearing about it had been mighty hard on the soul.

The girl and two boys shuffled past me, escorted by Lechemann and Johnson. "He said we belonged to him now," the older boy told Lechemann. "I didn't want to be a slave."

"I want my mama," the younger boy said. He raised his voice. "I want my mama!"

"We'll need to find out if they have any relatives in the area,"

Major Candon said to Lechemann. "You and Johnson take them into Hutchinson."

The girl sobbed nonstop, stumbling often even though her gaze was locked on the ground in front of her. By the stains and rips in her clothes it was easy to assume that she had been mistreated badly while in the custody of the group. My blood boiled. She couldn't have been more than twelve or thirteen years old.

"We got no one here," the older boy said. He looked to be about ten or eleven.

"If you can't find any of their family take them to Mankato. Take them to my wife," I said to Lechemann.

Lechemann nodded. He put his hand on the girl's shoulder to comfort her and she jerked away, terrified. The older boy took her hand and she gripped it so tight that her knuckles turned white. "It's all right, Missy," the boy whispered, leaning closer to her. "It's all right."

The girl's thin shoulders were wracked with silent sobs. She stumbled again and Lechemann reached out to catch her when it looked like she would fall. The girl cringed and squeezed her brother's hand so tightly that he winced in pain. He tried to pry her fingers loose but she would not let go.

"I want my mama," the younger boy wailed. "I want my mama!"

Major Candon stepped in front of the girl, crouching down on his heels even though it meant having to look up at her. "I know this is a difficult time for you, child," he said. "We want to punish the men who did this to you. If you can point him or them out to us now we can testify for you and you won't ever have to see them again. Can you do that for me?"

The girl shrank away from the major, trying to put her younger brother between him and her. "I know which ones," the oldest brother said. "They, uh, hurt her right in front of us."

"Let's start with your names," Major Candon said.

"Nordkopf," the boy said. "Billy Nordkopf. My brother is Heinrich. Missy's real name is Emily."

"Anyone got paper?" Major Candon asked over his shoulder. The younger boy had his face pressed into his sister's skirts and appeared to be calming.

Knobel stepped up, pulling a letter he had started to his mother out of his pocket. "I only got as far as the date and salutation," he said.

"It'll do," Major Candon said. He turned back to Billy Nordkopf. "Tell us what happened. And then point out the men who hurt your sister."

"They killed my family, sir," Billy said.

Major Candon nodded. "Just one thing at a time, son," he said. "I'm just hoping to save your sister from having to go into a courtroom and facing these men again. Can you help with that?"

Missy raised her head, looking over Major Candon at the men standing in shackles. "Him," she said, raising a trembling arm and pointing it at a man with blue streaks down his cheeks. "And him," she said, moving her arm, stopping when her fingers pointed at Walking Moon."

The younger boy had been sniffling but had stopped begging for his mama while they were talking. He looked back at where his sister was pointing. When he saw the Indian men who had abducted them he started to cry again.

"I want my mama," the younger boy wailed. He raised his head and yelled to the sky. "I want my mama!"

Chapter Twenty-Seven

Isaac

"Bannister?" I called out a bit louder.

Bannister stirred. He turned from his side to his back, looking up at me with blurry eyes. He squinted, trying to see who I was.

"Is it time already?" he asked.

"Tomorrow," I said, moving up to the bed. He looked very rough. I reached down and felt his forehead. At least there was no fever. "Your fever's broken," I said in relief. "Are you up to eating some dinner?"

"It might have been better if I had died," he muttered.

"But you didn't," I said. "As long as you have another day there is hope."

Bannister stared at me. "I've never liked you, Isaac," he said.

"I know," I said. "Eating will help. Can you get up?"

"I'd have thought you'd be agonizing over losing your children," Bannister said, studying my face.

"I am," I said.

"You're going to do something stupid," Bannister said, struggling to sit up. "Aren't you?"

"No," I said, shaking my head.

"I've never liked you but those children deserve better than being shipped off," Bannister said. He shook his head. "Mighty fine children you have, Isaac."

"If you can get some food in you you'll feel better," I said, backing away from the bed.

The smell of old vomit permeated the room. If I didn't get out of there I was going to add to the bucket. I backed out of the room and hurried down the hall. Mistress Meadows was in the kitchen when I returned.

"How is he?" Mistress Meadows asked.

"Fever's broke," I said. "Ma'am."

Mistress Meadows nodded. "That's a relief," she said. "I want no more delays." She studied my face. "You're more calm than I expected."

"Yes, ma'am," I said, looking everywhere but directly at her.

"The way you love your wife and children I expected trouble from you," Mistress Meadows said.

"No, ma'am," I said. "I know what's what."

"Do you?" Mistress Meadows asked. "You went by the train station. Again."

"Yes, ma'am," I said. They were watching me. I should have expected that. "I couldn't help it. That train's going to take away my family."

Mistress Meadows frowned. She sniffed the air and turned her attention to Betsy. "Do I smell ham?" she asked Betsy.

"There's a ham in the oven, ma'am," Betsy said.

"Has that fever addled your brain, girl?" Mistress Meadows said. "I clearly requested baked chicken for dinner tonight."

"Need it for stock," Betsy said.

Mistress Meadows frowned. "Stock? For what?" she asked.

"Stock, ma'am," Betsy said. "Lots of extra mouths to feed."

"Stock?" Mistress Meadows muttered. It was easy to see that she had no idea what went into stock but she didn't want to admit it. She looked over at Arice stirring the oatmeal. "Is that oatmeal, Betsy?"

"Yes, ma'am," Betsy said. "Lots of extra mouths to feed."

"Where are Constance's blacks?" Mistress Meadows asked,

looking around the kitchen. Her gaze landed on Sam. "You, boy. Go fetch them."

Sam jumped to his feet and hurried out of the kitchen without hesitation. Benji followed him unbidden. Arice took a step toward the door but caught my glare and turned back to stirring the pot of oatmeal on the stove. Bannister stumbled into the kitchen. Mistress Meadows physically recoiled at the sight and smell of him.

"How dare you enter the kitchen in that condition," Mistress Meadows yelled at Bannister. "You can wait in the stable until you go." Bannister shuffled through the kitchen on his way outside. Mistress Meadows fanned her hand in front of her face as he passed her. "Oh, the difficulties I must bear," she muttered.

Master Meadows returned home for dinner. Constance joined her parents for dinner and then visited with Mindy. The two women were in the salon. Constance sat next to Mindy on the sofa with her arm over the slave woman's shoulders, their heads bowed near each other. Both were crying.

Constance always did have a soft heart. I heard her comforting Mindy as I walked by in search of Master Meadows. "Papa says I have to sell you, Mindy," Constance said in her light, wispy voice. "I should tell him no. I would tell him no if Lawrence had not agreed with him."

"Is all right, Miss Constance," Mindy said, sniffing loudly. "I just don't wanna go. I like it in your house, Miss Constance."

"Oh, Mindy, I shall miss you so," Constance said, sobbing.

They sat with their foreheads touching. I hurried past the doorway, uncomfortable with so much emotion. The whole house was charged with emotion that night. It was almost too much to bear.

Master Meadows was in his office, trying to avoid all the emotion. I stopped at the open door. He looked up in surprise when I knocked on the doorframe.

"Yes?" Master Meadows said curtly.

"Pardon, sir," I said, remaining in the doorway. "May I speak with you?"

Master Meadows waved his hand and I stepped into the room. "If you're here to beg for your family it won't do you any good," he said.

"Yessir," I said, standing in front of his desk. I reached into my inner jacket pocket and pulled out a piece of paper. I set the paper on the desk. "A while ago I asked you if I could buy my family. I have the money." I leaned forward and pointed to the paper I had just set on the desk. "See. That's four thousand two hundred eighty-eight dollars and fifty cents. It's yours in exchange for my family's freedom."

Master Meadows sat frozen, looking up at me, not even looking at the paper. "Where did you get that kind of money?" he asked in a cold voice.

"I earned it," I said.

"Bullshit," Master Meadows said, bolting upright and picking up the paper. He studied it then looked up at me. "What is this?"

"Master Meadows, the elder Master Meadows, gave me a weekly allowance," I said. "I saved most of it. Then I invested it. This is the total. It's yours for my family's freedom. You're going to sell them anyway."

I waited while Master Meadows digested what was happening. He sat back in his chair, staring at the piece of paper he held. He looked between me and the paper several times. After several minutes had passed he tossed the paper on the desk.

"It's mine anyway," he said. "You don't own anything."

"No, sir," I said, shaking my head. "You can't get to it without my say so."

"You think you got me over a barrel, do ya?" Master Meadows said.

"No, sir," I said. "I'm offering to buy my family. That's all."

"What about you?" Master Meadows said, brow furrowing.

"I didn't have enough money to buy me as well," I said. "It's enough to free my family."

"Uncle William gave you an allowance," Master Meadows muttered. Master Meadows picked up the piece of paper again, staring at the number in the bottom right hand corner. "Very well," he said. "Sending them to Kentucky is a risk."

Relief flooded me. My legs trembled yet I felt buoyed with exhilaration. Master Meadows had agreed. My family was free! I would send them up North. When President Lincoln freed the rest of us slaves I would join them up North. If the South won I would run away and join them up north.

The next morning the rest were taken to the train station and shipped off to Kentucky after Betsy made breakfast for everyone. Bannister was still in rough shape but able to walk to the carriage to be driven to the train station. Betsy, Mindy, Dorathea, and Thomas walked beside the carriage. Tildy stood with the children gathered around her, watching them leave.

"Tell me again why we're not heading for the train," Tildy said, gaze locked on the subdued figures of the people being taken away to be sold.

Tildy had not been as excited as I had expected at the news. She was angry with me that I had not told her my plans even though I repeatedly explained to her that I had not said anything in case it had not worked. I had not wanted to get her hopes up for nothing.

Instead of dancing in jubilation at the news that our family was not going to be split up and sold on the auction block, Tildy had been as somber as death. I have to admit, my enthusiasm was quelled by watching the others being taken away.

"Master Meadows agreed to free you for the money I gave him," I said.

"What money?" Tildy asked. "Where'd you get the money to buy us? Did you steal from him?"

"No," I said. "It was money I invested. Money from the elder Master Meadows."

Tildy shook her head. "Don't feel right," she said, pulling Shonny and Benji closer against her. "Did he give you that paper then? That paper that says we free?"

"Not yet," I said. "The lawyer will have to draw it up."

"Don't feel right," Tildy muttered. She turned back to the house, taking Shonny's hand while Benji fell back to walk with the rest of the children.

After so much commotion in the house for several days the house was eerily quiet. Mistress Meadows expected Tildy to make luncheon. I told Tildy that she didn't have to take orders from Mistress Meadows any more. Tildy was free.

"I don't feel free," Tildy said, filling a pot with water.

"As soon as Master Meadows gives me the papers I will send you north," I said.

"North?" Tildy muttered. "But you'll still be here."

"For now," I said.

Tildy shook her head. "I don't trust that man," she said. I picked up the pot and set it on the stove. "Until he tells me himself I'm free and hands me those papers, not gonna feel free."

"He agreed to it," I said. "As soon as he hands me those papers I want all of you on a train north."

"North?" Tildy muttered. "What am I going to do up north? Without you?"

"It'll be all right, Tildy," I said. "I have some money set aside. You'll wait for me up there. As soon as I can I'll come as well."

"Why can't we just stay here?" Tildy asked.

"It'll be all right, Tildy," I said. "I won't feel you're safe until you are up north."

"Where you getting all this money?" Tildy asked.

"I earned it," I said.

"Where we gonna go?" Tildy asked.

Nothing I said would settle her doubts. The idea of leaving me and going north did not sit well with her either. It was the only way I felt they would be safe, up north where we could be free.

For several days life was back to normal, minus Bannister and Betsy. Tildy was working long days to do the work of all three. The hired servant Mistress Meadows had said was coming never did come to the house. Sam and Benji helped with cleaning and Arice and Willie helped in the kitchen.

They hadn't sold Lucas. He was too close to retirement and they knew no one would buy an old man nearing the end of his days. It wasn't worth the cost of the ticket to send him to Kentucky.

The second day I asked Master Meadows when the papers would be ready to sign. "I'm working on it," Master Meadows said. "You'll need to transfer the money to my account first."

"Yessir," I said. A knot formed in the pit of my stomach.

"Any other monies I should know about?" Master Meadows asked me.

"No, sir," I said.

"There better not be," Master Meadows said. "James said you were eyeing the cash drawer at the tannery office. Have you been helping yourself to other cash?"

"No, sir," I said. "I just closed that drawer. Didn't seem right to be sitting open with all that cash in there."

"I'm going to have the books audited," Master Meadows said. "If I find any discrepancies you'll regret it."

I knew that there would be no discrepancies found but I still felt the sweat drip down the back of my neck. All that mattered was that my family would be safe.

"You go ahead and transfer that money, Isaac," Master Meadows said.

"Yessir," I said. I looked up and met his gaze. "I'll send it to the lawyer so he can make a receipt."

Master Meadows frowned. "No need for that, Isaac," Master Meadows said.

"I'd feel better, sir," I said.

"Very well," Master Meadows said, looking away.

A whole week after Master Meadows had agreed to free my family for the monies I had told him that I had earned by investing my saved childhood allowance the lawyer came to the house. Master Meadows sat behind his office desk while the lawyer took a seat in front of the desk. I stood.

"Here we are," the lawyer said, pulling out a receipt from his portfolio. "Funds have been transferred to this account."

Master Meadows took the paper and nodded as he reviewed it. He smiled and leaned back in his chair. "Very good," he said. "Do you have time for some tea?"

"No," the lawyer said, standing. "I have another meeting in a bit."

"Where are the papers?" I asked.

"What papers?" the lawyer asked.

"Emancipation papers for my family," I said.

"Oh, that," the lawyer said, shaking his head. "Since you are property anything you own belongs to Mr. Meadows. You can't buy slaves with money you don't have."

I felt like someone had punched me in the gut. Roaring filled my ears. Master Meadows had taken the money but backed out of the agreement.

"Oh, that reminds me," the lawyer said, opening his portfolio and pulling out another piece of paper. "The insurance papers you wanted me to look over. The coverage should include the train being derailed by Union troops."

It took every ounce of my strength to not dive over the desk and choke the life out of Master Meadows. I could not speak. I could not move. All I could do was tell myself to not attack him. After all that he was still sending my family to Kentucky.

"See there," Master Meadows said to the lawyer with a smile. "He's a good boy. He does what he's told."

The lawyer nodded but looked uncomfortable. "Might be a good idea to lock him up until they're gone," he said.

"He'll be fine," Master Meadows said. "Won't you, Isaac?"

"Yessir," I said through gritted teeth.

Master Meadows stood and walked around his desk. I remained frozen while Master Meadows walked the lawyer out of the office and out of the house. He had taken the money. Master Meadows had promised to free my family but had only delayed shipping them away until he could get his hands on the money.

I had to do something. I couldn't give up. I just didn't know what to do. My knees collapsed and I knelt on the floor, overcome with emotion. Master Meadows returned to the office, stepping over my legs as he walked to his desk chair.

"Be a man," Master Meadows said as he sat. "At least try."

I had failed. Too late I realized that I should have asked someone to buy them for me. But who to trust? I had no rights. Anyone else could have taken the money just as Master Meadows had.

"Don't ever try anything like that again," Master Meadows said. "You will do as you are told and nothing else. Understand? If you ever do anything behind my back like you did with that investment I will punish you so badly you'll beg for death. But I won't kill you."

I nodded, not trusting myself to speak. Somewhere, deep in the recesses of my mind I scrambled to come up with a way to yet save my family. I could not lose them.

"May I at least spend this last day with my family?" I asked. It was not easy to speak calmly.

Master Meadows considered. "There's some deadlines getting mighty close," he said, shaking his head. "Save yourself the emotional turmoil of sulking all day. Concentrate on your work."

"You were willing to allow me time last week when the plan was to send them away," I said. Arguing with Master Meadows was a risk I had to take.

"Well, see there," Master Meadows said. "You already had your farewells last week. Get to work."

Chapter Twenty-Eight

Hank

Though the Ninth Minnesota Regiment of Volunteers arrived late to the War Between the States we weren't new to battle. Dealing with the Sioux uprising had given us a lot of experience. A lot of mistakes were made there, more lives lost than needed to be.

An uneasy sense of normalcy returned to many refugees from the Redwood River Area, enough for some to return to their homestead and start rebuilding. A lot of people never returned. Dad and Hans returned to the farm in the spring. Dad was impatient to get crops in the ground. Mom followed them a few months later.

The girl and two boys we had rescued months ago from Walking Moon's band of Lakota were staying with my family and went out to the farm with my parents. There was still a search going on for their family but no luck.

The girl, Missy, gave birth to a little boy nine months after her abduction. She didn't want anything to do with the child that had resulted from her ordeal. That was to be expected since she was just a child herself and the baby had been a result of brutal rape.

Katherine made arrangements for the baby to be adopted by a couple up in St. Paul but before they arrived Catches Pebbles came looking for the baby. Katherine told me what happened because I wasn't there when Catches Pebbles visited her.

"Is he Walking Moon's child?" Catches Pebbles asked, staring down at the baby.

"Maybe," Katherine said. "He was one of them who raped her."

"I will take him," Catches Pebbles said, standing as if to take the baby that minute.

"Wait," Katherine said. "You can't just take him."

"Why not? He is unwanted by his mother. He is half Indian," Catches Pebbles said. "I will give him to my mother to replace her son."

In the end Katherine decided that maybe it was for the best for Catches Pebbles to take the child. Catches Pebbles left with the baby, heading west to Dakota Territory.

Caroline and Katherine stayed in Mankato. Katherine wanted to remain by me. They had nowhere to go in New Ulm anyway. Piotr decided to permanently remain in Mankato since his practice was doing so well. Many survivors were not ready to risk returning to their homesteads. Many never returned but new settlers arrived once the Lakota were driven away.

Wilhelm was released from the Union army just weeks before we got our new orders to head to Missouri. He arrived in Mankato a few days before I left. He had lost a leg and spent months recovering in a farm house down in South Carolina. I managed to see him before my company left Mankato.

He was half the man physically than he had been when he left New Ulm. My vibrant, hearty, warm brother had been replaced with a man who was little more than a skeleton with guarded eyes who seldom spoke. Caroline's eyes were red from crying but she didn't cry in front of her ailing husband.

"Wilhelm," I said in greeting, settling into the chair next to his bed.

My brother made no recognition of me. Caroline came into the room with a tray with a bowl of soup and sat on a chair on the other side of the single bed. She smiled warmly at Wilhelm, stroking the side of his face. Wilhelm blinked and turned to look at her.

"You need to eat, dear," Caroline said.

She filled a spoon and put it to his mouth. Wilhelm obediently opened his mouth. After a few spoonfuls he reached for the spoon. Caroline let him have the spoon and set the tray on his lap so that he could continue himself. She pushed him up, fluffing the pillows behind his back.

"The woman attending him pinned a note to his jacket," Caroline said, pushing the tray closer to his stomach to catch the soup dripping from the spoon as he ate. "There was a welt and bruise on his head. They thought he was dead at first so he was left to lie in the field for days. His leg became infected."

"Gangrene?" I said.

Caroline nodded. "It was left too long and festered," she said.

"Better to lose leg than arm," Wilhelm said.

"Yes, dear," Caroline said, stroking his head. She looked over at me. "He says that a lot."

"Wilhelm," I said softly.

Wilhelm turned his head and stared at me blankly. Somewhere a light flickered in his eyes. "Hank," he whispered. "Hank."

"It is good to see you, Wilhelm," I said.

"Wilhelm Hansohn," Wilhelm said, frowning. "James is down. James is down. I can see his eyes when I shot him. Coming right at me. Too late for James."

Wilhelm's hand holding the spoon trembled, shaking so badly that the soup splattered across the tray until the spoon was empty. Caroline took the spoon from him, having to pry his fingers from it. Wilhelm stared at me.

I reached over and took Wilhelm's hand in mine. "It's all right, Wilhelm," I said. "You're home now."

Wilhelm's hand lay limp in my grasp. "Home," Wilhelm whispered. He stared into my eyes. "Home. Is it over?"

"It's over, Wilhelm," I said.

"They killed James," Wilhelm said. His face grew wild looking and he shook his head back and forth. He looked like he was suffering intense pain. It was a pain invisible to anyone but him. "They killed Robert and Jenkins. Frank's head just exploded. I can still feel his brains on my face."

"You're home, Wilhelm," I said. During his sudden bout of terror he squeezed my hand so tightly that I worried bones were broken.

Wilhelm sighed. It was as if all the pain, the horror, and the trauma came out of him in that long exhalation of air. The spark in his eyes died as well. He slumped back against the stack of pillows holding him upright in the bed. He stopped squeezing my hand. Wilhelm stared up at the ceiling.

"Better the leg than the arm," he muttered as he shut down again.

"You're home, Wilhelm," I said, squeezing his hand.

Wilhelm did not say anything. He stared at the ceiling, his hand limp in my grasp. Caroline moved the tray from his lap to the small bedside table.

"We can finish your soup later," Caroline said, stroking Wilhelm's face.

There was no response from Wilhelm at Caroline's words or touch. Caroline stood, her skirts rustling with the movement. She gestured at me to follow her from the room. I grudgingly set Wilhelm's hand down on the bed. He did not move his hand from where I placed it. He did not move or register that he even noticed as Caroline and I left the bedroom.

"Will he ever be himself?" I asked Caroline once we were out of the room where Wilhelm lay staring at nothing.

Caroline shrugged. "The doctor said that with time he can improve," she said. She took my hand. "That was the most response he's given since being home. Thank you."

I pulled Caroline into my arms, comforting her as she shed the tears she had held back while in the room with Wilhelm. Her shoulders shook and she pressed her cheek against my shoulder. She had grown so thin that she felt so fragile in my arms.

"It will be all right, Caroline," I said. "He's only been home a few days. With time he will be all right."

Caroline nodded against my chest. She sniffled and straightened, pulling back, and holding her head high. "Thank you, Hank. I truly hope so," she said. "He is not the first one to come home shattered in the mind as well as the body. I shall do my best to find my husband in the stranger who returned."

"He's still there, Caroline," I said. "Down under that pain. You will find him and help him return."

"Lydia is afraid of him," Caroline said. "I tried to get her to go in to him, hoping that he would respond to her but she refuses. It's the nightmares. Every night he wakes up screaming. Scares all the kids."

"Maybe if I went in with her?" I thought out loud.

"No," Caroline said, shaking her head. "I won't force her. When she's ready."

"You sent word to the farm?" I asked.

Caroline nodded. "I suspect your mom will arrive the moment she receives the news," she said.

Katherine's chin trembled when I told her that we had received our orders, that we were heading south at last. She tried so hard to be brave about it that it hurt me even more to have to tell her farewell. Seeing Wilhelm scared her that I could return in the same condition. She didn't say so but it was clear to see. How could she not look at my brother and not worry that I suffer the same fate?

"Be careful," she whispered.

"I have Guhrt," I said, hoping to tease a smile from her before I left. "He won't let anything happen to me."

"Is he really the mystery angel on everyone's lips?" Katherine asked. "We still hear new stories of him, in the middle of everything the night New Ulm was attacked."

"He is," I said. "Do you still plan to stay in Mankato when I go?

You could go stay with Mom and Dad."

Katherine nodded. "I can't leave Caroline alone," she said. "It will be a while before Wilhelm will be ready to travel again."

"Maybe seeing familiar things will ease his troubled mind," I suggested.

"I will talk to her about it," Katherine said, looking down the hall in the direction of the bedroom where Wilhelm rested. Caroline was back in the room trying to get him to eat more soup.

"I would feel better having you closer to my parents," I said. "And I think it would do Wilhelm good as well."

"It is safer here," Katherine said. "But I will talk to Caroline."

Once again I had to say good-bye to my family. I was confident that I would only be separated from them for a few months.

We marched out of Mankato, heading for Fairfield, Iowa to get loaded into box cars. From Fairfield we headed to Galesburg, Illinois, packed into empty freight cars. From Galesburg we headed into Missouri. It was a lot of backtracking but still faster than making the trip on foot.

The horses made the trip with us in their own cars. Shadow was back at the farm with Dad. The horse I used was military issued along with my uniform and boots. He had been assigned to me when we went to Mankato, a well-built bay gelding who was steady if not quick on his feet. Most importantly, he remained calm during gunfire.

Though we were infantry, not cavalry, we had needed horses to fight the Lakota and somehow they had managed to come along with us when we headed south. I think Major Candon just included them in his shipping arrangements and no one thought to question it.

The trip south was long and boring. We sat about cleaning equipment, sleeping where we could find a spot out from underfoot, and talking. Billy Williamson was a talker. For some reason he had attached himself to me and I couldn't turn without bumping into him most days.

Billy was an all right fellow for the most part. He followed orders and was reliable. It was his nonstop talking that got under my skin. He was always talking about nothing. Just nothing. All day long.

It was tough to get mad at Billy though. He was always in good spirits without a mean bone in his body. Guhrt really liked Billy and encouraged his tales of nothing. Sometimes it seemed that Billy's rambling was music to Guhrt's soul. Billy would get going on one of his stories and Guhrt would smile and listen to every word, even encourage him by asking questions.

With the rattling of the train car it wasn't always easy to clean guns but we did it. Rule of thumb when relying on a weapon, clean it and clean it some more. Guhrt was a master at tearing a gun down and assembling it again quicker than most could even get it taken apart. Billy was even faster than Guhrt. Billy could tear a gun down, polish it, and assemble it again faster than Guhrt could tear down and assemble.

So we sat about in the rattling train car as it clanked along the rail lines, heading from Minnesota to Missouri after a year's delay. Missouri was a federal state so we weren't really heading into The South but more battles had already been fought in Missouri than any other state.

Johnson was watching Billy clean his gun. Billy had laid out a rectangle of leather to keep pins and gun parts from rolling away and slipping into cracks in the car's floor from the vibration. "Plum amazes me every time," Johnson said, shaking his head as he watched Billy's hands fly through the motions.

"My mom's cousin's brother's wife could do it faster than me with one arm tied behind her back," Billy said. "She could spit farther than a mule as well." He chuckled. "Old Millie wasn't much to look at but she could sure whip your butt."

"Wait," Johnson said, cocking his head as he pondered Billy's words. "Wouldn't that just be your mom's cousin's wife?"

"Old Lizzy?" Billy said. He had not stopped working as he talked and he slid the barrel into the stock in one sure movement. "Nah. Old Lizzy shot a bear once and the recoil put her on her backside. Never touched a gun after that. Used a hatchet to chase the bears away."

"No," Johnson said. "You said your mom's cousin's brother's wife. The brother would be the mom's cousin so it would just be your mom's cousin's wife."

"Well, see, the thing is, I got a complicated family," Billy said. "My mom has three brothers and four sisters but two of the brothers were from a former marriage so they have different moms and dads. One of the sisters is really an aunt even though she's younger than my mom but her folks were killed in a steamboat accident."

"Well if she's an aunt she's not a cousin," Johnson said.

"Well, they have the same mom but her dad is also her dad," Billy said.

"Who's dad?" Lechemann asked. Billy and Johnson had gained an audience. Even those napping opened one eye as they listened.

"My mom and her sister have the same dad," Billy said.

"That's often how it works," Guhrt said with a grin.

"Exactly," Billy said.

"Then how can she be an aunt to your mom if she's a sister?" Lechemann asked.

"Exactly!" Johnson said.

"Her mom was my mom's sister," Billy said.

"So she was her cousin?" someone else piped up. It was Bederman, napping in the corner until the conversation started. He leaned up one elbow and faced Billy.

"Wait," Johnson said, holding up a hand. "What about the cousin's brother's wife?"

"Old Millie?" Billy said as he rolled up his leather into a roll and tied the attached cords around it to hold it into a roll. "She's still alive and kicking. Must be ninety if she's a day."

The train engines slowed. The train whistle sounded, long and piercing, three times, a pause, and another long burst. The rail car swayed and rattled then it's connecting hitch slammed into the car in front of its hitch with a bang. There was a long series of bangs as the cars came to a stop.

Lechemann slid open the car door and we peered out. Major Candon walked beside the train, heading back from the engine. "Stretch your legs, boys," Major Candon said. "Half an hour and we're on the move again."

"Better to get back to the car in twenty," I said as everyone moved to the door.

I had somehow become the squad leader. The men had chosen me several months ago. The position came with a nominal bump in pay, which gave me more wages to send home. Guhrt slung his rifle over his shoulder and jumped across the gap to the platform. We were in one of the cars near the engine. The platform extended to the car behind ours then stopped. The cars beyond that car had a longer drop to the ground so the men were slower at exiting their cars.

Guhrt headed to the open area beyond the train station with Billy trotting at his heels, ducking through a split rail fence surrounding the field. They loped through the tall grasses and vanished into the tree line. A cow in the field stood watching them as it munched on grass.

Major Candon came up to me, having watched Guhrt and Billy cross the field. "He better not scavenge any of the locals' livestock," Major Candon said to me.

"He knows better, sir," I said.

Major Candon had a view of the countryside from his car. The officers had a train car with upholstered benches and windows. "Lots of farms in the area," Major Candon said. "Not much free land."

"He's stretching his legs, sir," I said. "If he only sees cows and pigs then he'll return empty handed."

"Good man," Major Candon said, gaze where Guhrt and Billy

had vanished. "Guhrt's a good soldier."

The rest of us wandered in the opposite direction, walking through the small town. The sign at the station had said Macon City. The townspeople stared at us.

"I thought Missouri was a Federal state," I said to Major Candon, feeling uncomfortable with the cold reception we were getting.

"They're worried our arrival could mean fighting coming to their town," Major Candon said. "There was a battle just north of here not too long ago."

Word must have spread that we were just passing through. Eventually several women appeared with pitchers of cold, clean water. Our men appreciated the water and thanked the women profusely. I accepted a ladle of water in appreciation. It was as sweet as nectar.

Twenty minutes passed quickly and we headed back to the train, mingling next to the tracks. I kept an eye out for Guhrt and Billy as the minutes steadily ticked away. With only two minutes to spare they came into sight, loping across the field with the cow. They reached the train just as the whistle sounded to signal to board.

"Cut it close there," I said as we climbed back inside the stuffy box car.

Guhrt grinned. "Plenty of time to spare," he said.

The train whistle sounded again and the conductor walked past our car, heading for the engine after checking the train. The box car shuddered and clanged as the engine started out again. We left the door open for the air and spotted the man in coveralls standing at the switch. He raised his hand in a wave as we passed him. The train picked up speed.

"What'd ya get?" Johnson asked Guhrt.

Guhrt emptied his canvas bag. Three frogs hopped away and there was a mad scramble to catch them. In addition to the frogs there was a squirrel and a handful of speckled eggs, too small to be from a chicken.

"I shouldn't have taken the squirrel," Guhrt said, staring at the dead squirrel. "No way of cooking it."

"You'll eat raw frogs though?" someone asked.

"Sure," Guhrt said. "The eggs taste mighty sweet straight out of the shell."

"Kind of late in the year for eggs," Lechemann said, studying the eggs dubiously.

"I know," Guhrt said. "Lucky find." Guhrt enjoyed his snack of frog legs and bird eggs without anyone else taking up his offer to share.

Billy decided that it was a shame to waste the squirrel and decided to build a fire in the box car to roast it. While Guhrt skinned the squirrel Billy rummaged through his belongings and found a tin can of beans. He opened the can, leaving the lid attached by not cutting about an inch along the top and passed it around. Everyone took a bite to help empty the can.

Once the can was empty he stuffed it with straw from the floor and used his knife to shave off wood from the wall of the box car. He stuffed the squirrel meat inside the can, piling more straw and wood shavings on top then lit it with a match. Once smoke started trailing out of the can he pushed the lid down.

That was a strange smell coming out that can for almost an hour. Mixed in with the scent of burning bean juice, straw, and wood was the undeniable scent of cooking meat. We all watched in fascination. When the smoke had dissipated and Billy decided it had been enough time he dumped the contents of the can onto the floor, licking his burnt fingers.

The squirrel flesh was charred on the outside and a roaring red on the inside. Billy picked through the pile of burnt lumps for the pieces of squirrel meat. He offered up pieces of the scorched squirrel but there were no takers, not even Guhrt.

The third piece he bit into he spit back out. "Wood," he

muttered, tossing the piece aside. "Now my cousin's uncle's cousin would eat charred wood but I never acquired a fondness for it myself."

There was a scorched ring on the box car floor where the tin can had sat and less than an hour after eating his scorched, rare squirrel Billy ran to the car door, pulled it open enough for him to fit through, and squatted with his rear end hanging out. He was lucky he didn't fall out with all the rattling and banging the train car was doing.

Macon City was the last stop before St. Louis. The train had to stop several times to fill with water for the steam engine but we stayed inside our cars during those short stops. As we neared our destination a somber unease settled over the occupants of the rail car. Twice we passed areas that clearly appeared to have seen conflict.

Trampled fields had not been replanted. Scorch marks were visible on a partial rock wall in front of a burnt house. The battles had not been recent but recent enough to leave a lingering imprint on the countryside. The sight had a sobering effect on all of us in that box car. Even Billy was quiet.

Chapter Twenty-Nine

It was the beginning of October of 1863 when we arrived in St. Louis. We arrived in St. Louis hungry and tired. We lined up in the mess hall and got served cold beans and half a loaf of stale breach each. Once we were done eating we settled into our new temporary barracks.

Our orders were to guard the railroads in Missouri. Sherman was dependent on supplies coming in on the rail lines from the north and west while he was busy destroying the rail lines of the south and east.

Gradually Company C and Company K headed west through Missouri, providing security for the rail line running from St. Louis to Jefferson City, where we were to join up with the Missouri boys.

As we followed the rail line from St. Louis we saw several plantations with a lot of black farm hands. The conditions those poor souls endured struck me hard. We had camped within sight of one such plantation and witnessed the feeding of the children of those farm hands.

A man approached a series of wood troughs that at first glance had looked to be feed troughs for pigs. The man carried a bucket of some watery gruel which he poured into the troughs. Those poor little beings went down on their knees and scooped up the gruel with their hands. Some children just put their faces in the wood troughs and ate.

Guhrt stood next to me, staring at the scene with a face gone hard as stone. "If I hadn't seen it myself I'd never have believed such a thing," he said, spitting to the side.

Several of our companions had gathered around us, staring in open shock. The man with the bucket stopped and looked back at us for a moment. His attention turned to a small boy who had not joined his fellow children to the troughs. He kicked the boy then walked away.

Guhrt and Lechemann both took a step forward. "Don't," Major Candon said, stopping them in their tracks.

It was difficult to watch and not do something. My insides twisted at seeing those children being treated worse than animals. "How can anyone treat a human being like that?" I asked, gaze locked on the children struggling to get their share of gruel from the troughs.

"We can't interfere," Major Candon said. He kept his back to the scene.

"I cannot stand by and do nothing," Guhrt said, looking down at Major Candon.

"But you will," Major Candon said. "Break camp. We're headed west again."

"That boy is going to die if someone doesn't help him," I said, watching the small boy the man had kicked. He was just sitting there, bereft of enough energy to even crawl to the wood feed troughs.

"We have orders," Major Candon reminded us, looking at each man standing there with anger and disgust in our hearts. "The only way to save those poor souls is by winning this war. That's our job. To win this war."

There was a lot of grumbling around me as everyone watched that boy and the children being treated like animals. Some men turned away, unable to watch. Many men clenched their hands into fists at their side, unable to look away, yet unable to do anything to help.

I could not look away. Every nerve in my body screamed to go to those children, to save that little boy. An older boy crawled over to the boy I had my gaze on and held out his hand, cupped and palm up.

The older boy put his hand up to the weak boy, pushing the boy's head back and pouring some of the watered down gruel into the little boy's mouth. He swallowed some of it but most of it dripped down the sides of his mouth.

Walking away was the most difficult thing I'd ever done. We had our orders though. Not only were we not to interfere but we had a job to do. I looked back at Guhrt who was still standing there watching the plantation yard.

Black men and women were heading out into the fields, some with baskets in their arms, some with large sacks hanging from their necks, and some with hoes, walking right past the children without even looking at them. A black man with a whip followed them, occasionally swinging the whip to crack it.

"How can they ignore them?" Guhrt asked.

"I suspect they have no choice," I said. "We have to go, Guhrt."

"I hated killing those Lakota," Guhrt said, watching the field hands move out over the fields. "I don't like to talk about it because it made me feel dirty inside. Even though I knew I was saving the lives of those settlers, pulling the trigger and knowing that I ended a man's life was a terrible burden. But that man there, that one who kicked that little starving boy, him I want to kill."

I hadn't killed anyone. There had been skirmishes between soldiers and Lakota in other companies where men had died. The few groups of Lakota my company had hunted down had surrendered without struggle. Most of our time was spent guarding prisoners and then guarding the Lakota families being removed from the agency.

Eventually Guhrt managed to control his desire to go across the fields to the plantation yard and turned his back on the children with regret. We broke camp and headed west, following the rail line.

We saw more plantations but they were too far away from the

rail lines to see much more than black people out in the fields with the ever present whip holder. Most often the man wielding the whip was black and not white. He would crack that whip over the bent backs of those field hands as if he was earning a penny for every snap.

A few days later we set up camp by a river. It was next to a ford so the bank was flat and graveled with river stone. There was a bend in the river to the north of our camp, blocking the view upriver. Major Candon sent a few of us up to scout out the area around the bend.

Guhrt and Billy ducked into the trees as soon as we were out of sight of the camp. Johnson and I kept walking, looking for any sign of anyone else in the area. Food was always in shortage and we all appreciated Guhrt's finds, even if it was a frog. Frog legs were edible when cooked over a fire.

Across the river there was movement. The leaves of a tree branch shook. Johnson and I both crouched and eyed the trees where there had been movement. It could be a person or an animal. I couldn't see anyone and wondered for a moment if I was jumping at shadows. A face appeared between a tree and a shrub. He was wearing a gray cap and gray jacket.

We all stared at each other in silence for several heartbeats. I raised my rifle, hand trembling as I tried to find the trigger. The man in gray stepped out from the trees onto the river bank, hands out to his sides. I kept my rifle pointed at him but kept my finger well away from the trigger. I didn't dare take my eyes off the Rebel to see if Johnson had also raised his gun. I figured he had.

The man in gray looked back at us with eyes as wide as saucers. The river was too wide to cross. He couldn't reach us and we couldn't reach him. After a moment of staring at us he ducked back into the trees and vanished.

"Think he was a deserter or a scout?" Johnson asked, lowering his rifle.

I shook my head. My heart was pounding. I lowered my rifle, studying the opposite bank of the river. There was no movement or sign of anyone there. Without discussion Johnson and I both stood and hurried back in the direction of the camp near the ford, keeping a watchful eye on the opposite bank the whole time.

We reported to Master Candon what we had seen and he sent out a dozen men on horseback to investigate, along with six of us to search along the river bank on the side where the Rebel had been. We forded the river and walked along the opposite shore, passing the spot where we had spotted the man.

There was no sign of any hidden Rebel force. Satisfied that he had been alone we headed back to camp. The riders had returned, also reporting no sign of any Rebels. Guhrt and Billy returned with three rabbits each. Our company had rabbit stew for dinner that night. A few of us lucky ones even found a piece of meat in our bowl of stew.

When I settled down on my bedroll that night I couldn't fall asleep though my body craved sleep. Facing that Rebel across the river had been the most terrifying experience of my life. It wasn't that he would harm me that scared me. It was facing the possibility of having to shoot him that scared me.

Until that day I hadn't given much thought to shooting a man. The idea was some far away future that I hadn't dwelled on, just a matter of killing the enemy. Facing that man, who was as scared of us as we were of him, had brought to mind that the enemy was just some wide-eyed man wearing different colored clothes.

We arrived in Jefferson City in early November. Back home winter would have been full upon us but down in Missouri it was not even cold yet. In fact, it was even hot some days.

There were more dark faces in Jefferson City than there had been in St. Louis. The townspeople treated us all right. Not as welcoming as they had been in St. Louis but not interfering with us in any way. Once again, our presence stirred uncertainty. For the most part they chose to just pretend we weren't even there.

Instead of only walking or riding the rail lines we were now also to board trains traveling west and riding them back. We were to be headquartered in Jefferson City for a few weeks while we kept the Rebels away from the rail lines. There had been several incidents where Rebels had managed to steal trains and sabotage rails so it was a serious task. Our two companies had joined up with the Missouri boys.

At the start of the day I assigned the men who would ride the trains out and which trains. I'd been promoted again. This time it wasn't just a vote of the men as to who they wanted as leader. I was a lieutenant now. Every morning I was to send out the men on my list. I made a point to mix up the duties so that the men didn't get stale sitting on a train day in and day out.

I was at the train station on the first day after we'd arrived in Jefferson City, trying to make sense of the chaos. We'd missed the first train out because our watches were set to a different time than it was in Jefferson City and the train was running on Chicago time. I had a mob of men in blue mingling about the train station and a train gone from the station without an escort.

After hours of going through my lists and assigning men to the next scheduled trains I had managed to work through the confusion and gotten everything straightened out.

It was the first time I had really looked up from my stack of papers, my notes scribbled all over them, when I noticed the frail, elderly black woman sitting on a bench next to the train station. At least a dozen benches were located near the station building, stretching out along the sidewalk in front of the grassy lot next to the station building.

All the benches were the same, a slatted seat with two boards attached at the rear for a back rest. She was sitting on the bench farthest from the station, out in the direct sun, when there were several empty benches under the shade of the canopy extending from the building over the station's platform.

"Excuse me, ma'am," I said, taking off my hat and bowing my head. "But there's benches in the shade right there. Can I help you to one of them?"

The woman looked up at me. Her eyes were rheumy and her nose almost as large as her face. Her ears drooped down to the collar of her dress. Her fingers were wrapped around the cared wood ball head at the top of her cane. "You talk funny," she said.

"Yes, ma'am," I said, nodding. "That's sun's mighty warm even if it should be winter."

She licked her two remaining front teeth, her head bobbing as she studied me. "Them's white benches. I'm not white."

"But they're in the shade," I said. "Surely it's all right for you to get out of the sun."

"Been in the sun all my life," she said. "Where you from?"

"Minnesota," I said.

She mouthed the word. "Never heard of it," she said. "Is that in the country?"

"Up north, ma'am," I said.

She smiled. "I made it ninety-five years before a white man called me ma'am and you gone and done it three times now," she said. She reached out and patted the back of my hand with her hand. She had a cold hand. "You're a good boy. Let me be now."

"Yes, ma'am," I said. Short of picking her up and moving her there wasn't much more I could do.

I kept an eye on her between rounding up the next batch of riders. I didn't see the heavyset black woman approach the bench but I saw the two of them walking away. The frail, old woman had her arm wrapped around her companion's elbow, leaning quite heavily on the other woman. They walked very slowly. A shuffling step, a pause, and another shuffling step. I was relieved that she was not alone.

The next morning things went more smoothly. I had made a

timetable to keep track of the different times the train ran on and adjusted my watch to match the time in Jefferson City. The first train pulled out with its escort of blue uniformed men aboard.

A tall, black man in a cotton suit hurried toward the train station. He caught my eye. First, he was as tall as Guhrt. Second, he was the most well-kept man I had seen since leaving home black or white. His hair was cropped short to his head. His shoes had a shine and his jacket did not have a wrinkle. He glanced up at me as he walked by but was quick to avert his gaze.

I looked down at my own dusty jacket as I stroked the facial hair covering my chin. There was no reason not to present a better image. The train station clerk stared at me when I asked him where I could find a laundry.

"Over on Becker Street, I guess," the man said.

"Becker Street?" I asked, hoping for more information.

"Yes, Becker Street," the man said. He turned and walked away from the ticket window.

The immaculate black man was walking towards the train station again, going back in the direction he had come from, carrying two leather bound ledgers tucked under his armpit.

"Excuse me, sir," I said, stepping in his path. He glanced behind him, confused. "You there, with the books," I said. He looked up at me in surprise.

"Me, sir?" he asked in confusion.

I smiled. "Yes, you," I said. "Can you tell me where Becker Street is?"

"Yes, sir," he said. He twisted and pointed slightly behind him to the left. "Four blocks east and you'll be on it, sir."

"Thank you," I said. I turned and walked away. I was thinking our whole company could use some clothes laundering.

There was a rhythm to the town that became apparent as the days passed. Our arrival had stirred things up but eventually the routines settled back to normal. The station clerk only stayed around the ticket window fifteen minutes before a train was due and vanished ten minutes after a train left. Where he went was hard to say. Maybe he was sleeping back in the bowels of the building.

The same tall young black man walked past every morning empty handed then passed through again seventeen minutes later with his leather bound ledgers. At the end of the day he reversed his path, going past carrying his ledgers and seventeen minutes later heading back the way he came empty handed.

Every day at noon a man with bushy whiskers and eyes so recessed his bushy eyebrows almost hid the eyes came and stood on the station platform, watching us. He never said a word, just stood and watched us. Soot soiled his bare shirt sleeves and oil had stained his denim pants. At first I thought he was a train mechanic or car man but he never approached a train in my sight.

Early in the afternoon on days it wasn't raining the same frail woman escorted by her heavyset companion slowly made her way to the last bench in the row of benches extending from the train station. The fragile woman sat while her companion went off on errands, perhaps to visit a family member or friend. Some days the companion carried parcels when she returned to collect the feisty old woman but as often as not she returned to the bench bare handed.

The second time I saw that little old woman sitting in the beating sun I was not the only one bothered by the sight. I noticed Pete Mason and Jim Anderson, both in Company C, studying the bench after she left. I walked over to see what they were up to.

"An awning," Jim said, running his hands down where the back rest connected to the seat. "It's a firm holding. Can support the weight of something simple."

"Canvas and barrel staves," I said, thinking about it. Pete and Jim both looked up at me in surprise, not having noticed me approach. "See what you can do," I said, leaving them to the task.

They found some curved barrel staves and lashed them to the ends of the bench. Pete draped a piece of oiled canvas over the curved wood staves while Jim lashed it firmly in place. The little old black woman and her dark skinned companion arrived while I was looking over their work. Jim was still lashing the canvas to the staves. The bench was perfectly shaded from the afternoon sun.

The two men nodded their heads at the old woman then trotted over to the waiting train when the whistle blew. It was ready to depart and they had to board and take their stations.

The frail old woman stared at the bench with its awning, looking at me thoughtfully before sitting. She leaned back on the backrest, looking up and around at the canvas curved over the bench. Guhrt's head would have brushed the canvas but she was so small and slight that she had plenty of room and the awning did not block the view she enjoyed from her afternoon seat.

She smiled. Her smile turned into a grin. "Mighty fine," she said to me. "Mighty fine indeed."

The ticket clerk appeared. He rushed to the bench, sweat beading on his balding head. "What are you doing?" he yelled. He was looking at the black woman sitting on the bench. "How dare you interfere with railroad property?"

He reached for the awning, his intention to tear it down clear. I stepped between him and the bench. "Let it be," I said. "You touch it and I'll break your fingers."

The man took a step back, sputtering. "Well, I, I never," he said. "She's not even a customer."

"This bench is now under Union protection," I said. "You interfere and I'll have you arrested." I looked over at the platform and spotted William Mason, Pete's brother. "Mason!"

Mason trotted over to me. He saluted. "Yes, sir."

"I want you to guard this bench," I said. "If anyone interferes with this awning, you shoot him. Understood?"

"Yes, sir," Mason said without batting an eye. He promptly took a station next to the bench, staring straight ahead.

The ticket clerk glared at me. He licked his lips. "It's a bench," he muttered.

"Is it worth your life?" I asked.

The man backed away then turned and hurried back to his ticket window. Mason relaxed once the clerk was gone. "Do I really have to stay here?" he asked.

"Just keep an eye out in case he returns," I said.

The heavyset woman had stood nearby watching the whole episode with wide eyes. "Would ya'all really shoot him?"

"Only if he touches the awning," I said.

The fragile old woman chuckled. Then she laughed. She laughed so hard that tears ran down her face. "I'm so glad I lived so long so I could see that," she said. "Young man, you are a wonder."

"Don't encourage him, Lisbett," the heavyset woman scolded the old woman. "He's going to bring trouble on our heads."

"Anyone bothers you, just tell me," I said. I tipped my hat and went back to my duties.

The awning remained intact the entire time we were stationed in Jefferson City. The ticket clerk was not so eager to face two companies of Union soldiers as he was ready to bully a ninety-five year old woman.

Chapter Thirty

Guhrt, Billy, Lechemann, Mason, and I were walking from the barracks to the train station after eating lunch at the mess hall. There was a lot of talk of how General Sherman was making it his sole mission to destroy the rail lines over in Alabama and Georgia. Well, his mission seemed to be to destroy any lines in a Rebel state.

"Sherman's got a thing for railroads," Guhrt said

The statement made everyone laugh. "All we gotta do is keep these tracks in one piece while he's out blowing up the rest," Lecheman said. There was more laughter.

Guhrt and I realized at the same time that there was someone walking behind us. I realized that we were blocking the whole sidewalk, walking abreast as we were. The man with the ledgers was walking behind us, staring down at the sidewalk in front of his feet and almost stepped right into us when we suddenly stopped. Startled, he looked up and stepped back, intending to go around us.

"He looks just like Edward Patrice back in Mankato," Billy said, staring at the black man behind us. "The smithy."

"He does!" Guhrt said, eyes widening. He turned to me. "Even their hair is the same, all curly. Except Edward's is blonde. Do you think that means Edward is a negro?"

"And Edward Patrice has arms the size of Lechemann's legs," Billy said. "And Edward Patrice has missing teeth. His two front ones. Someone said a mule kicked him. Right in the face. Knocked out the top two. That's because they stuck out over his lower lip. Kinda hard to miss 'em when they stick out like that. Looked like a rabbit. When he had those teeth. Which he doesn't anymore."

"I think it means that we're all men of God and the color of our skin doesn't make us more or less than our neighbor," I said. Several of the other men nodded thoughtfully. I was uncomfortable talking about the man as if he wasn't even there when he was right there. I looked at the pleasant, well-groomed man. "Are we blocking the sidewalk, sir?"

"Excuse me, sir," he said, ducking his head and averting his gaze. "I was just thinking hard. Don't pay no never mind to me. I'll be out of your way."

He hurried around us and continued on his way. We resumed walking, trailing him now, almost keeping pace. We continued our banter as we strode along the sidewalk toward the train station. Once we reached the platform we stopped while he continued walking.

I turned slightly and watched the young man hurrying along his way. "Can you feel it, Guhrt?" I asked.

Guhrt nodded. "That's a man with a heavy burden on his shoulders," Guhrt said.

"Lots of that going on down here," Lechemann said.

"My mother's brother's son kinda looks like Edward Patrice," Billy said. "I wonder if he's a negro, too."

"How do you even know what you're talking about?" Mason asked, eyeing Billy with suspicion. "You're just making it up. Aren't you?"

The rest of us groaned, knowing what was coming. Billy proceeded to explain to Mason in detail his complicated family situation. The rest of us hurried out of ear shot, scattering in all directions to escape, leaving Mason trapped with Billy filling his head with how his mother's brother was not his uncle by way of marriage to a second cousin. I felt bad for Mason but he brought it on himself.

Only a day later the ledger man walked through the train station. I was trying to calculate the time variance between Jefferson City and Memphis, which was where the next train was coming from, when I looked up and saw him. He took a deep breath and slowed his steps as he neared me. The soles of his shoes actually scraped the ground as he dragged his feet slower and slower.

I watched him approach me, curious. I cocked my head slightly, wondering what he was about. It looked like he was trying to work up the courage to talk to me. I watched and waited, making no move to startle him away.

Suddenly he picked up his feet and hurried past me with long, ground-eating strides. He had made the decision to not approach me. I nodded my head at him in greeting as he passed then turned back to the men waiting for instructions.

The boys from Missouri Regiment didn't like the way we were going about things so there were some changes made. First off, we started splitting into smaller groups and instead of riding the trains we were to be stationed at various locations along the rail line.

In general there wasn't a lot of conflict with the Missouri companies but there were quite a bit of differences of opinion, even in interpreting orders. I'm not saying that Minnesotans are so much smarter than the boys down south but those southern men sure did things in a way that was not efficient or even the best way of doing it, in my opinion.

More Union soldiers came into Jefferson City and they went out almost as soon as they came in. Major Bloom of the Missouri Volunteers took over assigning the men along the rail line. He was an arrogant ass and even his own men didn't like him all that much. Twice he put down the same group of men for two different locations.

When his aide pointed out the error the major got all huffy. "If these men don't know they can't be in two places at the same time it's their problem," he said.

We were getting ready to ship out in two days, for guard and garrison duty in some small town forty miles west of Jefferson City and had no other duties until that time. Several of us were down at the train station, biding our time, when two armed men escorted a black woman with several children onto the train's platform.

The conductor and ticket clerk were having a heated discussion with the armed men, apparently over where they would be seated and that they were armed. The men were both gray-haired with dried, wrinkled leather for skin. The woman was crying and hugging her youngest child while the other children clutched her skirts.

There was fear in those faces. Dust kicked up from all the activity at the station coated their hair and faces. Tears streaked that dust. From a distance it looked like their faces were melting.

"What's going on?" Guhrt said, standing up straighter.

"They're taking them to Kentucky," Major Bloom's aide said. "Putting 'em on the auction."

"Selling them?" Billy asked. He shook his head. "Mighty strange. Selling people. I never thought about buying someone."

I watched the family. The woman didn't even seem to be aware of her surroundings. She stood with her head hanging, clutching the small child so tightly that the little girl squirmed in her grasp.

"Will they be sold together?" I asked.

The aide shook his head. I can't remember his name. Fair enough fellow. I just can't remember his name. John or James, most likely.

"Most likely not," the aide said, watching the family with their escort along with the rest of us, not left unaffected any less than us.

The mother was gripping her children so tightly because she knew that it wouldn't be long before her babies would be ripped away, likely never for her to see her children again. The oldest boy stood with his head high and his shoulders straight. His arms were filled with several clothe wrapped bundles. The next oldest boy also held a bundle with one hand and clutched his mother's skirts with the other hand.

For a moment I imagined Katherine and my children. Though I was away from my children I knew I would return to them. I knew that they were with their mother. I knew that they were surrounded by family who loved them and would care for them. Imagining losing my children caused a band of pain to tighten around my chest.

I finally understood my mother's pain in losing her baby girl all those years ago. Even though she had the rest of her children to care for, the pain of losing her child had seared her to the soul, a wound that she may never have recovered from. She may have had bouts of keeping the demons at bay sober but she always returned to that bottled form of dilution of her pain. All those years and the pain never left her.

"How much must we see while we are able to do nothing?" Guhrt muttered, gaze locked on that poor family's misery.

An agreement was reached between the conductor and the armed men and the family with its escort left the platform, heading for the rail car farthest to the end. One of the armed men opened the box car and set his rifle inside then climbed up inside. He leaned down and took the hands of the woman while the other armed man hoisted her up, still holding his rifle. The oldest boy climbed up and pulled his brother up while the man still on the ground picked up each child and set him or her inside the box car.

Except for the fine dust and soot kicked up around the train, that family was the picture of cleanliness and health. Their limbs were long and straight, their eyes clear and alert. That was a healthy group of people, well-tended and well-cared for. I wondered how long before those little children were dependent on eating watery gruel from a pig trough.

Major Bloom was walking our way. "Lieutenant," Major Bloom snapped without stopping. His aide fell into step beside him.

Seeing the slave family boarding the train on the way to be sold had a somber effect on all of us. Even Billy was quiet for a while. He kicked the dirt. "Pointing guns at children," he muttered, shaking his head before wandering away.

I took a few steps along the platform in the general direction of the end of the train, glancing off and on at that box car. There was no sign that there was even anyone in there. If I hadn't seen them go in there I wouldn't know they were there. But I did know they were there. It just wasn't right to stand by and do nothing but we had our orders.

The ledger man approached the train station. He was running. I was so used to seeing him in the morning and end of day that I glanced up at the big clock on the train station in surprise, thinking the day had somehow already passed.

The clock showed two minutes before two o'clock. I looked back at the ledger man. The man was running right to me. I came to full attention in surprise. There was no doubt that I was that man's destination. The train whistle sounded, warning any passengers not yet boarded that the train was heading out in just a few minutes.

Chapter Thirty-One

Isaac

I managed to get through the day, though my brain was in a fog. I did not pass the train station to the tannery when I returned the ledgers and I did not go out of my way to do so. I hurried home to be with my family.

We did not sleep all night, unwilling to lose those precious moments we had left. Sam managed to stay awake but the smaller children fell asleep one by one. We were all on the big bed, huddled together in a clump of entwined arms and legs. Tildy had packed a spare set of clothes for everyone but that was all they'd be taking.

"You can write to me," I said, stroking Tildy's hand. "Tell me where you're at. Write more than once, just in case."

"How am I gonna send you a letter?" Tildy asked. "You think my new owner will give me paper and pen and a stamp?"

"I'll be right back," I said, sliding gently out of the tangle of arms and legs.

I went into the office and took two envelopes and two pieces of paper. Master Meadows did keep stamps at the house. They were on my desk since I did all the mail. I put a stamp on each envelope and addressed the envelopes to make sure they were addressed properly so they'd be delivered all right.

When I got back to our cabin I realized that I should have done the same for Sam but it was too late to go back for more envelopes and Master Meadows might notice four stamps missing even if he wouldn't think much of two stamps gone. I gave Tildy one of the envelopes and Sam the other.

"We'll be together again," I said.

Tildy stroked the side of my face, studying my features as if to commit every nuance to memory. "I hope so," she whispered. She did not sound as though she believed that to be so.

I did not go into the office that next morning. Master Meadows came looking for me. "I thought I told you to work as normal," he said from the doorway.

"It's my last hours with my family," I said.

"That's no reason for your laziness, boy," he said in a hard voice. "You think you're more important than my business? More important than my employees? Get to work."

Reluctantly I kissed Tildy farewell, gave each of the children a long hug and kiss. I was crying like a baby by the time I held Sam in my arms. I had failed to protect them. I had failed to save them. I pulled Tildy into my arms again, holding her tight. She trembled in my embrace.

"I will find you," I whispered in her ear. Tildy nodded, crying too hard to speak.

Master Meadows grew impatient and barked my name. I followed Master Meadows into the house and down the hall to the office. The morning crawled. I stared at the papers on the desk in front of me, unable to see the writing for the tears blurring my vision. I heard the voices of the men arrived to escort my family to Kentucky.

Master Meadows left the office without a word. I stayed at my desk though I wanted to jump up and race out of the room. How could I sit at my desk in that room and do nothing while my family was taken away? Yet I sat there, trying desperately to think of a way to save them still.

I had to believe that the North would win and President Lincoln would free all the slaves and not just the ones in the Rebel states.

They would be safe. They would be safe until I could find them.

Fear outweighed my positive thoughts. I imagined my poor Arice being beaten for her moods. I imagined my sunny Shonny's spirit broken, starved and whipped until she was a shadow of herself. Benji sold to a plantation where he was worked in the fields from dawn to dusk. Sam as well. Will sold to someone like Rockforque.

At the noon hour I went to the kitchen for lunch. The servant woman the Meadows had hired to replace their slaves was standing at the stove and looked up at me in surprise. "What are you doing in here?" she asked.

"I am here for my lunch, ma'am," I said, head down.

"No one told me about feeding no blackie," she said. "You get on out of here."

"Yes, ma'am," I said, backing out of the kitchen. I almost bumped into Mistress Meadows coming into the kitchen, my attention on the woman glaring at me with a ladle raised as if to defend herself from me.

"What's going on here?" Mistress Meadows said, ducking around me before I could bump into her.

"You said you were selling all your blackies," the woman said, scowling at Mistress Meadows.

"All but him," Mistress Meadows said. "And old Lucas in the stables."

"Well, I don't want him in my kitchen," the woman said, chin rising.

"He has to eat," Mistress Meadows said, startled. She strode all the way into the room, looking at what was cooking on the stove. "Give him some soup and a hunk of that bread."

"And where is he going to eat that?" the woman asked.

"At the table," Mistress Meadows said, gesturing to the planked kitchen table across the room. "That's what it's for."

The woman's eyes narrowed but she scooped a ladle of the soup from the pot simmering on the stove and dumped it into a bowl. She tore a chunk of bread off a loaf and dropped it into the bowl right on the soup. She stepped back.

"Go ahead," she said to me. "Take it. You expect me to serve you, too?"

Reluctantly I stepped close enough to the woman to snatch the bowl. I backed away from her and went to the table. She had not given me a spoon but I was not about to ask her for one or get one for myself from the rack next to the stove. I ate the soggy bread and drank the soup directly from the bowl.

Mistress Meadows was having a heated discussion with the hired servant. I ate as quick as I could and escaped. I went to the cabin behind the house. It was empty. They were gone. The children's pallets were neatly stacked against the wall. I stood in the cabin for a long time, thinking and thinking.

"You need to ask for help sometimes," Lisbett had said.

It was a risk. There was something about those men, though. They were different. If I asked him for help and he said no I didn't think he would turn me in. It was my only chance left. I had to risk it. I slid my hand under the mattress and my fingers touched the canvas bag I kept there. I pulled the bag out from under the mattress.

I didn't know what would happen in the hours ahead but if I was captured with the canvas bag it would be found and taken but I couldn't leave it in the cabin or it would be found and taken. I took out the key and put it on a piece of string around my neck, under my shirt.

Lucas was sitting in one of the stalls in the stable. He looked up at me when I entered the stable. "They're gone?" he asked.

I nodded. Lucas' shoulders shook and he dropped his head. His gnarled hands clutched a bridle strap.

"I need your help, Lucas," I said. I pressed the canvas bag in his hands. "Can you guard that for me until I come back?"

Lucas looked up at me. His eyes were red. "You gonna do something stupid?" he asked.

"Maybe," I said.

He nodded. "I'll watch this for you," he said. "I always knew you'd eventually do something stupid. 'Bout time."

Master Meadows had not returned to the office. I glanced at the clock on his desk. The train was scheduled to leave at two o'clock and it was just past one o'clock. It would take me at least nine minutes to walk to the train station from the house.

"What are you doing?" Mistress Meadows asked from the office doorway.

I looked up in surprise. "Looking at the time, ma'am," I said. It was the truth.

"Mr. Meadows was called away," Mistress Meadows said, studying me with narrowed eyes. "He asked me to keep an eye on you until he returns."

"Yes, ma'am," I said, stepping around the big desk and sitting at my desk.

"You're not going to do anything, are you?" she asked.

"About what, ma'am?" I asked.

"Your family," she said. "My husband thinks you'll try something rash. I don't think you will."

"No, ma'am," I said. I had opened the newspaper and folded it so that it fit neatly on my desk before going to lunch. I did not look at the open newspaper, giving her my attention though my gaze remained averted from her.

"What do you do in here all day?" Mistress Meadows asked, stepping further into the room.

"I check the figures in the business ledgers," I said. "I go through the financial reports, ma'am."

Mistress Meadows rolled her eyes. "How droll," she said. "My head hurts just thinking about all those numbers."

The clock was facing Master Meadows' chair so the clock face was not visible from my desk. I could hear the steady click click as the clock hands moved around the clock face. I waited for her to leave, aware of each passing minute. I glanced at the newspaper for a moment, considering what financial news that I could talk about that would bore her enough to leave the office.

"I see you're just like Mr. Meadows," she said, laughing. I looked up in surprise before averting my gaze. "All you care about is work, work, work. You go ahead and make my husband lots of money. That's what you do, right? Make him lots of money?"

She laughed again, in an especially buoyant mood. She walked back to the doorway, pausing to look back at me with a toothy grin. "They should be on the train by now," she said. "Too late for you to do anything. Not that I thought you would."

The moment she stepped through the door I looked up at her back. I looked back at my desk and counted to twenty, ticking the number by tapping the desk top with my finger. I looked up again. The hall was empty.

I jumped to my feet and ran out of the house. I ran all the way to the train station. The train was still there, at the platform. Smoke and steam surged up above the engine in a white puff growing bigger and bigger as the engineer stoked the engine. The whistle blew. My heart raced and my feet flew.

He was there. Standing slightly apart from the others. I took a deep breath and ran up to the blue coated soldier. I ran right up to him. He watched me approach, cocking his head slightly as he realized that I was running directly to him.

I took a deep breath. My legs trembled so badly I was not sure I would not fall down. "I need your help," I said. I gasped for air between the words.

"What is it?" the soldier asked.

"My family," I said. My voice broke. I cleared my throat. "My family. My owners are sending my family to Kentucky to be sold. I need help."

The soldier studied me as he listened. He nodded when I finished. He turned his head, gazing out at the men wearing blue coats filling the area around the train station. "You think I can help you free them?" he asked, turning his head back to face me. "Is that what you're asking me to do?"

"I'm sorry," I said, backing away. My heart was pounding in my chest. "I just needed help."

I hurried past him but he stopped me with his hand on my arm. "Wait," he said.

"I'm sorry, sir," I said quickly, trying to sidle out of his grip without actually confronting him in any way. "I just needed help. For my family."

"They're sending them by train?" he asked.

"Yessir," I said. I took a relieved breath when he dropped his hand. "Sorry to bother you, sir. I'll be on my way, sir." I took three steps away.

"A woman with three boys and two girls?" he asked.

I nodded in surprise. He looked past me to the last car of the train. I followed his gaze. "They're already aboard and the train is ready to head out," he said. My heart plummeted. I was too late.

"I'm too late," I said. There was a roaring in my ears as the reality sank in. I was too late. My family was gone.

"I'll see what I can do," he added.

I looked up at him in surprise, afraid to hope. "Can you stop the train?" I asked.

"They have an armed escort," he said.

Several other blue coats noticed us standing there and three of them approached. I recognized them from the first day I had met the man. More men wandered over to the growing crowd around me and the man.

"What's going on, Hank?" the tall man asked, looking at me even though he was talking to Hank.

"The man asked for my help," Hank said.

I wanted to find a hole and crawl into it. Next they would call the sheriff and I would be hauled into the city center for public display and punishment as a runaway. More men gathered around us, curious as to what was going on.

"We gonna help him?" a slender, young man said, eyeing me with interest.

"They're taking his family away from him," Hank said. "Sending 'em to Kentucky to go up on the auction block."

"We're going to help him," the tall man said, nodding.

"I'm in," the slender man said with a grin.

"How we gonna help him?" the tall man asked.

"We're going to have to stop the train," Hank said. The engine whistle sounded again, three loud blasts.

I stared at the man, unable to believe my ears. "You'll help me?" I asked in surprise.

"We'll do our best," Hank said.

"Probably not the best choice we'll make this year," the tall man said.

"You don't have to help, Guhrt," Hank said.

"You think I'm going to let you have all the fun?" the man called Guhrt asked. It was not easy to understand him. His accent was very heavy. It was like his tongue was sticking to the top of his mouth as he talked and he said the words wrong but if I concentrated I could understand them anyway.

More men were looking at us, more than just men wearing blue coats. The train was chugging and the cars rattling as the train engine started moving. He said he'd help but they were just standing there while the train left with my family aboard.

We had the attention of more people. Someone was bound to tell Master Meadows that I was talking to the Union soldiers. The train was moving, leaving the station. The men in blue were just standing there. I could not linger any longer.

"I have to go," I said, spotting someone I recognized.

"Go?" Hank asked. "Where are you going?"

"Home," I said, watching the train pull out of the station. Tears rolled down my cheeks. I had been too late.

"Fight's not over yet, son," Lechemann said.

"I don't understand," I said, looking at the faces surrounding me. "The train is going. It's too late to stop it now."

"It's just leaving the station," Guhrt said. "We've got plenty of time."

"But it's gone," I said. Could they not see that?

"We'll head for Bonnets Mill," Guhrt said. Hank nodded in agreement.

"We need horses," Hank said. He turned and looked out at the gathering crowd of blue coated men. "If you're not with us, at least don't interfere."

Almost all of the men took a step forward in unison. Hank grinned. He turned to me while two dozen men started running away from the train station, the tall man Guhrt leading the way.

"Can you ride a horse?" Hank asked me.

"Where are they going?" I asked, watching the running men.

"To get horses, of course," Hank said. "We can't catch a train on foot."

I stared at the man in wonder. "Truly?" I asked.

"Train is slow, makes a lot of stops," Hank said. "We'll ride ahead and stop it.

"Can you ride a horse?" he asked again.

I nodded. I'd been on a horse a few times. I'd stay on one if I had to tie myself to it. "Yes," I said.

Chapter Thirty-Two

"I never caught your name," I said to the black man standing in front of me, holding out my hand for a handshake.

"Isaac," he said, taking my hand and shaking it. "My name is Isaac."

The thunder of hooves filled the area around the train station. The men who had gone to get horses returned, riding their horses and leading more saddled horses behind them. They rode right over the railroad tracks.

"He can use my pony," Billy said.

"You're not joining?" I asked in surprise and a little disappointment.

"He needs a good horse under him," Billy said. "And I have a ticket clerk to take care of here."

"I'll go round back in case he tries to slip out," Pete Mason said.

"I'll help," John Clerick said. Clerick was from Company C.

Guhrt rode up to me and handed me the reins to my horse. "Give him Billy's horse," I said as I swung into the saddle. I looked around at all the eager faces ready to rescue this man's family. I saw several men from Company C mixed in with my Company K boys.

Isaac mounted Billy's horse. He seemed to know what he was doing but he was not a confident horseman. I nodded at Lechemann then jerked my head towards Isaac. Lechemann nodded, riding up next to Isaac. Lechemann would catch him if he fell off Billy's horse.

One thing about all those months and weeks of guarding rail lines was that we knew every inch of that track between St. Louis and Jefferson City. The trains had to follow the tracks and the tracks had been laid to follow the terrain as well as stop at several towns along the way.

Isaac looked worried as the minutes ticked since the train pulled out of the station but the rest of us knew that we had plenty of time to get ahead of the train. Thirty-eight of us plus Isaac headed southeast out of town, skirting the town itself, the Missouri River to the north, keeping the horses to an even lope so as not to tire them out. We had to stick to the road for a time to cross the bridge over the Osage River.

An easy lope was manageable for Isaac as well. He bounced a bit as we got started then found his seat and settled back, relaxing in the saddle. He would do all right as long as we stuck to the roads. Guhrt led the way. Eventually he rode far enough ahead that he vanished out of sight.

It wasn't long before Guhrt turned back and gestured to a stretch of rolling meadows. "If we cut through here we'll come out ahead of them just after Bonnets Mill," he said.

The rail line swung in an arc up to Hermann before swinging back down south. Though Bonnets Mill was on the upward swing, the train stopped twice for water and passengers before reaching Bonnets Mill.

"Good idea," I said. "I was thinking of going straight across to Franklin but we don't want to stop them in a town."

It took less than an hour of hard riding to reach the rail lines east of Bonnets Mill. We were well ahead of the train and had time to get into position. Boulger and Thomas wanted to pull up the rail lines to stop the train.

"We don't want to wreck the train," I said. "Just stop it."

"They'll have to stop," Boulger said. He was a lean man with long sideburns and a moustache almost as long as his beard. "We'll warn them. Just pull up a few ties. Something easy enough to fix once we pull the woman and children from the train."

I reconsidered. It was a good plan. "Okay," I said, as if they had been asking my permission. Though I wasn't the highest ranking man in the group I had become the natural leader of the expedition.

Boulger and Thomas nodded and went to work pulling spikes out of one of the railroad ties until they could knock it out of position. It was taking longer than expected and someone spotted the train's steam cloud heading our way. The rest of us fanned out, forming an arcing line and rode towards the train. I rode right down the center of the tracks, waving my arms above my head to catch the engineer's attention.

The engineer sounded the train whistle repeatedly. I waved my arms and stood up in my stirrups, looking behind me to see the progress the men were making almost a mile behind us. They'd pulled up one tie. One was enough. The engineer must have spotted the men holding up the tie also because the brakes suddenly made a screeching sound as metal scraped against metal.

The train gradually slowed. We cleared the tracks and the train rumbled to a stop less than a half kilometer from the gap in the rail line. Plenty of room. The engineer poked his head out the engine's window.

"What the hell are you doing?" he yelled.

"Loose tie," I said, riding right on past him to the last car on the train.

The men escorting the family opened the box car door and were looking out to see what was going on. One of the men jumped down to the ground and walked towards us.

"What's going on?" he asked as we rode up to him.

"We're here to take the woman and children in that box car," I said.

He frowned looking around at the almost forty armed soldiers surrounding him. "Take 'em," he said. He had been hired to escort slaves, not fight off Union soldiers.

"Tell your partner to disarm and send them out," I said.

"Hey, Burt," the man yelled over his shoulder. "Put down your rifle and help the blackie and her offspring off the train."

Before Burt could do as directed, Isaac rode his horse up to the open door and held out his arms. A little girl threw herself into his arms. It didn't take long for men to ride up behind him and take their turn helping a child step from the box car either in front or behind them onto their horse.

The woman was the last one out. She stood in the open box car door staring down at the man waiting to help her onto the horse. She shook her head, eyeing the animal with trepidation. Isaac rode up to the other side of the soldier waiting to help her. He was a Company C man and I couldn't place his name.

"You can do it, Tildy," Isaac said.

The soldier slid back over the saddle back and patted the saddle seat. "Just slide on down," he said.

Tildy shook her head again. The man in the box car with her grabbed her by the waist and lifted her up and dropped her on the saddle. Her skirts billowed up around her waist, exposing her legs all the way to her thighs. Tildy leaned over the horse's neck, wrapping her fingers in the mane. Startled, the horse threw its head back, cracking Tildy in the nose. She yelled in panic and pain. It all happened in a few seconds before the soldier had time to react.

The man wrapped his arms around her waist, pulling her upright, and turned the horse away from the train. I could hear him talking to the frightened woman. "I got ya. I got ya. It's all right."

Isaac rode beside them. "She's never been on a horse before," he said.

"I'm figuring that out," the soldier said politely.

"I'm sorry," Tildy said over and over again.

"Nothing to be sorry about," the soldier said. "Just relax."

"Now what?" Guhrt said, riding up next to me during the commotion. He had the oldest boy behind him, still clutching those bundles, but calmly and easily sitting on the horse.

I really hadn't planned that far ahead. All I had been thinking was to get them off that train. It was clear what the next step had to be though. "They have to go north," I said. "To Minnesota. First, tell Boulger and Thomas to replace that tie while we get clear of here."

Passengers in the first few cars were looking out the window. Several had their heads stuck all the way out to their shoulders, looking back at the commotion.

"Minnesota?" Guhrt asked in surprise, watching the woman, terrified of being on a horse. "How they gonna get all the way up there on their own? We can't take 'em. That's desertion."

"We can walk," the boy behind Guhrt said.

"No," I said. "You'll never get far enough fast enough on foot." First we had to get away from the train. I twisted in my saddle, looking back at Boulger and Thomas. The engineer had walked down the tracks to investigate the missing railroad tie. "John and James, help them get that tie back in place."

Even as they galloped in that direction the engineer headed back to the train engine and Boulger and Thomas mounted their horses and headed to rejoin the group.

The woman in front of the soldier closed her eyes when he touched his heels to his horse and the horse leaped forward. She wasn't screaming anymore though. In fact, she had her mouth squeezed shut and her face twisted into a grimace but she was not making a sound and she was letting the man hold her without any struggle.

We rode northwest, heading for Bonnets Mill. We had to get across the Missouri at a bridge. It was too wide to try to ford. The people in Bonnets Mill had not heard news of what had happened. We got looks as we thundered through town but they were curious looks and we passed without incident.

We stopped a few miles north of Bonnets Mill near a deserted farmstead, dismounting to stretch our legs and work out a plan for the next step. The house had been partially burned down years ago and only the wall facing the road remained standing. Weeds were already growing up through the two steps in front of the front door's threshold. Isaac caught Tildy as she slid sideways out of the saddle. She wrapped her arms around her husband and sobbed in relief.

While the family comforted each other and celebrated their blessings, the rest of us worked out a plan. I sent someone back to town to buy them whatever foodstuffs he could find that wouldn't spoil so they could avoid towns as long as possible. We were going to give them three horses. They would have to ride double and the littlest one ride with someone already doubled up.

"The man can manage," Guhrt said. "And the oldest boy said that he spent his whole life on horses and he looks like he has. They'll manage."

I felt bad that we volunteered the least valuable horses but it was the best we could do. Everyone chipped in a few cents and a dollar here and there so that they could buy more food along the way. No one had a map though.

"How are they going to find their way without a map?" I wondered aloud. I didn't feel right about turning them loose to wander on their own but we couldn't escort them all the way up to Minnesota either.

"I have paper," Isaac said. "I'm familiar with the geography of Missouri and Iowa. If you can draw where this New Ulm is we can manage."

I took the paper and pencil from his hand. The step in front of the abandoned house provided a flat, almost smooth surface for writing. I drew the shape of Iowa the best I could then marked Hermann some distance below the southern border of Iowa and New Ulm up north of the northern border of Iowa.

A crowd gathered around the steps as I drew with men

volunteering what they knew of the location of rivers and towns along the way. Isaac stared at the paper as I worked, listening carefully and nodding. Jackson handed him his compass.

"Just keep heading north," Jackson said. He pointed at the compass needle. "That always points north."

Isaac nodded and slipped the compass in his pocket. I straightened and handed him the map. "If you can't find Katherine or Caroline in Mankato go to New Ulm. Once you get to New Ulm just ask for the Hansohn homestead. It's a few miles west of town."

Isaac took the paper, folded it, and stuck it in his jacket pocket. He looked around at all the men who had jumped in to help him rescue his family. Emotions overtook him for a moment and he couldn't speak. His oldest boy stood next to him and he put his right hand on the boy's shoulder and gave it a squeeze.

"Words can't express my total gratitude," Isaac said. He paused and took a deep breath. "I can never repay what you men have done for me. You have given us our family back."

I reached out to shake his hand and he let go of the son's shoulder to shake my hand. "I wish we could do more," I said. Mumbled agreements sounded around me.

I put the collected money in his left hand. "For supplies along the way," I said. Isaac stared at the pile of coins and the few paper bills "It's up to you to get them the rest of the way. Good luck, Isaac."

I headed for my horse and mounted. Several men stepped up behind me and shook Isaac's hand. He was crying. A line formed and every single man shook that grateful man's hand before heading for their horses.

"I'll catch up with ya," Guhrt said. "I'll just get them on their way is all."

When the last man had mounted I waved farewell to the family and led the way back to Jefferson City. If we rode hard we could be back before dark or at least not too long after dark. We could stick to the road going back since we didn't have to beat a train.

We did make it back to Jefferson City after the sun had set but a nearly full moon with an early rising lit up the road ahead of us well enough to see by. Major Candon was not very happy when he saw us, though he did not know completely what had transpired, he had an idea. The ticket clerk had broken free of the storage room that Billy had locked him in and gone straight to the authorities.

"You'll give me a full report in the morning for what took you out of Jefferson City all afternoon," Major Candon said.

Guhrt returned a few hours after us. "Got 'em heading in the right direction," was all he said before rolling over on his cot and falling asleep.

First thing in the morning Major Bloom was at the barracks with a list of men he wanted held and court martialed. He was furious and would not listen to Major Candon when he tried to reason with the man.

"They stopped a train and assisted runaways," Major Bloom yelled, spittle flying everywhere. "Either lock up these thirty-eight men or I'll bring up charges on you as well."

"You missed us," Billy said, stepping forward. Pete Mason and John Clerick stepped up next to Billy.

"Be reasonable, man," Major Candon said to Major Bloom. "All these men did was escort a man to his family. They just happened upon the train before the train hit a loose railroad tie and fixed it for the rail line."

"That man was a runaway slave!" Major Bloom yelled. "I don't know if you buy that crap about coming across a broken tie but I sure don't. These men held up a train to aid runaway slaves."

"We have duties to uphold," Major Candon said. "I promise to get to the bottom of this but for now it has to wait. There's a war going on, Major Bloom. Have you forgotten?"

"Was a weapon drawn?" Billy asked, earning a glare from Major Bloom.

"You were not asked to speak," Major Bloom yelled.

"No, sir," Billy said. "Just thought I could help you out by pointing out the facts. See, that man, that slave you talking about. He missed the train and we all thought to help him catch it."

"You weren't even there," Major Bloom yelled.

"No, sir, I wasn't," Billy said, shaking his head. "But my friends here, they told me all about it. And I was there when we all decided to help."

"Then you're as guilty as the rest of them," Major Bloom yelled.

"I'm not denying it," Billy said. "Like my sister's uncle likes to say, 'If you got jam on your face, don't say you were in the ham but not the jam.'"

"You be quiet or I'll arrest you just for being an idiot," Major Bloom yelled. He stared at Billy for a moment. "What the hell does that even mean?"

"You know, you got jam on your face," Billy said.

"Shut up! Shut your mouth!" Major Bloom yelled at Billy. He turned to Major Candon again. "That slave belonged to Mr. Andrew Meadows," Major Bloom yelled. "And he's mighty put out that Union soldiers aided a runaway slave." Billy opened his mouth but Major Bloom glared at him. He pointed to Billy. "You, keep your mouth shut!" He pointed at Major Candon. "You arrest and detain these men or I will bring up charges on you as well."

"I'm not arresting them," Major Candon said. "Until you have proof that these men actually drew weapons to stop a train."

"Lieutenant," Major Bloom yelled. His aid stepped up. "Arrest these men for stealing the valuable property of Mr. Meadows and interfering in the functioning of a train in the process. If they resist, they will be shot."

"There won't be any resistance," Major Candon said to Major Bloom. He turned to us, looking around the group of men. "Cooperate with Major Bloom. I'll get you released soon."

"Yes, sir!" we said in unison.

The lieutenant held up a list of names. "When I say your name please step forward, repeat your name, then head over to the guard house," he said. "Thomas Guhrt."

Guhrt repeated back his name as he stepped up to the lieutenant. The lieutenant nodded as he made a tick mark next to Guhrt's name on the list.

"Jeremy Fields."

There was no response. The lieutenant looked around at the men gathered in front of him. He repeated the name.

A voice spoke up from the back. "I think he's in the latrine."

"Go ahead and mark him," Major Candon said. "Guhrt swing by the latrine on your way and collect Jeremy."

"Yes, sir," Guhrt said, heading out the door.

"Philip Henry Hansohn."

I said my name as I stepped forward then continued out the door after Guhrt. We walked together to the latrine. Guhrt knocked on the door of the first outhouse. "You in there, Jeremy?"

"That you, Guhrt?" a muffled voice replied.

"Head for the guard house when you finish," Guhrt said.

"All right," the voice replied. "It'll be a few minutes yet."

"Well, when you're done," Guhrt said.

One by one men exited the barracks, heading for the detention building. They were expecting us and directed us into cells as we arrived. It was crowded but none of us expected to be there overly long. There was a war going on, after all.

Chapter Thirty-Three

We were court martialed and sat in the guard house for two months. Major Bloom wanted us executed for war crimes but Major Candon was able to keep that sentence from being carried out. Though we had interfered with the operation of a train during war time no one had been harmed and the delay had been only a few hours so despite Major Bloom's desires, the crime did not warrant a death sentence.

Sitting in that cell, day after day, we remained in fine spirits. Even with Major Bloom coming to see us every few days, telling us he was pushing for execution for what we'd done. We had finally managed to help someone. Rescuing that family had been worth it all. It was the right thing to have done.

I did feel sorry for Billy's cell mates. He was down far enough that I couldn't hear him from my cell. It was a bleak and boring ordeal but I wouldn't have changed events for anything. I don't believe there was a man there, imprisoned, considering execution, that would have changed events.

A letter came from home over a month after sitting in that airless cell. Katherine had written to say that a black family had arrived in Mankato and been directed to the house. After a few days in Mankato they had gone on out to the farm outside New Ulm.

When I read aloud the news from my wife there was a great cheer that went through that prison house. More cheers echoed as word moved down the line of cells. Success fueled the soul.

Word reached the United States Senate that forty-one able-bodied soldiers of the 9th Minnesota Regiment were sitting in the brigade and demanded an explanation. The Secretary of War himself investigated then ordered our release. We returned to guarding the railways between Jefferson City and the western border of Missouri for a few months.

We headed for St. Louis May 26, 1864 to join Brigadier General Samuel Sturgis' expedition for the campaign of Mississippi and left St. Louis on the 31st. Our orders were to crush and defeat the confederate Major General Forrest. Over eight thousand men moved out under Sturgis' command.

One June 10th, at the battle of Brice's Cross Roads (Guntown) the 9th charged and routed a body of the enemy, yet despite the superior numbers under Sturgis' command, the confederates controlled the battle. Six straight days of heavy rain had made the roads muddy messes and we were bogged down.

General Sturgis ordered a retreat, convinced that we were outnumbered and facing annihilation. When it became evident that we were routed, the infantry cut loose the horses and mules pulling the artillery and wagon trains and thus managed to escape. There were still a thousand men on foot after two thousand horses were recruited from the harness.

By the end of the day we covered the retirement in good order for 23 miles, when we became separated from the main column. We succeeded in reaching Collierville, where we met a train with reinforcements.

In that affair the Ninth Minnesota regiment's loss was 286 killed, wounded, and missing, 233 captured. Company K's loss was five men.

The adjutant-general of the state, in his report of the affair, said: "That this disastrous undertaking did not result in the entire loss of the whole force, is mainly due to the gallantry of the officers and men of this 9th regiment."

The noise and smells were the most noteworthy things about engaging in battle. Though fear pumped the blood at a faster rate, the need to do what was required outrode the fear.

When the canons fired at us, the balls would often land in the dirt, spraying dirt out all around it. Then the dirt would rain down back on us with that distinctive sound as the dirt hit ground or trees or bodies, living or dead.

The smoke from the musket rifles a lot of soldiers had the misfortune to have to use, filled the air as the paper and gunpowder burned. By itself, a paper wrapped musket shot was but a poof of smoke. Multiply that by thousands of guns and hundreds of rounds each gun and within hours the field was sometimes too smoky to even see across.

Then there was the smells from the wounded men. Blood had its own smell. Sometimes a bullet struck a bowel, releasing the rank odors from within. Many men loosened their bowels in their death. Gangrene smelled of rotting flesh. Men lay in the battlefield, sometimes for days, their flesh rotting around their wounds.

The constant boom of canon fire was the worse. The short tap of a rifle near and far I'd gotten used to hearing all around me but that canon fire meant a cannon ball could land anywhere, sending men flying backwards or just killing them where they stood.

I saw Knobel get his legs shot out right from under him. Both legs just gone. He bled out in short time. Jenkin got shot in the side and then in the hand. Angry, fired up on adrenaline, he jumped up and ran right into the enemy's midst. They shot him until he fell and didn't move again.

I can attest to the gallantry and fortitude of the men of the Ninth Regiment as we engaged in battle with confederate forces at Brices's Cross Roads. It was unfortunate that our first full-fledged battle against the confederates was not a victory for our side but it was not for a lack on our part.

We returned to Memphis, attached to the 2nd brigade, 1st division, 16th army corps, and were sent to Mississippi in June. We participated in the battle of Tupelo and in the Oxford raid; joined the

Missouri campaign in September and October, and were in the battle of Nashville in December, where we were in a series of charges in which many prisoners were taken, Company. K especially performing excellent work on the skirmish line.

In a charge the following day the colors of the 9th were the first planted on the enemy's works, the regiment capturing 2 battle flags and 550 prisoners, to which the 9th added 150 more during the day.

The 9th joined in the pursuit of Hood and went into quarters at Eastport, Jan. 9, 1865.

The 9th were in the campaign of Mobile and siege of Fort Blakely and Spanish Fort; were then ordered to Montgomery, Ala.; thence to Selma, and on May 19, to Marion.

I was taken prisoner at Nashville, along with Guhrt, Billy, Lechemann, Pete Mason, and a hundred other men. We were sent to Andersonville, also known as Hell on Earth. Pete Mason was the first to die at Andersonville. When we arrived there were guards but no fences. Pete stepped over to the stream to collect some water to rinse Billy's wound and the guards shot him dead. He had stepped over the dead line. We hadn't known of such a thing.

Billy had been shot in the shoulder during battle and died two days after we arrived in Andersonville from the infection that had spread from his untreated wound. After a few months in Andersonville we were all in a bad way.

There was little food, none of it nourishing, and disease was taking a toll on those who hadn't even been injured during the battle. With such close quarters and lack of sanitary conditions, life in the prison was killing men at a faster a rate than in battle. At least on the battlefield there was a sense of purpose. There was no purpose in being pushed into a stockade and left to the mercy of the elements.

The once robust Lechemann was the next one to die. He had caught some lung disease in the prison and after a few weeks of coughing up blood he breathed his last breath. His own mother would not have recognized him. Between the lack of nourishing food and the disease he was but half his normal size, if that.

Somehow Guhrt and I managed to survive. It was only survival. It was hard to even think for lack of food. My ribs were clearly visible as the muscle on my body melted away. The hunger faded long before the stench of rotting bodies, vomit, and diarrhea. My feet were rotting from standing in wet mud.

The only escape from the harshness around us was sleep. Most prisoners slept most of the day as well as all night. The lucky ones had tents to protect them from the elements. Some poor souls had no shelter of any form.

I saw a man who was prepared to meet his maker, going so far as to lie on his worn blanket, over against the stockade wall where the chances were less of being stepped upon, with his arms folded over my chest. He had to use his hand to close his own eyes in preparation for the final moments before he breathed his last breath.

If not for Guhrt, I felt I'd be in that position eventually. He managed to secure a tent and even some boards that we laid on the ground in the tent to get us up off the ground. There were gangs of men going about robbing the weaker of anything valuable, food being the most valuable of all. We were fortunate to not be set upon by any of those men.

Men were dying by the scores. Some soon after arriving, from their battle wounds, others from the deplorable conditions were we forced to endure as war prisoners. The days of amiable prisoner exchanges were gone once negroes joined the Union side and took up arms against the confederates.

Newcomers shared news of what was going on outside the prison walls. Whole towns were being burned, women and children left to starve. Our own Union soldiers were robbing and looting before burning those towns.

Guhrt and I were both able-bodied enough to be selected for burial duty but we didn't dare leave our tent unattended so only one of us went out at a time. It was a grim and brutal task, digging holes then burying the starved and rotted bodies but it got us out of the walls for a time.

Never mind that there were armed guards surrounding us, ready to shoot to kill with any misinterpreted movement, it was a chance to stand on ground that wasn't churned mud, a chance to clear the nostrils of the stench permeating every inch of that prison. The dead bodies we buried smelled so strongly that the smell often caused men to gag but it was a different odor than inside the stockade walls.

After a few more months we were too weak to go out on burial detail anymore. Pretty much we just settled in and waited to die. I could feel a sickness settling over me. The complete lack of vegetables in our starvation diet was making my gums rot and my limbs to twist.

I was surprised one day when a man approached our tent and told Guhrt and me to report to the hospital. There were men a lot worse off than us who had crawled to the hospital gates and been turned away.

We hesitated in leaving our tent unattended, afraid there'd been a mistake and once we arrived at the hospital gates we would just be turned away. The man said it was all right, he'd stay and keep an eye on our tent until we returned. So we went, feeling that the medical attention was worth the risk.

We had no change of clothes since arriving and no matter the effort we made to take care of our clothes, wearing them twenty-four hours a day for months on end had worn them thin. Guhrt's trousers were thinner than mine and had shredded. The sores on his legs were visible, oozing liquids and smelling mighty fierce.

The guard at the gate took our names and let us through. I didn't think it was possible but the hospital smelled even worse than the other side of the prison. Men filled with gangrene lay about on the ground, inside makeshift tents, and a few on cots in the building itself. I was afraid we had stepped from approaching death to certain death.

The doctor had us lay on cots inside the building as he examined us. He cleaned the sores on Guhrt's legs then put a blue bottle to his lips and told him to drink it all. After he looked at me the doctor gave me a similar blue bottle and instructed me to drink it all. It tasted vile but I obeyed.

Within minutes of drinking the contents of that blue bottle I was feeling death taking its grip. I was convinced that I had been poisoned but I could not speak to accuse the man of his black hearted deed. The doctor pulled a blanket over Guhrt's face just before I closed my eyes and breathed my last breath.

A woman came up beside me. She smelled of soap and horse, a smell so out of place in that world of stench that it pulled me from leaving my body that day. First, she put her hand on my heart, looking for a sign of life in me. Then she raised my head and poured nourishing broth down my throat.

I was still convinced I was going to die, but that woman was just as convinced to drag the life back into my body. I don't know who she was. I couldn't see her face. I'm convinced that she was an angel. It wasn't my time to leave my earthly vessel no matter that I thought it was.

The nourishing broth that the angel had been forcing down my throat was stirring life back into me. I could feel it working its magic. I could lift my head enough to turn it and look around me. That was the limit of my strength and that effort drained me of any more energy.

We were in the back of a wagon traveling on a road but I was barely jostled. The back of the wagon was filled with straw and the straw was covered with several layers of good, wool blankets. Guhrt was lying next to me on that bed of straw and wool. More wool blankets covered Guhrt and me. It was hard to tell if the wagon was even moving, it was such a cushioned bed someone had made for us.

The wagon stopped and the driver came around back with a woman. I thought I was hallucinating at that moment. My eyes strained to make out the woman's features in the dim light of twilight. Or maybe I had died and it grieved me to see that my mom had gone on ahead of me to the afterlife because it sure looked like her standing behind the wagon. I turned my eyes because it was too much effort to turn my head. There was a tall black man standing next to Mom.

"Did I die?" I asked. "Are you dead, too?"

Chapter Thirty-Four

"You're alive, Hank," Mom said.

The black man helped her climb up into the back of the wagon then handed her a pot. "Stay alive a while longer, sir," he said. It was difficult to make out his features but that voice sounded familiar.

Mom used a ladle to feed me broth from the pot then stepped over me to feed Guhrt also. I wanted to ask her who else was in the wagon with us but I had again used up my energy and I fell asleep before I could form the question.

It was in the light of the next day that I fully saw the man traveling with us. It was Isaac, the slave I had helped in Jefferson City the year before. Or had it been two years? It felt like a lifetime ago.

We traveled all the way across Georgia, Alabama, and up through Tennessee in that wagon. When it rained the black man covered the back with a tarp to keep us dry. Every morning Mom made fresh broth before we started out on the road again and every day Mom fed us broth from her pot until we were strong enough to start eating more substantial food.

It took a while for my stomach to accept more than the broth. Of course, Guhrt was able to eat sooner. That wagon moved steadily through the countryside all day and well into the night. When I was able to sit up I watched the passing countryside.

Too often we drove right past bodies lying about. They were in ditches. They were out in fields. We passed burnt farm houses, burnt towns, and burnt fields and forests. Twice they pulled the tarp over us when they spotted soldiers on the road but surprisingly we were never stopped or bothered.

Finding more substantial food was not always possible along the way but they managed somehow to find people willing to sell something for us to eat from time to time. The two of them had learned the art of scavenging as well, finding peanuts and pecans in the cover of darkness.

Guhrt and I were both wearing civilian clothes, wool trousers and cotton shirts. "We're out of uniform," I said to Mom when she came back to feed us again. "We can't be out of uniform."

"There was nothing left of your uniforms," she said. "This is what I had. There weren't any uniforms handy to be had."

Once we encountered a field with pigs wandering freely. It had grown dark and we could see their white shadows shining in the burnt out field. They were moving about, rooting and eating something. Isaac managed to secure a pig and Mom butchered it.

That pork was the first meat I'd had in half a year. As bad as I felt for stealing a pig from an honest, hard-working farmer, that pig gave my life back to me. We ate as much as we could and hoped the rest would store long enough to eat the rest of it.

The next day we passed a long stretch of more burnt out fields and the skeletons of trees between the fields. White skulls were visible, scattered about by the cloven hooves of more pigs eating the rotting corpses.

A few days after leaving Andersonville, Mom told us what had happened. They had been watching the prison and seen us out on burial detail. Mom managed to gain an audience with Captain Henry Wirz, begging the Swiss man to at least allow her to take the bodies of her son and son-in-law when they died.

"But we didn't die," I said. "Did we?"

"I bribed the doctor to give you something that made it appear that you were dead," Mom said. "Two thousand dollars, I gave him. For each of you."

I stared in stunned silence. "Where did you get such a sum?" I asked.

"I paid it," Isaac said.

A slave having that sum of money was even harder to grasp than my parents coming up with that sum of money. That my mom had traveled across a country torn with war with a black slave who was a runaway and risked being captured at any moment was beyond my comprehension at the time. I seriously considered that I was in fact lying on a muddy knoll inside Andersonville dreaming the whole thing.

"We have to return to our regiment," I said when I was well enough to realize that we were heading for Minnesota.

"When you're well enough," Mom said.

"When we reach St. Louis," Isaac said. "I have a favor for you in St. Louis."

"The 9th is back in St. Louis?" Guhrt asked in surprise.

"I don't think so," Mom said. "They're down south somewhere. In Alabama maybe. You're in no condition to join them yet. But there's soldiers in St. Louis. We'll take you to them."

By the time we reached St. Louis I was strong enough to walk beside Isaac into the bank. That was his favor of me, to go into a bank with him, pretending to be a customer. A security guard stopped us in the foyer, eyeing the pair of us with suspicion. Per Isaac's instructions, I asked for a Mr. Poole.

"He can't be in here," the guard said, looking at me but meaning Isaac.

"I have been ill," I said. "I require his assistance in case I collapse again." The guard eyed me, not wanting to allow Isaac in the bank but uncertain about my condition. "Just fetch Mr. Poole. Tell him a friend of Mr. William Meadows seeks his assistance in a financial matter."

"Stay here," the guard said.

We waited right where we stood until the guard returned with a short, balding man. Mr. Poole looked us over, taking a second look at Isaac. "This way please," he said, gesturing behind him.

We followed the frail man back to a private office. He bade us sit and left us. He returned with a lock box and a piece of paper in his hand and shut the door.

"I was deeply saddened to hear of the death of Mr. Meadows," Mr. Poole said to Isaac. "You have the box number and your key?"

"Yes," Isaac held up a small key. "I will be closing this account," he said.

Mr. Poole nodded. "Please sign here. I will take care of the refund of the rent paid on the box. When you are finished just leave the box in the room with the key," he said. "You can collect the monies owed you at the teller's window."

Once Mr. Poole left the room, shutting the door behind him, Isaac took a deep breath and inserted his key into the lox box. He sat for several minutes with his hand on the box lid, working up the courage to open the box. Inside was a canvas bag. Isaac took the bag out of the box and slid it into his inside jacket pocket.

"Thank you," he said, standing. "I could not have retrieved it without you."

Isaac waited while I went to the teller window and asked for the envelope Mr. Poole had said would be there. I gave the envelope to Isaac and we left the bank. Mom and Guhrt were waiting outside with the wagon.

We approached Fort Jackson and Isaac stopped the team before reaching the gates. "Officially you died at Andersonville," he said. "They would never know if you went on home."

"I would know," I said.

"As would I," Guhrt said, climbing down from the wagon.

Isaac nodded, one corner of his mouth curling up in a half smile at the answer. I climbed down from the wagon after Guhrt. We shook Isaac's hand farewell. I hugged Mom for a long time, finding it unbearably difficult to leave her that day.

"I still can't believe you came for me," I said, holding her back at arm's length. "The risks were so great."

"I couldn't let Isaac go by himself," she said. "As soon as he heard you were at Andersonville and reports grew worse in the newspapers about the conditions in those prisons and of the treatment of the prisoners of war he was bound and determined to reach you. I had to accompany him. It was the only way."

"I'd have never reached you without her," Isaac said. "She's a mighty brave woman. I see where you got your courage, sir."

"We pretended he was my slave, escorting me to my ailing sister," Mom said.

The dangers they must have faced terrified me yet gave me a profound admiration for the both of them. They were not yet out of danger either. Not until they crossed into Iowa did I feel they could really be out of danger.

"Stay here," I said to Mom. "It's safer here."

She shook her head. "He's not safe here," she said. "I'm not going to abandon him now after all he went through to rescue my boy." She kissed my forehead. "We got this far. We'll be fine from here."

"I have to know," I said to Isaac. "How did you ever come to owning such a sum of money?"

My conscience was bothering me, thinking that the man had paid for our freedom with stolen funds. It was the only way I could imagine the man had been able to get his hands on the money.

"I earned it," he said. "It was not stolen, if that's what you're thinking."

"It will take me a long time to repay you," I said. "But I will make payments until the sum has been repaid."

"It was my debt," Isaac said, shaking his head. "I was but repaying my debt to you."

"That is too much money," I said, shaking my head. "I was but helping a neighbor. You owe me nothing. I will repay you."

"It was my debt to you," Isaac insisted. "I will not take money from you."

"You may discuss it at length another time," Mom said. She looked up at me, cupping my jaw with her hand. "I cannot bear to think of you going back. My only consolation is in believing that this brutal war is nearly at an end."

In that she was right. We reported to the commander at Fort Jackson in July of 1865 and went directly to the infirmary. By the time we were mended enough to rejoin our regiment it was August and the war was declared over. We were sent up to Fort Snelling to await the rest of the 9th regiment. The 9th were mustered out at Fort Snelling, Aug. 24, 1865.

Epilogue

The canvas bag was heavy in my pocket, its weight a constant reminder that it was waiting for me. As much as I wanted to see what Master Meadows had put in the lock box all those years ago, I needed to wait for the right time to open the bag to see its contents.

When I was finally alone, in a small room at a boarding house in northern Iowa, I pulled out the canvas bag and poured out the contents. Several picture frames slid out with their backs facing me. I turned the top frame. An old man stared back at me. I turned the second frame. A young black girl stood holding a young white child up for the camera.

There was a letter. I opened the envelope and straightened out the creases in the letter, gaze drifting back to the pictures as my fingers smoothed the letter flat.

Dear Isaac,

I would call you son but really you are my brother. I recognized my father in your face that day I bought you from the auction block. That you were from Summerset Plantation removed any doubt. I confronted him with it one day. Shortly after my mother's funeral, which I was not welcomed to attend, I went to her grave to say my farewells. He found me there and we argued. We always argued. He denied at first that he had fathered you then in a fit of anger he blurted out that he had sold you to get your reminding face off the plantation.

I tried to buy your mother from him but he would not sell her to me. Later he sold her to prevent my getting my hands on her. A spiteful old man to the end.

The picture of your mother was from several years before you were born. She was nanny to my brother's children from the time she was eight years old. It's the only picture of her and that's only because Andrew was not cooperating for the photographer so Eveline was recruited to calm the child.

I am not confident that you shall ever hold this correspondence in your hand but maybe the day shall come. It's good for a man to know where he comes from. I always tried to do my best for you, giving you the life you deserve as my family. I have learned that I have a heart condition and don't know how much time I have left on this Earth. You will be upset with me for leaving you to Andrew but he's a good man and he'll keep you safe.

Sincerely Your Brother,
William Meadows

I picked up the picture frame of the man who Master Meadows claimed was my father. I did not know that stern-faced man. As far as I was concerned, Master Meadows was my father. He raised me and loved me. I forgave him for not freeing me, believing he sincerely believed that keeping me as a slave protected me. I did not agree with him but I forgave him.

There was another envelope that I had missed. Inside was a stack of bearer bonds. I flipped through the bonds, adding up the numbers printed on them. I was an even wealthier man than I had thought. That was, if the bonds maintained any value after the war.

I had given the younger Master Meadows part of the money that I had earned from investing with his hundred dollars from the household account. It seemed fitting to attempt to buy my family's freedom with those monies. The money I had earned from investing the hundred dollars that the elder Master Meadows had put into that bank account for me was sitting safely in a bank in St. Paul, Minnesota.

Money was green. With the anonymity provided by the power of using my signature no one ever saw the color of my skin. Green was a color that opened doors.

Even better was living in Minnesota where the color of my skin has not been what people have rated my value as a man upon. Tildy doesn't like the cold but we both like the people so we will stay.

###

Shades of Right is based on a single real event. There really was a slave who approached some soldiers of the 9th Minnesota Regiment at a train station in Missouri and asked for help.

Though Missouri was part of the Union slavery was still legal in the state. However, slaves could not be bought and sold in Missouri during that time so it was common to ship slaves to Kentucky to sell them.

Those men of the 9th Minnesota Regiment really did help that slave save his family by holding up the train carrying them to Kentucky and were court martialed for it. When I heard of this incident I was immediately intrigued. How brave that man was to approach complete strangers for help, risking so much if they chose instead to report him to the local law.

Having grown up in Minnesota, descended from German immigrants who moved into the area between Big Stone Lake and Hutchinson, this story has a personal connection for me. I've known a lot of Minnesota men who could step back in time and step forward on that train station platform, willing to help a neighbor. Everyone's a neighbor to Minnesotans.

Isaac and Hank are how I imagine these men to be. Who they really were is a mystery.

Other Books by Robyn Braemer

The Heart Key
The Horse Keeper
Dark Thunder
Huron: Descendants

Books by Robyn Kaech

Runaway Pinkerton
This Moment
Jewel of Baleria

Robyn lives in northern Minnesota with a very large dog and a very large cat. When not writing Robyn is exploring with a camera in hand and constantly flexing creative muscles in a wide variety of artistic interests. She worked in the digital mapping field for over sixteen years and when that chapter closed chose to embrace the opportunity to focus on writing novels.

Visit Robyn on Facebook. **Author - Robyn Braemer**
https://www.facebook.com/Author-Robyn-Braemer